World of Calliome

SCARS OF THE SUNDERING
BOOK 1

MALEDICTION

Second Edition

SCARS OF THE SUNDERING
BOOK 1

MALEDICTION

Hans Cummings

Scars of the Sundering
Book 1 – Malediction
Book 2 – Lament
Book 3 - Salvation

Hans Cummings

This is a work of fiction. All characters and events portrayed in this book are fictional, and any resemblance to real people or incidents is purely coincidental.

ISBN: 978-0-9847205-6-9

Electronic edition available through Amazon.com,
Print edition available through Amazon.com and fine booksellers everywhere .

Edited by Laura K. Anderson
http://rootshalfhidden.com/

Heraldy by
Axel Löfving

Cover design by Eric Hubbel
http://hubbelcreative.deviantart.com/

Cartography by Anna B. Meyer
http://http://ghmaps.net/

Cover Art by Lily Yang
http://www.lilyyangart.com/

World of Calliome Logo by Gwyneth Ravenscraft of G-Sharp Productions
http://www.g-sharpproductions.com/

ACKNOWLEDGEMENTS

For Tink, without whom this would not have been possible.

Thanks to Michael R. Hicks, J.A. Konrath, Chuck Wendig, and Michael A. Stackpole for encouragement, advice, and inspiration. You all help give me the drive to make this possible.

Special thanks to Mike Wolff, Craig Majors, Rabia Gale (Lady Q), and the fine folk in the Fear the Boot and KindleBoards message board communities for all their encouragement and feedback.

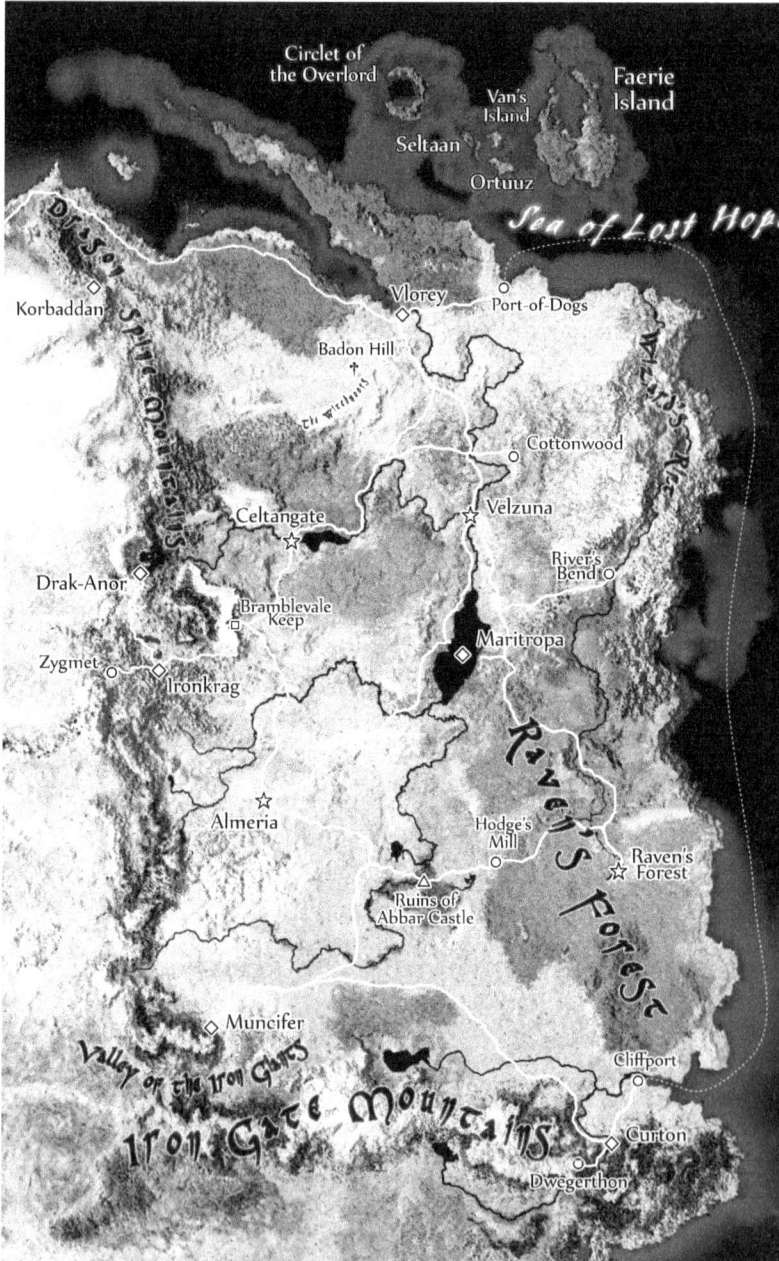

Chapter 1

The minotaur stopped at the edge of the great pit. Consuming the scant light in the tunnel, it threatened to swallow him as well. He rubbed his right horn, feeling the cool gilded tip against his fingers. Alongside him, Kale kicked a stone into the hole. It clattered against the sides as it fell. After searching for an alternate route, the minotaur determined descending the hole as the only way forward.

"Come on, Pancras!" The diminutive lizard-like creature, who, according to legend, descended from dragons, gestured for his friend to follow him. The minotaur sighed, running his hoof along the edge of the precipice. The black-and-red striped drak jumped into the unnaturally dark void. "It's not that deep! You were right!" Kale's voice echoed up from below.

Pancras suspected the darkness was magical in nature. Dwarven lights, powered by the Soul Forge, dotted the tunnels of the city, illuminating the upper part of cavities such as the one before him. Shaking his head, he tapped a piece of rubble at the edge. It vanished into the blackness. *Sometimes I think Kale is braver than he is smart.*

The scraping of a boot behind him interrupted his mental debate on the prudence of following Kale. Smoothing the front of his gold-trimmed violet robes, he faced the hairy creature behind him.

"I'm Edric. I've been ordered to go with you." The dwarf ran his fingers through the frayed braids of his beard, evidence that he had not groomed himself in days.

Inadvertently standing downwind, Pancras wrinkled his nose as the pervasive odor of stale ale, which clung to the dwarf, wafted past him. He and Kale could handle whatever they encountered, but since the dwarves sent a helper, he would put Edric to work. *The smelly bugger can distract the ghouls at least.* He nodded, pointing toward the darkness. "Fine. Get in then."

Edric shrank away from Pancras. "That hole? Why in the name of Adranus's beard would I do that?" Easing forward, he peered over the edge into the blackness, running his fingers through his facial hair. "What's down there?"

Pancras sighed. "Were you not told why we're here?"

The dwarf shook his head. "Nah. They don't tell us much when we're being punished. You fellas are from Drak-Anor, right? I figured you being here with us dwarves was your punishment for something or other, and I got stuck here with you."

I suppose being here is a punishment of sorts. "Lord Sarvesh asked Kale and I to help your Seer-King with this ghoul problem as a gesture of goodwill."

"Ghouls?" Edric stepped away from the hole. "I heard about some problems down here, but nobody mentioned ghouls. I don't mess with no undead beasties."

"Well, that's the job." He gripped Edric's collar. The dwarf squirmed, thrashing. Holding him at arm's length, Pancras dropped him into the hole. After taking a deep breath, he jumped in after the dwarf. For a brief moment darkness enveloped him.

Unprepared for the impact of hooves to ground, he collapsed onto his knees. Kale, busy helping Edric to his feet, shook the dwarf off his arm, then rushed to his friend. Pancras waved him off. There wasn't much Kale could do to help him up anyway since he stood only as high as the minotaur's waist.

"When did we get a dwarf?"

"He arrived just after you jumped down the hole. Ordered to help us." There was a time not so long ago when Pancras would have needed a translator to understand the dwarf's language. However, when Lord Sarvesh became leader of Drak-Anor, he required his closest advisors, and anyone else who was interested, to learn Dwarvish.

"Help us, huh?" Kale offered a clawed hand to the dwarf. "I'm Kale."

Staring at the proffered hand as if it might bite, the dwarf shook it with obvious reluctance. "Edric."

Pancras eyed the rocky ceiling above them, noting the dark void encompassed only the hole. *Hmm. It is indeed magical.* Standing in an unlit, rough-hewn tunnel wide enough for only two side-by-side, the minotaur crouched to keep the tips of his horns from scraping the ceiling.

Shaking his head, Edric examined the walls with a gloved hand. "This is not dwarven work. Look at these markings." He pointed to a pattern on the wall. "This tunnel was dug by claws."

Kale probed the area with a clawed finger, then faced Pancras. "Dug? So the ghouls came in from outside Ironkrag?"

"Yes. We have ghouls coming in from outside. Ghouls of goblin, drak, oroq, and dwarven origins, yes?" Ticking his fingers, Pancras recited the names.

"That's what Sarvesh said." Kale drew one of the many daggers from his bandolier. "But where do they come from? The dwarf ghouls, I mean. Dwarves turn to stone when they're dead, right?"

Edric nodded. "Yes. Fuel for the Soul Forge. I have never heard of a dwarf being so afflicted." He regarded the black hole above them. "I wish I'd repaid that bastard moneylender now. They sent me here to get rid of me."

Grinning, Kale raised himself on tiptoes to put his arm around the dwarf's shoulder. "Don't worry. Pancras and I have some experience with this. Ghouls are nothing."

The dwarf pulled away from Kale. "It ain't the ghouls I'm worried about. It's what's making them."

Pancras nodded, chewing his upper lip. "Edric speaks wisely. A vampire could do this. Perhaps a necromancer. There are older and fouler things that could so corrupt a dwarf as well. The ghouls are a symptom of the problem. Our true foe is much more dangerous than a pack of mindless flesh-eaters."

A clicking sound from up ahead interrupted his musings. Although a variety of creatures made their homes in dark places of the world, Pancras had not encountered any that made such a distinctive sound.

Dropping to a fighting stance, Kale peered ahead. "What's that?"

Pancras eyed Edric. The dwarf shrugged. The minotaur drew magical energies to him, preparing them for use on whatever lay ahead, the tips of his horns glowing with emerald light as the swirling tendrils of aether converged.

He nodded. "Let's proceed then."

Moving alongside Kale, Edric drew his sword, a short and angular weapon designed primarily for chopping and slashing, typical of the type of brute-force weaponry dwarves preferred. They crept forward, guided by light from the magical foci on Pancras's horns. Although the minotaur was accustomed to living underground, he noticed the air in this tunnel felt uncharacteristically oppressive and thick.

The tunnel descended as they advanced. The subtle downward slope became more pronounced the farther from Ironkrag they explored. Pancras sniffed the air, recognizing the faint stench of decay. The clicking in the distance continued, growing louder.

"This is worse than Deep Road patrol," the dwarf complained.

With every step forward, the clicking sound grew louder and the odor became stronger.

Stopping, Edric held up his hand. "Feel that?"

Pancras and Kale stood motionless. The minotaur felt nothing out of the ordinary. "What?"

"Vibrations. In the stone. Feels like machinery ahead."

Kale nodded at the minotaur. "Hey, maybe it's not such a bad idea to have a dwarf along after all, huh?"

Pancras frowned. "I never said it was."

"Where do you suppose this tunnel goes, anyway?" Kale peered into the darkness. "We've walked a ways already, and we're going deeper and deeper. I'll bet we're already below Deep Road."

The underground thoroughfare connected most of the dwarven cities, from Dwegerthon in the Iron Gate Mountains to Ironkrag and Korbaddan in the Dragon Spine mountains in the northwest. Although he was unsure how far under the mountain Deep Road extended, Pancras agreed Kale was probably correct.

"Let's keep going." Gesturing for Kale and Edric to lead the way, he concentrated on keeping his magic at the ready, cursing himself for not bringing Kale's sister who specialized in combat sorcery.

The tunnel continued its descent, turning sharply before opening into a cavern. The misty glow of phosphorescent moss covering the distant ceiling looked like purple clouds in an impossibly dark sky. The clicking echoed throughout the chasm.

"Whew! I thought something stank." Kale waved his hand in front of his snout. "It reeks in here."

"Oh." Edric sniffed the air. "I thought that was the two of you!"

"Ghouls are close." Pancras pushed past his smaller companions. "Be on your guard."

As they moved deeper into the cavern, the minotaur felt the ground vibrating through his hooves. Ahead, boulders the size of drak houses dotted the chamber, and a shadowed recess lay at the center of the floor. Upon reaching the end of the path leading to the depression, he peered over the edge into a shaft.

Downward pointing spikes lined the sides of the pit. A pool of scarlet liquid churned at the bottom. The bloodlike substance rose to the sides, creeping upward almost like ivy, yet it moved in a way that suggested thought, purpose.

It was then Pancras realized: the spikes were teeth.

***

"What is that?" Kale bumped into Pancras. Gasping, the minotaur took hold of him. The drak observed spikes and a red morass at the bottom of the pit. Pulling on Kale's bandolier, Pancras dragged him away from the edge.

"Bloodmaw."

"What?" Kale adjusted his dagger belt.

"It is a beast born of chaos." Pancras stroked his chin. "It should not be in this world."

Edric looked over the edge. "That thing's making the ghouls?" The clicking noise echoed up the bloodmaw's pit.

"No, no. I don't think so. It can corrupt, though, corrupt and devour. When the world was sundered, the shards of Calliome were surrounded by elemental chaos. Scholars called it the Maelstrom. Those rifts were all sealed with the healing of the world, but as with all grievous wounds, some of the scars festered and allowed bits of chaos to seep through, much like the portal to the Fae Realm in Drak-Anor. They allow what's on the other side passage to our world. This chaos beast"—Pancras gestured to the bloodmaw's pit—"must have come through one of those festering sores."

"How does it make that—?" Kale noticed movement out of the corner of his eye. Dozens of ghouls, hunched over with their knuckles touching the ground, shuffled toward them out of the darkness. Their dirty, elongated nails resembled talons. Ghouls that were once dwarves, draks, and even minotaurs and humans, trudged toward them. He tapped Pancras on the hand.

"We have company."

The dwarf spun, brandishing his sword.

Pancras faced the ghoul horde. "Aita's bloody bones!"

Ghouls closed in from all sides, moving toward them with purpose. Kale drew a second dagger, crouching into a combat stance. "Why aren't they attacking?"

The glow from the tips of Pancras's horns intensified. "They are being controlled."

"Indeed." A mellifluous, malicious voice answered. The language it spoke sounded strange to Kale; yet somehow he understood it. The air around them grew ranker and as cold as the deep of winter. A shadow rose from behind the pack of ghouls surrounding them.

"Welcome, Necromancer. Come to join my ever-growing army?"

Kale shuddered, his stomach twisting in knots. Every fiber of his being screamed for him to run and hide or cower in fear at this twisted abomination in the shadow. Yet, his brain commanded him to stand fast with Pancras.

The minotaur stepped forward, interposing himself between Kale and the shadow. "We come to destroy it."

The shadow laughed. "The three of you? You would make fine additions, despite your foolishness." The figure moved forward, revealing its true form: that of a slime-covered humanoid. Shadows cloaked it like billowy clouds of soot and ash. Kale found himself instinctively shrinking away from it, although he had never seen anything like it. Its slavering maw snapped. Hissing at the trio, it bared its teeth.

Pancras planted his hooves firmly into the ground. The emerald glow at the tips of his horns flared.

Kale shielded his eyes against the glare as Pancras threw open his arms, chanting, "*Aita pairnei piso tee dyaenamee pou eiche klapei.*"

Growling, the shadow charged the minotaur. Kale leapt forward, throwing a dagger in its direction. He threw two more from his bandolier before touching down. The daggers punched holes through the shadow. Hissing, the wounds sealed themselves with a puff of greasy smoke.

"*Ypoloipo, nekrees psychees. Peegainete sto aionio yeapno sas!*"

A burst of emerald flame cascaded across the ranks of ghouls. Screeching, they clawed at their skin as brilliant green flames consumed them. Edric stood at the edge of the bloodmaw pit. Although his legs trembled, he stood fast. Together, Kale and his companions held their ground.

The minotaur's horns continued to glow. "*Aspida tou ravematos.*" The shadow beast slammed to a stop inches from Pancras's face. A thin shell with a kaleidoscope of colors playing across its surface, like the rainbow on a bubble of soap, surrounded his friend.

Stepping back, the shadow creature shook itself. Growling, it swiped at Edric, as one might swat a fly. The dwarf dove to the side, rolling into a crouch, then pointed the tip of his sword at the shadow.

"You are a worthy opponent, Necromancer. You speak with the voice of Aita. A pity. You could be so much more than you are." The shadow beast's sugary tone crawled under Kale's skin. He shivered, feeling the desperate need for a bath.

"What I am is enough for me."

Kale poised his daggers for another throw. For all the good it will do. The shadow beast lunged forward attempting to drive Pancras into the bloodmaw.

"*Skia veema.*" The minotaur vanished just as the beast reached him. Unable to stop its momentum, it tumbled over the edge. Pancras reappeared next to Kale. The trio listened to the beast howl in rage at the bottom of the pit.

"Fooled by a childhood trick." Tugging at Kale's bandolier, Pancras gestured at Edric. "Come, we must find a way to seal the rift before it climbs out. The bloodmaw won't devour that thing. They're probably working together."

***

Pancras easily destroyed the undead, simply by recalling the energy used to create them. Channeling that energy, he erected a shield before the shadow reached him, but the demon was strong, and its impact against the shield nearly caused its collapse. Luckily, he used the demon's own shadow to step through and avoid its next charge.

His cleverness did not come without cost, though. Pancras, tired and hungry, felt as if his last sleep and meal were weeks ago; when, in reality, they were but a few hours past. Magic taxed the wielder, particularly when fighting a strong foe and using different effects in rapid succession. Pancras willed his legs to carry him forward.

A shadow demon, a chaos rift, a bloodmaw. I hope those hairy little cretins appreciate this. No wonder the Seer-King didn't send his own dwarves down here. I'll bet the old bastard suspected something like this and asked for Sarvesh's help because he views us as expendable.

"How in the name of Pacha's blue bollocks are we going to destroy those things?" Edric jogged to keep up with Pancras.

"That is a very good question." The minotaur slowed his pace. *One for which I do not have an answer. I can seal the rift... if we can find it.*

The three skirted the edge of the bloodmaw's pit. Pancras heard the shadow demon scrambling against the sides, roaring. He hoped the downward-pointing teeth hindered its progress long enough for them to find something, anything useful to hinder it from following them.

He stumbled over a boulder, exposing a cave rat that then scurried for cover. Pancras saw a glint of metal up ahead. He surged forward to find part of an unattended digging apparatus churning away at the rock. Locked in place, the digging bit spun fruitlessly just above the dirt as it had for gods know how long. It appeared to be dwarven in make, but it was a style he had never seen.

Edric approached it. "Wow, this thing is old. There are a few of these back in the city, but we don't use them anymore." He ran his hands along the machine. "These date back to before the Sundering."

"Wow." Kale's widening eyes gleamed with the wonder of a child experiencing their first snowfall. "How does it work?"

Edric climbed onto it. "I'm not sure. These are from before my time. The controls don't look that different than some of the machines we have now. Well, except it feels different, if that makes sense? Can you feel it?"

When Pancras placed his hand on the machine, he felt arcane energy running through it. "The magic is old. How do the ones you have currently work?"

"There's a bunch of springs, clockwork gears, that sort of thing. I think they draw power from the Soul Forge, but I don't really know much about that." Edric pulled a lever. The machine lurched forward, spewing bits of rock and dirt and leaving a gouge in its wake. After he pulled another lever, the machine turned toward the bloodmaw pit, chewing its way forward.

Edric jumped off the machine. "Seems a shame to waste such fine craftsmanship, but I suppose it might do some damage if we let that beastie chew on it a bit, eh?"

Pancras nodded. "It should buy us some time. I'm sure that shadow demon won't be pleased when a giant dwarven machine falls on its head."

"I don't know. My daggers went right through it like it wasn't even there." Kale tugged at Pancras's sleeve. "Hey, look! There's another tunnel behind the machine!"

Phosphorescent fungi covering the cavern walls and ceiling spiraled into the tunnel, like a whirlpool.

Pancras led Edric and Kale into the passage through curves that descended deeper underground. The weight of the earth above pressed in all around them. Suddenly, the ground shook, and they heard high-pitched wailing.

Grinning, Edric eyed Pancras. "I'm guessing that bloodmaw beast didn't like the meal I gave it."

Shaking off the debris that smacked him in the head when it fell from the ceiling of the passage, Pancras continued forward. He tapped his hoof against the ground, noting the surface felt more like metal than packed dirt.

"Eww! Pancras, the wall is furry!" Kale recoiled, bumping the minotaur and pushing him into the opposite wall with a squish.

Pancras came away with bits of fur stuck to his robes. "We're close to the rift. See its effect on the environment?"

The tunnel grew brighter as they followed it to its termination in a small chamber. At its center, a glowing slash hovered about a drak's height from the floor. Pancras moved closer to examine the coruscating, writhing river of light.

The floor beneath the rift churned. It bubbled as if the metal were boiling, but Pancras did not feel heat from the seemingly molten metal. He found it difficult to look directly into it; yet he felt it tugging and pulling at his eyes. Piercing the ceiling of the chamber, dozens of shadowy tendrils rose like smoke. A thick fleshy column descended from the ceiling into the heart of the pulsing light.

"There! The bloodmaw is still connected to the rift." Standing before the swirling miasma, Pancras gathered threads of magical energy. He spread his arms, looking over his shoulder at Kale and Edric. "I'm going to close it. Whatever happens, you must make sure nothing interrupts me."

Kale drew two daggers. "What happens to the bloodmaw if you close the rift while it's still in it?"

"It might be cut in half. It might be ejected all together."

"Ejected?" Edric, adjusting his grip on his sword, stood next to Kale. "On our side or the other?"

"Yes." Pancras moved his hands in the complex patterns the ritual required. *Sealing the rift should be like sealing any other magical portal... I just hope I have strength enough left to do it.* He chanted under his breath, raising the volume of his voice to match the intensity of the arcane energy. "*Stenee pyealee, stenee pyealee...*"

***

As Kale listened to the minotaur chanting, he wished his sister could be with them. *Deli would burninate anything that attacked us right now!* He flipped one of his daggers in the air, catching it by the handle.

Shuffling his feet, Edric fiddled with the hilt of his sword. The dwarf muttered to himself. "Should've stayed at the pub. Never dealt with this stuff at the bottom of a bottle. Warm beds, happy whores, maybe get a job, pay off my debts, but not this. Never this."

The air crackled. Kale surveyed the room. The walls seemed to undulate, but he wasn't sure if that was an effect of the energy in the air or if the walls were actually moving. Reflecting he understood little about raw chaos, he wished Pancras would hurry.

Gelatinous sludge squished between his toes as the floor oozed up around his feet. Yelping, he shook the goo off them in a sort of hopping dance. One of the walls erupted in a shower of blood and ichor, swirling toward the rift like a tornado.

"You have to stop him, Kale."

The drak gasped. Delilah, his twin sister, appeared before him. Her crimson and ebony scales appeared dull and ashen in the sickly light of the rift. Leaning on her skull-topped staff, she flashed her eyes at him.

"Come, Kale." Smiling, Delilah held out her arm for him. "Let's leave this nasty place. Come away with me."

Kale glanced over his shoulder at Pancras. The necromancer gave no indication he saw or heard her. *It sounds like Deli… but it doesn't.* He stepped toward her. Putting her arm around him, she hugged him close, tickling his ear with her muzzle.

"It ain't real!"

Deli jerked backward, squealing, when Edric hacked her arm with his sword. Black ichor spewed from the ragged stump as he sliced through skin and bone.

"Deli!" Kale lunged toward Edric.

The dwarf caught the drak's arm poised to stab him with a dagger. "I told you, it ain't real. Look!"

As Kale's attention wavered, Delilah's form dissolved into a tentacle that retracted into the wall. Shuddering, he pushed Edric away. Two more tentacles shot from the wall toward Pancras. Shouting, Kale leapt toward them, slashing with his daggers.

Tentacles descending from the ceiling snagged Edric. Muttering a string of expletives, the dwarf raised his sword. Each slice produced a splash of ichor, like grease from plump sausages. One of the tentacles wrapped around Kale's ankle, then hoisted him into the air.

Slashing at the tentacle that held him, Kale's dagger drew a line of burning fire across his leg. He cursed at his clumsiness. The tentacle flicked him like a bit of mud on a shoe. Screaming, he sailed through the air into the rift.

Kale's vision exploded into flashes of green, yellow, and silver. He wheeled through what seemed like eternity in a realm where up and down were the same as left and right. He could see the flavor of ripe apples and roasted meat. When he opened his mouth, Kale found he could not cry out. He could only smell the sound of Pancras's chanting.

Through to the other side of the rift he flew. After crashing into a metallic wall, Kale's world went dark.

***

Pancras caught a glimpse of the little drak dangling by his ankle. If he stopped to help Kale, the incantation he wove to seal the rift would be ruined, and he would have to start over.

Suppressing uncertainty the ritual would work, he repeated the words, continuously. He poured every bit of arcane energy he could muster into the rift. "*Stenee pyealee, stenee pyealee.*" He had encountered only one magical portal in Drak-Anor, and although he studied it intermittently over the last several years with the help of the sorceress Delilah, he never tried to close it. The theory behind the process, until now, he had not tested.

Through the air, Kale sailed past him into the rift. Pancras's heart skipped a beat, but he willed himself to concentrate on the task at hand. If he sealed the rift with Kale inside it, the drak would be trapped in elemental chaos for eternity. However, leaving the rift open risked destruction to Ironkrag and maybe even Drak-Anor. As much as it pained him to admit it, closing the rift was worth the life of one drak or even all three of them.

The air crackled as lightning arced across the room. The kaleidoscope of colors caused Pancras's head to ache. He saw no sign of Kale but noticed Edric struggling with a veritable forest of toothed, suckered tentacles. Pancras felt the portal's tenuous connection with the Mortal Realm weaken.

The wispy tendrils of shadowy smoke coalesced into a familiar, demonic form. Pancras redoubled his efforts to end the ritual. "*STENEE PYEALEE!*"

Splurrrt-woosh! Air rushed past them as the rift contracted with a sucking sound. Pancras felt a force slam into him, driving the breath from his lungs. After a flash of light, the chamber fell still. Edric's sword clanged to the ground as the tentacles he fought vanished. The closing rift bisected the bloodmaw: the part in the rift no longer visible, and the part still within Calliome mortally wounded. After slithering through the hole in the ceiling, it crashed to the floor with a grotesque, wet plop.

Working to catch his breath, Pancras fell to his knees. Smokey tendrils wafted from his limbs, gradually growing nebulous until they vanished completely. Although the shadow demon disappeared when he closed the rift, it was no guarantee he eliminated the threat. He heard the dwarf getting to his feet behind him. He didn't see the drak. "Kale?" Pancras called in a raspy voice.

"Ow."

Upon stepping around the bloodmaw's carcass, Pancras found Kale curled up against the wall, holding his head and moaning. Kneeling down next to him, the minotaur put his hand on Kale's shoulder. The drak's scales felt feverish and uncomfortable to the touch.

"Kale? Can you move?"

"Can I?" Kale lifted his head as if lead weights were attached to it. His eyes seemed different to Pancras, although their color had not changed. "Yes, but I don't want to. I hurt, Pancras. I feel like I'm burning up from the inside out."

"It'll pass." He helped Kale to his feet. *I hope.*

"What now?" Edric poked at the remains of the bloodmaw with his sword. The angular blade sank into the carcass like a knife through a quivering bowl of jelly. Grimacing, he yanked it free, then shook the slime off it.

Pancras scanned the room. There was still no sign of the shadow demon. "Let's try to head back to Ironkrag. You dwarves can probably deal with any remaining beasties down here. I recommend collapsing these caverns entirely." Although he figured the dwarves would ignore his advice, he gave it anyway.

"They sent me down here to get rid of me. I bet they never thought I'd come back."

"Why is the room all twisty?" Staggering, Kale held his head. Pancras moved to lift him, reaching under the drak's arm. Given his propensity for sausages and cheese, Pancras expected the drak to feel heavier.

"If nothing else, you have quite a tale to tell."

"Aye."

The three made their way up the twisting tunnel into the main chamber where Pancras had destroyed the ghouls. The cavern was quiet and still, with only the phosphorescent glow of fungus providing light, no creatures stirring, not even cave rats. In comparison to the cacophony in the cave earlier, to Pancras's ears the trio's breathing was deafening.

By the time they returned to the tunnel leading to Ironkrag, Kale's body had cooled. He demanded he be allowed to stand on his own.

"I can walk! You can't carry me into Ironkrag. We'd never live it down!"

Pancras lowered Kale to the ground before the drak, risking injury, squirmed free of his arms. He kept a close eye on him, nevertheless, in case the effects of the chaos rift were permanent.

He took a deep breath as the area of darkness at the end of the tunnel came into view. "Let's just get this report to the dwarves over with. Then we can go home."

Chapter 2

After several hours asking the same questions over and over again in the Dwarf Council chamber, the Seer-King seemed satisfied with the group's resolution of the problem. Pancras declined an invitation to stay and feast with the dwarves, so he and Kale could get an early start on the multi-day trek home. As they trudged up the mountain path, the forged, black gates of Drak-Anor came into view. Deep shadows shrouded the pass as the sun descended behind the mountains. A cold wind blew down from the peaks, heralding the approach of winter.

Pancras welcomed the coming snow. It blocked the mountain passes, making the city quiet without innumerable travelers afoot. Although many found winter boring in comparison to the other seasons, he looked forward to the time it afforded for contemplation and relaxation in front of a crackling hearth.

He sighed. He wanted nothing more right now than a goblet of mulled wine and a warm bed, but Sarvesh would want to be apprised of their mission under Ironkrag. With Kale bouncing alongside him, the minotaur wished for some way to tap into the drak's boundless energy. He continued forward, heartened by Kale's seemingly complete recovery from exposure to the energies of the rift.

"Come on, Pancras! We're home!" Kale bounded ahead, waving for the minotaur to keep up. Pancras smiled.

"Go on ahead." He waved for the drak to go without him. "Find your sister and have a drink. I must meet with Sarvesh."

As he passed through the gate, the guards nodded in recognition. Most of his minotaur kin gave him a wide berth, but they always treated him with respect. Pancras suspected it was more out of fear that he would turn them into zombies than actual admiration for his abilities.

Of course, I would never turn them without their permission. Pancras rolled his neck. He had not created undead in several years, not since the Battle of the East Gate. Pancras allowed his thoughts to wander to that day when the forces of Drak-Anor defeated the warlock and his army of oroqs who wanted the underground city and its resources for themselves. The citizens transformed Twilight Dungeon, a destination ruled by whomever wielded the most power, into Drak-Anor, an independent city interested in trade and goodwill with its neighbors. That was the day the Earth Dragon came.

Terrakaptis made his lair in the caldera of the extinct volcano above Drak-Anor. He tended the new World Tree growing in the rich soil. Pancras didn't see the Earth Dragon much. He felt uncomfortable, like a potential meal, around a creature who was only one generation removed from the gods, and he suspected his necromancy made the dragon uncomfortable as well.

"Pancras! Oh, Pancras!"

Releasing the memory, the minotaur focused his attention on the three-legged, tentacled creature waddling toward him. Bargle was one of several Golguthrons who kept Drak-Anor clean, eager to eat the refuse, cast-off, and sewage created by the myriad creatures living in the city. *'Tis a motley bunch we have living here.*

"Bargle. I'm on my way to see Sarvesh now." He hoped the revelation would stave off conversation.

No such luck.

"There are some men here to see you. I think they're waiting with Sarvesh."

"Who?"

"Men. Humans, I mean. I thought they were dwarves at first, but they're tall, like the werewolf girl."

Aeryn. Probably off scouting the lower trails. "Then what makes them dwarf-like?" Pancras scratched his head. He often found Bargle's logic difficult to follow.

"They're hairy. Great long beards!" Bargle waggled his tentacles to demonstrate. "What do they want?"

Pancras frowned, shrugging. "I have no idea; I haven't spoken to them yet. I certainly didn't invite them here. I don't know any humans."

The last bit wasn't strictly true. It would have been more accurate for Pancras to say he didn't know any humans who would visit him unannounced.

"All right, thanks, Bargle. I will see what they want."

Pancras left the golguthron and continued on his way. The minotaur wound his way through the city market, ignoring merchants hawking their wares at him. Sarvesh, an Unseelie Fae, preferred to spend much of his time in the chamber where councilors from Drak-Anor's various districts of mostly minotaurs and draks gathered. Because he did not want to be seen as a ruler disconnected from his people, Lord Sarvesh involved himself in the daily affairs of the city, unlike the previous ruler.

Erected from hewn stone blocks, the council tower stood only a few stories above the tallest buildings at the far end of the city market. Because it was barely half the height of the cavern in which it sat, an outsider might overlook it.

Pancras entered the tower, then followed the outer corridor toward the stairs that led upward. Poking his head into the council chamber, he hoped, despite the late hour, to find Sarvesh there. Indeed, towering over two humans attired in mouse-grey robes, Sarvesh flapped his wings at a lazy pace. A flame danced on the end of his tail.

Taking in a deep breath, he strode into the council chamber. "I have returned from Ironkrag, Lord Sarvesh.

The ghouls are no more." He spoke in the Drak language, unconcerned with whether the humans understood him.

"Pancras!" Spreading his arms, Sarvesh met the minotaur halfway across the room, then embraced him. "I assume by your demeanor that all went well?"

Pancras shrugged, noticing out of the corner of his eye, the humans vying for their attention. He ignored them. "As well as could be expected. There was a shadow demon, an army of ghouls, a chaos rift, and a chaos beast." Pancras scratched his chin. "Nothing we couldn't handle."

Sarvesh's smile faded. Stepping closer, he lowered his voice. "By the gods, my friend… Are you putting on a show for the humans?"

Pancras nodded. "Of course. They might not understand my words, but I don't want to appear as exhausted as I am. It was unexpectedly challenging. We were fortunate."

Sarvesh smiled. "I knew I could count on you." He clapped Pancras on the shoulder. "Now then, these humans say you must answer charges of some sort." Sarvesh moved behind them.

The shorter human, a man with a long, grey-streaked blond beard, cleared his throat. "We represent the Arcane University." His voice, shrill and uneven, possessed no trace of accent as he spoke in Drak, "You are delinquent on your dues and, thus, are in violation of the oath you swore when you accepted our training."

Pancras ground his teeth. *Seriously? They traveled all this way to collect my dues. Since when did they care about that?* "Fine, I'll pay them. How much?" He reached into his money pouch, searching for coins.

The taller human's shaggy, brown beard bounced as he spoke, "One thousand, three hundred eleven crowns, after penalties, fees, and expenses."

Nodding, Pancras fumbled with his pouch for a moment before his eyes widened. "Crowns? Gold crowns?"

Sarvesh whistled. "At ten to one silver to gold, that's over thirteen thousand talons. No wonder there are so few wizards. Who can afford the fees?"

"The money"—the blond-bearded human waved his hand—"is inconsequential at this point. Your negligence in paying the dues, as I mentioned earlier, is a violation of the Wizard's Oath."

Rubbing his right horn, Pancras chewed his lip. He hadn't expected officials from the Mages Guild to come after him. "You never seemed to care about this before. What's different now?"

"Our Lord, Archmage Vilkan Icebreaker, the Manless, has instituted some changes with the blessing of the Duke of Muncifer."

Pancras bit his lip until he tasted blood. "What happened to old umm"—he snapped his fingers—"What was his name? Archmage Golovin?"

The brown-bearded human's eyebrow rose. "Oh, he died. Several years ago."

"Pancras is my valued advisor." Drawing himself up to his full height, Sarvesh spread his wings. Flames trickled along their edges. "As you no doubt overheard, he just returned from an expedition helping our neighbors in Ironkrag with a sticky situation."

Examining Sarvesh's expression, Pancras could not determine whether the display was in anger or an attempt to intimidate the humans.

The blond-bearded human did not back down. "Which is why he is being given the option to present himself before a tribunal. If he were considered a true renegade, we would be authorized to kill him."

"Fine." Pancras spread his arms, bowing. "I present myself before you for judgment. I apologize for my neglect and will be happy to pay any penalties and fees as well as my dues forward for at least a decade." *I have no idea where I'll obtain that amount of money, but hopefully Sarvesh will back me.*

Brown Beard chuckled. "That's very nice, but we are not your tribunal. You are to present yourself to the Tribunal of the One at the Arcane University in Muncifer on the first day of Spring's Dawning."

"Muncifer? Spring's Dawning?" Pancras's mouth dropped open. "That will require me to leave in the middle of winter to have even a prayer of reaching Muncifer in time."

Blond Beard nodded. "Hm, yes. I imagine the snows can close down these mountain passes. I expect you should leave quite a bit sooner than midwinter. If you do not appear at your tribunal, you will be branded a renegade and hunted down. Understand?"

Pancras's ears flattened. Although he could dispatch one or two Slayers, wizard hunters employed by the university, he understood how the Arcane University handled renegades. One or two Slayers would be followed by others, endlessly. He would never be able to show his face in the civilized world again, not that he had any intention of leaving Drak-Anor. However, now, it appeared he would not have any say in the matter.

"Very good, then." Clasping his hands together, Brown Beard nodded. "Be well and have a safe journey!" The two humans exited the council chamber, leaving Pancras alone with Sarvesh.

"If it was that important, you'd think they'd clap you in irons and lead you to Muncifer themselves." Sarvesh stared after the men.

"That's too crude for them. They assume every user of the arcane arts will be mindful of their oaths and do the honorable thing." Pancras scuffed the tip of his hoof on the floor. "They were quite serious about sending Slayers."

Sarvesh put his hand on his friend's shoulder. "They'd have to get through our gates to get to you."

"Yes." Pancras nodded. "I can't endanger anyone here over thirteen hundred crowns. I'll just go, pay the fine, and return here as quickly as possible."

"And the punishment?"

The minotaur shrugged. "How bad can it be? If they kill me or somehow render me unable to use magic, they're not going to get any more money from me. What's the expression? One cannot squeeze blood from a stone?"

"Famous last words."

***

To Kale, entering the Bloody Spike was like coming home, more so than was stepping through the gates of Drak-Anor. He and his sister spent most of their free time in the pub; it was his happy place, and after what he experienced in the chaos rift, he needed his happy place.

He didn't want to admit it to Pancras, but he still felt as if his blood were on fire, and his vision had not yet returned to normal either. He saw auras around everyone. Although he didn't understand their significance, he decided to ignore them until after he had an ale with his sister. *Besides, Deli might be able to tell me something. She's smart about this magic stuff.*

He found Delilah at their regular table and her staff resting against an adjacent one. Where Kale was striped black and red, Delilah was striped red and black, although she was quick to correct anyone that her coloring was actually crimson and ebony. The skull topping her staff appeared to stare at the mug of ale in front of her and the steaming plate of sausages in the center of the table.

Leaning an elbow on the tabletop, the drak seated alongside Delilah cradled his chin in his hand. He stared into her eyes, enthralled. A golden glow surrounded each of them, but it faded after Kale rubbed his eyes. The aroma of sausages wafted past Kale's nose, causing his stomach to grumble. He felt as if he hadn't eaten in days. Since Sarvesh engaged in trade agreements with Celtangate and Ironkrag, the quality of food available in Drak-Anor improved immeasurably. Kale wasn't sure he wanted the other drak sitting so close to his sister. Narrowing his eyes at the stranger, he approached, realizing, only after seating himself, that he knew the dark-scaled drak.

"Welcome home! How did helping the dwarves work out for you?" The drak raised his mug.

"You remember Zarach, don't you, Kale?" Smiling, Delilah squeezed her brother's hand. Kale reached toward the plate of sausages.

"Watch out! They're hot." Delilah swatted at Kale, but he snatched up a sausage before her hand reached his.

"They're not so hot." Kale bit into the roasted tube of meat. Grease spurted down his chin, dripping onto the table.

He felt Delilah's eyes on him. Zarach waved over one of the servers, then pushed a mug of ale toward Kale. "Are you all right?"

Kale shrugged, chewing on the savory meat. "I watched Pancras kill hundreds of ghouls, ran from a demon, got tossed through a chaos rift, you know, just a regular, boring day."

His sister stared at him. "You… were tossed through a chaos rift? What happened?"

Kale regaled them with the story of finding the rift and fighting off aberrations as Pancras closed the fissure and killed the bloodmaw. "We never did find out what happened to the shadow demon. Maybe it got sucked back through the rift."

Delilah nodded. "That's possible. Maybe it's out there still, pestering the dwarves."

"Maybe." Kale hoped it didn't follow them home. Grimacing, he arched his back. He felt sore and stiff, probably from hitting the wall. *At least the food is good.* He examined the mug of ale Zarach gave him, sniffing it before taking a sip. To his surprise, it tasted like ale humans brewed—crisp, bready, and refreshing, like rays of sunshine after a week-long storm. Years of drinking that fermented mushroom juice, reminiscent of soggy, moldy paper that the dwarves called ale, pained his palate.

Stabbing pain shot through Kale's head. Squeezing his eyes shut, he whimpered, stifling his reaction in front of Zarach. He felt his sister grip his hand again.

"Kale, are you sure you're okay? What's wrong?"

He shook his head. "It's nothing. Nothing. Just sore from getting tossed around." When he opened his eyes, the auras disappeared, but his throat and lungs burned when he inhaled.

"Nothing, my butt. You're ashen and panting." Delilah picked up her staff. Wisps of blue aether swirled around her. "*Ageliofedros.*" A fuzzy blue boggin, little more than an orb of teeth with legs, popped into existence on the table. Delilah snapped her fingers in front of it. "Fetch Jared. Tell him my brother is sick."

The boggin yipped, hopped off the table, and sped out of the pub. "I don't need a healer. I just need to rest. And food. More food." Kale tore into another sausage.

Kale changed the subject to one of his sister's favorite topics: herself. "So, what's with you two?"

"We're just enjoying a drink together." Delilah set down her staff.

"And sausages, huh?" Kale ate another one. "Was this your idea, Zarach?"

Zarach's eyes flicked from Kale to Delilah. His mouth opened and closed and then opened and closed again wordlessly. He seemed unsure of what to say. Delilah patted Kale's arm. "Why are you acting like this?"

"Why? Why?" Kale felt a flash of anger toward his sister. "I… you—" Another pain lanced through his head. He dropped the sausage, then clutched at his face. His skull throbbed as if impaled by a sword. Then, as quickly as it was upon him, the pain disappeared. Panting, Kale found himself on the floor. He stared at his sister who crouched over him.

"Hey."

"Kale!" Delilah cradled his head.

"Get off me! Help me up!" Kale struggled to his feet. Zarach and Delilah sat him in the chair. The Bloody Spike seemed quieter than he remembered. Looking around the tavern and feeling the glare of onlookers, he blushed.

"I'm okay. The pain's gone. Sorry about that. I don't know what's happening."

"That's why I called Jared." Delilah pulled her chair next to Kale's, keeping a firm hold on his arm. Kale nodded. *Was I mad at her? Why was I mad at her?*

"You don't look well." Zarach stood next to Delilah. "Maybe I should go see what's keeping Jared."

Kale waved a hand in protest. "No, it's only been a few minutes. Sit down. I'm sorry if I said anything that—"

"No, it's fine. I know you and your sister are close."

"What's all this then?" The human's Drak words cut through the silence of the tavern. Relieved everyone's attention turned toward the entrance, Kale reached for a sausage. Two robed, bearded humans approached them.

Delilah moved toward her staff. Upon noticing it lay beyond her reach, Zarach passed it to her. "What are humans doing here?"

"We're from the Arcane University. We saw your messenger, a clever, if unorthodox conjuration." Raising an eyebrow, the brown-bearded human scratched his chin. "Where did you learn it?"

"Not from the Arcane University, hmm?" The other human leaned forward, staring at Delilah.

"No, I've lived here all my life." The eye sockets of Delilah's staff glowed blue, and Kale noticed thin tendrils of aether forming around it. "I learned from books, scrolls, and relics left behind by people like you who used to invade our homes and slaughter our people."

"Natural talent?" Cocking an eyebrow, Brown Beard glanced at Blond Beard. "Impressive but not unheard of among draks."

"It falls under the third statute of the Rose Concordat as enacted by Gerold the Craven. You know, The Manless will want his code enforced."

Kale looked from human to human. He had neither heard of the Rose Concordat nor the Craven Mage. He glanced at his sister.

Delilah regarded the men through narrowed eyes, baring her teeth. "We're not beholden to your laws, no matter where you're from."

Blond Beard shook his head. "All practitioners of the arcane arts are beholden to the Rose Concordat. It is what enables us to coexist with the Slayers. To be a renegade, is to always be hunted."

Brown Beard nodded in agreement. "The archmage will show lenience toward you, of course, since your ability is natural and he has a soft spot for dragon kin." He ran his fingers through his beard. "Why, I bet he would allow this drak to simply begin paying dues from this point forward and take the oath."

Delilah tapped the butt of her staff on the ground. "I'm not taking any oath."

"Indeed?" Brown Beard cocked an eyebrow. "Do you know the minotaur Pancras?"

She nodded. *What does Pancras have to do with all this?*

"Speak to him. He will be traveling to Muncifer very soon to face his tribunal for negligence of his oath. I suggest you accompany him."

Blond Beard wagged a finger. "It would be most unfortunate if we had to enter you into the rolls of the renegades. Once the Slayers hunt you, there are no second chances."

Kale heard the sound of leathery scales sliding across the floor behind him. Suri, the medusa who ran the Bloody Spike and snake-haired consort of Sarvesh, slithered up to the two men.

"How dare you come into my establishment and threaten one of my customers!" She toyed with the chain holding her veil in place, a subtle threat Kale knew from experience she carried out on unruly patrons.

The two men bowed to Suri. Brown Beard spread his hands. "We offer no threat. We suspected this drak was unaware of the Slayers and the Arcane University's renewed position on renegades. We sought to educate and encourage, not threaten."

Blond Beard nodded first at his companion, then at Delilah. "As we said, if you present yourself at Pancras's tribunal, we can resolve this with a minimum of fuss. We are all comrades, we who weave the mystical fabric of the arcane. There is no reason for hostility between us."

Brown Beard bowed again. "We shall take our leave. We must be on our way to Celtangate in the morning."

After turning in unison, they left. Suri turned to Delilah. "What was that all about, anyway?"

Jared entered the Bloody Spike, carrying his satchel of herbs and medicines. Kale slumped in his chair. *This relaxing evening is anything but.*

***

The next morning, Delilah visited Pancras to tell of her encounter with the two wizards. She berated him for not letting Kale and her know about his predicament. "When were you going to tell us? Or were you just going to leave without saying goodbye?"

The necromancer puttered about his laboratory, organizing the things he wanted to take with him on his journey and deciding the fate of the things he must leave behind. He had always dabbled in alchemy, but since he stopped creating undead years ago, his collection of instruments and reagents more than doubled. Noting the unsuitability of most of it for travel, he wavered with indecision over taking any of it.

Sighing, Pancras leafed through his scrolls. "It was late. I was tired, tapped out. After telling Sarvesh about what happened under Ironkrag and dealing with those humans, I came straight back here and went to sleep." He smiled at Delilah. "Believe me. It never crossed my mind to leave without saying goodbye. Anything I can do to delay my departure is welcome."

Placing a hand on her hip, Delilah pointed her staff at Pancras. "Ever thought of not going?"

Yes. For a moment. "Not really, no. It's not worth the trouble the Slayers would bring here were I branded a renegade."

"The city would band together for you." Delilah tapped the butt of her staff against the floor. "For us. We wouldn't stand alone."

"And they would die for us because we didn't pay a fine." Pancras sighed, pulling three scrolls out of the pile. After carrying them over to a small chest, he placed them inside. "No, no, I will not ask anyone to do that for me. Nor should you. It is unfortunate they discovered you. I hoped you would be spared the petty tribulations of the Arcane University and the Mages Guild, but what is done is done. We must deal with it."

"Do you really think they would send these Slayers after us? Just for a bit of coin?"

"There was a time when I would have said no. That's why I haven't paid in so long. I don't know anything about this Manless chap, the new archmage. I am not willing to call his bluff."

Delilah slumped. "I guess I need to go with you, then. How far away is Muncifer?"

Pancras rifled through a trunk until he located an object to help him navigate throughout his journey: a teardrop-shaped lodestone suspended from a string. "A long way. A couple of months overland if we can secure some horses or mules. If we have to walk the entire way?" He threw up his hands. "We'll never get there on time."

"When are we leaving then? Today?"

Pancras shook his head. "No, I need to get my affairs in order. Probably tomorrow." He groaned. Setting a departure date felt final.

"I'll be ready." Delilah left him to his packing. He took stock of his beakers and decanters, his jars of reagents, boxes of scrolls, and his wardrobe. He would have to leave behind almost all of it. He shuffled through his robes. Because of their weight, he couldn't take more than a few extra sets.

Fingering the gold trim on his purple robes, he decided to take the dark malachite ones with silver trim for daily wear. The black-and-silver and purple-and-gold ones would do for more formal occasions. *Will I ever see my possessions again? It's a long way to go.*

***

Delilah stomped past the guards at the entrance of the minotaur labyrinth where Pancras lived. *Stupid humans and their stupid rules. Who are they to dictate to us?* She understood his point of view, though. The minotaur was right; the guards and warriors of Drak-Anor would fight Slayers who came for them, and neither of them had the right to ask anyone to risk death for them. She thought they could evade these Slayers indefinitely, but she decided to defer to Pancras's judgment.

Her brother was her more immediate concern, his erratic behavior and pallid scales the obvious result of being tossed through a chaos rift. She needed to ascertain he would be all right before she left him.

Delilah and Kale did not spend much time apart, and the thought of leaving her brother for months twisted her stomach into knots. She moved toward the city market, past the Bloody Spike and the series of caverns where the draks made their homes, although the twins had not lived within the drak community for most of their lives. Shortly after they were hatched, they were cast out of their own clan for superstitious nonsense regarding their status as twins hatched from the same egg.

She arrived at the small home she shared with Kale at the far end of the market near the council tower. What was once little more than a hole in the ground, another antechamber in the vast system of caverns, tunnels, and lava tubes that made up Drak-Anor, was now a homey hole, filled with Kale's tools, half-completed machines, and the scrolls and books from which she taught herself sorcery. Her eyes lingered on a beat-up codex she acquired from a trader a few years ago, a lexicon for the common trade language used by surfacers. She picked it up. *I guess I need to buckle down and study this.*

Kale lay in his bed. They slept in the back room, each on opposite sides of the hearth. Perking up when she stuck her head through the door, he shoved aside his blankets.

"Hey. What's going on?"

Sitting on the edge of her bed, Delilah flipped through the lexicon. "I'm leaving with Pancras tomorrow."

Furrowing his brow, Kale sat upright. "I thought you weren't going?"

"Stupid Pancras made me feel guilty." She shut the book, then tossed it on her pillow. "He made a good point: if they send Slayers after us, a lot of people will die in the fight."

"Oh, well, then I'm going with you!" Kale rolled out of bed, bouncing into Delilah.

She put a hand on his chest. "Jared said you needed rest."

"If you were going to Ironkrag or maybe even Celtangate, I'd let you go without me, but Muncifer might as well be the other side of the world. Do you even know how far away it is?"

Delilah slumped. "Pancras said a couple of months. If we can find horses." Resting her elbows on her knees, Delilah held her head in her hands.

Kale sat next to her on the bed. He put his arm around her, then rested his head on her shoulder. "We need to stick together, Deli. We're a team."

Delilah loved her brother, but his determination to tag along now twisted her guts more than the thought of leaving him behind. She thought of Zarach and the conversation her brother interrupted last night.

"Kale, have you ever thought about taking a mate? Maybe starting a family?"

He lifted his head off her shoulder. "Well, sure, but none of the clans here in Drak-Anor want anything to do with us." He picked at his claws.

"That's not exactly true. The Stoneclaw clan might."

"Might what?" Cocking his head, his eyes widened. "Hey! That's Zarach's clan!" He leapt to his feet. "Did you mate with him? Were you going to abandon me?"

Delilah stood, placing her hands on her hips. "Kale! What I do with him is none of your business, and I would never abandon you!"

"You did, didn't you!" He peered at her stomach. "Are you going to hatch a bunch of draklings?"

Throwing up her hands, Delilah groaned. "No! I told him if anything like that were to happen, Stoneclaw would have to take you in too." She took his hands. "It's like you said: we're a team."

Kale curled his lips. "I'm not mating with Zarach and you."

"Don't be stupid. He's not coming with us. It'll be Pancras, you, and me. Apparently." Delilah dropped Kale's hands, then left the bedchamber. She rooted through the closest pile of books and scrolls.

"Do…" Kale leaned against the doorway. "Do you think Stoneclaw clan has any females for me?"

"Probably." Delilah didn't want to spend the rest of the day talking about a possible future with the Stoneclaws. Sighing, she moved to another pile. "Look, why don't you go talk to Terrakaptis?"

"Oh, yeah, good idea. Let him know we're leaving." Kale strapped his bandolier across his body. "Maybe he'll give us a lift. Muncifer is a lot closer if you're flying!"

Delilah nodded. *Fat chance of that, but at least you're out of my scales for a while.*

Chapter 3

With his anxieties over his sister's blossoming relationship with Zarach Stoneclaw forgotten, Kale raced through the tunnels leading upward from Drak-Anor to the caldera of Bloodplume.

The tunnel led to a ledge which wound around the interior of the main lava shaft. Sunlight streamed in through the opening at the top, giving warmth to the cool, late-autumn air. Boughs of the World Tree, its violet leaves as bright and vibrant as the day it sprouted, cloaked part of the shaft in shadow.

Kale climbed the path until it terminated in the caldera. The sloping sides of the crater cradled the World Tree like a stone cup. Underneath, the Earth Dragon's treasures glittered in the sunlight, sparkling in the dappled shade of the tree like stars on a moonless night.

The dragon lay on a boulder in the sun, soaking up the warmth like a cat. His scales, gleaming like polished rosewood, appeared supple and yielding, but they were harder than forged iron. The Earth Dragon, offspring of Rannos Dragonsire and Gaia the Earth Mother, lived through the Sundering over seven hundred fifty years ago, but he had not revealed his exact age to Kale.

Clearing his throat, Kale hoped the sound would rouse Terrakaptis. The dragon's eye snapped open. Upon seeing Kale, he stretched.

"Ah, my little drak. Come to see me again? How long have I slept?" He sat up.

"About six months this time."

Lowering his head, the dragon studied Kale. "Not so long, then."

"My sister and I have to leave for a while." Kale explained about the human wizards and their upcoming journey to Muncifer. "I'm sorry we'll have to put off the adventure you talk about a bit longer."

"It is I who must apologize. You've waited patiently to travel with me for years. It takes time to fully awaken from centuries of slumber." Terrakaptis yawned, displaying teeth as big as Kale. "When you return, you will be ready to journey with me to wake my brothers and sisters."

It was supposed to be the very next spring. Then the next, and the next. Kale shrugged. "I don't know how long it will be. Muncifer is a long way."

"No matter how long you take, it will be a short while to me."

"I don't suppose"—Kale shuffled his feet—"I don't suppose you could fly us there?"

Terrakaptis shook his head. "No, little one. Robbing you of this journey would do you a disservice. I sense something about you, a coming change. I smell… chaos. You need this time. Besides"—Terrakaptis drew himself up, covering the drak with his shadow—"I am a dragon, not a pony."

Kale bowed, remaining prostrate. "I'm sorry. I didn't mean to offend. I just thought… it can't hurt to ask"—he peeked up at Terrakaptis—"right?"

The dragon's deep, booming laugh shook the leaves of the World Tree. "Of course not, little drak."

He turned his back to the drak to rifle through the piles of treasure surrounding the base of the tree. "I have something here to aid you on your journey." The dragon's head disappeared from sight. Kale dodged platters and goblets made of precious metals that the dragon flung over his shoulder.

"Ah ha!" Terrakaptis emerged from the pile, holding a golden box dwarfed by his claws. He placed it on the ground before Kale. Intricate carvings covered its surfaces, and cutaways in the side panels revealed complex mechanisms within. Kale picked it up with one hand, noting the box felt lighter than he expected.

"What is it?" Kale inspected each side, turning it over in his hands.

"A puzzle box, created by a drak craftsman during the Age of Legend."

"Before the Sundering?" Kale whistled. If what the dragon said was true, the box was over a thousand years old, yet it appeared to have been recently crafted. He could not find a latch. "What's in it? How do I open it?"

"I do not know." Terrakaptis stretched, bringing his head near Kale. He flicked through another pile with one claw. "It's a puzzle. The challenge and reward, I suspect, lies in solving it. The contents could be even older than the box, or newer. It might be nothing, or a trinket, or a forgotten memory. I'm sure you have tools with which to tinker during your journey. I have something for your sister as well."

Kale stood transfixed by the box. Through the cutaways, he observed clockwork mechanisms below the gears and wheels, which must have taken tiny hands years to install.

"Here it is." Terrakaptis pulled a book out of the pile, then slid it to rest before Kale. Tarnished silver clasps held the darkened cracked leather cover closed. Kale read aloud the Drak writing on the top. "Grimoire of Gil-Li the Graven." He eyed Terrakaptis. "A book?"

"Mm, yes, a book. A vast codex, also from the Age of Legend, written by one of the foremost scholars of the arcane arts in that time, Gil-Li the Graven, a drak of some renown, as I understand. I never met her myself. The tome came to me through one of my followers. He said she bequeathed it to the ages, in penance for her failure to prevent the doom to come." The dragon shrugged. "I assume she was referring to the Sundering. It's possible he killed her and took this as a prize for me. It's irrelevant now. It belongs in the hands of a drak. I'm sure Delilah will learn well from it."

The leather creaked in protest when Kale lifted the cover of the book. Upon noting the fragility of the pages within, he closed it. "Thank you. I'll take it to her right away."

"Tell her to be wary. Gil-Li's knowledge was vast. She lived an unnaturally long life. It was said she was born in the Age of Dreams." Terrakaptis tapped the cover of the book. "There is power to be unlocked within that could conquer nations."

Kale's eyes widened and he stepped away from the tome.

Terrakaptis laughed. "Or, maybe those are all just stories! There is magic in it, for sure, some of which was lost to the world, but the power to change history? I suppose that all depends on who reads it, hm? Oh, there is just one more thing." Terrakaptis poked Kale in the chest. "*Draevyehfehdin*!"

Tendrils of green, blue, and red swirled overhead. Buffeting the drak as they encircled him, they converged on the Earth Dragon's claw. Amidst a burst of multicolored light, Kale stumbled backward at the dragon's touch. Tipping his chin toward his chest, he viewed the smoking rune emblazoned on his scales.

"There, just in case. Now, should you happen upon any of my kin, you have been marked."

Kale brushed the smoke away. Surprised he felt no pain from the brand, he studied the figure. "Marked? What do you mean?"

Terrakaptis yawned, crossing his arms. "You have been marked Draevyehfehdin: a friend and kin of draev, dragons. They will at least talk to you now before devouring you!" Chuckling, Terrakaptis closed his eyes. "Now, you should go, my little drak. Go have your adventure. When you return, we will embark on the journey to awaken my kin!"

Pancras hefted his pack. It was still heavier than he liked. If he had a horse-drawn cart, he wouldn't be worried, but he must hike down the mountains before acquiring one became a possibility. No one in Drak-Anor sold pack animals, and the only ones in Ironkrag belonged to traders who used them for commerce. He doubted he could persuade anyone to part with their animals for a fair price.

Sighing, he rummaged inside his pack to find what he might leave behind. Pancras withdrew his crucible, then tossed it aside, but he left the mortar and pestle. He leafed through the scrolls in his pack, removing all the necromantic ones. Since he no longer created zombies and skeletons, he wouldn't need them. Leaving his prized scrolls pained him; yet he wondered if the meager weight savings was worth it. *Maybe I can sell them to someone at the Arcane University. A set of robes, perhaps? The black robes? No, that's foolish. I need those.* He returned the scrolls to the pack and scanned his room.

Flickering candles provided dim illumination. The popping fire in the bedchamber took the chill out of the air, warming even his library far down the hall. Pancras approached his tool shelf. Knives, snips, hooks, and probes used to gather and test reagents lay scattered about. He sighed. Alchemy required many more tools and accoutrements than what he needed when he practiced necromancy.

"It's still too damned heavy!" He stood up. Kicking his pack, his hoof clipped the edge of his mortar with a clink. "I hate traveling."

"Having trouble letting things go?"

The minotaur flinched, jingling the gold rings in his ears, upon hearing Sarvesh's voice. He did not expect such stealth from the seven-foot tall, hoofed faerie.

He faced his friend. "It's difficult deciding what to bring and what to leave behind."

Carrying a small chest into the room, Sarvesh spread his wings for balance. His hooves clopped on the stone floor as he moved. Nodding, he placed the chest on the workbench. "You won't be gone forever. Just take that which you cannot live without."

Scratching his head, Pancras pulled a stool over to the bench and sat down. "That's what I'm having trouble deciding. It was easier when I practiced necromancy. I could always have my undead carry things for me."

"You won't be alone, so you need not bring everything. Besides"—Sarvesh pulled a stool alongside the minotaur, then slid the chest toward his friend—"you can buy anything you find you need while on the road." He tapped on the chest. "Enough to pay for your and Delilah's dues, your fines, advance dues until you're dead, probably, and enough extra for any incidental expenses you'll accrue. Silver, gold, and gems for those who will take them."

Pancras gripped the top of the workbench to steady himself. "I… I don't know how to thank you." He fingered his gold earrings. *These might fetch a good price in an emergency as well.*

Waving a hand, Sarvesh shook his head. "No thanks needed. If we had paid you a regular wage all these years, you probably would have earned more than the contents of this chest anyway. You've been here what? Twenty years now?"

"Twenty-five." *Has it been that long?* Hearing himself say the words somehow gave them veracity. He had come to know their leader in the past ten years or so, but Drak-Anor and its environs had been his home for much longer. "You know, when you first arrived, we were sure you would become the next Twilight Overlord. We expected you to knock old

Bonehead's skull off the first day he waved his mace in the air and yelled at you."

Sarvesh nodded. "Believe me. There were days I wanted to. But I didn't want to be Overlord."

"Those reluctant to lead often make the best leaders. I knew you weren't a demon the first day I met you, although I wasn't quite sure what you were. At that point, fae other than elves had been gone from the world for so long, most people forgot there were other fae."

Sarvesh shifted on his stool. "You knew, huh?"

"It was obvious to me. Demons can be terrible or beautiful to behold, but all of them exude an aura of fear, a sense of… wrongness. They twist one's stomach in knots and make one want to hide in a hole where one cannot be found." Pancras chuckled. "You can be intimidating, but you're not terrifyingly fearsome."

"Well, thanks." Sarvesh smirked. "You know the dwarves used to call me a demon of flame and fury?"

Pancras chuckled. "I remember Delilah telling me about that."

"What am I going to do without you and Delilah around?"

"You'll manage." Pancras smiled. "Maybe one of the faeries who enter our realm through the nexus can help you out."

Sarvesh threw back his head. "I liked it better when there was no nexus for other faeries to come through. Some days Drak-Anor feels like a parade of fae weirdness. They can't just pop in and be on their way. No, they have to leave chaos in their wake." Few remained in Drak-Anor more than one or two days before moving out to find forests and glens in Calliome where they were needed, as living underground did not appeal to them.

"Fae are born of chaos. You're a living example of that." Pancras referred to the cloven hooves, wings, and horns that made his friend resemble a demon rather than what most surfacers thought of as fae.

"Logical arguments are not particularly comforting, Pancras." Sarvesh laughed. The two friends sat for a few hours reminiscing about the days the elders would have called better times but which Pancras and Sarvesh knew were just fleeting snippets of their lives.

***

Leaning against the rock wall, Delilah tapped her foot and waited. Kale paced in front of her. The sun warmed the morning air around the entrance of Drak-Anor as it crept across the sky, ascending toward its zenith. Two minotaur guards, leaning on their halberds, chatted alongside the forged gates.

Delilah noticed her brother's new marking. "What's that? On your chest?"

Kale looked down, rubbing the sigil branded on his breast. "Oh, Terrakaptis put it there, in case we happen across any dragons. Since he's sleeping and we can't go with him to wake his kin until after we get back, he thought it was a good idea to mark me as a friend, so they don't try to eat me."

"Do you think we'll run into any dragons?" Delilah scratched the back of her neck. "The plains don't seem like a good place to hide and sleep for centuries at a time."

"There's plenty of hills and gullies to hide in. Besides, I stopped trying to figure out Terrakaptis years ago. When he's half-asleep, it seems he talks in riddles. I don't know." Kale stopped pacing and faced his sister. "Where is he?"

Glancing back toward the city's entrance, Delilah peered into the darkness. She shrugged. "I don't know. Do you think he left without us?" She didn't think that was the minotaur's style, acknowledging she didn't know him half as well as she should.

"He wouldn't do that." Kale scanned the city entrance with his sister. She saw minotaurs and draks meandering about but no one who resembled Pancras. Delilah adjusted the straps on her backpack where they dug into her shoulders. She leafed through the ancient tome the night prior and anticipated the opportunity of their upcoming journey to further explore the secrets within. However, at the moment, the Earth Dragon's precious gift felt like a boulder.

Hearing the sound of jingling bells from the mountain trail, Delilah turned her attention away from the mountain. A pair of elves approached, riding in a cart pulled by a shaggy horse. The animal was larger than any of the draft animals the dwarves used, standing twice as tall at its withers as Delilah.

"Hail, Drak-Anor!" One of the elves raised his hand to wave at the minotaurs guarding the gate. He shouted in the common trade language that gave Delilah such trouble, although basic greetings she understood. The tips of his ears peeked out from locks of wind-blown hair. The teal skin of his face seemed as smooth as porcelain, and he appeared frail enough that a minotaur could snap him in half like a twig.

While holding the reins in one hand, the other elf waved. "Hail! We bring autumn ale and wine from Celtangate!"

"Any elf bearing wine and ale is welcome here." One of the minotaurs approached the merchants. The other, shouting up at the guard tower flanking the city entrance, summoned laborers to unload the cart.

"Dammit, Deli! A new delivery of wine and ale, and we're going to miss it!" Kale gazed with longing at the barrels, sighing as if mourning a lover seen only in fleeting glimpses across a crowd.

"I'm sure there's ale in Muncifer, Kale." Upon returning her attention to the city entrance, Delilah saw Pancras trudging toward them. He carried a pack on his back large enough for one of the draks to ride in.

"Sarvesh is busy with a council meeting. Suri and Glykeria are dealing with some minor disaster at the Bloody Spike involving golguthrons, a barrel of soggy bread, a drak, and a minotaur; I didn't ask for details. Some things are best left unexplained. At least Kale has come to see us off."

"Not hardly. I'm coming with you!"

Grinning, Delilah hugged Kale. "Won't this be great, Pancras? The three of us, together!" Truth be known, Delilah was worried. Most of her friends hadn't even heard of Muncifer, let alone knew in which direction it lay in relation to Drak-Anor.

"What? Why? You're not recovered nearly enough from that business with the chaos rift."

Mere mention of the rift seemed to cause Kale pain, and he winced, withdrawing from Delilah's hug. "I'm not leaving my sister."

Nodding in agreement, Delilah eyed Pancras. "And I'm not leaving my brother." *If I'm going into the unknown, it will be with him at my side.*

Pancras slumped, surrendering to the weight of his pack.

"Come on, Pancras." Kale took the minotaur's hand. "This will be a great adventure!"

Blowing a raspberry, Pancras shook his hand from Kale's grip. "Adventure means discomfort, danger, and desperation. These are not things I willingly seek out." Pushing past the drak twins, he sidestepped the elven traders' cart.

Delilah pointed, opening her mouth to reply, but she decided any retort would be fruitless. She followed Pancras, nearly colliding with him when he turned to admire Drak-Anor one last time.

"It has been my home for so long. Now, I feel like I may never see it again."

"We'll be coming home soon, Pancras." Delilah took his hand. Meeting her eyes, he shook his head.

Kale caught up to them. "Yeah, it's just a trip to Muncifer and back, right?"

"For you, perhaps. I don't know what awaits me there. It was my home before I came here. I left for a reason." The minotaur's face twitched, and he stared with unfocused eyes into the distance, rubbing his right horn. "I don't want to go."

Delilah studied his face and then regarded the only home she'd ever known. She lived in Drak-Anor for all of her life and had never traveled anywhere except Ironkrag, once, a decade ago. The world lay ahead, a great unknown, and like Kale, she eagerly anticipated the adventure, despite her anxieties. The two guard towers stood on either side of the forged gates, spires piercing the sky, monuments to the day Sarvesh truly became their leader and named the city Drak-Anor. However, most minotaurs still grumbled in their ales about living in a city called "Home of the Draks."

Pancras gazed at the city gates. His ears drooped as he shuffled his feet. Sunlight flashed off his earrings of gold and silver, and his fur-trimmed purple robes ruffled in the breeze.

Delilah tugged at his hand. "We're with you, Pancras. We'll make this journey together, the three of us, and we'll stick together. You're not alone out here."

***

Pancras regarded Delilah and her brother. *Drak twins of crimson and ebony, black and red, and—odd, I don't remember Kale having a tattoo on his chest. It looks draconic.* He chuckled, deciding to let the questions he had about Kale's new symbol lie. *My friends.*

"Yes, yes, thank you. Let's be on our way. We should reach Bramblevale Keep in a week." He pulled his hands away from the draks, wiped his nose, and hefted his pack. Taking a deep breath, Pancras turned away from Drak-Anor. He set out on the road that would take them within a day of Ironkrag before turning east and out of the Dragon Spine Mountains. Kale and Delilah followed behind him.

Sighing, Pancras took comfort in the knowledge that no matter where he went, as long as they were with him, a part of home was with him too.

As they strode, the sun continued its journey across the sky, warming the brisk mountain air. In the valley below mist shrouded the plains of Etrunia, and bright colors in the forests blazed forth in unparalleled glory, heralding the slow change from summer to autumn. The drak twins sang songs to pass the time, and once the chill of morning burned away, Pancras hummed along too.

"This fresh air is great." Delilah inhaled deeply. "It's been too long since I've been outside the city. Too many stinky minotaurs in there."

"Hey!"

"Sorry, Pancras, but it's true. You don't bathe enough."

The minotaur considered himself fastidious, more so than his brethren. "I reckon I bathe as often as you." He glanced back at his companions.

"I'm sure she didn't mean you, Pancras." Kale gave his sister a playful shove.

"We don't have fur stinky things can stick to." Delilah returned her brother's shove.

Sniffing himself, Pancras shrugged. "Well, I don't smell anything offensive."

"You're probably the best-smelling minotaur in the city."

"Someone's coming!" Kale pointed to the road ahead.

Pancras shielded his eyes. A small figure trudged up the road toward them. As it approached, he identified the sole character in traveling gear. "It's a dwarf for sure, but I don't think it's a trader. An envoy, perhaps?" They waited for the dwarf to reach them.

"It's Edric!" Kale waved at the familiar figure. The dwarf, alongside whom they fought a few days earlier, nodded to Kale and Pancras. Unlike their first meeting, he wore his beard neatly braided with brass beads adorning it, and more pouches than could be practical hung from the belt around his hips. Pancras supposed the ornaments weighted the beard to keep it from blowing around in the wind.

"What brings you to Drak-Anor?" Kale greeted the dwarf in Dwarvish.

The dwarf ignored Kale's extended hand. "The elders weren't pleased I survived our little adventure. They decided to follow my family's lead and just outright banished me this time." He spat on the ground. "Aita take them all." He regarded the trio. "Where are you three off to? Back to Ironkrag?"

Pancras shook his head. "I have an errand in Muncifer."

Delilah tugged at Pancras's sleeve. In Drak she urged, "Let's go. We don't need a smelly dwarf hanging around with us."

The minotaur eyed Edric. "Why come to Drak-Anor? Wouldn't Celtangate be better for you?"

"It's a home for misfits, right?"

Frowning, Pancras resisted the urge to toss the dwarf off the mountain. "We do not think of ourselves as misfits. Most citizens of Drak-Anor are minotaurs and draks. You would be the only resident dwarf, aside from Ironkrag traders passing through."

"Oh. Well, maybe I should come with you to Muncifer."

Shaking her head, Delilah tugged at Pancras's sleeve again. The minotaur shook her off, addressing her in Drak,

"Look, he's probably just going to follow us if we don't let him tag along."

"Fine!" Delilah huffed, throwing up her hands in resignation. She burst past Pancras, pulling Kale with her.

Pancras observed them for a moment before he felt Edric's eyes on him, awaiting a response. "Sure, I guess. But I'm in charge of this expedition, understand?"

"In charge? Of going to Muncifer on an errand?" Edric snorted. "I'll try to keep my ambition in check."

Pancras moved to catch up to Kale and Delilah. *Great, sarcasm from a dwarf. All I need now is a blizzard before we are clear of the mountains.*

***

"Hey, why are you so set against Edric joining us?" Kale resisted his sister dragging him down the mountain road, finally wrenching his hand free from her grip. "He helped Pancras and me with those ghouls."

Delilah again noticed Kale wince at the mention of his latest adventure with Pancras, although his grimace lasted only a fraction of a second. She decided to keep an eye on her brother. "Look, it's going to be hard enough, the three of us going to Etrunia. From what I hear, no one outside of Muncifer likes minotaurs, they barely tolerate draks, and everyone thinks dwarves are greedy little thieves. If an elf or a human, or even that werewolf, Aeryn, wanted to tag along, I wouldn't have a problem with it. At least they could be helpful." Delilah looked over her shoulder toward their companions.

"You've never had a problem with dwarves before."

Frowning, Delilah pursed her lips. She pulled him farther away from Pancras and Edric and tried to stay out of earshot. "I'm scared, okay?"

"Of Edric?" Kale scratched his head.

"No. Do you even know where Muncifer is? Now that we've started, it's a great unknown before us." Delilah hated admitting her apprehension, and she abhorred the thought of anyone else learning of her fear.

"Pancras knows. He's not going to let anything happen to us. Besides, we've been on Deep Road dozens of times. Out here, we don't have to worry about cave-ins, giant hungry lizards, or anything like that." Grinning, Kale spread his arms, although Delilah thought she saw a hint of a wince at first. "It's the whole world, Deli."

"Yeah, no walls. No ceiling." She'd been outside before, but just that one time coming back from Ironkrag, and it was years ago. At the time, Kale occupied her thoughts, since she believed him dead, and she never really noticed the vastness of the land beyond Drak-Anor. A part of her wanted to clutch the road, crawling on all fours, for fear of flying into the great blue void above her.

"Hey, you two, don't make a habit of getting too far ahead." Pancras and Edric caught up to them. "Once we're out of the mountains, it will be too easy to become separated and lost if you do that."

Sticking out her tongue, Delilah put her arm around her brother. "Very well, Father. We won't wander."

Kale wiggled free from her arm. "Careful, Deli. My shoulders are sore." Grimacing, he rolled them. "I hit that wall pretty hard."

Pancras knelt to examine Kale. "Are you sure you're up for this? It's not too late to go back."

"No—I mean, yes, I'm up for it." Kale bobbed his head.

"Let's just get on with this, Pancras." Delilah tapped the butt of her staff against the ground. Aside from the backpack holding the grimoire and a belt pouch containing leather polish and some money, it was all she had. She couldn't imagine needing anything else. Kale, on the other hand, festooned with bulging pouches, appeared to have packed every tool, probe, and lockpick he owned in anticipation of whatever they might encounter. She chuckled, regarding the comical image of her laden sibling.

Chapter 4

As Pancras led them away from Drak-Anor, Kale tried to concentrate on something other than the sudden pain that coursed through him. His blood felt as if it was on fire, but he was sure the sensation would soon abate. It never lasted longer than a few minutes. *I hope Deli doesn't notice.*

Drak-Anor's healer, Jared, found nothing wrong with Kale other than the expected bumps and bruises one might acquire when running from ghouls and being tossed by slimy tentacles around a room with stone walls.

By the time the sun reached its zenith, most of Kale's discomfort subsided to a dull ache. Although he noticed a new twinge localized near his shoulder blades, he assumed the strain occurred while carrying the massive tome from Terrakaptis to his sister.

So the days went, cool and sunny, followed by clear and cold nights. Delilah happily cast a spell here and there to short-cut the fire building process and set alight their campfires. The four of them spent the majority of their time practicing the common trade language of Andelosia. Dwarvish and Drak were fine for the mountains, but down on the plains, most humans spoke only their regional dialects and the trade language.

They snacked during the day while on foot, cooking only when they stopped to make camp each night. Pancras, determined to reach Bramblevale Keep as quickly as possible, kept a brisk pace. The sooner they purchased pack animals to carry their gear and possibly themselves, the better chance they had of arriving in Muncifer in time for the tribunal.

Kale didn't much notice if the days and nights became colder as time passed, but Pancras explained that lower elevations tended to be warmer and that cold days approached. Most of the time, though, Kale felt hot, and his back ached. The clockwork box gifted to him by Terrakaptis was not heavy, but after nearly a week of carrying it, it felt like it would crush him.

The road took them east out of the mountains, and they found themselves on the outskirts of the Celtan Forest. Ahead lay Bramblevale Keep. A stone wall surrounded the blocky, masonry building. Men with bows patrolled the battlements between the guard towers that stood at each of the wall's four corners. A moat surrounded the wall, and a tree-lined avenue spurred from the main road in front of the keep, leading them toward a drawbridge.

Bramblevale Keep marked the northern edge of Etrunia, or if one hailed from Celtangate, the southern edge of that city-state. Neither expended resources to properly garrison the keep, and as a result, the Lord of Bramblevale was loyal to neither, despite his troops originating from both.

Traders passing between Ironkrag and Celtangate avoided the keep more often than not. Upon spotting guards above the gate with their bows trained on the troupe, Kale understood why.

Pancras held up his hands as three guards approached. "Greetings, men of Bramblevale. My companions and I seek to trade."

The men eyed them with suspicion. One wore a tabard emblazoned with Etrunia's blue-and-red coat of arms, featuring a white medusa head; the other two wore the grass-green and yellow griffon of Celtangate. Unsheathing his sword, the Etrunian veteran, a grizzled, old man with one eye, regarded Pancras. "We do not trade with monsters from the mountains."

Edric snorted, brandishing his weapon. "Who are you calling a monster, longshanks?"

The three guards drew their swords in unison. Pancras moved between Edric and the guards. "Peace! Stand down, now! We are passing through on our way to Almeria and hoped to buy horses to speed our journey. That is all!"

"Buy?" One Eye raised his sword. Kale noticed the archers on the battlements nocking arrows and taking aim. "With gold plundered from the dead, no doubt."

As One Eye gave the command to fire, Kale tackled his sister, shielding her with his body. He heard Pancras intone, "*Aspida tou ravematos*" just as the arrows flew. The missiles bounced off the shimmering green shield between Pancras and the humans. Edric charged toward the three guards, but he jerked to a stop when Pancras seized his collar.

"We do not want a fight. It is clear we are not welcome here, even if our intentions are peaceful." Pancras retreated, dragging Edric with him. Standing, Delilah shoved Kale aside, then brushed herself off.

Another volley of arrows flying toward the four companions fell short, stopped by the arcane barrier.

"Let me blast them, Pancras." Delilah stabbed the butt of her staff into the ground, her eyes sparkling with an azure glow.

"No." Wisps of emerald aether wreathed his head as Pancras concentrated to maintain the shield. "No, we are departing as we came: in peace." He bowed to the humans, never taking his eyes off them.

The humans, to their credit, did not pursue, despite launching a few more volleys of arrows that seemed to intentionally fall short. Pancras continued backward until they reached the intersection of the avenue and the road that connected Almeria and Celtangate.

"Where to now, Minotaur? Celtangate?" Edric sheathed his sword once they were out of range of the keep's archers, although Kale doubted that it would have provided protection had the bowmen shot at the dwarf.

Pancras allowed the magical energies to dissipate. "No. I'm not willing to waste that many days to risk being turned away at their gates. We'll proceed to Almeria on foot. Surely there will be farms or inns between here and there where we'll be able to buy horses."

Kale faced Pancras. "How far away is Almeria?" He didn't relish the thought of all that walking.

Pancras turned to the south. The sun continued its relentless march across the sky toward the mountains on the western horizon. "Probably two weeks or more by foot. It's been ages since I've come this way." He sighed, slumping. "Maybe the snows will hold off until we reach Almeria."

Edric sniffed the air, gazing back at the mountains. "Doubtful. Why in Tinian's name did you pick such a foolish time to begin?"

"It wasn't my choice. I must reach Muncifer by Spring's Dawning. If we can find horses on the way or in Almeria, there should be no problem. If we are forced to walk the whole way…"

"Our feet will be killing us by the time we get there." Delilah passed Pancras. "What are we waiting for? I'm not standing around to get caught out here when the snows come!"

***

Loath as he was to do so, in order to reach Almeria, Pancras turned his back to Bramblevale Keep. Now that he knew how the humans there regarded him and the draks, he feared they would send out hunting parties to cleanse the world of the vile "monsters of the mountains." He hoped news of the last five years of peaceful trade among Celtangate, Ironkrag, and Drak-Anor had reached the borderland folk, but obviously they were either ill-informed or did not care.

Even though Celtangate probably would not turn them away, Pancras felt the risk didn't justify the extra time to backtrack. Upon finding no sign of pursuit from Bramblevale Keep as twilight approached, Pancras breathed a sigh of relief. The first of the evening stars twinkled overhead. Despite dark clouds gathering over his shoulder in the peaks of the Dragon Spine Mountains, Pancras relaxed. *As long as the clear weather holds, we should make good time.* Scowling, he slapped at an insect buzzing around his head. *I hate the outdoors.* Already dirt clung to the hems of his robes, and he thought he saw the telltale loose strands of fabric that would become a full-blown fray by evening.

The fair weather continued, and within a few days, the trees and hills of the borderlands gave way to the plains of Etrunia. The road on which they traveled would take them straight to the gates of Almeria, the Etrunian capitol, and from there, Pancras would decide whether to travel overland to Muncifer or follow the more circuitous trade route.

For now, that decision could wait. Pangs of hunger twisted the minotaur's stomach, and the farther they walked, the more his thoughts turned to food. Edric, as it turned out, was a decent scrounger and trapper, and given Kale and Delilah's prowess hunting cave lizards in the deep caverns beneath Drak-Anor, they enjoyed fresh fare almost every night.

Two days out of Bramblevale Keep, Delilah pointed toward the eastern horizon. "What's that over there?" The midmorning sun passed behind a puffy cloud, casting dark shadows over the landscape. Squinting in the direction Delilah pointed, Pancras spotted the silhouettes of four spires rising from the plains against the azure sky. A thin wisp of smoke climbed from between the spires, thinning as it made its way higher and higher until it vanished.

"A roadside temple of some sort to one of the lesser-worshipped deities, perhaps? There's a fire." Pancras figured a lone traveler stopped to rest at one of the many shrines dotting the landscape.

Delilah stepped off the road and advanced toward the spires. "Let's check it out. It's not that far away."

"We don't have time for this!" Pancras stopped, exasperated. In truth, the shrine, or whatever it was, was not far enough away to significantly delay them, but myriad dangers could lie between the road and it.

Beaming, Kale ran after his sister. Pancras looked to Edric for support, but the dwarf bolted after the draks. Dropping his hands to his sides, Pancras let out an exaggerated sigh, then trotted after them.

Arranged around a central boulder with a large bronze disk embedded in its surface, each stone spire stood as high as Pancras's head. The bas relief on the disk depicted a curly-haired, bearded man drinking from a wine goblet. Nearby, a log popped in the fire. A hooded man knelt in front of the altar, paying his respects to Dolios, Lord of Language, Commerce, and Travel.

The man glanced up as the travelers approached him. Keeping his eyes fixed on the drak twins and Pancras, he stood, nearly tripping into the fire as he backed up with his hands held high in front of him.

"No, no, no!" He turned, then ran. "Don't kill me!"

Pancras, his mouth agape, watched the man flee. Delilah huffed, crossing her arms over her chest. "I'm not sure whether I should be relieved he didn't attack us or offended that he ran."

Edric tossed a coin into the tarnished brass collection bowl attached to the boulder just below the bas relief. The vessel rang like a bell as the coin bounced into it. "Surfacers."

Sniffing the air, Kale giggled. "Maybe the dwarf-stink made him take off."

"Drak teeth and minotaur horns, more like!" Edric wheeled on Kale.

Pancras scowled. "Let's just leave an offering and go. There are still several hours of good daylight." He saw no sign of the frightened man. Pancras did not want to risk him returning with hostility in his heart, or worse, returning with a pack of humans ready to end a perceived threat to travelers in Etrunia.

"What do we leave?" Kale patted the pouches on his belt, searching for something appropriate.

"Just toss a coin or two in there." Edric touched the bas relief before stepping away from the shrine.

Kale pulled a dull golden coin from a pouch, then tossed it in the bowl. It rolled on its edge for a moment before toppling onto its side. "I hope that's enough. It'll bring us good luck, right?"

Pancras snorted. "Sure, if you think Dolios really cares about two draks, a minotaur, and a dwarf making a journey to Muncifer."

"I'm a gambler." Edric looked over his shoulder as he marched toward the road. "Dolios looks after my kind."

Following behind Edric, Pancras overheard Delilah whisper to her brother, "Yeah, that's why he got kicked out of Ironkrag."

***

As the rain poured down, Delilah pondered the fruitlessness of leaving an offering for the god of travelers seeking good fortune. For the past three days, rain fell from the sky nonstop, a deluge of damp sadness that greyed out the sky and sun, transforming all but the rockiest parts of the road into a muddy morass. Edric bought oilcloth cloaks for them from a trader caravan a day down the road from

Bramblevale Keep, but even those provided scant protection from the downpour.

At the moment Delilah hated mud between her toes, almost as much as she hated Dolios and Tinian and all the gods that controlled the weather. As they trudged along the road, Delilah entertained scenarios during which she met each of the weather-affecting gods, compelling each in turn to slog for days in a chilly deluge.

Kale's chipper attitude did not help Delilah's outlook. Even as she stood shivering, Kale reminded her he felt comfortable. She derived her only glimmer of joy watching the downpour transform the dwarf's formerly tidy beard into something resembling a drowned rat. It clumped together in strands, and he stopped every few hours to wring it out. Still, Edric uttered not a word of complaint, and Delilah looked to Pancras to share her misery.

Shuffling under a cloak not quite large enough to cover him, the minotaur slumped as though his rain-soaked robes bore the weight of all the world's worries. Observing water dripping from his snout as he moved forward like an automaton, Delilah was no longer certain that being covered up in this dreadful weather provided any benefit.

They found nighttime harder to endure than the day, when at least walking helped keep the cold from seeping into their bones. By the fourth day, no one spoke; it took too much effort and distracted them from ignoring their misery.

That afternoon, pinpoints of light appeared on the horizon, remaining as they continued along the road. Perking up, Pancras stepped up the pace, leading them onward.

"Finally! Do you see it?" Pancras pointed toward the outline of a building which appeared from the mist.

Delilah squinted, trying to make out details. "Is that a farm?"

Edric looked back at her. "It's an inn, lass. We've reached the river."

"At last, a reprieve from this gods-cursed rain!" Pancras trotted toward the inn. "We're almost halfway to Almeria now!"

The inn, a blocky, two-story, L-shaped building, sat across a central plaza from the stable. Delilah observed two carts in front of the barn and a man with the collar of his long coat pulled over his head dashing toward the main building. Torches flanking the doors sputtered and smoked in the rain. A sign flapped in the wind above the door, its rusty hinges creaking in protest. Delilah did not understand the writing on it. She figured it was written in either the common trade language or an Etrunian dialect, neither of which she had learned to read while she practiced speaking the trade language with Pancras.

Delilah heard the din of the tavern through the mullioned windows, although the splattering rainfall and the sploshing of their feet through puddles drowned out intelligible conversation. Glancing back at them, Pancras stopped in front of the door with his hand poised over the handle. Nodding, he opened the door.

The aromas of roasted meat mingled with burning wood and sweat from men in heavy woolen cloaks. The hearth sputtered at one end of the room. A frail man with the barest wisps of hair stooped, tending the fire. Opposite the hearth, a younger, lanky man stood behind a sturdy oaken bar, turning his head toward the newcomers.

When the four travelers entered the inn, the myriad conversations halted. Heads turned, and Delilah felt dozens of eyes staring, judging. She smelled their fear.

Swallowing, the man behind the bar set down the mug he had been cleaning. He gripped the edge of the bartop with white-knuckled hands. "Your kind ain't welcome here. We don't want any trouble."

"That's good." Upon withdrawing a small bag from his pouch, Pancras tossed it in his hand to emphasize the coins inside. "We're not looking for trouble, just shelter. As to our kind, you would turn away paying customers?"

Pancras approached the situation with more diplomacy than Delilah would have. She felt like torching the whole building just for their attitude. Then again, her way would have them sleeping out in the rain. The man standing behind the bar scowled, rubbing his chin. He looked to the room, seemingly seeking advice from the patrons.

"The dwarf can have a room. The rest of ya's stay in the stable."

Delilah tapped the butt of her staff on the floor. "We're not animals, you stupid, skinny, son-of-a-bitch!"

The barkeep raised his eyebrows, appearing to not understand Delilah's Drak outburst. She felt Pancras place a hand on her shoulder.

"We are emissaries from Drak-Anor on our way to Muncifer." Pancras maintained an even tone and spoke slowly as if addressing a child. "We do not wish special treatment, just the same accommodations any other patron of this fine establishment enjoys. We want rooms with beds, and we will want to eat hot meals. It is cold outside. We're just travelers, like everyone else here, I suspect."

"You'll kill us in the night!" One of the disheveled men shouted from across the room. "You'll suck the marrow from our bones!"

Fire burned in Delilah's belly. Her thoughts turned toward summoning a swarm of boggins to devour the rude man. The small furry balls of teeth and hate would make short work of him and everyone else in the tavern. Pancras squeezed her shoulder.

"We are neither oroqs nor ogres. We don't eat people."

Leaning in close, her brother spoke out of the side of his mouth. "Bargle does." Grateful Kale whispered in Drak, Delilah kicked him.

A younger man, seated alone near the bar, cleared his throat. "Let them stay, Josef."

"Quiet, Ivan. They're beasts. They should stay with the beasts." The barkeep spat on the floor for emphasis.

"They're customers, with money. I took a caravan up to Drak-Anor last year. Remember? The old ways are changing." He pushed his chair away from the table and stood. "I'll give up my room if I must."

Josef shook his head. "I can't put your wife out in the rain. She's with child. It's not right."

"Exactly. Josef, it's going to be a harsh winter." Ivan approached the bar, then placed his hand on the barkeep's arm. "Don't turn away the coin."

The older man nodded. "Fine." Wrinkling his nose, the corners of his mouth turned downward. He faced the dripping-wet travelers. "Let's see this money. I'm not taking any of your scrip."

***

Kale watched Pancras drop a handful of coins into the barkeep's outstretched hand. Enticed by the prospect of hot nourishment, his stomach rumbled as the aromas of roasting meat wafted across the room. The constant rain made building a fire outside difficult, if not impossible, and although he never felt as uncomfortable in the wet cold as everyone else, he would enjoy sleeping indoors once again.

After Ivan pulled extra chairs to his table, he beckoned for the travelers to join him. Kale took Delilah by the arm, motioning for her to sit next to him. Edric sat between Delilah and Ivan, and Pancras took the seat on the other side of Kale between him and the human.

Relieved his sister wasn't looking at him, Kale winced as he sat. The ache in his back became a distinct, localized stabbing sensation by the time they arrived at the inn. He didn't remember hurting his back in the fight against the ghouls or the shadow demon. Kale worried the pain could be related to his passing through the chaos rift rather than from hitting the wall.

He focused on maintaining a neutral expression as the innkeeper brought a round of ale to their table.

"Can't believe I'm reduced to taking money from draks and minotaurs to make it through the winter." He set down the tray on the table with enough force to slosh frothy ale over the sides of the tankards.

Delilah picked up a mug. "Then don't take our money and serve us for free."

"Our money spends just as well as money from humans." Pancras slid several silver talons toward the innkeeper.

Ivan distributed the rest of the ale to Edric and Kale. "You mentioned you were travelers? From Drak-Anor? Do you have any news?"

"No news. We're heading to Muncifer on business." Pancras brought the tankard to his mouth, sniffing it before taking a sip. "You say you're a trader?"

Ivan nodded. "Not me, personally. I run trade caravans, but I leave the trading to others. I've heard stories about Drak-Anor. They say it used to be a fiery demon's lair, full of torture and other evil things like that, and that some hero came by and freed all the slaves." He raised his eyebrows, regarding Pancras and the drak twins. "The stories didn't say the slaves were all minotaurs, draks, and dwarves, though."

Laughing, Delilah retorted. Kale nudged her, spilling her ale. She glared at him while drying her fingers.

After taking a long swig, Edric smacked his lips, then wiped froth from his mouth. "My people fought with them all the time, and even we don't hear such piles of horse shit."

Pancras tapped his finger on the table. "Tales often grow in scope and nature the farther from the source they're told. It would be more accurate to say that we draks and minotaurs of Drak-Anor threw down our own oppressors. We trade with Ironkrag and Celtangate now, so don't believe everything you hear."

A beanpole woman delivered a steaming kettle to the table, then tossed half a dozen bowls at them. "Eat up. The rabbit's fresh from today." She turned and left. Kale heard her mutter under her breath, "Probably."

Kale stood on his chair and peered into the kettle. It contained a thick brown sludge with hunks of meat and white and orange vegetables in it. He picked up a bowl from the table, plunged it into the kettle, then passed it to Delilah. She took the bowl from him and handed him an empty one. He served himself, then slid the stack of empty bowls to Pancras.

Ivan snapped his fingers to capture Josef's attention. "Bread? Spoons? Anything?"

Kale didn't bother to wait for either. He picked up his bowl and slurped the stew. He didn't know if the meat was rabbit, like the woman said, but he didn't know what a rabbit was anyway. Hunting along the journey thus far had yielded mostly squirrels, groundhogs, fish, and the occasional bird. Kale was surprised the stew didn't seem hot to him, despite the steam drifting up from the kettle.

"Slow down, Kale." Delilah grabbed his arm. "You can't be that hungry."

"I am!" Kale scarfed down a second bowl. As he reached to refill it a third time, he noticed his hands trembling. Heat rushed to his head, and the food in his stomach felt like piles of wet clay. Pushing himself away from the table, Kale lost his balance and fell backward. As Delilah and Pancras stood to help him, Kale scrambled away and ran out of the inn into the downpour.

Cool rain pelting his skin turned to steam as the water beaded and ran down his arms. Falling to his knees, he retched, spewing the now-boiling remains of his dinner onto the ground.

"He's burning up!" The minotaur grabbed Kale from behind, but with a yelp of pain, he dropped the drak.

Shutting his eyes, Kale tried to quell the twisting sensations in his gut. Upon sensing someone kneeling next to him in the mud, he cracked an eye to see Delilah peering at him. The worry etched on her face confirmed that he appeared as horrible as he felt.

"Here now, I'll not have your plague in this inn." Josef's voice came from behind Kale. "We need our health to get us through winter preparations. Take your vile sickness away from here."

Facing the inn, Kale witnessed Josef tossing Edric into the rain by his collar. "All of you!"

***

Pancras removed his cloak, then wrapped it around Kale. The stinging rain chilled him to the bone, and he cursed the gods for making the outdoors so miserable. After helping the drak to his feet, he guided him toward the stable.

"What are we going to do, Pancras?" Delilah followed behind him.

"We're staying out here for the night." He paused to pull open the stable door and ushered Delilah and Edric inside before entering with Kale. "We'll continue toward Almeria tomorrow, provided your brother is well enough." Pancras pulled the door closed.

"You think they'll mind us staying in here?" Edric wrung out his beard. "They all think the drak has some sort of plague."

Kale coughed. "I feel much better now, really. I'm hungry, though."

Pancras looked around the stable. The horses shuffled with nervous energy, stomping and snorting, seeming agitated by strangers in their midst. The thatched roof kept the rain out, and the patter of water hitting the roof created a relaxing roar. A flash of light flooded the room, followed by a booming peal of thunder.

"At least the rain will keep them from following us." Pancras sat down on the ground next to Kale, noticing rainwater no longer steamed off the drak.

"You hope." Edric pulled the door open a crack and peered outside. "If these humans get it in their head we're dangerous, they're going to come after us with torches and pitchforks. Mark my words."

"Then we'll leave as soon as the storm lets up a bit. There used to be all sorts of farms and villages along this road. Maybe we'll find another place where we can hole up and work out a plan." Pancras removed his cloak from Kale's shoulders and shook the rain off it. After folding it in his lap, he rubbed the drak's back. He felt two lumps where Kale's shoulder blades should have been.

"Kale? What are these?" Pancras lifted Kale's cloak. The drak's back featured two mounds running alongside his spine.

"What? I don't know. My back's been hurting."

Delilah moved to examine him. "You didn't say anything? What's wrong with you? What are they, Pancras?"

The minotaur palpated the bumps. "I don't know."

Kale winced, shifting beneath his touch. "Stop it! That hurts."

Edric shut the door. "Hey, if he's really sick—"

Kale snatched his cloak from Pancras, drawing it tight around him. "I'm fine. Leave me alone."

"Well, there's something wrong with you!" Standing, Delilah eyed Kale. She placed her hands on her hips. "Why didn't you say anything about this?"

"I didn't know! I thought I was just sore from being tossed around the other day."

"The hot flashes, these strange deformities on his back"— Pancras shook his head—"It's more than just having been in a fight. Possibly something to do with the chaos rift." He gestured for Delilah to sit down. "I don't think it will affect us. I need to think on it."

"It will if he changes into some devil-beast." Edric sat against the stable door, as far away from Kale as he could. Fairly confident Kale wouldn't become demonic as Edric presumed, Pancras could not say exactly what was happening to his drak companion.

"I'm not going to become a devil-beast." Kale circled the stable.

Pancras watched him pace. If the chaos rift indeed caused the malady from which he suffered, Pancras was certain it wasn't contagious. If it was some sort of plague, however, they were all in danger. He ground his teeth. Concentrating magical energies, the tips of his horns glowed with an emerald light. He focused on the auras of the life around him. Scintillating patterns surrounded the horses and donkeys. He found Delilah's fiery glow almost blinding to behold. Near the stable door, dark greys and violets washed over Edric, like a deep pit of depression and suspicion. Pancras turned his gaze toward Kale.

Viewing the shifting morass of colors and shapes surrounding the drak, Pancras's eyes ached. The more he tried to focus on details, the worse his head throbbed from the effort. He rubbed his eyes, trying to clear the images from his vision, but they lingered on the backs of his eyelids, like the spots that remain when one gazes too long at the sun.

"Were you just magicking me?" Kale poked Pancras in the shoulder. "Hey!"

"I was just trying to determine if your illness is magical in nature, Kale."

Delilah pulled her brother away from Pancras. "Is it?"

When Pancras opened his eyes, he found spots dancing in his vision. He nodded. "It appears so, though I can't be sure of its exact nature."

The dwarf snorted. "So? Are we all going to catch it and die?"

"I doubt it. We'll find a way to rid you of this, I promise." When Pancras patted Kale's shoulder, the drak's aura flared in his vision again. A shadowy claw lingered on Kale's shoulder before dissipating like smoke in the wind. Pancras gasped, withdrawing his hand.

"What?"

Pancras blinked to clear his vision, hoping no one else had seen the figure. "Nothing, just lingering pain from the magic. Whatever has afflicted you is chaotic in nature. Of that, I am sure. It responds unpredictably to divinations."

Another rumble of thunder in the distance shook the building. Edric pulled the door open again to look outside. "The storm's moving off."

Donning his cloak, Pancras stood. "Let's get moving. If these people truly fear us, it would be best not to be caught in their stable."

Chapter 5

T hat place over there looks like a good spot to make camp!"
Delilah pointed with her staff toward a crumbling tower
on top of a nearby hill. Overrun with weeds and vines, the
path leading away from the road toward it appeared as if it
had not been used in years.

"That's pretty far from the road, don't you think?" Edric
stomped his feet in an attempt to keep warm. Although
the rain stopped a few hours earlier, the chill in their damp
clothes lingered. Pink clouds in the eastern sky heralded the
approach of dawn, but Pancras needed rest.

"It's close enough." Delilah pulled her brother along
toward the tower. Since his episode at the inn, she had not
allowed him to wander farther from her than arm's reach.

Edric knitted his brow. "I don't trust nothing made of
stone that humans built. That thing's falling apart!"

"At least we can be fairly sure there won't be any rude
humans to throw us out."

Pancras clapped Edric on the shoulder. "Kale has a point
there. It's just for a few hours. Hopefully it will shelter us if
the skies open up again."

The dwarf grumbled all the way to the building. The
door, once sturdy, iron-banded oak, now rotted off its hinges.
They found the interior overgrown with weeds and cobwebs.
Pancras viewed a crumbling spiral staircase leading up,
and he noted the building's dark interior proved that some
semblance of the roof remained intact.

"*Dapane phlogone.*" Delilah held her staff before her.
Azure fire shot from the eye sockets of the skull atop it,
clearing the weeds and cobwebs. Pancras hoped she didn't
destroy the supports to whatever roof remained. Thick, acrid
smoke poured from the interior.

Delilah stepped back to view her handiwork, nodding in appreciation. Upon not hearing any screams, Pancras sighed in relief. The sorceress hadn't bothered to check for vagabonds occupying the ruined tower, although the condition of the surrounding area suggested it was well and truly deserted.

"Pacha's blue bollocks, are you trying to burn it down?" Edric waved his hand in front of his nose, fanning away smoke that seemed to drift his way, no matter where he stood.

"Calm yourself, Dwarf." Delilah pushed Edric away from her. "*M'poy'rieni aerha.*" A breeze swirled into the tower extinguishing the remaining fires and dissipating the smoke. Pancras held his cloak and robes to keep them from fluttering in the wind.

"There! Now we don't have to worry about creepy-crawlies while we try to sleep!" Delilah grinned, tapping the butt of her staff on the ground. "*Fos.*" The skull emitted cool, blue light.

Pancras followed her inside. Thick ash covered the floor, and burnt vines clung to the walls. Appearing sound, the roof seemed none the worse for having had a fire lit under it. Upon noticing the thick wooden beams across the ceiling supported by heavy stone columns, he concluded Edric's complaints about the quality of human engineering were misguided.

Pancras spread his cloak on the ground and sat upon it. Edric cleared a spot by the doorway, kicking the still-smoldering fragments of the rotted door out of his way. Delilah helped Kale find some comfort, then they drifted off to sleep.

***

Pancras's rhythmic breathing helped Kale doze, but the images in his mind prevented restful slumber and his head thrashed while he slept. Through the haze of partial consciousness, Kale felt his gut ablaze, but he felt powerless to relieve the discomfort.

He soared over the watchtower in circles above it as the light of the sun crested the eastern horizon. Feeling himself pulled toward the southern mountains, trails of fire followed in Kale's wake. Below him, he viewed the vast expanse of the Etrunian plains.

Wait a second… I can't fly…

Kale dropped, spiraling out of control. Careening toward the ground, he awoke with a start to sunlight streaming through gaps in the roof and birds chirping merrily outside. The stench of burnt foliage from the night before still lingered in the air. Panting, he checked to ensure he had not awakened his companions. He found Delilah curled around her staff and Edric, with his chin on his chest, dozing by the door. Although Pancras appeared asleep, the tips of his horns glowed, and swirls of red and emerald energy wreathed his head.

Upon crawling over to his sister, Kale shook her shoulder. "Deli. Deli, wake up!"

Delilah cracked an eye and stared up at her brother. "Go 'way."

"No, wake up." He turned her head toward Pancras. "Does he do magic in his sleep?"

Yawning, Delilah sat up. "Hey, that's weird." She rubbed the sleep out of her eyes, clearing the cobwebs from her mind. "No, that's not normal."

Delilah scooted closer to Pancras to poke him with the butt of her staff. "Pancras, wake up! Pancras!" She jabbed him in the ribs.

The minotaur groaned, then rolled over. Delilah glared. "Pancras! You're sleep-magicking or something. Wake up!" She kicked him in the rear.

Upon hearing Edric stirring, Kale glanced in his direction. The dwarf regarded the draks with a frown. "Can't you two be quiet?"

While Delilah continued berating Pancras, Kale dragged himself to his feet, then moved to the door. Through squinted eyes, he spotted someone approaching. Nudging Edric, he pointed in the direction of the figure lumbering toward them. The dwarf rolled on his side to look outdoors, shielding his eyes from sun glare with his hand.

From the doorway, they watched the disheveled figure shamble closer and closer. Its dirty, torn clothing hung loosely from its limbs, and silver tufts of hair protruded in multiple directions from its grey, saggy skin. Kale's eyes widened when he realized the human was not alive.

"Deli, wake him up! There's a zombie coming!"

Delilah huffed, nearing the door. "He must be necromancing in his sleep. I keep poking him, shaking him, and yelling in his ear, but he won't budge." Pointing her staff at the approaching figure, wisps of blue energy swirled around her.

"*Dapane phlogone!*" A stream of azure flame shot from the eyes of the skull atop her staff, hitting the zombie dead-center in its chest. Igniting, its body erupted in flames. Its skin blackened before sloughing off, as its body continued to burn. Undaunted, it continued forward, finally collapsing, its body consumed, mere steps from the door.

The draks dashed over to Pancras. Together, they shook the minotaur.

"Enough! I'm awake!" Pancras pushed them away. Using the stairs to help himself stand, he sniffed the air. "What's that stench?"

Edric thrust a thumb over his shoulder. "Burnt zombie."

"You were necromancing in your sleep." Delilah jabbed Pancras in the gut with the butt of her staff.

"Nonsense." Pancras grimaced, moving the staff aside. He passed Delilah to see for himself. "Maybe it just wandered by. Don't humans have superstitions about the dead stalking the moors?"

Edric nodded. "Yeah, but its broad daylight. Those superstitions are about nights on the marshes."

"Your horn tips were glowing and everything, Pancras." Kale shoved his head under the minotaur's arm to peer outside.

Pancras turned around, rubbing his arms. "I remember having a dream. It's fading fast. There was a shadow… and a voice. A raspy, female voice. It felt urgent, but I don't remember what it said. And claws, lots of shadowy, smoky claws, like that shadow demon we fought, Kale. You remember?"

The drak nodded.

Edric pulled his things together.

"I knew I should've gone with you two. One adventure without me, and you're both cracking up!" Delilah put her hands on her hips.

Kale gave his sister a playful shove, giggling. "I'm not going crazy, Deli."

Rubbing his snout, Pancras frowned. "Nor am I." He regarded the ceiling. "Perhaps it is this place. Let's continue our journey."

Pancras gathered his cloak, then left the tower. Kale sighed, rolled his shoulders, and stretched. The discomfort he felt during the night subsided, for the time being.

Cocking her head, Delilah put her arm around Kale. "How are you feeling today?"

Kale took her hand, leading her outside. "Better. Almost normal. Maybe the worst is over."

***

"Oh, Kale." Delilah followed her brother into the field. "Why did you have to say that? You know things are going to get worse now!" Grinning, she punched him in the shoulder, then ran after Pancras. She wanted to celebrate her brother's assertion he felt better, but she didn't quite believe him. Although Delilah understood less about chaos magic than Pancras, she did not believe such afflictions cured themselves overnight.

She caught up to Pancras and Edric in time to hear the dwarf regaling the minotaur with outlandish stories he heard from human traders about the moors. Ignoring them, she turned her thoughts to home. Zarach wasn't thrilled when she told him of her intention to leave with Pancras and Kale, but he understood her desire to keep the humans off her back.

Still unaccustomed to the brightness of the sun, Delilah wiped her eyes. It made her head throb; yet she appreciated the crisp, cool air.

"At least it's not raining, right?" Kale bumped into Delilah, causing her to stumble.

She glared at him. "I was just thinking how I almost preferred it. The sun is stinging my eyes."

Kale flipped up the hood on his cloak. "You have one of these, you know?"

I hate him. Delilah pulled the hood over her head. While it shielded her eyes well enough, it made the heat feel even more oppressive. She ignored his attempts to engage her in conversation. Eventually, he joined Pancras and Edric who were comparing tales they had heard about human lands.

The group marched onward down the road, over the low hills and through the grassy plains of Etrunia. Delilah saw what she thought must be farmhouses or trading outposts near the horizon, but Pancras seemed to want to stick to the road. She, herself, did not desire for the group to press their luck at these places after the welcome they received at the inn. Pancras led them off the road only to make camp as the sun dipped behind the western horizon.

No zombies assaulted them in the evening, and Delilah kept a close watch on both Pancras and her brother to make sure neither one of them caused any strange occurrences.

The next day went easier for Delilah. Puffy, white clouds blocked the sun for a good portion of their journey, and she felt comfortable enough with Kale's health to divert from the road alone to hunt down some game. The dried foodstuff they brought with them was decent enough, but Delilah wanted some variety, not to mention fresh meat. By the time they made camp again, she managed to scorch two long-eared rodent-like creatures to death, then presented them to the group.

"I hope these are edible. They looked like rats, but with longer ears."

"Daft girl, those are rabbits!" Edric took them from her, tasking himself with skinning them. "Get a proper fire started. These will roast up nicely! I don't suppose you caught any wild ale while you were out there?"

Delilah thought about it for a moment before realizing Edric didn't actually expect her to catch ale. She made a rude hand gesture toward him. Meanwhile, Kale searched for dry brush and twigs.

"There's not much here, is there?" He held up a handful of grasses. "Can we make a fire with these?"

She wrinkled her nose, flicking them with her fingers. "I don't think they'll burn long enough."

Pancras pointed past Edric. "I saw a grove of trees over there. Help Edric. I'll fetch some wood. I should be able to carry enough to last through dinner, at least."

When Delilah approached Edric to help him with the rabbits, he waved her away. "I don't need your help." Glancing up from his work, he shouted after the minotaur. "Bring back a couple of stout sticks for skewers!"

Observing her brother withdraw the puzzle box Terrakaptis had given him, then fiddle with it, Delilah approached. So far, Kale had not progressed in finding a way to open it, but he insisted he would figure it out eventually. Delilah sat next to him and rummaged through her own pack, finally opening her trade language lexicon. *May as well make the most of this waiting.*

***

Pancras heard Edric's request for sticks and quickened his pace. He didn't think there were animals large enough to be a threat to him living in the plains of Etrunia, although he couldn't say the same for the copse of trees. He preferred staying with the rest of the group and felt a bit exposed out alone.

Dark hollows in which creatures could shelter or lie in wait for prey often risked an element of danger; however, the minotaur's expertise lay with deep caverns over wooded areas. He hoped the creature making the knocking sound somewhere in the canopy was innocuous in nature and not some fierce beast that dined on minotaurs. Pushing away anxious thoughts, he decided to focus on birds singing cheerful, lilting songs in the distance.

At the edge of the grove, Pancras found sufficient deadwood to start a fire and even a few larger pieces they could snap into smaller ones to keep it fed well into the night. He found a few long branches that would have made excellent skewers, but he had no tool with which to cut them down. Running his hand along a branch, he regarded the top of the tree. Its broad, green leaves swayed in the breeze, a hypnotic dance born of nature.

Nearby, the sound of a snapping branch froze the blood in Pancras's veins. He felt the fur on the back of his neck stand on end when he peered into the underbrush for whatever caused the disturbance; however, the canopy kept most of the sunlight from reaching the ground, and the thickness of the undergrowth occluded the area at least a dozen feet into it.

A cold breeze picked up dead leaves from where they had fallen, swirling them around Pancras's feet. Realizing the birdsong stopped, he felt a shiver creep down his spine. After several minutes of staring into the trees and surrounding underbrush, he relaxed. Whatever made the noise was not coming after him. *Or, if it is, it's more patient than I am.*

Pancras backed away from the grove, then headed toward the campsite. Keeping his pace steady, he moved somewhat faster than normal. When he arrived, he found Delilah studying her language book, Kale examining his puzzle box, and Edric skinning the second rabbit, having already finished dressing the first one.

"Here's all the wood I could gather." The minotaur dropped the bundle of sticks and branches in a pile near the area Edric had cleared for use as a fire pit. "I couldn't find anything usable as a skewer without cutting it from a live tree, and I didn't have an axe."

Edric grunted, wiping his knife on his trousers before yanking the rest of the skin off the rabbit. He tossed the furry bundle onto the pile with the rest of the leavings. He waved his knife at Kale. "Put the box down, and go find me some good-sized rocks, why don't you?"

The drak's mouth formed a thin line. "Go find your own rocks. I've almost got this first layer figured out."

Delilah snapped her book shut, then shoved it in her pack. "Come on, Kale. I'll help you. Besides, I want to talk to you in private. "She seized Kale's arm, then pulled him to his feet. He tossed the puzzle box on top of his pack, scowling.

Pancras knelt to examine the rabbit skins and entrails. "Can we do anything with these?" He lifted one of the hides, its fur scorched in patches where Delilah had attacked it.

Shaking his head, Edric hacked one of the rabbits into pieces. "If the drak hadn't burned it to a crisp, we might be able to sell the pelts, but they're not worth anything now. Can you use the entrails to tell our futures?"

Lifting a rope-like loop of intestine, Pancras shook his head. "I know the techniques, but they're not accurate. Most divinations are little more than educated guesses, anyway." He tossed the bloody bit back into the pile. "Besides, I don't need a rabbit's guts to tell me we're in for a lot of discomfort and misery on this journey."

***

"What's this about, Deli? That fuzz-faced dwarf can find his own rocks!"

Delilah ignored her brother's complaints until the tall grasses hid the campsite from their view. She picked up a fist-sized smooth rock, searching for more like it. "I want to talk to you." She found a second slightly larger but flatter one. "Without them around."

Kale knelt down and scratched around a large rock protruding from the ground. "Fine, what?"

Delilah knelt beside him, then lifted his chin until their eyes met. "How are you feeling? Really, Kale. No bravado this time."

Jerking his head away, Kale glared at her. "I'm fine. Honestly, today I feel fine. My back is still sore, but not like it was the other night."

Delilah moved his cloak aside to examine the lumps on his back. She thought they seemed slightly larger than when Pancras first discovered them, but they did not appear inflamed. She put her hand on his head, prompting him to back away from her. He felt warm, but not feverish.

"You're not cold? Too hot?"

"No! Well, I think I'm warmer than I should be, but it's not uncomfortable, especially if I leave my hood down." Kale returned to his knees, continuing to scratch the dirt around the rock, clearing away enough to free it. Wriggling, fat, pink worms fell off the bottom. He stuck out his tongue in disgust before brushing them off.

Delilah seized one of the worms. As she watched it wiggling between her fingers, her mind wandered to a time when she and Kale, just hatchlings, sustained themselves by scratching up the dirt in the caves of Drak-Anor to expose them. *That was a long time ago*. She popped it in her mouth.

"Ugh. Still tastes like dirt." After chewing it, she swallowed.

Nodding, Kale moved to another spot to gather a couple more rocks.

"You're really okay? You'll tell me if you start feeling worse, right?" Delilah followed him.

"It won't do any good if I do. We don't have a healer with us, and Pancras doesn't know what's wrong with me."

"Yeah, well, I want to know so I can worry properly." Delilah picked up another rock. "Think we have enough?"

"Probably. What does he want with these anyway?" Kale cradled the collection in his arms as they trekked toward the camp.

"I bet he misses home. Dwarves probably use them as pillows." Laughing, Delilah imagined Edric handling them like precious gems. The image of him sleeping on and around the dirty rocks they found had her giggling all the way back to camp.

When they returned, they found Edric had finished butchering the rabbits. He was talking to a seated Pancras, who held his lodestone in front of him, gesturing toward the south.

"We got your rocks!" Kale and Delilah dumped them in a pile near the center of camp. Edric sorted through them, humming and nodding.

"Okay, you've earned your dinners. These will work perfectly!" The dwarf arranged the roundest rocks in a circle, placing the flatter ones on the inside. He then proceeded to stack up the wood, first the smallest twigs for kindling and then the larger branches. When he finished, he stepped aside, gesturing to Delilah. She pointed her staff at the fire pit.

"*Aktina tees pyrkagias!*" A thin finger of fire shot forth from Delilah's staff, setting the kindling alight.

"She's handy to have around, huh?" Kale helped Edric carry the rabbit pieces and arranged them on the flat rocks.

"I guess you're both useful at times."

Delilah stuck out her tongue.

Pancras gathered everyone around the fire. Already the rabbits were hissing, and the campsite filled with the aroma of roasting meat. "I've been trying to keep track of how far we've come and how far we've yet to go. The inn was about halfway to Almeria. Obviously, it would've been faster to cut overland as soon as we emerged from the mountains, but I hoped for a warmer reception at Bramblevale Keep."

Smelling the aroma of roasting rabbits, Delilah's stomach knotted in anticipation. She smacked her lips, ogling the sizzling meat. Edric stooped, flipping and repositioning them to keep them from burning.

"Do you think someone will sell us horses in Almeria?" Kale, resting his hands on his belly, watched Edric work. Delilah figured he must be hungry since he drastically reduced how much he ate at each meal since the incident at the inn.

"I hope so."

Snorting, Edric stood. "More likely than not, they'll run us off just like those gits at the keep."

Pancras shook his head. "I don't think so. When I passed through there last time, minotaurs and draks lived there. Not many, mind you, but it didn't strike me as a particularly xenophobic town."

"Times change." Edric returned his attention to tending the meat.

Delilah glanced at her brother. Engrossed in watching Edric cook dinner, Kale was oblivious to his sister's anxieties. She couldn't help but worry about their fates if Almeria turned them away before winter arrived.

**

Kale's stomach rumbled. He pressed his hands against it, hoping to quiet it. His hunger urged him to snatch the still-cooking rabbits and consume them all, but his experience in the inn made him wary of indulging in that fashion. He returned to his bedroll, then picked up the puzzle box.

He turned it over in his hands, trying to find the side he examined before their rock-hunting expedition. Every side appeared almost identical with their subtle differences invisible to the untrained eye. He noticed a tiny lever on the side facing him. With the greatest of care, he stuck a claw through the gold lattice to move it. With an audible click, the gears sprang to life and turned, then stopped with another click.

"What was that?" Pancras glanced up from his pack.

"My puzzle box. I found a lever!" Kale brought the box over to Pancras. "It made the gears on this side move a little but didn't do anything else."

"What does that thing do anyway?" Edric poked one of the large pieces of rabbit with his knife. "What's it for?"

"I don't know." Shrugging, Kale regarded the box. "Terrakaptis gave it to me. He said the reward was in figuring out how to open it."

"Looks like you solved a piece of that puzzle." Pancras smiled.

"Yeah…" Kale wandered back to his bedroll, peering at the puzzle box as if the intensity of his stare would unlock its secrets.

"The rabbits are roasted. Let's eat!" Edric whistled, beckoning them. He held up a steaming leg impaled on his dagger.

After Edric distributed the rabbit, they all sat around the fire tearing into the hot, sinewy meat. The dwarf didn't have much with which to season it as it cooked, but the hot meal helped lessen the weariness of the day. Kale fought the urge to wolf it down, forcing himself to take small bites and chew them thoroughly before swallowing. The last thing he wanted was a recurrence of the vomiting scene at the inn. Kale slowly adapted to the heat his body seemed to generate, but the pain in his shoulders irritated him. They ached while he was up strolling around, and he feared the discomfort would limit him if they encountered any situations requiring quick movements or outright fighting.

The rest of the evening passed without trouble from Kale's stomach or curious animals wandering into the camp. As they ate, the King and Queen, Calliome's twin moons, shone down brightly from the sky. By the time they turned in for the night, clouds obscured the moons. No rain came, though, and save for the morning dew, they awoke dry, well rested, and ready to resume their journey.

Pleasant, though more temperate, weather accompanied them for the next few days. Cool autumn winds blew puffy clouds across the sky, creating patches of shadow that kept the sun off their backs. A herd of grazing animals with which Kale was unfamiliar, but which Edric and Pancras called blackbucks, paralleled their course for an afternoon. Delilah wanted to go hunting, but they had no means to preserve the excess meat.

After traveling a few more days, evidence of civilization appeared in the distance across the fields. They noticed what appeared to be several farms and homesteads, the smoke from their chimneys wafting up into the sky in lazy columns. The road widened, and wheel ruts from caravan wagons became more prominent.

"Do you think we should move off the road, Pancras?" Kale fretted about the reactions of passersby, should they encounter any.

"You're worried they might attack us?"

Delilah tapped the butt of her staff on the ground. "They'll be sorry if they do!"

Pancras frowned. "We should try not to antagonize anyone right now. I think if they see us traveling along the road, just the four of us taking our time, they may not assume we mean to harm them. After all, if we really wanted a fight, hiding in the grasses would be smarter. Out here, in the open? I think we'll be better off."

"I agree." Edric nodded. "At worst, they'll just ignore us or give us the cold shoulder. Hopefully."

It was the "hopefully" that worried Kale. If what Pancras told them about Almeria was true, they could expect a somewhat tepid welcome, but not a hostile one. If Pancras was wrong, however, an encounter with a guard patrol might prove disastrous. His fears were unfounded, however. Over the next few days, the patrols and traders they came across either ignored them or offered greetings in passing.

Road traffic increased in proportion to their proximity to Almeria. Nearing the city, the plains gave way to hills. As they crested the rise, the capital of Etrunia came into view.

Chapter 6

A dark grey stone wall, punctuated at regular intervals by towers, surrounded Almeria. From the troupe's vantage point on top of the hill, Pancras spotted streets winding through cramped, half-timbered buildings and low walls separating sections of the city. A multi-spired palace surrounded by a gleaming-white, crenelated wall stood at its center. He noted fenced-off fields, wooden buildings, and a makeshift marketplace beyond the main gates outside the city proper where caravans made camp and sold their wares.

Almeria appeared larger than Pancras remembered it, yet with the passing decades, he supposed his memory to be faulty. He led Edric and the drak twins down the hill toward the city. Kale and Delilah gaped at the stables and trading posts flanking the road on their approach to the main gate. Pancras sniffed the air, noting all the familiar stenches of city life hanging thick on the breeze, mingling with the fresh fragrances of harvest crops for sale in the makeshift market ahead.

Most of the merchants they encountered had little interest in engaging a traveling group of draks, a minotaur, and a dwarf. One drak proved the exception. "Hey! Hey! You've come far? We don't see your kind here much, unless you're from here. Did you just leave from another gate and circle around? Hey! You two have stripes! You must be important!" The drak with scales of sunset orange and a circlet of tiny horns upon the crown of his head wore a simple brown leather jerkin cinched around his waist by a braided belt.

Pancras held up a hand to silence the drak. "We're not from here but would appreciate anything you can tell us about the city."

The merchant grinned, still staring at the striped drak twins. "It's Almeria! Capital of Etrunia—"

"We know that much." Gritting his teeth, Pancras willed himself to be patient. "We need lodging for the night"—he steeled himself for the drak's response—"and we'll want to buy mounts that can carry us to Muncifer before the winter snows fall."

The drak beckoned the trio to follow him. "Lodging, mounts, yes!" Laughing, he led them to a cart overflowing with textiles. "Get to Muncifer before it snows? Not even if you cut across the country. You'll be snowed in before you reach the halfway point at Ice Crown."

"Can I interest you in some fine linens? Hand woven tapestries? Bolts of silk or wool?" Circling his cart, the drak showed them each type of fabric in turn.

"This is really nice." Delilah held a bolt of verdigris silk in her hands.

Pancras pulled her away from the cart. "Nothing right now. We've come a long way and would just like to find an accommodating inn."

The drak scratched his head, appearing confused. "I'm sure there are some, but I… my memory—the name was on the tip of my tongue…"

Pancras pursed his lips, reaching into one of his pockets. Upon fishing out a silver talon, he flipped it through the air toward the merchant.

Snatching the spinning coin from the air, the drak grinned. "Oh yes, now I remember! The Sleeping Viper is friendly to our sort."

"Oh, and what sort do you think we are?" Delilah stepped toward the merchant, pushing her snout against his.

He back-pedaled, raising his hands in submission. "No offense, of course. I simply meant us draks." He nodded toward Pancras. "And minotaurs. Most inns will happily accommodate the dwarf, but many people are not intelligent enough to appreciate what fine qualities we bring as customers, if you know what I mean."

Putting his hand on Delilah's shoulder, Pancras coaxed her away from the merchant. "We understand. Could you tell us how to get there?"

"Oooh, the memory's a little faulty there too. I don't get to that part of town very often, you see—"

Pancras gave him another talon. "Funny how silver seems to help."

"Silver's very pure. It can drive the were- out of a werewolf, you know!" The drak took the coin and slipped it into his pocket. "Enter through the main gates, like you were. Then follow the main road until you reach the Commerce District bath house. You can't miss it. There's a fountain out front and everything. Almerian Spring Way runs right behind the bath house, so you'll want to turn there and follow that, it's a really curvy street, until it reaches the Foundry gate. Go through the gate. Then go left and hug the wall until you find the Broken Tree. You can't miss that either. It really is a broken tree. There's sort of a courtyard around it, but if you go past the smithy, the blacksmith, not the armory or the minotaur smith that only makes axes and swords, about three buildings down is the Assassin's Dagger. Right next door to that is the Sleeping Viper."

Narrowing her eyes, Delilah glared. "You have memory problems but you can recite all that so precisely?"

He held up the silver coin, winking at Delilah. "Silver is a cure-all. Say, you look like a pretty discerning female, if you fancy some company sometime—"

Kale darted forward, interposing himself between his sister and the merchant. "She won't. Come on. Let's go, Deli."

"I don't need you to protect me, Kale." She turned her back on the textile merchant, then stomped toward the city gates.

Pancras and Edric shook their heads. Pancras put a hand on Kale's shoulder as he passed, and together they entered Almeria.

***

I can't believe Pancras let that drak scam him out of two talons! He didn't have memory problems. He just wanted to get paid to help us. The nerve of some people. Scowling, Delilah entered the city, hoping one of the guards would challenge her. To her disappointment, they didn't even give her a second glance as she strode past them and under the open portcullis. Regularly spaced holes dotting the ceiling of the gatehouse indicated a second open portcullis. Beyond that, the sprawl of the city beckoned.

Having spent the majority of her life in Drak-Anor, Delilah had limited experience with cities. In contrast to the buildings mostly carved out of the rock of the mountains in Ironkrag and Drak-Anor, all the buildings here were free-standing, mostly with two or three stories and sloped roofs. Staring at the architecture, she flinched when she felt a hand on her shoulder.

"Come on, Delilah. Let's try to find this inn." Pancras led them down the street. Men, women, and children packed the avenues in front of them, carrying tightly wrapped bundles or otherwise going about their daily business. Towering above the crowd, a few minotaurs were easily visible, but even they stepped aside when the crowds parted to make way for a city guard on a horse or trader's cart.

The din of dozens of simultaneous conversations seemed to bounce off the walls of the buildings. Not only did everyone in Almeria seem to speak louder than did the people of Drak-Anor, there were so many more of them. She was disappointed that she didn't see any draks, though.

"Come on, Pancras. Can't you go faster?" Kale bumped into Delilah, seizing her arm to keep from falling.

"He can't strong-arm his way through the crowd, Drak." Edric stopped beside the twins. "This place is more crowded than Ironkrag. Stinks too."

Kale gawked, lifting Pancras's sleeve to see past him. "How do they clean the place? Do the golguthrons come out at night?"

Shaking his head, Pancras regarded his shorter companions. "No golguthrons here. That's probably why it stinks so much."

A cart exited the building in front of them. Once it was in the street and moving, Pancras stepped past it. Delilah noticed they had moved from the packed-dirt road to one covered with small cut stones. She couldn't see what held them in place, but she noticed they were worn down and smooth. Large blocks placed at regular intervals cut across the street at the same height as the walkways adjacent the buildings. Not until she observed pedestrians crossing the road atop the blocks and cart wheels passing in the spaces between them, did she understand their purpose.

Over the din of the crowds, Delilah heard the sound of splashing water. Just past them, she saw a marble carving of a nude human woman. The figure, standing a head taller than the minotaur, held an ornate ewer that spilled water into a pool at its feet.

"Is that a fountain? This is the bath house, right?" Delilah tugged at Pancras's sleeve. The building behind the fountain connected to a sprawling complex constructed of gleaming-white-and-pink marble. Chimneys atop the red tile roof belched out clouds of white smoke.

"I think so. We need to find the street that runs behind it… There it is!" Pancras pointed ahead. Delilah did not recognize the words painted in red script on the sign. The lexicon she used to learn the common trade language was written in Drak, phonetically, to teach her how to pronounce words, not to read them. *So that's what it looks like written. It's more delicate than I imagined.*

Almerian Spring Way ran alongside the bath house before turning behind it and winding its way through various half-timbered houses. The group passed a few gardens with sprawling trees that peeked over the tops of the walls that surrounded them, as well as several boutiques. Delilah guessed each shop's specialty from the pictures painted alongside the words on each of their signs. The candlemaker's sign showed a lit candle, the baker's sign displayed a loaf of bread, and the butcher's shop depicted a haunch of meat. Delilah figured at least one of the shops was an apothecary or alchemist. At least that's what she thought the mortar and pestle signified. A trio of draks stood in front of another shop, arguing about the quality of copper in the pots from the snippets of conversation she overheard. She tried to establish eye contact, but they took no notice of the passing strangers.

The street they traveled on passed through a residential section. Ahead, Delilah recognized the wall described by the drak merchant outside the city. The smoke of industry rose above it from more chimneys than Delilah could count, forming a nebulous black haze that clung near the highest rooftops. *Edric will probably feel right at home here.* The ringing clang of hammers on anvils provided a background cadence to their march along the road. Around one final bend, Delilah noted the Foundry Gate, little more than a passage through the wall, contained portcullises on either side. She didn't notice any murder holes above her, but she also did not see a gatehouse from which guards might defend this particular entrance.

A minotaur leaned against the wall next to the passage, cradling a halberd in his arms. The tunic of the city guard hung over his mail. He straightened his posture as they approached, moving his halberd to a defensive position. "Hold there, what's your business here?"

Clearing his throat, Pancras dusted his robes. He tilted his head in a bow toward the guard. "We were told the Sleeping Viper was through this gate in the Foundry District. We were told they would be happy to accommodate us."

The guard looked them over. "New in town, eh?" He snorted. "You could do better than the Sleeping Viper. Who told you to go there?"

"A drak fellow." Edric stood next to Pancras.

"Yes, it was a drak merchant." Pancras nodded at Edric, then the guard. "I believe he was a mercer, just outside the main city gate."

"Well, like I said, you could do better than the Sleeping Viper. You'd have to split up, though. The Grand Duchess is owned by a minotaur, so you'd be welcome there. The draks, however"—he shook his head—"she doesn't like them at all. Across the street The Manticore & Dragon Inn has short beds for the small folk."

After sharing a look of concern with her brother, Delilah tugged at Pancras's sleeve. She didn't like the idea of splitting up, not on their first night in a new city. Pancras acknowledged her with a nod.

"I think we'd prefer to stay together for now."

Shrugging, the guard leaned back against the wall. "Suit yourself." He confirmed the drak's directions and bade them good day as they passed under the Foundry Gate.

***

Kale wrinkled his nose. The air in the Foundry District became fouler and fouler the farther into it they traveled. The odor of soot and brimstone reminded him of the forges back home, but the scent of something else he could not identify combined with it.

"Clear below!" A man leaned out the window of the upper story of the building ahead of them, then dumped the contents of a chamber pot out of the window. Kale recognized the source of the other odor as the fetid sewage splashed into the street, collecting between the cobbles and running along the sides of the raised walkways.

Gripping her brother's hand, Delilah jumped up onto the raised promenade, avoiding a small stream of foul-smelling, brown water.

"This must be the garden spot." Edric pinched his nose closed as they passed under the building from which the man had dumped his chamber pot.

"These people really need to get some golguthrons in here. It would be so much cleaner." Delilah regarded the area in disgust. "I wonder if we could convince some to come here to work. I bet we could make a fortune!"

"I don't think they would be welcome here." Pancras stepped up onto the raised pathway. "Even if they were willing, they don't fare well under the sun."

Ahead of them, Kale spotted a jagged tree stump. It appeared, quite literally, like a giant had broken the tree in half, leaving behind the part rooted in the ground. A circular pattern of cobblestones surrounded the trunk, and several minotaurs and humans congregated in groups, conversing amongst themselves. Gesturing for Edric, Kale, and Delilah to wait where they were, Pancras approached the group of minotaurs. When he returned, he pointed to one of the side streets.

"The Sleeping Viper is that way." He led them down the road past the smithy. Kale heard the ringing of a hammer beating metal into shape. A red brick chimney built into the side of the wooden building spewed black smoke. Just after the hammering stopped, the hiss of hot metal plunging into water could be heard in the street.

Edric stared at the smithy as they passed. His shoulders seemed to slump. When he noticed Kale's eye on him, he straightened up, averting his eyes.

"Missing home?"

"A little, but not because of the smithy." Edric took a long drink from his waterskin, then wiped his mouth. "I was just wondering if my life would've been different if my family had been smiths instead of traders. My sister and father kept busy traveling all the time while Mother watched the shop. Perhaps keeping busy in a forge might've kept me out of trouble." He shrugged. "Doesn't matter now."

"I don't know." Kale glanced over his shoulder at the smithy. "You could probably learn to become a smith. You're still pretty young, I think, right? There's time."

"Aye, time's aplenty. The spirit is not willing, though."

"We're here." Delilah tapped Kale's arm to get his attention, then gestured toward the sign ahead. The rough-hewn sign hanging from a pole above an iron-banded oak door jutted beyond the building. Kale couldn't read the words painted on it, but the stylized image of a snake was clear.

A bell jingled as the swinging door pulled a chain attached to the jamb when Pancras opened it. Entering the inn, Kale surveyed the dim vestibule, noting well-worn bare, wooden floors stained with water and ground-in dirt and a rack with blunted iron hooks attached to the far wall. The clomping of hooves on wood heralded the arrival of the Inn's proprietor, a hulking minotaur, wearing a greasy leather jerkin and kilt Kale thought might once have been green and blue. On the same side as his missing horn tip, a gnarled scar drew a pale line down his face, crossing a milky-white eye.

He grunted upon noticing the four travelers occupying his vestibule. "What do you want?"

Pancras cleared his throat. "Lodging."

The scarred minotaur narrowed his eyes. "Yeah? Who sent you?"

"We didn't get his name. A drak textile merchant set up outside the main city gates said you could accommodate us."

"Two draks, a dwarf, and a minotaur?" The innkeeper looked at each of them in turn. He grunted again. "I have beds for you. A half-talon per day. Each. That's for the common room. You're responsible for your own washing, your own meals. I got beds. That's all."

Pancras reached into his pouch, withdrawing two silver talons. He handed them to the proprietor.

"Common room?" Delilah stood toe-to-toe with the scarred minotaur. "My brother and I want our own room. I'm not sleeping with them!"

"A talon a day for private rooms." He turned, then ambled down the hall, pausing to look back at them. "Each."

Pancras handed him two more talons.

Kale leaned over to his sister. "This guy's not very happy, is he?"

"None of your business, Drak. I may not be able to see out of one eye, but I can still hear just fine."

Edric chuckled as the minotaur led them toward the back of the inn. A set of rickety stairs led up. He pointed to a door under the stairwell. "Privy. Your rooms are up. Take whichever ones you want. No one else is here right now. Keys are in the locks. Beds should be clean and have fresh linens. If you need anything, you can call me. I'm Scar."

That's original. Kale ascended the steps to the second floor of the inn. They creaked with each footfall, but they felt solid enough. As noisy as the treads were, Kale did not want to take the rooms closest to the stairway, so he kept ahead of Pancras and Edric and advanced to the far end of the hall. True to Scar's word, a key protruded from the door lock. After turning the key, he opened the door.

A musty odor pervaded the air of the spartan room, and motes of dust danced in the light afforded by the window opposite the door. Kale noted the lone bed pushed up against one wall. At the foot of it, he found a three-drawer chest about his height with a wash basin and pitcher on top. A full log rack sat on the floor next to the fireplace built into the wall opposite the window. Delilah passed Kale and hopped up on the bed.

She leaned over, peering out the window. "Not much of a view."

Kale approached to see for himself. The window overlooked an alley, across which lay an overgrown garden surrounded by a crumbling wall. Holes in the tiled roof of the building adjacent to the garden allowed Kale to see inside it. Vines covered the structure and snaked through the broken windows.

He heard Pancras clomping around in the room next to theirs. *I suppose it could be Scar. I won't be able to tell them apart just by listening to their footfalls.* He opened the window and stuck his head through to examine the facade. He could scale the wall if he needed to sneak out, but it wouldn't be easy.

"Do you think we're going to have to stay here all winter?"

Delilah removed her pack, then withdrew the books from it and placed them on the bed. "I figure Pancras will want to stay here until we learn our way around the city. We don't want to get trapped out on the plains when it snows, though I really don't see how staying here will be any better."

"Well, here, at least we'll have a roof over our heads. If it's cold, we can just huddle around the fireplace. Out there, we'll have to scrounge for wood, and it'll be wet—"

"Yeah, yeah. I know all that." Delilah dismissed his explanations with a wave. "I just don't want to stay here all winter. It's kind of a dump."

Kale sat next to his sister on the bed, lowering his voice. "I wouldn't say such things so loud. Scar will hear you!"

"I'm not afraid of him."

"I know. Nothing much scares you, does it?" Kale rested his head on his sister's shoulder, then closed his eyes. His back ached, and he still felt warmer than he thought he should, but as long as Delilah was with him, Kale supposed they would figure things out together.

"Not much, no." Putting her arm around Kale, Delilah hugged him. "But I miss stupid old Sarvesh and blubbery Bargle."

"Me too."

"I don't think we'll ever see them again, Kale."

Kale leaned into his sister. "Nah, once this business in Muncifer is over, we'll go home. I bet we'll even get some mighty steeds to speed us home." He laughed. "I really don't want to walk all the way back."

"I'm with you there, Brother."

***

When Pancras finished sorting through his pack, he laid it on the chest of drawers and left the room, locking the door behind him. He thought about checking on Edric and the twins, but he decided to go downstairs to talk to Scar first. He found the innkeeper in the kitchen, sitting alone at a small table. Scar held a thin, black-bladed knife in his hands, whittling a block of wood. Pancras thought the figure resembled a horse, but, from his position in the doorway, he was too far away to ascertain.

Scar glanced up from his carving. "What?"

"I wanted to let you know the accommodations are acceptable and to give you payment for the next few days in advance, if that's all right. Also, the draks are sharing a room, if you want to factor that into your calculations." Upon entering the kitchen, Pancras placed a gold talon on the table.

The proprietor grunted. "It's up to you what you do with your money."

Pancras lingered as Scar resumed carving. Pausing his work after a minute, he eyed Pancras. "Do you need something else?"

"No, not really. I was just wondering about you. Where—"

"Not your business. I don't know you, and I don't want you to know me. You paid for rooms. I provided them. That's all we need from each other. Agreed?"

"Yes, of course." Pancras bowed, backing out of the kitchen. "Good day."

No wonder the guard said we could do better. After ascending the stairs, Pancras proceeded down the hall to Kale and Delilah's room. He knocked on the door. Upon hearing the patter-clicking of clawed feet approaching the door, he waited.

Opening it with a jerk, Kale greeted Pancras. "Hi! What's your room like?" The drak invited him in.

Noting similar accoutrements and their arrangement, Pancras smiled. "Just like this one. I think they're all the same. I was thinking we should go to the tavern next door, have a few ales, get some food, and work out a plan for the next few weeks."

"Good idea." Delilah hopped off the bed. "It'll be nice to eat something we didn't have to catch and cook."

After reminding the draks to lock up before they left, Pancras went to Edric's room to gather the dwarf. Together they all went to the Assassin's Dagger. The tavern seemed quiet from the street. Pancras regarded the image of a dagger burned into the oaken door before opening it. With a bar top running almost the length of it, the narrow common room of the tavern stretched back to the far end of the building. Round tables filled the room, save for the front of the hearth, which was left clear to give the tavern keeper room to stoke the fire. A centerpiece featuring skulls with hair of clumpy melted wax adorned each table. Flickering candles atop the skulls provided dim illumination, barely adequate to stave off the darkness.

Behind the bar, a portly, monolithic human, rubbing the bar top with a dirty cloth, flashed a gap-toothed grin at the travelers as they entered. "Ah, good, the first customers of the evening! I am Janek. Welcome! Welcome!" He gestured to the empty room. "You may sit anywhere you desire."

He waddled around the front of the bar toward them as they chose a table near the hearth. "Ale? Wine? Dwarven spirits?"

Edric's face lit up. "You have dwarven spirits?"

"Indeed, I do, Master Dwarf. Fine bottles from Dwegerthon. Only the best."

"Ale for us." Delilah pointed at herself and Kale.

"For me as well." Pancras fished a talon out of his pouch and pressed it into Janek's hand.

"I want some of those spirits, but I'll need an ale as well." Edric glanced around the table at the twins and Pancras. "To wash it down!"

Janek laughed. "Of course, of course. I'll bring your drinks right out. Now, Lenka has prepared several fine dishes tonight. We have roasts of beef and lamb with the last of the summer vegetables, and I think a shepherd's pie."

"Lamb for me." Eating the meat of bovines made Pancras uncomfortable. Although minotaurs resembled cows, they weren't actually related to them. Nonetheless, eating beef felt too much like cannibalism to Pancras.

"Us, too!"

Edric nodded. "Is it lamb or mutton? It seems late for lamb."

"Oh yes, of course, it is mutton. My apologies." Janek bowed to the dwarf.

"I'll have beef, then."

"Very well. I think they're not quite ready, but you're welcome to sit and drink while Lenka finishes up in the kitchen. Other patrons will be arriving shortly." Shouting toward the kitchen that guests were hungry, Janek bowed to the table, then went behind the bar to fetch their drinks.

By the time their meals arrived, half the tables were filled. The patrons, a mix of humans and minotaurs, most of whom were dirty and loud, demanded ale and food. Janek served them all with a smile and a laugh. A far better fare than Pancras expected to find in the working-class part of town, steaming platters filled with meat and vegetables brought to their table smelled of herbs and spices.

As they ate, Pancras considered what they would do. Money wasn't an issue with the boon he received from Sarvesh before leaving Drak-Anor. "We need a plan. We're going to be here until the snows thaw. I think it would be unwise for us to do nothing but sit around our inn or wander the streets aimlessly."

Edric nodded in agreement. "Aye, maybe I can find a gambling house or something."

"That doesn't sound like a very good idea. You might need that coin for the trip to Muncifer." Pancras chomped on a steaming tuber. "Unless you plan to stay here."

"I could. I might." Edric shrugged. "No offense to you three, but there's no reason for me to keep dogging your heels."

"I think we should spend a few days looking around town, seeing what's here." Kale paused to finish his mug of ale. He swayed a bit as he set his mug down.

Pancras felt a bit lightheaded and fuzzy; the ale seemed stronger than the brew served in Drak-Anor. "Maybe an opportunity will present itself."

Delilah waved down Janek and ordered another round. "We should definitely try to find a nicer inn. The bed is okay, but Scarface has the personality of a rock. Not a nice rock, the nasty kind you overturn and find all sorts of gross, crawly things under."

Pancras chuckled. He didn't want to judge Scar too harshly without knowing what perils the minotaur had seen.

"Maybe we should try to find that other inn tomorrow, the one the guard mentioned," Kale stifled a belch, noticing it seemed to burn in his throat. He coughed to clear it. "What was it called? The Grand Duchy?"

"Grand Duchess." Pancras nodded. "It's a good idea. I don't hold out hope for that one, though. With a name like that, it must be very expensive."

"I think we should split up." Delilah helped herself to more mutton. "We can cover more ground that way. We can meet up here for dinner again and share what we've learned."

Edric pushed himself away from the table. "I'm going to go learn right now. See you tomorrow. I'll be here at sundown." He tossed a talon on the table, then left the tavern.

"Do you think he'll really come back?" Kale watched Edric go.

Delilah shook her head. "He'll probably find a bunch of dwarves in town and stay with them. He doesn't fit in with us." She surveyed the room. "And we don't fit in anywhere."

Pancras didn't necessarily agree with that sentiment. Just because they hadn't seen many draks and minotaurs didn't mean they didn't belong. They hadn't seen enough of Almeria to know whether they would be outcasts the entire winter.

"I think tomorrow we should stick together. None of us know this city well enough to not become lost. It would be very easy to wander into a dangerous area. We'll need each other's strengths." Pancras pushed away his now-empty plate.

"Maybe the grump can give us some pointers." Kale reached across the table to Edric's abandoned meal, pulling the plate toward him. The dwarf ate all the meat, but he barely touched his vegetables. Kale consumed them with gusto.

"It's worth a shot, I suppose." Pancras didn't hold out hope of obtaining useful information from Scar. He merely hoped they could make it through the winter without any unfortunate encounters like the one at the inn several weeks earlier. Pancras decided to start by going straight to bed, hoping the night would pass without incident.

Chapter 7

As Pancras slept, strange images entered his mind. Despite being aware of his dream state, he lacked the ability to escape it, finding himself forced to witness the scenes unfold. Darkness seeped into the room, and the shadows seemed to dance, although there wasn't any music. Kale stood in the doorway, mouthing words Pancras could not hear.

The darkness crept toward Kale. The drak, oblivious to the danger, advanced into the shadow, then emerged as a skeleton, crumbling as Pancras reached for him. Seeing his own hand transform into a shadowy talon, Pancras gasped.

Entering the room, Delilah witnessed the disintegration of her brother's form. Screaming, her eyes melted in their sockets, then flowed down her cheeks. The scales flaked off her body, leaving raw, wet muscle behind before they, too, puddled on the floor of Pancras's room.

He awoke with a start. The soft glow of dawn poured through the window, drawing his eyes to the dust on top of the chest of drawers. Gasping for breath, Pancras threw open the sash without bothering to put on his robes. The brisk air, hitting him like a fist to his chest, helped clear his head. He then approached the basin and pitcher atop the chest of drawers. *Naturally, it's empty. I don't know what I expected.*

Yawning, Pancras rubbed the sleep out of his eyes. While dressing in his malachite robes, he thought he saw movement in the shadow he cast on the floor. He shook his head to clear his sleep-addled mind of lingering dream images.

After wandering downstairs, Pancras remembered Scar saying the inn would not offer any sustenance with which to break their fast. He neither found Scar in the kitchen, nor any bread on the table. Snores from the common room indicated they were no longer the sole tenants of the Sleeping Viper. Peeking inside the doorway, Pancras found Scar with his chair leaning against the wall, snoring with his mouth agape, oozing drool, as well as two humans slumped over tables, asleep. Rather than disturb the innkeeper and risk his ire, Pancras returned upstairs and roused Kale and Delilah.

By the time they left the inn, Scar had not yet risen, and although the sun was still low in the sky, the blacksmiths were already hard at work. Their cacophonous clanging was enough to cause his head to throb, and Pancras was eager to search for other lodging in a quieter part of the city.

"Do you think our stuff will be okay?" Delilah regarded the Sleeping Viper. Already, the streets teemed with people going about their daily routine.

"Should be, if you locked the door to your room." Pancras patted his pocket to ensure it still held the key. They followed the street until they reached a large thoroughfare. After Pancras made a few inquiries of a nearby guard, they headed toward the Commerce District.

Over the din of the crowd, a clarion called folk to worship. From the tight streets of the Foundry District, Pancras couldn't see which temple summoned its devoted. Most people around them seemed to ignore its call. With the rumbling of distant thunder promising to put a damper on the morning, Pancras urged Kale and Delilah to move faster, although they did not know where they were headed, exactly.

Despite the crowds, Pancras enjoyed returning to civilization. Considering himself ill-suited for the wilderness, he always felt more comfortable around buildings and shops and vendors hawking their wares than he did sleeping under the open sky and fending off swarms of midges.

I hope there are shops with reasonably priced clothes in my size. He glanced down at the mud-stiffened, ragged hems of his robes. He tried to limit what he wore during their travels so at least one set of robes remained in decent condition. Now that the prospect of obtaining horses or a cart to take them to Muncifer come spring seemed likely, he figured a few extra pounds of clothing would not unduly burden him.

Streets in the Commerce District all ran toward the city market, which was open daily. The market itself, a large, gated area, featured stalls from which farmers from the surrounding area sold their wares, produce, and livestock. Merchants who owned shops in the city preferred locations closer to their stalls in the open-air market, and many merchant families maintained ownership of their properties from generation to generation.

Towering, gilded gates featuring statues of Dolios, god of travel and commerce, and Anetha, goddess of civilization, marked the entrance to the city market. Pancras led the twins inside. Vendors selling everything from weapons and armor to fine clothing, baked goods, cheeses, fresh vegetables, livestock, and more filled the area.

Pancras reached into his pouch, then handed Kale and Delilah a handful of coins. "Let's do some shopping while we're here. We'll meet at that pie vendor over yonder when we're finished."

***

Stowing the money in his pouch, Kale gawked. "Have you ever seen anything like this, Deli?"

A human's pack smacked Delilah across the snout. Rubbing it, she glared daggers at the oblivious man. "No. We're the smallest things here, Kale. We'd better move it before we get squashed!"

Dodging a different human, who rushed past carrying a basket of small, red fruit, Kale splashed in a puddle he hoped was water. Delilah pulled him by the hand through the crowd. They paused in a covered stall filled with jars and urns.

The shaggy, bearded man tending the stall held out an earthenware jar toward them, tilting the lid. "Black lotus? Stygian, the best!"

Delilah held up her hand, shaking her head. "Perhaps later. Look over there, Kale!" She pointed to a stall filled with clothing.

They dashed across the street. Kale admired each mountain of cloaks arranged by color and type of fabric. The merchant dozed on a stool nearby, awakening with a start when Delilah tapped her leg with her staff. Delilah held up the fraying hem of her cloak. "Got anything in our size? Ours are getting a little threadbare."

Rubbing the sleep out of her eyes, the woman nodded. "I have some cut for children." Her eyes narrowed. "You can pay, yes?"

Kale jingled his coin purse. "Of course we can!"

Satisfied, the woman described how her cloaks were the finest in the city. Her performance was similar to that of all the merchants around her. Kale found a hooded, dark-brown wool cloak that suited him and watched passersby as Delilah spent what seemed like hours trying on various fabrics and colors until she ended up with a fur-trimmed forest-green mantle. Supposedly, it was made especially for a nobleman's daughter who tragically died in a runaway cart accident. In his mind Kale questioned the veracity of her story, but Delilah nodded sympathetically as the merchant told the tale.

"Are you ready to go? We need to meet up with Pancras, and I'm getting hungry again."

Delilah twirled. "This is fantastic. Now I'll be warm all winter!"

By the time they found their way back to the pie vendor, they found Pancras waiting for them. The baker chatted as he pulled a steaming, golden brown pie out of the small, brick oven set up in front of his stall. Pancras dropped a silver talon on the counter.

"Svarog here says these are the best meat pies in the city."

"That's right." The baker broke the talon in half, then returned half to Pancras. "Only the finest chickens and lambs go in my pies."

Kale couldn't deny they smelled delicious. The aroma of spiced chicken with fresh herbs wafted past his nose. "Everyone here says their wares are the finest in the city."

Svarog laughed. "That's right. Everyone is the best! All our wares are better than everyone else's, but my pies are better than that pig Yuri's!" He made an obscene gesture at a tavern across the street.

"Well, it's a good thing we purchased yours, then." Holding the pie with the edge of his cloak, Pancras led Kale and Delilah to a nearby stoop. "I see you two purchased new cloaks and robes. Anything else?"

"We didn't have time. It took Deli all that time just to find the right robe. She tried on everything that woman had. Twice!"

Delilah stuck out her tongue at Kale. "Some of us are more discerning than others. I wasn't going to be satisfied with the first ratty cloak I came across."

"It's not ratty!"

His sister did not often indulge her vanity, and Kale liked her new cloak, so he let the matter drop. When they finished eating, the three set off together. They still needed to find a better inn. That task proved challenging. The inns that catered to minotaurs were unwilling to accommodate draks. The inns that accommodated draks did not have beds large enough for minotaurs. A few inns demanded they leave as soon as they entered their doors, and they still had not found The Grand Duchess or The Manticore & Dragon Inn.

Kale wasn't sure he wanted to go look for the latter two, since it would mean sleeping in separate buildings. He agreed with Pancras that they should stick together for safety.

As the afternoon waned, they decided to return to the Assassin's Dagger, eat, and plan for the next day.

"Hopefully, Edric will have some good news for us." Kale gathered up his new cloak as he tiptoed through a puddle.

"If he even shows up." Delilah pulled Kale to a stop in front of their inn. "Go on ahead, Pancras. I want to check on our stuff."

The minotaur nodded, then proceeded into the tavern.

"I just have a funny feeling, Kale. Like we've been robbed." Delilah entered the inn. They heard Scar arguing with another customer about lumpy beds in the common room. A heavy thump followed Scar's roar. Kale hurried upstairs after his sister.

I hope she's wrong.

***

Delilah approached their room with trepidation. She pulled the key out of her pouch, then unlocked the door. To her surprise, her pack lay where she left it. She took a running leap onto the bed, causing the pack to bounce to the edge of the mattress. Lunging to grab hold of it before it fell, she felt a twitch in her back as the book-laden pack lurched to a stop.

The new pain was proof enough of the pack's contents. Groaning, she hauled it toward her.

"Are you coming? Pancras is waiting for us next door." Kale leaned against the door, lifting a foot to pick at his heel. Delilah sympathized. Walking on the cobbles all day made her feet hurt, too, and she was pretty sure there were pebbles embedded between some of her scales.

"I just wanted to check on my books. It doesn't look like anyone disturbed our stuff." She moved the pack to the center of the bed, then hopped onto the floor. She held her staff. *It's just dinner.* Deciding to leave it behind, she tossed it on the bed.

"Who would? They'd have to contend with Scar. He'd probably gore them and grind their bones to bake into bread." As he said it, Kale's face fell. He breathed an audible sigh of relief when he saw no one behind him.

Delilah peered into the hallway. "Expecting Scar to be there?"

"Yeah, I'm a little jumpy all of a sudden. My scales are crawling, like someone is watching me." Kale shivered, rubbing his arms. "Let's go eat. I'm hungry."

"Good idea." Delilah pulled the door shut, then locked it. Together they went next door to the Assassin's Dagger. Pancras was already seated at the same table they used the night before. Tankards of ale awaited Kale and Delilah. Several other tables were occupied by patrons, but the raucous crowd had yet to arrive.

"I got us a pork roast to share." Pancras raised his mug to the draks. "It should be out soon."

Kale clinked his tankard against Delilah's. "I have to admit, the fare is better than what we get at home."

"Maybe you should learn how to cook." Delilah grinned at her brother. "I'm sure Suri would give you a job."

"I like what I do." Kale worked on keeping the siege engine defenses working properly in Drak-Anor. Delilah helped with that, too, but since they no longer fought with the neighboring dwarves, they didn't have to perform as much upkeep.

"Where's Edric?" Glancing around the tavern, Delilah didn't see their dwarf companion.

"He hasn't shown up yet." Pancras glanced at the window. Waning light foretold dusk's approach.

Lenka, Janek's rotund wife, weaved her way through customers milling around the bar and brought their roast. A kerchief held her stringy hair out of her face, and her weathered skin told of a life of hard work. "Here you go, dearies. One leg roast with all the trimmings."

Orange, yellow, and green vegetables surrounded a steaming, pink roast. Its surface flaked with herbs and spices and its aroma made Delilah's mouth water and stomach grumble. Pancras carved a hunk for Kale, then one for her, and finally one for himself. As she prepared to dig in, a shadow crossed over her, looming between her and Kale.

"That's my table."

Delilah regarded the bare-chested minotaur. Prominent veins traveled alongside knotty muscles. He had matted, brown fur, and the tips of both horns had broken off, leaving jagged edges. His bloodshot eyes glared down at them, and his notched, torn ears twitched.

"Now"—Pancras set down the knife, then held up his hands—"We sat here yesterday, and Janek there said we could sit—"

The minotaur slammed his fists on the table, spilling Delilah's ale. "I don't care with that fat, greasy human said. I sit here. Everyone knows it. Move your scrawny asses before I eat them for dinner!"

The tavern fell silent. Delilah felt everyone's eyes upon them. She reached for her staff before remembering that she left it in the room.

"Ktinos! They're paying customers." Lenka placed a hand on the minotaur's arm. "There are plenty of other tables."

Ktinos shoved the proprietor's wife. "Don't touch me, Woman."

"There's no need to get angry." Pancras pushed himself away from the table, standing with deliberate movement. He gestured at their empty chair. "We have room for one more."

"I don't share!" The minotaur shoved Delilah backward, upending her chair and launching her into the next table. Stars exploded in her vision. Through the haze, she saw customers jump up and scatter. Some backpedaled to the far side of the tavern while others bolted out the door.

"Deli!"

Rolling over, she looked toward her brother. With drawn daggers, Kale snarled, leaping at Ktinos. He sunk one into the minotaur's arm down to the hilt and hung on. Thrashing, Ktinos roared. He grabbed Kale by the waist, trying to pull him away, but Kale bit the tip of his nose. Delilah noticed the tips of Pancras's horns glowing.

Bellowing, Ktinos lifted Kale by his neck. Kale's eyes bulged as the minotaur squeezed him with hands as big as the drak's head. Delilah tried to push herself to her feet, but her arms wobbled. She blinked, attempting to clear her vision.

Kale howled. Then, coughing, he exhaled a gout of flame into the minotaur's face. With a high-pitched, primal scream, the minotaur tossed Kale away, swatting at his face. He ran through the inn, flailing his arms as the stench of burning fur filled the air. Flames wreathed his head, climbing higher and higher until they licked the ceiling. The minotaur ran headlong into the stonework hearth. Crack! His flaming head smacked the stones. He fell to the ground, his wails of agony trailing off as smoke and fire seared his throat. The tavern's customers watched in silence as his head continued to burn. Finally, Lenka, snatching ale from the nearest table, doused the flames.

Delilah rolled onto her back. "What—by Maris's bloody spear, what just happened?"

Kale trembled. His eyes darted from the dead, but still twitching, minotaur to his sister and back. "I don't know, Deli."

***

Kale trembled with such intensity he couldn't see clearly. When he spat to clear the taste of brimstone from his mouth, his smoldering spittle left a black scorch on the wooden floor.

"Have you ever done that before?" Pancras kept his eyes on Kale while leaning around the table toward Delilah.

Shaking his head, Kale reached for the tankard of ale closest to him. "I don't even know what I did."

"You breathed fire." Pancras knelt alongside Delilah. She winced when he touched the back of her head. Dark red liquid glistened on his fingers.

"Deli, are you all right?" Kale stared wide-eyed at his sister's blood on Pancras's hand. "You have to be all right."

Staggering to her chair, Delilah nodded. "I'll be okay. It's just a bump."

Janek approached their table, clapping his hands and calling for everyone to go about their business. "You might think about leaving here now. Ktinos was a brute, for sure, and I'll vouch for you that it was self-defense, but even that doesn't get very far these days."

"We have to leave town?" Kale's stomach knotted. *No, no, we can't! We'll die out on the plains when it snows. We can't get to Muncifer before winter.* He tugged Pancras's arm. The necromancer chewed his bottom lip, rubbing his right horn.

"We have nowhere to go. Nowhere we can get to before the snow falls." Pancras shook his head. "We'll try to reason with the authorities. It's our only chance."

That didn't sound like a good idea to Kale, but he was willing to go along with Pancras. He regarded the dead minotaur. *Maybe he's right. What's happening to me?* He rubbed his chest. His lungs burned, although the sensation faded when he concentrated on ignoring it.

"Nuts to that." Delilah stood up, but the room spun, and she gripped the table to keep from falling. She sat down again. "There's got to be another village or something around here." She eyed the proprietor. "Right?"

The human scratched his head. "A few farms here and there, and Fallow Gulch about three days west of here."

"Three days. We can make that. It won't snow in three days." Delilah reached across the table and took Pancras's hands. "We can't be at the mercy of these humans, Pancras. You know they'll just see us as monsters. They always do."

"Here now—" Janek protested at the guards bursting into the tavern. One of the humans who fled the initial confrontation pointed at their table. Drawing their swords, several guards surrounded them. Another approached Ktinos's body, gagging at the sight of charred flesh.

Kale prepared to rise, but a glance from Pancras told him to stay put. The minotaur gestured for Delilah to remain seated as well. "We don't want any trouble."

A burly, middle-aged guard approached the table, regarding the three in silence. His stringy, salt-and-pepper hair peeked out from beneath his helmet, and his threadbare tunic clung tight to his armor, threatening to pop its seams. Sniffing, he smoothed his drooping mustache. "You three are under arrest." He gestured to the other guards. "Take them away."

***

The door slamming shut on Pancras's cell sounded like a pealing bell announcing a momentous death. The guards stripped him of his clothes, jewelry, and even the gilded tips of his horns, and he stood literally and figuratively naked with only a trussed bedstead and waste bucket as his companions.

Kale and Delilah occupied separate, but nearby, cells. They, too, were stripped of their possessions, but as for clothing, they had only their cloaks. Delilah sat on her cot, holding her head and groaning. Kale paced, wringing his hands. Gripping the bars, he stuck his snout between them.

"What are we going to do, Pancras? You know they want to string us up. You heard them talking."

The possibility the humans would refuse to listen to reason crossed his mind. He lied anyway. "It's just talk, Kale, to intimidate us. You acted in self-defense. They must see that."

"I didn't do anything! Not on purpose, anyway."

"Everyone says that, at first."

In the cell next to Kale's, a drak with burnt-orange scales stepped out of the shadows. From her temples two horns ran back along her head curling under her ear fringes. Leaning against the bars, she grinned. "I'm Kali, in here for yet another misunderstanding. How about you?"

"I melted a minotaur's face off." Kale's head drooped. He slid down the bars until his butt hit the floor, then drew his knees up to his chest.

"Nice! Magic?"

"We're not sure how it happened." Pancras rattled the cell door to see how secure it was. There was some play, but it felt solid.

"You have stripes, huh?" Kali nodded toward Delilah, who regarded the other drak female with narrowed eyes. She faced Kale. "Is she your mate?"

"Sister."

"Hm, striped siblings. Your clan must think you're something special. Strange they'd let you run around a city like this."

Pancras didn't like where the conversation seemed headed. "What do you want from us?"

"From you, O Mighty Hairy One? Nothing. I just haven't had anyone to talk to in a while."

Frowning, Pancras sat on his bunk. "You're asking more questions than talking."

"You can't learn nothing by keeping your mouth shut." Kali tapped the bars of her cell with a claw.

"Sure you can. You should try it." Delilah hopped off her cot, then yanked on her cell door. As with the door on Pancras's cell, it rattled but did not open. "We need to get out of here before the humans decide to be done with us."

Kali chuckled. "They've already made up their minds. Whatever's going to happen to you is going to happen. If you're lucky, they'll waste enough time that I can get you out of here once they cut me loose."

Pancras rubbed his right horn. "No, we must bide our time. I need to think." He didn't doubt Kali's word that the humans already decided their fate, but he did not relish a jailbreak as the answer. He didn't want to be on the run from the law while fighting to survive winter in the wilderness. Pancras took stock of his cell. The stark and uncomfortable conditions beat freezing to death on the plains.

"Suit yourself." Kali shrugged, chuckling.

Kale approached her. "How could you help us, exactly?"

"We don't need her help, Kale." Delilah rattled the cell door to get his attention.

"Sure you don't."

The door to the holding area opened. A guard entered. "All prisoners on your cots! Move it!"

Waiting until the three draks were seated, he proceeded into the holding area. "Three of them now... which one of you is Kali Blackclaw?"

The orange-scaled drak raised a clawed hand. "That'd be me, Chief."

"All right, you're done. Stay on the cot." He approached her cell to unlock it. Pulling it open, he waved his cudgel. "Out you get. The Master Jailer has your possessions. Collect them on the way out."

Kali hopped off the prison bed, smoothed her brown, leather jerkin, and sauntered past the guard, winking at Kale as she passed him. "If you get out, come see me at the Assassin's Dagger. Just ask the barkeep for me by name. That's Kali Blackclaw, Stripey."

The guard pushed her. "Keep moving."

Delilah neared the cell bars. "Hey, you have to let us out too. All we did was defend ourselves from that mad minotaur!"

Slamming his cudgel against the bars, the guard wheeled on Delilah. "On your cot, Worm!"

Glowering, Delilah did as he ordered.

Pushing Kali out of the holding area, the guard looked over his shoulder at the three prisoners. "The magistrate will hear from you in the morning. Keep quiet until then."

"He'll hear what idiots you are!" Clenching her fists, Delilah approached the bars again. "If we had our foci, we'd blast this place to rubble! Our minotaur's a necromancer! You'll be lucky if he doesn't raise an army of zombies and raze this city to the ground!"

"Delilah!" Pancras fought to keep his voice steady. "Quiet!"

"What? These idiots—"

"Necromancy is punishable by death in some cities." Rubbing his temples, Pancras put his head in his hands. *There's no situation that can't be made worse by an excitable drak.*

"Yeah, well, they're still lucky." Delilah paced in her cell. "Gods, my head hurts." Furrowing her brows, she faced her brother. "How are you, Kale? Your aches and pains? Better? Worse? Talk to me."

Kale kicked his feet, dangling them over the edge of the bunk. "My back still hurts. Other than that, I feel pretty good."

A small window at the far end of the holding area provided the means for Pancras to approximate the time of day. The rainbow colors of dusk shone through when they were arrested. Now, the area beyond the window appeared pitch dark, and lanterns at either end of the holding area provided scant light.

When it became apparent he could not accurately track the passage of time after the sun set, Pancras stretched out on his cot, covering himself with a moth-eaten blanket as his only protection against the cold. His hooves hung off the edge of the prison bed.

Sleep did not come easily to Pancras that night. He tossed and turned, unable to find a comfortable position. The murmured conversation of the drak twins added to his anxiety. *Life was simpler when all I had to do was create a few skellies now and then. Study my magic, fend off a few dwarf attacks, and everybody left me alone.*

"Pancras? Are you awake?"

Kale's whispers cut through the minotaur's thoughts. Pancras considered not answering. *Maybe if they think I'm sleeping, they'll be quiet.*

"Pancras? Hey!"

"Yes, Kale?"

"Deli and I have been talking."

"I know. It's keeping me awake." Pancras rolled to face the wall. *By what foul sorcery do they still have enough energy for this?*

"We have a plan to get us out of this place. We'll have to leave Edric behind, but we think he'd do the same in our place anyway."

Pancras couldn't disagree with that sentiment, but he still thought they would be better off not trying to escape.

"When they come to feed us, Deli will pretend she's dead, because she hit her head, right? They'll collect her body and when they take her outside to dump her, she can go back to the inn, get our stuff, and break us out with her magic."

He didn't want to say it was a stupid idea. Portions of it had merit. He rolled over. The draks' eyes glowed in the darkness of their cells, reflecting the dim light of the lanterns.

"There are a lot of things that can go wrong with that plan. What if they dismember and burn the corpses of their prisoners to keep them from being raised by a necromancer?"

"Oh…"

"We can't just sit here, Pancras!" Delilah's voice, a hiss, dripped with anger and frustration.

"Go to sleep." Pancras didn't think they would listen to him, but he wanted to close his eyes. "Things will be clearer in the morning."

"They'll come to take us to our executioner in the morning!" Delilah banged on the bars of her cell. The sound cut through to the base of Pancras's spine.

"Shut up for a minute and think!" Pancras clenched his teeth. "If minotaurs and draks are treated as poorly as everyone here has said, then do you really think they'll care that much about one ill-tempered minotaur being killed in a bar brawl?"

"You know, he's got a point, Deli."

"Kale—"

"Yes, I have a point. Now be quiet. It's bad enough I'll have to face the magistrate without my clothes. I don't want to face him exhausted as well."

Pancras heard nothing more from the draks after that, but neither did he get his wish for even the most minimal sleep. With dawn's light came the sounds of the city through the jail walls, and the jailers followed soon after.

"Minotaur! Sit up." The mustachioed guard who arrested them entered the holding area with two guards wielding pikes. They brandished them through the bars of his cell. Pancras complied with the guard's order. Another guard entered holding shackles and leather straps.

"You're coming with us this morning. Someone wants to talk to you." The guard opened Pancras's cell, allowing the man who held the restraints to enter. Kale and Delilah rolled out of their cots. Before they made it halfway across their cells, the guard ordered them to return to their bunks.

He pointed at Pancras. "Muzzle him."

***

"See? I told you!" Delilah hurled her waste bucket across her cell as the guards led Pancras away, shackled and muzzled. It splintered against the stone. *Glad that was empty.*

"What do you think they're going to do to him, Deli?" Kale paced the floor.

"They'll probably skin him for a rug. We'll be next!" Delilah considered sending a message to Edric. She concentrated on the wisps of magical aether permeating the world. Minus her staff, her focus, she found it difficult to grasp them with her mind, like holding smoke in one's hand.

Kale inhaled, puffing up his chest. Closing his eyes, he exhaled. A jet of flame shot across his cell and into the next. With a yelp, he clamped his mouth shut with his hands. Trembling, his eyes widened. He turned toward his sister.

"You can do that whenever you want now?"

Lowering his hands, Kale nodded. "I guess I can." He gulped. "What's happening to me, Deli?"

As much as she felt excitement for her brother's new and interesting ability, a fire-breathing drak was not a normal occurrence. Recognizing he was frightened, she tried to avoid upsetting him further. "Maybe it has something to do with that chaos rift? You haven't been quite right since that."

Kale sat down on his cot. "Should we try to bust out of here or wait for Pancras to come back?"

"I guess we should wait. The guards said someone wanted to talk to him. If they're going to execute him, hopefully they'll bring him back here first." Delilah sat cross-legged on the floor. *I wish I had my lexicon, or my grimoire. This is too boring. If I had my staff, we'd already be on our way out of the city.*

A guard entered the holding area, interrupting Delilah's thoughts. He carried two steaming bowls. Wooden spoons stood in the paste-like gruel. "Stay on your cots." He sat the bowls down in front of Delilah's cell, unlocked the door, and then slid one of them into her cell with his foot. He locked up, then did the same at Kale's cell.

"Eat up. Next meal will be at dusk."

When he turned to leave, Delilah approached the bowl of gruel. It resembled wet horse feed. "Hey, what did you humans do with Pancras?"

"The minotaur? Took him away. Didn't tell me where. Eat." He locked the holding area door behind him.

After crouching in front of his bowl, Kale stirred it. "What is this slop?"

Tasting it, Delilah pursed her lips. She expected a foul flavor and instead discovered the slop had no flavor at all. "Prison food. Yum, yum."

Chapter 8

L eave him here. Uncover his mouth."

The guard removed the muzzle from Pancras's snout, shoved him into the room, then shut the door behind him. Pancras stumbled forward, tripping over his shackles, but he managed to remain upright. Hand-cut rugs covered the floor in front of a crackling fireplace. Candles burned in sconces on the wall, casting scant light, and a window on the far side of the room allowed rays from the rising sun to enter. Pancras smelled herbal incense smoldering. A small table, the sort at which two people might sit to share drink and conversation, sat in the center of the room.

A man sat at a writing desk, scribbling on a piece of parchment. After setting down his quill, he arched his back, working out the kinks in his knotted muscles. Turning, he regarded Pancras. He appeared to be someone of authority, based on his attire. Admiring the human's fashion sense, Pancras noted the robes he wore resembled his own.

"Ah, the minotaur." Upon standing, he bowed. "I am Prince Gavril."

Pancras returned the gesture. *The Prince of Etrunia himself? What is this about?*

"You may have heard that I am a man of little patience. I will not waste your time with false pleasantries. Your loud drak companion says you are a necromancer." Maintaining eye contact, he paced the floor between them.

Pancras ran his hands down his chest, wincing as fur caught in his shackles. *How did he find out about that so quickly?* He sighed. "I was once, yes."

"Once?" Prince Gavril stopped before him. "Have you forgotten all your skills?"

"No, I simply have not practiced them recently."

"Very well. What is your purpose here in Almeria? As you may have surmised by now, your kind is not welcome here."

Pancras licked his lips. "When we arrived, I was not aware Almeria's stance toward my people and draks had changed. We only wished to winter here. We are on our way to Muncifer, and I know you know how deadly the cold and snow can be in the dark of winter's night."

Prince Gavril resumed pacing. "I speak of necromancers, not minotaurs and draks. Even now, I have councilors who are incredulous I have not put you all to death. Your existence is a crime to them."

Pancras opened his mouth to retort but held his tongue upon a gesture by the prince.

"I did not say I agree, but a man in my position can ill afford to anger all of his councilors. What is your name, Necromancer?"

"Pancras, First Wizard of Drak-Anor."

"First Wizard?" Prince Gavril cocked an eyebrow. "A political title. I have heard of Drak-Anor but know little of it." He gestured at the table in the center of the room. "Please, sit. I have a proposition."

Pancras could not imagine what the Prince of Etrunia wanted with him, but if it meant a chance to free Kale and Delilah and find Edric so they could be on their way, Pancras was obliged to listen. He would take his chances in the wilderness only if it meant avoiding the headsman's axe. Pancras sat at the table, wishing he had clothes. He felt exposed, vulnerable. The prince poured a brown liquid into two glasses and handed one to Pancras. The minotaur sniffed the contents. It smelled of oak and alcohol.

"I don't trust men who don't drink. Our spirits are strong and will keep you warm on cold nights." The prince drank the liquor down in one gulp. Pancras did the same, grimacing as the liquid burned its way toward his stomach.

"I want you to work a spell to make my wife barren."

Blinking, Pancras almost dropped his glass. He set it on the table. He knew of hexes that could have such effects, but he had not ever performed such spells.

"I can see you are confused. My wife shuns me every night unless she wants to conceive a child. Then, and only then, am I welcome in her bed. I mount her and deliver my seed. If she does not conceive, we try again. If she does, she has nothing to do with me until the next time she wants a child. As it would be improper for me to take a mistress, I find myself lacking when it comes to companionship at night, and believe me, even these halls grow cold in winter."

"I am not sure…" Pancras stalled. He didn't know what to say. He gave up necromancy for a reason. He tried to conceal his revulsion to the prince's request to render a woman—his wife, no less—infertile.

"I don't need you to understand, but I will explain further. When two people are wed in Etrunia, the man's possessions become his wife's. If I demand a divorce now, without cause, I will lose everything. My lands, my titles, my money. However, if I have cause, say, because my wife is barren, well, that's another matter. She will be cared for, of course, as will the children we have, but I cannot be obligated to stay with a woman who cannot produce heirs. As prince, I have a duty to spread my seed as widely as I can, provided it is with my wife."

"In exchange"—the prince offered more whiskey to Pancras, who declined with a shake of his head—"I will provide accommodations here in the palace for you and your companions until the snows thaw and you can resume your journey."

Pancras focused his eyes on the table, furrowing his brow in thought. "It is a difficult ritual, dangerous and time consuming. There is a risk to her."

"If she dies, I will be free to find a new wife." The prince smiled. "Of course, I could not allow the death of my wife to go unpunished."

There's the rub. Pancras stroked his chin. So far, Almerian hospitality left much to be desired. *But how could I trade this woman's fertility for our comfort?* He realized there was much more than that at stake. The authorities meant to jail them indefinitely or have them executed, and the Slayers would have an easy time of it if the archmage sent them after Pancras and Delilah while they rotted in a prison.

"Consider this, today, in your jail cell, Pancras." Prince Gavril leaned forward, grinning. "You all will likely hang from the gibbets if you don't perform this service for me. See what your companions think of that." The prince's eyes darted from side to side, and he glanced more than once over his shoulder, seemingly searching for eavesdroppers. Then, the prince lowered his voice. "But speak not of the request I made of you. No one must know. If anyone asks why you're here, claim to be ambassadors from… Drak-Anor, is it? I can guarantee you a slow and painful death if my wife or anyone else finds out."

***

After choking down what the prison classified as food, Kale returned to his cot. Counting knots in the wood beams that crossed the ceiling wasn't the most exciting activity in which to immerse himself, but it was the only entertainment available to him at present. Delilah wanted to work out an escape scheme, but Kale didn't want to risk the guards overhearing their plans, and he didn't want to sit on a hard floor to be close enough to whisper.

All things considered, he felt good. His insides didn't burn anymore, although his back still ached where the two lumps had formed. Kale dozed until the creak of the holding area door awakened him as it opened. After the guards escorted Pancras inside, one of them opened a cell for him, removed his shackles, then exited.

"Hey, you're back." Delilah traced symbols in the floor of her cell with a finger. "I notice they took the muzzle off."

Pancras rubbed his snout. "It was an odd meeting. Not with a magistrate."

"Oh?"

Cocking his head, Kale sat up. "Well, who then?"

"The prince propositioned me."

"He's into minotaurs? Huh." Kale shrugged. "Can you tolerate humans enough to put up with him?"

Pancras snorted. "Not that kind of proposition, Kale! He wants a favor from me, from a necromancer. In exchange, he's offered to let us stay the winter in the palace."

Kale jumped up, clapping his hands. "That's great! Let's get out of this place, then!"

Delilah stood up and nodded her agreement. "Yeah, whatever it is that you have to do, do it. The palace beats jail and that dumpy inn too."

"I was afraid you would feel that way." Pancras flopped onto his cot, covering his face with his hands. "I don't want to do what he wants."

"Well, what is it?" Kale couldn't imagine Pancras would risk their freedom just to avoid creating a few skeletons or zombies for the local ruler.

"I cannot tell you, but I don't want to do it."

Delilah rattled her cell door. "Hey, look at me. Don't get all worried about being proper. They'll keep us locked up and throw away the keys if they can. You need to do what he wants, or, at least, make him think you've done what he wants, and get us out of here. What happens if they keep us locked up long enough that we don't get to Muncifer on time?"

"They'll send the Slayers after us, and we'll be sitting ducks here in jail." Pancras paced. "Maybe I can find an alternative solution. I have time. I told him what he wants is complicated and time-consuming. It's going to take a month, at least, to pull everything together anyway."

The thought of living in the palace until spring made Kale want to jump and cheer. "Come on, Pancras, you have to at least say yes, even if you don't mean it. Once we get out of this jail, we can figure out what we're going to do after that."

"All right, all right. I'll agree to the terms. Maybe there's something more going on, something to which I am not privy, something we can use to our advantage once we are free from this place." Pancras rattled his cell door. "Guards! Guards!"

The holding area door opened. "Quiet! One more outburst, and you'll go hungry tonight!"

Kale shared a grin with his sister.

Pancras sighed. "Tell Prince Gavril I agree to his terms."

***

The guards brought all the trio's possessions into the holding cell, dumping them in a pile. While the minotaur and draks sorted through it, the guards brought two battered and bruised humans in, shoving them into the cells Kale and Delilah previously occupied.

The mustachioed guard banged his cudgel against one of the cells. "All right, you lot. I've orders to take you to the palace straight away."

"No way. We still have stuff at our inn." Delilah put her hands on her hips. "You're going to take us there, first.

I'm not leaving my staff and books with that brute one minute longer."

He raised his club to strike. Pancras stepped forward, pushing Delilah out of the way. "We all have valuables at the Sleeping Viper. The prince would be very displeased if we arrive unable to work because you refused to let us retrieve our possessions."

The guard lowered his weapon, considering Pancras's words. "We'll send someone 'round to collect your things. We have orders to deliver you"—he pointed at the minotaur—"right away."

Pancras put a hand on Kale's shoulder. "Go with the guards. Make sure they don't forget or miss anything at the inn. All my things are in my pack." He eyed the guard. "Acceptable?"

"Maybe I should go with them." Delilah watched her brother and the guards leave.

Shaking his head, Pancras followed their escort out of the holding area and up the stairs leading out of the jail. "Together, you two might scheme your way into more trouble. This way, Kale will return to us with the guards."

Delilah stuck out her tongue, then scowled behind Pancras's back. *He's right. We'd give those guards the slip and figure out a way to bust us all out of this mess. At least they didn't damage my new cloak.* Unaccustomed to wearing much clothing since draks didn't need to cover themselves the way softer-skinned people did, she adjusted the sash at her waist before running her claws over her belly. She strode forward, thankful she had chosen her new garment carefully, determined to look the part of a civilized wizard.

Pedestrians on the streets of Almeria gave their escorts a wide berth. Delilah appreciated the reprieve from pressing crowds. She tired of dodging relative giants oblivious to her presence. A rumbling knot in her stomach reminded her she had not eaten since the morning's gruel.

She tugged at Pancras's sleeve. The minotaur shuffled behind the guards, towering over his escorts. "Hey, do you think the fare at the palace will be good?"

"It should be. Nobility often eat better than the common folk. We may have to eat with the servants, but I'd wager it will still be better that what the average citizen eats." They turned a corner onto a wide, tree-lined avenue. Leaves of red, yellow, and brown swirled along the street, dancing on gusts of wind. The spires of the palace jutted above the surrounding wall, obscuring the rest of the palace grounds from Delilah.

The guards directed them to the side of the avenue as a gilded, horse-drawn carriage approached. Delilah marveled at the gleaming white coach as it passed, every surface covered with ornate carvings and gold accents. Sheer curtains drawn over the windows provided privacy for the passengers while allowing diffused light to pass through. To Delilah the carriage was large enough to be a drak house on wheels, although she suspected Pancras would consider it cramped.

As they crossed the bridge over it, Delilah noted with disappointment the moat that surrounded the palace wall contained only brown, murky water. *Damn. I hoped for some monsters or something waiting to gobble up invaders.* She noticed murder holes, similar to those at the city gates, as they passed beneath the gatehouse and its twin portcullises. Beyond the gatehouse, the palace grounds sprawled with fields of green. Groves of trees, their once-green leaves having given way to the multicolored palette of autumn, were surrounded by fields of late-blooming flowers. Watching draks and humans working alongside each other and tending the greenery surprised her.

The palace itself sprawled. Delilah lost count of the spires and turrets jutting up from the main structure. "You could put dozens of clans of draks in there!"

"Compared to the crowds in the rest of the city, this will feel spacious, indeed." Pancras pulled her close. "We may be going from one cage to another, Delilah, but at least this one is warm and has good food."

***

Glancing at the garden as they passed, Pancras identified half-a-dozen plants he could use for various potions and unguents. He expected they would be allowed free run of the palace grounds, but he suspected the prince would forbid them from going out into the city, at least, not without an armed escort. He could live with that until spring, but he feared the drak twins would chafe at those restrictions. Pancras also wondered about Edric. *Maybe Kale will see him at the inn.*

The guards led Pancras and Delilah up the palace steps to the gold-inlaid double doors that opened into the entrance hall. Pancras pulled Delilah by her cloak to keep the wide-eyed drak moving. A woman dressed in the garb of the Royal Guard approached them as they moved through the entrance hall.

"Hail, Borys!" She raised her hand in greeting to the mustachioed guard.

He bowed. "Lady Milena. Here are His Highness's new… patrons."

She regarded Pancras and Delilah before returning her attention to Borys. "There were three of them."

"The third went with two of my guards back to their inn to retrieve the remainder of their possessions. He should be along shortly." Borys saluted before turning on his heels and leaving Pancras and Delilah with Lady Milena.

"I am Captain of the Royal Guard. Lady Milena Trueblade, Protector of the Realm, at your service." Upon crossing her fist over her chest and bowing, her long auburn hair fell forward, obscuring her face. Standing, she brushed it over her shoulders with her free hand. "Follow me to your quarters, please."

Following Lady Milena through the palace halls, Pancras gripped Delilah's cloak to keep her from gaping at a painting of a long-forgotten battle. Gold-framed paintings and tapestries covered the walls, interrupted only by sconces in which glowing gemstones provided light. Beneath the sconces were marble busts of men and women.

"Former rulers of Etrunia." Lady Milena pointed to the sculptures as they passed. "Each one, immortalized in stone. My family has proudly served for five generations."

Pancras nodded. "Do you know anything about our service to His Highness?"

"Nothing." She held a door open for them. "I am not privy to His Highness's dealings. I serve Etrunia first, Almeria second, and the current ruling family third. My ultimate duty is to crown and country, not who wears it."

After they climbed a series of stairs, past a hall of mirrors, Lady Milena led them down a hall whose open archways overlooked the gardens. *It would be easy to jump that wall and escape into the flowers. Of course, one would have to contend with the drop and the outer wall.* The look on Delilah's face indicated she, too, might be mentally calculating a way to sneak out. He snapped his fingers behind him to gain her attention, shaking his head to discourage thoughts of escape.

"Her Highness, Princess Valene, enjoys walking this corridor. The open air is good for one's health, you know, especially during the crisp mornings of autumn and winter!" She glanced toward the sky. "We may get our first snow tonight. Can you feel it?" She stopped in front of a set of double doors, then withdrew a key from behind her tunic.

"Your quarters are here. You will all be sharing, but I trust you will find them spacious."

Spacious was not the word Pancras would have chosen. The room they entered seemed to be the hub for four other rooms. A multicolored, hand-cut woven rug, larger than most rooms in Drak-Anor, covered the floor of the parlor. A dining table constructed of dark, polished wood sat at the far end of the room in front of a pair of windows overlooking the back garden. Matching high-backed chairs surrounded the table; enough place settings for six people and enough space to accommodate at least another four by Pancras's reckoning. A smaller, ornately decorated round table stood in the near corner of the parlor, surrounded by four plush armchairs covered in velvet jacquard. Pancras could not identify the design on the table, but the repeating pattern on the chairs appeared to be some sort of stylized, ornamental flower. Two doors led out of the parlor on the wall to his left and right.

Delilah whistled, admiring the room. "Very fancy. But where are the beds? We don't sleep on the floor, even if it does have a nice covering." She flexed her toes on the rug.

Lady Milena pointed to the doors on the side walls. "Bed chambers on either side, as well as—she pointed to the farthest door on the right—"a bathing room." She approached a tapestry depicting a sumptuous feast that hung from the wall to the left of the bathing room door. Pulling a cord dangling beside it, she raised the tapestry to reveal a small door. After winding the cord around a hook, she opened the door. Pancras eyed the rope leading down the shaft. *Too small for me, but I'd wager one of the draks could fit if they didn't mind being cramped.*

"Nourishment will be delivered here. Servants will be by shortly to check that you're settling in. The kitchen does not take special requests, usually, but there are often limited choices each day." She closed the door, then lowered the tapestry. "You are free to go where you like in the palace. Guards will turn you away from forbidden areas like the royal chambers or the treasury."

"What of the gardens? We may also wish to go into the city at some point." Pancras examined a tapestry on the wall opposite the bathing chamber. It depicted a battle with three armies united against an army of skeletons and what he assumed were spirits or ghosts of some kind.

"My instructions were to keep you here. You will not be permitted to leave the palace."

"That's ridiculous! I thought we were guests, not prisoners!" Delilah stomped her foot for emphasis, but the plush rug dampened the impact.

"I know nothing of your arrangement with Prince Gavril. I was ordered to bring you here, nothing more." Lady Milena approached the tapestry Pancras examined. "This tapestry depicts the Battle of Badon Hill, the final defeat of the Lich Queen." She straightened, placing her hand on the hilt of her sword. "My father led the armies of Etrunia who fought alongside the free peoples of Vlorey on those bloody plains. He gave his life to help defeat that witch."

Mention of the Lich Queen caused a pang in Pancras's chest. He knew of the necromancer of the north, of course. She conquered nearly half of the continent with her army of the dead before the combined forces of Vlorey, Etrunia, Cardoba, and a smattering of aid from the elves of Celtangate stopped her. Nearly every living defender who fell became part of the Lich Queen's army.

Darkness engulfed Pancras's vision. He staggered, reaching for Lady Milena's arm to steady himself. A shadowy claw wrapped around her mail-covered arm in the place where his hand should have been. Before his eyes, her flesh, blackening, decomposed until nothing remained but red eyes in a gleaming white skull.

"Are you all right?" The captain's question snapped Pancras out of the vision. Delilah raced to the minotaur's side.

"He's tired. We're tired. We've been treated like dirt since we arrived here and spent last night in jail for the crime of defending ourselves." The drak regarded the room. "It looks like we've traded one cage for another, albeit a gilded one."

Pancras held Delilah by the shoulder. "No, it is all right. She is right, my lady. It's nothing, just fatigue." He bowed his head. "Thank you for your concern."

Lady Milena bowed. "I shall take my leave of you, then."

After she left, Delilah tugged on Pancras's arm. "Are you sure you're all right? You looked like you were about to faint, and the tips of your horns glowed. I don't think she noticed that. Most tall folk don't bother looking up."

"It was strange, like I was seeing her through someone else's eyes. I didn't feel like myself." Pancras rubbed his eyes. "It was nothing, fatigue. Like you said, we're all tired."

I hope whatever ails Kale isn't contagious. He sat down in one of the armchairs.

Delilah peered behind the food lift's tapestry. "How does one get an ale around here? We could use a drink."

An ale would hit the spot right now. "Kale could bring some back, if only we could send him a message. How well can you cast without your focus?"

Delilah shrugged. "Not good, but I can probably swing a messenger."

He hoped Delilah's brother stayed out of trouble. The drak twins were known for making mischief back home, but Kale was more of a practical joker than a conniver. Because schemes were his sister's forte, Pancras kept her with him to keep an eye on her. He thought it unlikely Kale could concoct an escape-from-Almeria plan without her. *I hope I'm right.*

Scar refused to let the guards accompany Kale up to their rooms. "Guards never help us. If you lot aren't here to arrest me or one of my guests, you can wait outside." Kale's escorts were not inclined to argue with the broken-horned minotaur who stood a head-and-a-half over them. The solitude suited Kale fine. His escorts, disinclined to provide more than non-committal grunts or one-word answers to his questions, didn't laugh at his jokes.

Kale banged on Edric's door before opening his own. As he crammed his possessions into his pack, he wondered how he would carry Delilah's and Pancras's belongings as well as his own. *Maybe Edric will help.*

He knocked again on Edric's door, but there was no sign of the dwarf. *Maybe he's gone next door for an ale.* For a brief moment, Kale entertained the thought of inviting his escorts for a drink, but he then decided they were poor company. He closed the door to his room, locked it from inside, and then opened the window. A blast of cold air whipped his cloak around. Dark clouds moved across the sky, laden with rain, or worse. Assessing the side of the building, he spotted a downspout that would help steady him during his descent down the half-timbered construction.

Kale pulled himself up on the window frame, then swung his legs outward. First gathering his cloak around his waist to keep it from snagging on the rough wooden edge, he then lowered himself. Hand-over-hand, he worked his way along the windowsill. Finding the downspout barely within reach, he took in a deep breath, then lunged at it. His claws made no purchase on the pipe, and he slid, scraping the conduit until his toes caught on a protruding support beam.

Taking a moment to catch his breath, Kale dared to look down. The street was still farther away than Pancras was tall, a longer distance than Kale cared to fall. He tightened his grip on the pipe and allowed it to support his weight. When he felt the danger of sliding the rest of the way had passed, he began his descent anew, breathing only when his feet touched the ground.

Looking up at the window to his room, Kale straightened his cloak. "That wasn't so hard." In the deserted alley, he heard the din of early drinkers in the Assassin's Dagger. Upon finding the kitchen door ajar, he ducked in. He dodged the cook's assistant, then hid behind a barrel of salt pork.

Lenka wiped her hands on a greasy apron before carrying a steaming platter with some sort of roasted bird on it into the dining area of the tavern. Kale took the opportunity to scamper behind her, ducking under a nearby vacant table. When Janek turned to reach a bottle on the shelf behind the bar, Kale climbed onto one of the stools. From his perch, he glanced from table to table, but he did not see Edric. He rapped his knuckles on the bar top.

"Oh, little master!" Beaming, Janek retrieved a tankard from under the bar. "I see the guards didn't give you too much trouble. What'll it be?" The proprietor looked over the crowd in the tavern. "Where are your friends?"

I guess I have time for one drink. "Just an ale, please." He tossed a half talon on the bar. "We're staying at the palace now."

Janek whistled. "Mighty fine. That must be quite a story." He drew Kale a tankard of ale.

"I was told to look for Kali Blacktalon, Blackclaw? Here?" Kale peered over the frothy mug.

Janek's cheerful expression fell. "Oh. I see." Clearing his throat, he jerked his head toward the back room. "Pull the tap on the farthest keg, the one marked 'Dwarven Winter Beer.'"

"Thanks!" Kale tossed another two talons on the counter. "There are two guards outside the Sleeping Viper. Ale's on me."

Kale sipped from his tankard on his way to the back room. Crates of linens and root vegetables surrounded extra chairs stacked on top of each other. Several stacked ale kegs obscured the near wall. Kale went to the one farthest from the doorway. Although he couldn't read the label, it was the only one with a tap.

He pulled it, hearing a click before the front of the keg swung open. A short passageway, too small for a human or minotaur but passable by a drak or even a dwarf, led Kale through the keg to a set of spiral stairs that plunged into darkness. Kale saw a light at the bottom and heard the sounds of laughter and conversation. He chugged his remaining ale, then wiped his mouth on his cloak.

The stairs took him to a room set up as a tavern in miniature. Ten draks sat around a table, laughing and conversing, paying him no mind. Two more chatted with Kali. Upon seeing Kale, she smiled and waved him over. Fine gold chains wrapped around her horns connecting to gold rings on her ear fringes added an air of sophistication to the same brown leather jerkin she had worn in the jail.

"I wondered if we would see you!" Kali stood, grinning. "Everyone! This is the drak I told you about. Kale, was it?"

He nodded at the group. The other draks greeted him with a glance or a raised mug and returned to their business.

"Where's your sister?"

"She's with Pancras at the palace. We're staying there now. There are two guards outside the inn next door waiting for me. I gave them the slip to see if our dwarf friend was here. You haven't seen a dwarf hanging around, have you?"

"Nah. The palace, huh? How'd you swing that?" Pulling out a chair next to her, Kali motioned for Kale to sit.

"Pancras made some deal with the prince. He couldn't say what."

Kali took Kale's hand. "We're going to become good friends, you and I." Her scales felt cool to him, but her hand felt soft. Softer than Delilah's. "We could use a friend in the palace."

Kale narrowed his eyes, withdrawing his hand. "Who's we?"

Clasping her hands together, Kali smiled. "Oh, we have a partnership. Mostly draks, though we've been known to hire some minotaurs as muscle. You may have noticed our kind are less than well regarded here in Almeria. Sometimes we have to…" Shrugging, she spread her hands. "Let's just say the humans aren't always willing to deal with us fairly, so we have to improvise a lot."

Kale understood. He was no stranger to having to sneak around larger people and sometimes procure materials without paying. It was less of a problem since Sarvesh founded Drak-Anor, but before then, he was forced to scrounge for his supplies most of the time. Gasps of alarm interrupted his reply. Several draks jumped up from their tables, drawing weapons, as a glowing, blue creature bounded down the stairs. Hopping on two stumpy legs, the furry ball bounded toward Kale, then bounced onto the table. The knives two draks threw at it passed through its body, embedding in the hardwood top.

Holding up his hands, Kale motioned for folks to shush. "It's just a message from my sister. It's not a real boggin."

The magical creature faced Kale. "Mistress Delilah and Master Pancras are comfortably awaiting your arrival at the palace and would very much appreciate you bringing ale for them." After delivering its message, the blue ball of teeth disappeared in a puff of azure smoke.

"Ale!" Kale threw up his hands. "Like I don't have enough to carry!"

"They can't get ale at the palace?" Kali scratched her head. "How odd."

"I don't know. I should get going. The guards are probably looking for me." Kale stood. "I don't want to get into any more trouble."

Kali accompanied him to the top of the stairs. After entering the passageway, she pulled him close. Kale's pulse quickened, and his breath caught in his throat when Kali nuzzled his ear. "I'll be in touch." She pushed him out of the keg, grinning as she closed the door.

Kale focused his mind on cheese and sausages, banishing lascivious thoughts of Kali, as he returned to the Sleeping Viper by way of the alley. He gathered their possessions, then met the guards out front.

"We were going to go look for you after we finished these." One of the guards tossed his mug toward the Assassin's Dagger. "How'd you get these to us? The woman said you paid for them."

Kale shrugged, staggering under the weight of three packs. "It wasn't easy. Shall we?"

Chapter 9

Pancras groaned. He had not intended to nap in the armchair, but he didn't fight the slumber that overtook him. Delilah rushed past Pancras in her excitement to greet whoever pounded on the doors. Her face fell when she opened them.

"What do you want?"

The servant bowed. "It is dinnertime. May I?"

"Let him in, Delilah." Pancras yawned. He stood up, stretching, then followed the human and drak to the dinner table. The servant stood by the tapestry in front of the food lift. After a few minutes of uncomfortable silence, during which the servant stared straight ahead while Pancras and Delilah alternated glances between him and each other, a bell rang in the distance. The servant pulled on the cord, raising the tapestry. He then opened the door and pulled the rope hand-over-hand until a platform containing a variety of platters and goblets appeared.

Setting the food on the table, he glanced around the room. "I understood there were to be three of you?"

"Yes, so did I. I wonder where he is, Pancras." Delilah peered out the windows. The minotaur wasn't quite sure of his bearings, but he was fairly certain the Sleeping Viper did not lie within the view from their suite.

"He'll be along." Pancras sat at the head of the table. "He needed to collect the rest of our possessions from the inn."

"Very good, sir." The servant returned to the food lift, rang a bell on the inside of the shaft, and waited until another tray was ready to pull up. "When you are finished, stack everything inside the lift, and ring the bell." He placed another covered platter and two pitchers of wine on the table. "Will there be anything else?"

"No, thank you." Pancras marveled at the multitude of serving dishes and plates arranged before him. The fare appeared to be far more than they could consume, even if Kale and Edric were with them.

"Yes! I want a bath." Delilah faced the servant. "How do you fill the basin? I have weeks of dirt ground into my scales."

"I will have someone draw your bath for you." He glanced over his shoulder as he left. "It will only be hot water, however. We don't have… whatever it is you people bathe in."

"Water!" Delilah shouted at him as he shut the doors. "We use water!"

Pancras lifted the cloche from one of the platters, revealing in the center a roasted bird set upon a bed of multicolored vegetables.

Grumbling to herself, Delilah returned to the table and sat just as there was another knock at the doors. Grousing with every step, she crossed the room to open them. She squealed when Kale, staggering under the weight of their packs, entered the suite. Pancras moved to help with their gear, but Kale ignored him, dropping their belongings just inside the entry way, then speeding to the table.

"I thought I smelled food!" He climbed into Pancras's seat and tore into the bird.

"Hey!" Delilah shouted from the entry doors. "Where's our ale?"

Kale shot her a withering glance while he ate. "I had to carry all three of our packs by myself. The guards didn't help one bit, even after I bought them ale."

"Oh well." Delilah's non-committal reply did not hide the disappointment on her face.

Pancras poured wine for everyone before he sat down. "Did you see Edric?"

"No sign of him. Janek hadn't seen him, and I couldn't get Scar to talk to me. When I told him we moved to the palace, he just grunted. He looked happy we were leaving, though. For someone who runs an inn, he sure doesn't seem to like customers."

Before they finished eating, servants appeared again to fill the tub. The ornately detailed, claw-footed copper bathing vessel stood large enough in which a human or both draks could sit upright but promised a cramped experience for Pancras.

"You know"—Pancras ran his fingers along a tooth-like detail near the rim of the bathing vessel—"it looks like a dragon's maw." Lavender-scented steam wafted up from the surface of the water. Delilah cast off her cloak and unbuckled the harness on which she attached her pouches and fetishes and then climbed into the tub.

Water sloshed over the sides as Delilah settled in. "Ooo, that's hot!" She shooed Pancras and Kale away with her hand. "You may leave now. I have serious thinking to do."

Chuckling, Pancras returned to the dining area to put the dirty dishes in the food lift. "Did you have any trouble? You took longer than we anticipated."

"No trouble, other than carrying three packs by myself. I stopped off for an ale at the Assassin's Dagger. I wanted to see that drak from the jail again."

Ah, so that's it. "That was dangerous." Pancras feared Kali Blackclaw was up to no good, and he believed Kale was ill-equipped to deal with such people.

"She wants to be friends." Kale's voice quivered with excitement. "There's a whole secret tavern under the Assassin's Dagger. It was full of draks!"

"Kale." Pancras took the drak by the shoulder. "Think about it. The Assassin's Dagger. A secret meeting room. Doesn't that sound strange to you?"

"Why shouldn't they have a place to have a few drinks without being hassled by the humans?"

"Janek seemed welcoming enough. Why would such a place be in his tavern?"

Kale scratched his head. "You… you don't think they're assassins, do you?"

"It's possible." Pancras stretched. Sleeping on the cot in the jail stiffened his muscles and caused pain in his lower back. "It doesn't matter right now, anyway. We're not going to be allowed to go back out in the city."

"What?" Kale nearly dropped the plate he was carrying. "We're prisoners here?"

"Guests, prisoners. Honored ambassadors is the term the prince wants us to call ourselves, by the way. It's all the same right now. I'll work on obtaining us a little more freedom tomorrow. I need to acquire some equipment if I'm going to work on this project for which the prince traded our freedom."

"Kali gave me the impression she could get into the palace if she wanted to."

Pancras put the last empty plate into the food lift and rang the bell. After closing the door, he lowered the tapestry. "If she can, you'll have your answer. I didn't get the impression that many people, be they human, drak, elf, dwarf, or minotaur were free to come and go from the palace as they pleased.

Kale seemed to consider Pancras's statement. He nodded toward the door that led to the bathing room. "Hm. How long do you think Deli will be? The water will be all cold and dirty by the time we get in there."

"Now that we have our foci back"—Pancras rubbed the tips of his horns—"I think between Delilah and me, we can use our magic to clean the water and re-heat it. The servants weren't too keen on bringing it up here in the first place. The less we bother them, the better, I think."

Kale tried to open the windows, but discovered they were locked. "Do you think we'll be able to get out of here, Pancras? Get back on the road to Muncifer in time?"

Pancras shared Kale's concerns, but he knew the draks looked to him for guidance and leadership. "I am doing everything in my power to ensure that we will, Kale. I promise."

***

No amount of dirty looks Delilah directed at the closed door quieted the sounds of Pancras and Kale cleaning up the dinner table. *At least I can't hear what they're saying.* The steaming bath reminded her of the volcanic springs in which they bathed and relaxed in Drak-Anor. However, Delilah preferred the mineral scent of the waters back home to the floral scent provided here.

Sighing, she sank deeper into the water. She concentrated on blocking outside sounds. While the hot water and steam dissolved the grime of the last several weeks, Delilah realized that this was truly the first opportunity to relax since they left home. She missed their friends, but as long as Kale and she were together, Delilah knew they would be all right. She couldn't help what became of Edric, though, and when she was finished with her bath, she picked up her staff.

Drawing tendrils and wisps of magical aether to her, Delilah directed them to coalesce in an area above the floor. "*Ageliofedros*." A glowing blue boggin appeared, hopping from foot to foot as it awaited her instructions.

"Find the dwarf, Edric of Ironkrag. Tell him we are no longer at the Sleeping Viper, we've moved into the palace, and he should come find us as soon as possible. Return with his response." Delilah sent the messenger on its way. *That'll be faster than combing the city for him, especially if we can't leave.* She considered the slight probability of the messenger not finding him, of course, especially if the dwarf were dead or a lot of Edrics from Ironkrag were in town.

The parlor lay deserted when she emerged. She didn't need to check the nearest bedchamber; she heard Pancras snoring as she approached the door. On the other side of the parlor in another room, she found Kale seated on the bed examining his puzzle box. Her brother looked up when she entered.

"Hello, Deli. I put your pack over there." He pointed to a chair next to the side table on the far side of the bed from where he sat. "I didn't know if you wanted to share a room or if you wanted one all to yourself. This place is huge, huh?"

"We can share. I've heard enough strange sounds that I don't think I want one of these big beds all to myself." Pulling up her pack behind her, she climbed up on the bed.

"I know what you mean." Kale nodded in agreement. Suddenly, he jumped to his feet, knocking Delilah off balance. "I unlocked another side, Deli! Look!" He held up his puzzle box for her inspection.

Delilah saw gears turn and a plate slide away from an inner mechanism, but she didn't understand his excitement. "So what does it do now?"

Scratching his head, Kale sat on the edge of the bed. "I'm still not sure. I have to get all six sides working in sequence before it'll open. I wonder what's inside."

"It's probably a joke. You'll spend all this time working on it, and it'll be empty." She hoped, for Kale's sake there was a point to the puzzle box, but it wouldn't be the first time Kale obsessed over a mechanical item that had no practical purpose.

Upon removing the grimoire from her pack, Delilah opened it. While they traveled, she spent most of her free time studying her lexicon so she could communicate effectively with humans. Now that they planned to stay in one place for a couple of months, Delilah wanted to study this arcane tome in depth. Already, glimpses of the ancient knowledge locked within tantalized the drak sorceress with its power and potential.

The words on the page shifted, flowing before her. The text rearranged itself as she read it, allowing her to read the equivalent of several pages of information before having to turn a page. Magical theory, from essays on the nature of wizardry and the ways its effects could be manipulated, to rituals covering mundane activities, like removing a stain from linen, to infusing life into that which was lifeless, the book contained more knowledge than Delilah expected could fit between leather covers.

She smiled to herself. *I know where I'm going to be lost while it's snowing outside. This gilded cage is no prison for me.*

***

Pancras tossed and turned. The fire in the hearth proved ineffective at removing the chill from the air, and the blankets upon his bed provided scant relief from the cold. Dark shapes crept toward him, shadowy figures with neither form nor substance. Yet, he felt them grasping at him, clawing, pulling him down into a shadowy pit.

Falling, the minotaur pushed past the discomfort of the breath caught in his chest and screamed. "*Seeko osta sto choma kai na ipakousoun tis entoles mo!*"

Pancras fell out of bed, gasping. The coppery taste of blood flooded his mouth as the floor rammed his bottom teeth into his tongue. Groaning, he pushed himself to his hands and knees before he pulled himself up, using the bed frame to steady himself.

He drank from the pitcher, swishing water in his mouth before spitting the bloody liquid into the basin. A thin line of light visible under the bedchamber door beckoned Pancras to pull on his robes and follow it into the common area. Dawn's first light streamed through the windows. Its orange glow, reflecting off the glistening white blanket of the season's first snowfall, set the town below ablaze.

Pancras stepped away from the windows, then left the suite through the double doors which led to the walkway overlooking the courtyard. A bitter wind blew through the arches, bringing with it the thick scent of burning wood from nearby hearths. The clouds that brought the snow moved away, disappearing over the horizon and leaving behind a clear, blue sky. The fresh snow cover made Almeria seem quieter, more peaceful than usual.

The fresh air cleared his head. Pancras replayed in his mind the dark, strange dream he had as well as the vision that befell him during his discussion of the tapestry with Lady Milena. Not one to have particularly vivid dreams, this recent trend unnerved him. Between Kale's affliction and his own experiences, Pancras thought Delilah might be the only one among them who was even remotely normal. *And then there's Edric. Has the dwarf abandoned us?*

Startled by the scuff of boots on the stone floor, he turned in the direction of the sound. A woman approached, her sepia-brown skin glowing with orange-red undertones in the morning sun. She wore a fur-lined, beaded, white gown, and her ebony hair, woven into a complex braid, hung down her back to her waist. Holding a steaming goblet, she regarded Pancras as if she were deciding whether she should be alarmed by the minotaur on the veranda or pretend he was part of the scenery.

Pancras bowed. "Good morning."

The woman tilted her head. "I am Princess Valene. Identify yourself, Minotaur."

"Pancras"—he considered whether to add his title, remembering Prince Gavril's instructions—"First Wizard of Drak-Anor."

"Ah, yes. One of my husband's new pets." She turned toward the city.

Unsure whether he should stay or retreat to his chamber, Pancras remained still for a moment. Her accent told him that Princess Valene was not a native of Etrunia. He thought she might be from the north, possibly Vlorey.

"Did that term upset you?"

"Your pardon, Highness?" Pancras bowed again. "I was unsure if it was proper to remain here. I was enjoying the fresh air for a moment."

"You may remain. For now." After sipping from her goblet, Princess Valene faced him. "Why are you here? What business have you with Almeria that is so important my husband would allow you use of a suite here in the palace?"

Pancras swallowed, fighting to keep his expression neutral. *How can I face you, you who are the reason I am here?* He found he could not meet her gaze, the jade eyes which regarded him with unspoken accusation. "We are ambassadors from Drak-Anor—"

"Do not insult my intelligence. That odious little troll would not accept ambassadors from a place he has barely heard of, not like this. Maybe if you were from Celtangate or even Ironkrag, I could believe it, but you are not a dwarf."

"Kind of you to notice—"

Princess Valene clicked her tongue. She poked him in the chest, forcing him to meet her gaze. She was tall for a human; Pancras stood only a head taller than she. "Let us speak plainly, Minotaur."

Rubbing his right horn, Pancras nodded. "Very well."

"My husband is a schemer. He is always plotting, always looking for an advantage. I do not know what his game is, what he thinks a minotaur and two draks will gain him, or over whom, but I will be watching."

"Your Highness, whatever it is you think your husband is plotting, I assure you, we have no involvement in it. In fact, our plan is to leave as soon as the snows melt sufficiently for us to travel to Muncifer safely." Pancras liked this deal with Prince Gavril less and less the more he thought about it. He never wanted to encounter his intended victim. Nausea at the thought of cursing this woman welled in the pit of his stomach.

"So you say." She stared at him for a moment, her eyes searching his face for the lie. "No matter. Tell me of Drak-Anor. It is relatively new, is it not? I don't remember hearing about it when I was growing up in Vlorey, and I heard many things whilst loitering around the docks."

Pancras appreciated the change of subject. Taking a breath, he noted the scent of wine and spices wafting from Princess Valene's beverage past his nose on the breeze. "The city has always been there, at least, longer than I have lived there. It's only been recently that we've come together behind a reasonable leader and removed the more destructive elements sharing our mountain home, the goblins and oroqs that infest the tunnels and caverns of the Dragon Spine Mountains."

"So you are not from there, originally? I thought I recognized your accent. Muncifer, is it not?"

"You are very wise, Highness."

"It is experience, not wisdom. I listened to many sailors from the south, many minotaurs, as they told their tall tales on the docks of Vlorey." She smiled, looking into his eyes. "Pity you're here under false pretenses. I might have enjoyed hearing your stories as well."

"Regardless of my true intentions"—Pancras decided to gamble—"It doesn't make my unrelated stories less relevant to your enjoyment."

"True." Touching his sleeve, she examined his jewelry. "You have a keener fashion sense than most minotaurs I've seen. Yes… I will be watching you."

Princess Valene drank from her goblet before nodding to Pancras. "I must assume my duties at court. We shall talk again, Am—no, I shall not call you Ambassador because we both know that is a false title. Pancras, First Wizard of Drak-Anor."

Pancras watched her glide down the corridor. He let out a breath, slumping. His burden just became much heavier.

***

After breaking their fast, Pancras and Delilah cleaned and re-heated the bath water so Pancras and Kale could have their turns. While the males bathed, Delilah studied her grimoire. It was midmorning by the time they were all ready to leave the suite. Delilah's messenger returned to them as they prepared to leave.

The electric-blue, conjured boggin jumped and yipped. "Mistress Delilah, Dwarf Edric reports that he has a good thing going at an unnamed gambling establishment and will be in contact later." It disappeared in a puff of blue smoke.

Kale nodded. "I'm glad he's all right."

Delilah harrumphed. "Yeah, he'll be in contact when he's run out of money and run up massive debts, I'll bet."

"That'll be his problem, Delilah." Pancras led the way through the palace corridors and down the spiral staircase to the main hall. "I need to speak to the prince about equipment for the research he wants me to do and see if I can get us permission to go out into the city. In the meantime, I want you two to explore the palace. Go everywhere they'll let you." Leaning in close, he lowered his voice. "Who knows, maybe you can find secret ways in and out of the palace, huh?" Pancras smiled, shooing them away, then continued toward the throne room.

Kale rubbed his hands together. "This will be great, Deli. It's like exploring the caverns around Deep Road, except there's nothing waiting in the shadows to eat us!"

"Just guards who want to stick us." Delilah returned the glare of a palace guard who watched them.

Kale wasn't worried. Lady Milena seemed nice enough from what Pancras told him. "So what if a few guards don't like us? We're ambassadors, right? They can't do anything to us as long as we don't do anything bad."

"I wish we could go outside the palace. The snow in the mountains near Drak-Anor is always severe and harsh, but it looks like it might be fun to go out in it here." Delilah glanced toward the palace doors and pulled her furred mantle tighter.

Kale took his sister's arm, pulling her toward an undecorated corridor. "Pancras will convince them to let us leave the palace. There will be plenty of snow. Besides, it's just cold and sticks to you and then gets all wet."

They wandered the palace for hours. It didn't take long for Kale to ascertain plainer rooms and unadorned hallways contained fewer guards and more idle servants. Decorated areas intended for visitors and those the royal family wanted to impress featured lavish embellishments and promoted the family's image.

Their explorations led to a heavy wooden door at the end of a dusty corridor. The pain in Kale's back returned, and he wanted to have another hot bath; the one he enjoyed earlier seemed to alleviate the discomfort. However, he couldn't resist the lure of the door.

"I think we've seen enough, Kale. You could draw a map of this place already!" Leaning on her staff, Delilah tapped her foot. Her claws clicked an impatient rhythm on the stone floor.

"Sure, except for this door." He opened it, revealing a set of stairs leading down. "Excellent! Are you coming? We could probably use some light down there."

"*Fos*." The top of Delilah's staff emitted a pale light. "You know, if they don't have those magical lights down there, it probably means no one goes down there anymore. If you're looking for things to eat you, that's where they'll be."

Grinning, Kale patted the daggers on his bandolier. "I have these, and I have you. Plus, I can breathe fire now."

"Great. You'll burn down the palace all around us."

Kale descended the stairs alongside his sister. "Stone walls won't burn."

The stairs led to a vast room supported by arches which seemed to extend beyond the reach of Delilah's light. Stone walls divided the room into alcoves, some filled with crates and chests. The air felt damp, heavy, and smelled like mold. Dust hanging in the air like a grey cloud veiled the light from Delilah's staff.

"This is the place where all the junk goes to be forgotten." Delilah turned around. "Let's go. There won't be anything good down here."

Unconvinced, Kale pulled on her hand. He glanced over his shoulder when she resisted. "Come on, are you scared? There's nothing bad down here. It's just… stuff."

"I'm not scared, Kale." Delilah snatched her hand away from her brother. "I'm tired, it's dusty, and I want to get back to my grimoire."

"Fine. Just make me a magical light, and I'll go on ahead." *If she doesn't want to share in the fun, she can go be grumpy by herself.*

"I can't just make a magical light for you like that. It takes the right materials, time, and a whole ritual! I'll work on one for you this week, though. I promise."

"Just a few more minutes, Deli."

"Oh, fine!" Delilah passed him, holding her staff ahead of her to light the way. Kale rushed to keep up with her. They advanced faster than he wanted to explore, but at least they moved in farther and away from the stairs.

"Fantastic. Another door." Delilah pointed with her staff. "Do you wonder what's behind that one? Maybe it's extra dust with double the mold."

Kale laughed, approaching the door. "It's probably just more storage. I wonder if they have any old crowns down here or anything like that. Ooh, maybe an old, forgotten ancient dagger from before the Sundering!" He opened the door.

Beyond it, they found a corridor lined with internment niches. Kale spotted ossuaries and urns, along with sarcophagi farther down. Frescos depicting the departed decorated the walls and ceilings. "It's a catacomb!"

"We shouldn't go in there, Kale."

He furrowed his brow. "Pancras said we could go anywhere the guards didn't forbid us. I don't see any guards. Do you?"

"Kale!" Delilah's expression told him all he needed to know. Spinning, he faced the ragged, half-rotten man charging at him. Kale ducked, then dove forward as the undead creature lunged with outstretched blackened talons.

Rolling into a kneeling position, Kale drew two daggers from his bandolier. The creature turned its attention to Delilah. Kale threw one of his daggers, striking the ambling corpse between its shoulder blades. Ignoring the wound, it swiped a dirty claw at his sister.

Delilah jumped backward, leveling her staff. "*Dapane phlogone!*" A stream of fire burst from her staff, engulfing the creature. "I told you things down here wanted to eat us!"

The undead creature spun around, flailing its arms as the flames consumed it. Kale leaped under it as it fell backward. Turning after Delilah helped him to his feet, he saw dozens of pairs of glowing red eyes in the darkness of the catacomb lumbering toward them.

"That's not good, Deli."

Delilah pushed him out of the way before raising her staff high. Swirls of blue mist surrounded her, fusing into a sphere in her palm. "*Ophayra!*" She tossed the coruscating orb toward the advancing mob. Kale slammed the door after they exited, holding it shut until an explosive concussion slammed into the door and he felt the heat of the flames through the wood.

"Let's go!" Seizing Delilah's hand, Kale raced out of the undercroft and up the staircase, continuing until they reached the main hall. Servants and guards gathered, all wondering what caused the boom they heard.

Kale pointed down the hall from whence they came. "Dead things! Under"—he fought to catch his breath—"under the palace… dead things!" He was not sure if he spoke drak or the common trade language. Seeming to understand the gist, the guards sped in the direction he indicated.

A few moments later, Pancras rushed out of the throne room, followed closely by an auburn-haired woman wearing the gleaming armor of the Royal Guard. "What's going on?"

"Delilah and I were just exploring the palace, like you said to. We were in this big underground vault thing when these undead things just attacked. They were zombies or ghouls or something, I don't know. They were nasty with long, black, claws, and their skin was rotting off."

The knight next to Pancras nodded. "The catacombs, in the undercroft. We've never had trouble with undead there before."

"I roasted them." Placing a hand on Kale's shoulder, Delilah straightened her back.

Pancras faced the knight after nodding at Delilah. "That would be the detonation we heard, Lady Milena."

"Wizardry?" Raising her eyebrows, Lady Milena regarded Delilah. "I hope you have not damaged the palace. The undercroft is very old. It has served as the foundation of not only this palace, but the one that was here before as well."

Pancras knelt and took each drak by the shoulder. "Are you two all right?"

Brushing away his hand, Delilah nodded. "We're fine. We may not see much action anymore, but we can handle a pack of ghouls. Or zombies, whatever they were. We didn't stick around to ask."

"Hey, Pancras. Do you think this has anything to do with those ghouls we found under Ironkrag? They never had problems either until recently, remember?"

Lady Milena turned her gaze toward Kale. "What's this?"

Pancras stood. "Shortly before we left to travel here, Kale and I, along with our dwarf companion, found and defeated the source of a new ghoul infestation in the caverns near Deep Road under Ironkrag. Something created them, even out of dwarves, but I believed we destroyed the creature."

Lady Milena shook her head. "I don't understand. Dwarves can't become undead?"

"Well, typically, when a dwarf dies, its body hardens and becomes like stone. To create an undead creature from a dwarf, one must work very quickly. One cannot just go into a dwarven crypt and raise an army. There are no bodies, per se, to work with, you understand."

"You sound as though you speak from experience." Lady Milena's hand dropped to the hilt of her sword. Kale noticed she adopted a defensive posture; she stepped back a half-step and widened the distance between her feet.

"Yes, well," Pancras rubbed his horn, lowering his head. "Drak-Anor was once a darker place." He noticed Lady Milena no longer stood close to him. "As one of Aita's faithful, I find it wise to know the ways of my enemies, yes?"

"Princess of the Underworld…" Lady Milena's eyes flitted from Pancras, down to the draks, and back. She regarded them for a moment before she relaxed. "If I find you have anything to do with this…"

Pancras held up his hands. "I have not." He placed one of his hands over his heart and bowed. "I swear it."

"Very well." Lady Milena turned her attention to an approaching guard. "Report?"

"We found several burned bodies, Lady Milena. They were all in the catacomb."

Kale wondered if the minotaur accidentally created them in his sleep again, like he did at the watchtower.

"They were burned beyond recognition, but other than some clawed tracks, we found no evidence of anyone having gone down into the undercroft in ages. We're conducting a search for the creatures that left those tracks in the dust."

Lady Milena coughed, pointing at the draks. "I think you'll find your culprits right here, Corporal."

"Oh, yes, of course. Shall I arrest them?" He moved to restrain Delilah, who responded by jumping backward and hissing. She held her staff ready.

"No, Corporal. They were given free run of the palace, and the undercroft was not off limits." She pointed at Kale and Delilah. "It is now, however, understand?" She returned her attention to the corporal. "Post a guard. Until we discover what exactly is going on here, I want no one going into the undercroft or the catacombs, clear?"

"Understood, milady!" After saluting, he left to carry out her orders.

"I suggest you two head back to your suite. You've made enough trouble for one day, don't you think?" Lady Milena glared at them with the judging eyes of a mother chastising her children.

"Suits me. I didn't want to go down there in the first place." Taking Kale's hand, Delilah dragged him toward their suite.

Kale glanced over his shoulder at Pancras as they left. The minotaur's shoulders slumped, and he rubbed his temples. "I think we shouldn't have gone down there, Deli."

"Told you so."

Chapter 10

Pancras didn't blame Kale and Delilah for what happened. He told them to explore as much of the palace as they could, and if the guards weren't guarding the undercroft and catacombs, the draks could hardly be expected to avoid the area.

From outside the doors to their suite, he gazed at the snow-dusted city. Much of what fell the night before was gone, but heavy, grey clouds in the distance promised another snowfall.

Lady Milena approached him. "I've just spoken to the prince. He wants you to go into the undercroft and ensure all those things are destroyed. I am to accompany you."

"Now?" Pancras rubbed his neck. "I was just about to eat."

"I have my orders." The Captain of the Royal Guard dropped her hand to the hilt of her sword. Pancras turned away from her, rubbing his right horn.

"Very well. Allow me at least to inform the draks where I'm going. I wouldn't want them to worry and start searching the palace for me."

"Yes, that is wise." Lady Milena banged on the suite doors. After a moment, Kale opened them. "Pancras and I are going into the catacomb to ensure your sister killed all those nasty undead. Don't wait up for him." She turned away from the door. Kale stared wide-eyed at Pancras.

"Save me something to eat, if you can."

"All right. Delilah wants to talk to you when you get back, so wake her up if you have to."

Waving in acknowledgment, Pancras followed after Lady Milena. He rushed to catch up to her, checking his pockets and pouches as he went. He didn't really need anything other than his arcane focus, the gilded tips covering his horns, but he found the various bits and bobs that found their way into his pockets always came in handy.

The stink of burnt flesh greeted them as they entered the dusty undercroft. Floating motes of dust that combined with lingering smoke formed a choking haze. Milena coughed, fanning her hand in front of her face.

"Have you any incantations that might help with this?"

"*M'poy'rieni aerha.*" As he spoke the words, tendrils of green formed near the tips of his horns. Pancras blew, his magically enhanced breath clearing the air.

"Useful stuff, wizardry." Milena drew her sword, then withdrew a glowing stone from her pouch. She held it high in front of her to illuminate their path.

"I have always found it to be so."

Pancras marveled at the vast number of crates stacked in the alcoves. "What are all these?"

"Mostly dishes and linens. Decorations, that sort of thing."

What possible use could they have for so much of it? There must be enough here for every family in Almeria. "Backups in case of breakage?"

Milena paused, allowing Pancras to clear the air again. "Every time a new family ascends to the throne, they replace everything imprinted with the old ruler's crest. Sometimes, they just replace everything. Can't be using anything to tie them to the old regime, you know. Over there." She pointed to a closed, heavy oaken door with her sword.

Pancras gestured for Milena to take cover behind him before he approached the door to the catacombs. While drawing upon arcane energy, he placed his hand upon it. "*Entipismos zompi. Entipismos zompi. Entipismos zompi.*" Chanting as he concentrated, he reached out with his mind, searching for the telltale signs of the undead. As unnatural creations, all undead were an abomination to the Earth Mother, and as such, they created negative space, a hole in the life-force of the world. Pancras interpreted negative results as a good sign.

"There's nothing immediately threatening beyond the door, nothing undead, that is. Detection is not perfect, especially the farther away from us they might be, but we should be safe to proceed for now."

Milena sheathed her sword before opening the door. "From how far away can your divination sense them?"

"I've never had to use it beyond a few dozen feet, honestly, although I expect I could sense the entire catacomb complex." Stepping around a pile of burnt corpses, Pancras pinched his nose shut against the odor.

After closing the door behind them, Milena again drew her sword. "Do not be so sure. The catacombs run under most of the city. The areas that connect to the palace's undercroft are supposed to be sealed off, but workers in the catacombs are notoriously unreliable."

"Can anyone who lives in Almeria be interred here?" Pancras followed her, careful to keep the wisps of magical aether swirling around his horns, ready to destroy any undead lying in wait.

"If one has sufficient money. Many families choose cremation as it is cheaper. Certainly, all the noble families have sections reserved for their use, near their estates, of course." She inspected an alcove, but upon finding only funeral urns within it, she returned to the main hallway.

"There have been plans for years to build a new palace near the north wall, surrounded by a mighty, impregnable complex, disconnected from the catacombs and inaccessible except through one gate. That sort of work is expensive, and the Duke of Muncifer and the minotaurs in charge of the Stonecutter's Guild are less than eager to negotiate lower prices with Prince Gavril. They don't like him much."

"Imagine that." Pancras chuckled.

Milena ducked under a cobweb, then turned the corner. More alcoves and burial niches stretched deep into the darkness. The farther into the catacombs they went, the staler the air became. There was something else in the air, a slight breeze, carrying with it a putrid stench.

"Do these catacombs connect with any sort of sewer system?"

"I'm not an expert, but I believe there may be some old cisterns and sewers that connect, why?" Milena faced Pancras, furrowing her brow.

"I smell something foul. It doesn't smell like death and decay." Movement caught Pancras's eye. He spun toward the flicker but saw nothing in the darkness.

"Probably a rat." Milena tapped his arm with her sword. "Let us continue."

"It seemed bigger than a rat."

"Where?"

Pancras pointed in the direction where he saw the movement. Milena moved past him and into the alcove. He waited while she inspected several internment niches. All contained ossuaries and offering bowls, except for one, which contained a full skeleton dressed in once-fine robes, now faded and moldy with age.

The only evidence Pancras and Milena found of movement was a disturbance in the dust. Neither could identify specific tracks. "One of the destroyed undead probably came from here." Milena sheathed her sword. "I am not certain there is any value in continuing further. Surely we've been down here long enough to attract attention should a ravenous beast wish to devour us, yes?"

"Most undead are attracted to life, unless their creator holds sufficient control over them. It seems likely they would have attacked by now." Pancras blew a thick layer of dust off the skeleton. *At least this fellow is resting peacefully.*

"Where did they come from, I wonder?" Milena stood next to Pancras, eyeing the skeleton. She cocked her eyebrow. "Doesn't it require a necromancer to create this kind of undead?"

Pancras coughed, shuffling his hooves. "Generally, yes. There have been exceptions. The Lich Queen, as an example, is said to have known a ritual that could empty all the graves in a city leagues away from her army and summon them to her side."

"I overheard guards talking. They say your drak friend claimed you are a necromancer." Seizing his shoulder, she turned Pancras to face her. Milena reached over her head, yanking one of his horns and pulling his head downward. Pancras grunted, squirming, but he could not free himself. The strength of her grip surprised him. "What is your game? Why are you here?"

"It's true, I once practiced necromancy, and I have created my share of skeletons to aid me in my work." He twisted again, but Milena kept a tight hold on his horn, gripping the other one with her free hand for more control. "But, I have not done so in years."

Pancras fought to control his breathing. The position in which she held him placed uncomfortable pressure on his neck and chest, straining the muscles in his back. When she wrenched him down, he felt a few of his vertebrae pop.

He could overpower the human, if he so desired. However, despite her distrust of him, he did not wish to risk injuring Captain Trueblade. If anything, he needed at the very least for her to tolerate his presence.

"Do you value the lives of your drak companions, Pancras?"

What do they have to do with this? "Yes, yes, they are as close to kin as I have."

"Then swear on their lives that these undead are not your creations."

It was an oath which Pancras could readily affirm. "I swear on their lives, I did not create these undead."

"Swear it again, by their names."

The minotaur raised an eyebrow when confronted with Milena's knowledge of the arcane. By demanding the draks' names of him, she guaranteed consequences if Pancras lied, assuming she could back up the oath with magic. He didn't think she wielded such capability, no one but the most powerful wizards did, but she knew an oath reinforced by magical compulsion carried greater impact when coupled to names.

"On the lives of Kale and Delilah Windsinger, I swear I have no involvement with these undead."

Milena released her hold on him. Pancras rubbed his neck, straightening. He expected to read contempt or anger in her expression. Instead, as she peered down the corridor, her face carried no lines to reveal emotion.

She motioned for him to advance ahead of her. "Let us leave this place."

Pancras led her out in silence, feeling relief she allowed the matter to drop. When they reached the main hall, Milena stopped him before he headed back to his suite.

"I will take you at your word on this matter, but I will be watching you."

Bowing, Pancras touched her hand to his forehead. "I understand, of course. Your dedication to your duty does you credit, Lady Milena." She nodded in acknowledgment, then turned away. Pancras returned to his room, and his thoughts turned to his now-cold dinner.

***

Delilah found she rather liked the plush armchairs in the great room of their suite. They were soft and large enough for her to curl up in completely with her grimoire. She enjoyed fewer distractions by the crackling fire than in the bedchamber where Kale experimented with his puzzle box. He muttered to himself when he worked on it, seemingly oblivious to her presence.

She lost herself in the ever shifting characters on the page. "How does it do that?" She traced the characters with a claw, but she could not keep up. When she closed her eyes, she still saw the images dancing on the edges of her vision. The characters formed new words she couldn't understand and fleeting pictures that vanished when she lingered on them.

Concentrating on a single symbol at a time, Delilah found she could sort of hold it in place long enough to examine it. The characters transcribed in this grimoire seemed to possess a type of power with which she was unfamiliar. She maintained her focus even as the doors of the suite opened. However, when a burst of cold wind caused the fire to sputter, her concentration faltered, and the symbol wriggled before it vanished.

Annoyed at whoever interrupted her studies, she opened her eyes. After shutting the door against the winter wind, Pancras greeted her with a smile. "I don't suppose you saved me anything to eat?"

Softening her scowl, Delilah pointed at the table. "Of course we did. It was some sort of soup. It's probably cold now, but it came in little iron pots, so you could probably stick it in the fire for a few minutes."

She closed her grimoire, latching the clasps, while Pancras brought his pot of soup to the fire to warm it. "Hey, Kale and I were talking while you were gone."

"Oh?"

"You sleep with your focus on, right?"

Pancras set the pot on the edge of the hearth, near the glowing embers at the bottom of the burning logs. The fire sputtered and crackled, its light casting prancing shadows about the room.

Nodding, the minotaur sat in the armchair next to Delilah. "Yes, I rarely remove it."

"Maybe you should. It might keep you from necromancing in your sleep." While she couldn't be sure whether Pancras experienced another episode of undead creation during the night, she and Kale agreed it couldn't hurt to take precautions.

"I'm not actually sure that's possible."

"Pancras." Delilah leaned her book against the chair leg. "What can it hurt?"

The minotaur fingered the tips of his horns, lost in thought. "Perhaps… my dreams have been dark of late. Very well." He smiled, nodding at Delilah. "I will remove them from now on."

"Good, we'll see if any more undead crop up here in 'civilization.' As nasty as some of the humans behave, I have to admit this is nicer than that grumpy minotaur's inn, huh?"

"The Sleeping Viper was adequate, but yes, this is nicer."

"When do you think—"

Knocking at the doors echoed through the parlor. Sighing, Delilah hopped off her chair.

Kale shouted from the bedchamber. "Can someone else get that?"

Delilah chuckled, opening the doors. The orange-scaled drak from the jail stood before her holding a spherical glass vessel. The retort and crucible, a tool of alchemy, featured a long downward-pointing spout.

"You! How'd you get here?"

"I have a delivery for Pancras. Some of the equipment you requested." Smiling, she pushed Delilah out of the way to enter the room.

"Just put it over there." Pancras waved in the general direction of the table. "Where's the alembic?"

Delilah didn't give her a chance to reply. Upon shutting the door, she placed a clawed hand on Kali's shoulder. "I didn't know you worked here in the palace."

"Oh, I don't. But you'd be surprised how easily servants will abandon their duties to the first volunteer to come along when they resent their job." She put the equipment on the table, then dusted off her hands. "Draks and minotaurs aren't very popular among the nobility."

"We've noticed."

Pancras leaned around the back of his chair. "How did you get into the palace if you don't work here, then?"

The drak shrugged, smiling. "It wasn't easy, but there are secret ways in and out of most of these old buildings if you're small, don't mind getting a little dirty, and don't want to be seen."

"So, either you're very odd and like to take over random delivery jobs, or you want something." Delilah put her hands on her hips. "So, what do you want?" Not even for a moment did she consider this a social call.

"Where's Kale?"

Delilah moved to put herself between Kali and the bedchamber door. Her eyes flicked to her staff on the floor near the armchair and then to the other drak. "What do you want with him?" *Pancras better back me up here.*

"You're the older sibling, aren't you?" Kali turned her back to Delilah. She approached the hearth. "I'm not going to hurt him. I just want to talk to him."

"About?" From his chair, Pancras watched her kneel before the fire to warm her hands.

"Who's here? Kale stood in the doorway. Oh, hi Kali!" He moved toward her, keeping his eyes fixed on the puzzle box he rotated in his hands instead of watching where he was going. Delilah put her hand out to keep him from plowing into her.

Dammit, Kale. "She was just leaving."

"I wasn't, actually. I wanted to talk to you."

"Oh." Kale felt his face grow warmer. "What's going on? Why is everyone so tense? I can't have friends visit?"

Kali cut off Delilah's reply. "They don't trust me. They think I'm some criminal mastermind here to abduct or murder you."

"Pancras!"

The minotaur snorted, grinning. "Not me." He rose from his chair to check his soup.

"Deli?"

Delilah felt Kale's eyes on her. Turning to face him, she put on her best innocent expression, clasping her hands in front of her chest. "We've had nothing but trouble since we arrived, Kale. I just want to keep us all safe."

Scowling, her brother held the bedchamber door open. He gestured for Kali to approach him. "You always get uptight when a female wants to talk to me, Deli. Kali is my friend, and we're going to talk. In private!" He punctuated his statement by slamming the door.

Pancras blew on his soup, sipping gingerly at the spoon. Raising his eyebrows, he regarded her over the steaming bowl. Delilah stomped across the room, then flopped into the chair.

"Stupid Kale. You weren't supposed to notice."

"Your sister doesn't seem to like me much." Kali sat in one of the chairs at the side table. Tossing his puzzle box on the bed, he took the seat across from her.

"She's worried about me getting hurt. That's all. Back home, most draks only talk to us when they want something. We're the ones they don't trust." Kale was accustomed to the derision he and Delilah received from the draks in Drak-Anor. It was the main reason they spent most of their time with Sarvesh and Pancras.

"Why is that? You both have stripes. I would have thought they would revere you."

"Yeah, well, they think because we hatched from the same egg, our curse is stronger than any special destiny we might have. We were cast out of Clan Windsinger as soon as we were old enough to fend for ourselves." Barely ten years old when their clan banished them, the twins wandered in the mountains, ultimately finding the city now known as Drak-Anor during the same year Pancras arrived, although they didn't know him at the time. It seemed like a lifetime ago to Kale.

"Twins?" Kali slouched in her chair. "They would have left you to die from exposure if you didn't have stripes."

"Yeah, that's what everyone kept telling us." Kale suspected were it not for their parents, the elders would have left them to die at birth anyway. Once they were old enough to fend for themselves, even their parents couldn't sway the elders from their decision. "Deli got to be good with sorcery, so we did okay for ourselves. We have better friends now than we would have if we'd stayed in that village."

Kali nodded, then withdrew a small box from her pouch. She set it on the table. "I have something I need help with." She smiled, regarding her hands. "I seem to have lost the key."

Laughing, Kale pulled the lightweight metal box across the table to examine it. He didn't see any hinges, but he noticed a seam that traveled the circumference of the box. One side contained a keyhole just large enough for Kale's claw. "Lost it, huh?"

He didn't believe her claim for a moment. "With all the draks in that secret tavern of yours, there aren't any who can pick a lock?"

She stroked his arm. "Sure. But I want *you* to do this one."

Shuddering, Kale pushed the box away. "I could. It looks pretty easy. Why should I? I'm not as naïve as my sister thinks I am. I just get excited."

Kali withdrew her hand, grinning. "I knew I liked you for a reason."

"I'm not saying I'm not going to open it, but I just want to know what you really want."

"Fair enough." Kali leaned forward, folding her hands together on top of the table. "Despite the name of our tavern, we're not assassins. We just ensure that the draks and minotaurs of Almeria get the things they need. Sometimes, humans aren't keen on letting us bring that stuff into town, or they don't want to sell to us. So, we use alternate methods of acquisition."

"So, you're thieves and smugglers?" Kale reflected on what life was like before the foundation of Drak-Anor. Draks, minotaurs, oroqs, and goblins all vied for the same limited resources. One had to be either strong or sly to get what one needed. Kale didn't always have his sister's sorcery to back him up, so he often resorted to sneaking around.

"Well." Kali pursed her lips, turning her eyes toward the ceiling. "If you want to be crass about it."

Kale picked up the box, then removed tools from his pouch and laid them on the table. Peering into the lock, he noted a few mechanisms inside that did not seem connected to the locking assembly. *A needle? I wonder if she trapped this on purpose.* Within a minute after he adeptly avoided the snare, of course, the lock clicked, and the top of the box popped open.

"Easy." He slid the box across the table to Kali. "Would I have been poisoned if I set off that needle in the lock?"

Smiling, Kali plucked a pearl ring from the box. She slid it onto her finger before closing the lid. "That would have been rude. Want some work? Think your sister might be willing to help us out?"

Kale considered her request for a moment. Whatever endeavor Kali wanted him to undertake would undoubtedly be more exciting than fetching supplies for Pancras, but he wasn't sure Delilah would be game. "I don't mind helping out, but I don't want to get involved in anything too serious. We're leaving for Muncifer as soon as it's safe to travel again. The prince says we're not allowed to leave the palace, so that sort of limits what I can do."

"There are ways around that. I can show you tonight, if you like."

The thought of being able to come and go as he pleased brought a smile to Kale's lips. He opened his mouth to reply, then remembered Pancras's arrangement with Prince Gavril and shook his head. "I'd better talk things over with Pancras and Delilah first. Pancras made some kind of deal to get us out of jail and in here. I think he's trying to get us permission to go into the city. I don't want to mess things up." He chuckled, scratching at a nick on the table. "This is much nicer than the jail or that inn we were staying at."

Kali stood, then sashayed past him, nuzzling his neck as she went. "Suit yourself. If you get a chance to wander around, you know how to find me. And if you want me to come back and show you how to get out on your own, I guess you'll have to ask your sister to send me one of those glowing, blue things."

Kale rubbed his neck where she nuzzled it, watching her leave. Her touch warmed him inside. It almost made him forget about the pain in his back. Delilah entered the room, as he stretched, wincing.

***

"Well?" Delilah tapped her foot, waiting for Kale to respond. Kali hadn't said a word either to her or to Pancras when she left. Delilah was sure the orange-scaled drak drafted Kale to be at the center of some nefarious plot.

"Well what?" Kale flopped down on the bed, then picked up his puzzle box.

"Are you going to run away with her and leave us?" Delilah clamped her hands over her mouth as soon as she uttered the words. *Stupid, stupid, stupid!* She knew her question was ridiculous, and she hated when her anxieties made her speak without thinking.

Kale rolled over on the bed to face her. He scooted to the end, hopped off, then hugged Delilah. "I'm not leaving, Deli. I promise. Even if she and I… if something—no, if anything like that happened, I'd make her come with us."

Delilah pushed Kale, causing him to stumble into the bed. "Fine then. What did she want?"

"She asked if we wanted to help her smuggle stuff for the draks and minotaurs in town. The humans don't treat them well, you know."

"I noticed." Delilah sat on the edge of the bed. "What did you tell her?"

"I said I'd have to talk it over with Pancras and you. I don't want to do anything to mess up the deal Pancras made, and I don't want to go back to the Grumpy Minotaur Inn."

Delilah hugged her brother. "I shouldn't have doubted you."

Kale nudged her before leaning on his elbow. "You're right. You shouldn't have. I'm not dumb."

A wave of guilt rushed over Delilah. He had a point. She treated him like a child. "I'm sorry, Kale. I worry about you, about us. This whole thing…" She waved her arms in the air, sighing. "There's so much that could go wrong, so many bad things that can happen, and you're still affected by that chaos rift thing." She lay on the bed next to her brother.

"Between you and Pancras, you'll figure out all this magical stuff." Kale turned his head toward her. "I'm just trying not to be bored while we're stuck here for the winter, you know?"

"I understand. I hope Pancras gets permission to leave the palace." Delilah rolled toward the edge, reaching for her grimoire before remembering she left it in the great room. "I don't think he's going to let us help with his little favor for the prince."

"Kali offered to show me the secret way she used to get in."

Facing her brother, Delilah's eyes brightened. "If Pancras doesn't have something for us to do by dinner tomorrow, we'll contact her."

***

The shadow invaded Pancras's dreams once again while he slept. Enveloping him like a cold blanket of sodden wool, it suffocated him. He fought to keep it at bay but could not summon his powers, for in his dream, he was naked. This vulnerability served to further enrage the shadow, and it pummeled Pancras with the sum of its fury until the light of dawn encroached, beating it back with its warm, life-giving light.

Pancras rolled out of bed, clutching his head. Throbbing at the base of his skull made his eyes feel as though they bulged and might at any moment shoot across the room. Bleary eyed, he fumbled with his focus, reversing the parts before he was able to fit them onto the tips of his horns.

Fresh air, that's all I need. He stumbled out of his bedchamber, clutching his robes. Kale and Delilah were already breaking their fast and waved to him from the table. He offered a feeble wave in response and stepped out into the corridor that overlooked the gardens. He remembered to don his robes just as footsteps on the stone heralded the arrival of Princess Valene taking her morning constitutional.

"Once again, I encounter a minotaur on my morning walk," the princess teased, her mouth upturning and her eyes twinkling. Her smile faded when Pancras stepped into the light. "You look terrible."

"I feel worse. I was hoping the fresh air would help." He leaned on the wall overlooking the garden. Fresh snow fell overnight, and the cold breeze blew the white powder into drifts across roofs in the city.

Princess Valene raised an eyebrow as she glanced over Pancras's shoulder. "Oh dear, a Royal Guard is coming, for you, I suspect."

The minotaur turned to see Lady Milena, with her hair frazzled and grey-purple bags under bloodshot eyes, approaching.

"Pancras. Your Highness." The knight bowed to her sovereign.

Princess Valene placed her hand on the captain's shoulder. "Good morning, Milena."

Milena turned toward Pancras. "Prince Gavril will see you now."

Blinking to clear his bleary eyes, Pancras squinted at Milena. "Now? I expected him to keep me waiting for at least another day."

"He said now." Milena gestured for Pancras to accompany her. He bowed to the princess, hearing her snort as he left with the Captain of the Royal Guard.

"Rough night?" Pancras hoped his restless sleep had not somehow affected Lady Milena.

"My duties do not end when we part ways. Also, I never sleep well after a visit to the catacombs."

"You know, if the prince would just let us go into the city and do our own shopping, he wouldn't have to bother with me at all."

"That is not my business."

Prince Gavril met them in an antechamber off the main hall, rather than in his throne room. Reading a document as he paced the floor, his lips moved in silence. Shaking his head, he rolled up the paper, then faced Pancras.

"Well, let's have it."

"Have what?" Pancras didn't understand the prince's question. He had stated his needs quite clearly in his request for an audience.

Prince Gavril coughed, then took a deep breath. "What is it you want?"

"You promised to hear my request to acquire my own equipment and supplies. The alchemy equipment delivered last night is a good start, but it is only a fraction of what I need for the"—Pancras's eyes flicked to Lady Milena standing at attention in the doorway—"for the project you want."

"And how am I to know you won't simply flee the city, hm?" Prince Gavril slapped his hand with the paper. "What guarantees will you give me, eh?"

Pancras didn't feel guarantees were needed. If the city was bogged down with snow and poor weather, the open country would be even worse. They would likely die of exposure within a few days if the weather became colder.

"I'm not sure what I could offer—"

Lady Milena cleared her throat. "Your Highness, if I might offer a suggestion?"

Prince Gavril addressed her in the tone of one scolding a child, "By all means, enlighten us."

"Perhaps Pancras could stay here while the draks go into the city, and vice versa."

Pancras nodded his assent. The draks could do little to help him search for supplies. In fact, they'd likely distract him. Furthermore, if they wanted to search the gambling halls for Edric, they certainly didn't need him around. For his part Pancras considered the dwarf competent to look after himself.

"Oh, very well. If it will get you working and keep you out of my hair. Lady Milena, you will accompany Pancras when he desires to visit the city. You can accompany the draks, as well, or find another guard to do it, but only you will accompany the minotaur. Clear?" Prince Gavril did not await her response before dismissing them with a wave of his hand. Brushing past them, he headed toward the throne room.

"Damn it." Lady Milena chewed on her bottom lip, glaring at the prince as he strode away. She turned her attention to the minotaur. "You do not look well. Are you ill?"

Pancras stifled another yawn and rubbed one of his eyes. "No." Pancras and Milena ambled down the hall toward his suite. A group of ladies-in-waiting stared at them as they passed. "I have a terrible headache. I haven't been sleeping well."

"I see. If it becomes chronic, I can contact my brother. He is a priest of Apellon, god of healers, light, and the arts. He knows a few teas that can remedy such ailments."

Pancras dodged a pair of giggling children running down the corridor. "Thank you. I shall keep it in mind."

He kept one hand on the wall as they climbed the spiral stairs to the wing that led to his quarters. The journey seemed arduous, and he felt as if he could sleep the rest of the morning if the shadows in his dreams would allow it.

"Will you want to go into town this morning?" Milena took his arm as they continued down the hall. He leaned on her for support until they reached his door.

"No, I want more sleep. You're welcome to come in and see if the draks want to, though."

Milena's expression told him in plain terms what she thought of that. "I will look for volunteers among my guards for them. There are a few who are sympathetic to the draks in town."

Pushing the door open, Pancras offered her a smile. "That would be most appreciated."

Chapter 11

Delilah was seated across the table chatting with her brother when Pancras staggered in. Her eyes followed the minotaur who headed for his room.

"Hey, Pancras!" Delilah tossed a sweet roll at him. Striking him in the shoulder, it adhered to his robes for a moment before falling onto the rug. His eyes, following its journey to the floor, remained fixed on it for several moments after it landed. He turned his gaze toward Delilah.

"What's the news? Can we leave yet?"

Kale hopped down from his chair to retrieve the sweet roll. He bit into it on his way to the table.

"Yes, with supervision. Lady Milena is looking for a couple of guards to volunteer to escort the two of you. We can't go together. If you go, I have to stay here. You have to stay here if I go." He pushed open the door to his bedchamber.

Delilah hopped off her chair and followed him. "So, are you going? Can we go?"

"I am going back to sleep. There's a thick blanket of new snow out there right now. I'm sure Lady Milena will be by when she has found someone willing to escort you." He fell into his bed, covering his head with his arm.

She poked the minotaur, eliciting only a grunt and a swatted arm in response. She returned to the table, closing his door behind her as she left, then helped her brother load up the food lift with dirty dishes.

"He passed right out."

"I'm not surprised. You didn't hear him yelling and screaming last night?" Kale yawned. "I hardly slept."

"Nope." After climbing into the armchair in front of the fire, she opened her grimoire.

"What are we going to do today, Deli?" Kale sat in the chair across from her, nursing a mug of mulled wine."

"I'm going to sit here and try to read until Lady Milena comes back and tells us who will take us into the city." She turned to the page where she left off. The symbols danced on the page as if awaiting her attention. "Then, I'm going to go look for stuff."

"What stuff?"

"I don't know. Something, anything. I'll know it when I see it. Besides, I need to make you a glow gem, right? So you can wander around the catacombs and other dark places without me." She returned her attention to the page, trying to wish her brother into silence.

"Aren't you worried I'll run off with Kali? Or we'll do stuff alone in the dark down there?"

Delilah closed her eyes, sighing. When she opened them again, she found her brother staring at her. "I told you, I don't really care about that, but if it'll get me some peace and quiet so I can study this"—she tapped the open page of her book—"then you can run off with her right now if you want!"

Kale kicked her dangling leg, retreating before she could retaliate. *Brothers!*

***

The next several days passed slowly for Kale. He knew better than to spend the entire time harassing his sister. Although Lady Milena found two volunteers willing to take him and Delilah into the city, the accumulation of falling snow prevented them from leaving.

Gaining permission to leave the palace but being unable to exercise it was worse in Kale's mind than not obtaining permission in the first place. He felt more trapped now than ever. Try as he might, Kale was unable to convince Delilah to continue their explorations of the castle. His puzzle box provided only a few hours of diversion at a time before he became bored.

"Kale, fetch me a bucket of water, please," Pancras called from his bedchamber. He spent the first couple of days of the snowstorm converting the extra space in his room into a makeshift laboratory. Kale didn't think he would want to sleep in a room with all that equipment, but Pancras seemed accustomed to it. Retrieving a bucket they acquired from the kitchens for such a purpose, Kale descended the stairs and proceeded to the palace entrance. Swinging the bucket, he hummed.

"Still too much snow out there, Drak." The guard smirked at Kale. "I don't see your escort, either."

Kale pointed at the bucket. "Not leaving. Getting snow."

"Snow? What for?"

"Water!"

After the guard opened the door for him, Kale plunged the bucket into a snow drift. He scooped up as much snow as the bucket would hold, then nodded his thanks to the guard.

"We have wells for that, you know."

The wells from which the palace staff drew their water were located in the lower levels, near the kitchens. "This is closer and cleaner. The well water smells funny."

"So do draks!" The guard called after him. Kale offered the guard an obscene gesture, ignoring his laughter. By the time he returned to the suite, he spotted Lady Milena ahead of him, knocking on the doors.

"Looking for us, or for Pancras?" Kale held the door for the guard captain.

Upon finding Delilah still seated in the same spot with her head in the grimoire, Kale set the bucket of snow on the hearth. Pancras emerged from his bedchamber.

"Kale, do you have that bucket of—oh, Lady Milena. I didn't hear you come in."

The captain greeted Pancras with a bow of her head. "I have spoken to the guards I know to be sympathetic toward draks and have found two to escort them into the city once enough of the snow clears."

"Excellent!" Pancras wiped his hands on his robes, stepping toward the bucket. "This is snow!"

"It becomes water when it melts, Pancras." Kale pointed to the bucket. "It just hasn't gotten that far yet."

Pancras growled. "I know snow melts into water, Kale."

Delilah snorted, burying her snout deeper in her tome. Lady Milena crouched in front of the fire to warm her hands. "We've had reports that snow packing is proceeding well. We should be able to open the palace gates tomorrow."

After heavy snowfalls, people in Almeria worked together to tamp the snow in the streets. They worked their way through the city on the main roads first, then up to the palace, and, finally, to the secondary roads and alleys. When their work was finished, the compressed snow was equal in utility and hard as a dirt road, a second road laid on top of the cobbles of the first.

"Excellent. I need to do some research." Pancras sat in the armchair next to Delilah. "You mentioned your brother is a priest of Apellon, yes?"

"Yes, that's right." Milena, rubbing her hands together, glanced up at Pancras. "Still having headaches?"

Pancras scratched his head. "No, not since that one night. The project I'm working on… I need to speak to a priest of Apellon, since you don't have an Arcane University here with its extensive library. Cybele would probably work, too, maybe even Aurora."

Kale eyed Pancras upon hearing of his malady. Apart from appearing a bit disheveled, Pancras seemed normal.

Why does he need to see priests of those gods? I thought he worshipped Aita.

"There are temples to all three in Almeria. Are you working on some sort of love potion? Cybele won't help with that, unless you're looking to woo the farm animals or crops." Milena's upper lip curled in disgust.

"Nothing like that. I don't work in magic that can control minds and wrest people's will."

Milena stood, a hand on her hips. "What is this project you're working on?"

"I cannot say. Ask your prince."

She huffed. "Perhaps I will. I will be around to escort you into town as soon as they open the gates." She stalked out of the room, clenching her fists.

Kale tapped Pancras on the knee. "What about us? We're tired of being cooped up in here."

"You can go when I get back. I shouldn't be long, and then you can take as much time as you need."

"Suits me." Delilah slammed her book shut. "If you two are going to keep talking, I'm going into our room to study this."

"Fine, Grumpy-butt!" Kale stuck out his tongue at his sister. She picked up her grimoire before turning her back on him, muttering under her breath and slamming the door behind her. Kale knew he shouldn't antagonize her, but he found it far too easy some days.

"See what I mean?"

***

After warming himself sufficiently in front of the fire, Pancras took the bucket to his bedchamber. Most of the snow melted, yielding more than enough water for his purposes.

Because he had not yet acquired all the components to perform complex necromancy, such as that required to fulfill Prince Gavril's demand, he set up a rudimentary alchemy lab in the interim. If he recalled correctly, subtle curses affecting a victim's long-term health required some sort of material object, a fetish or elixir, in order to function. He scrounged sufficient ingredients around the palace to make a few simple restorative potions.

He didn't regret leaving most of his necromancy notes and books behind in Drak-Anor. The discomfort of carrying the extra weight was hardly an incentive to bring them just in case they were needed. Besides, he found the prince's request abhorrent, and he intended to drag his feet for as long as possible. Not having them in his possession worked more to his advantage than not.

The priests of Apellon, Cybele, and Aurora all offered cures for infertility. At least, Pancras hoped they did. He hoped to utilize them to reverse-engineer a solution. Grimacing, he picked up his mortar and pestle. Even in the days when regularly he created zombies and skeletons to help him in his lab or send into battle, he would have found the idea of making someone barren without their knowledge or consent repulsive. He felt that sort of curse crossed the line.

Still, what choice do I have? Jail? Execution? I have a responsibility to Kale and Delilah. Maybe I can find something that will seem to work temporarily to give us enough time to get away from Almeria. Pancras did not think Prince Gavril would send his army after them, and he intended to leave no trace of the curse he was about to create, so there would be no evidence. Hunting them down would make Prince Gavril appear petty and vengeful. Given the growing dissatisfaction in Almeria among draks and minotaurs with the manner in which humans treated them, he thought Prince Gavril could ill afford to further antagonize them.

Pancras expected he could develop a solution by spring. Being permitted to go into town was the first step. He, too, wanted to stretch his legs and explore Almeria. He sympathized with Kale and Delilah's frustration over being cooped up in the palace. *Strange, back home I was content to stay in my laboratory for days, even weeks. But here, I'd rather be out in the city than in this lab.*

He scraped the mash off his mortar into the small cauldron in which he intended to brew the potion. Using a ladle Kale acquired from the kitchen, Pancras added water into the cauldron, then stirred it with a spoon. *Hopefully no one in the kitchen will come looking for these implements.* He rubbed some dried lavender leaves between his hands, crumbling them into the cauldron. He didn't have a means of boiling the mixture yet, apart from setting the cauldron on the hearth, and that sort of uneven and irregular heat was not suitable for the delicate art of alchemical brewing. Potions required steady, even heating or they became unstable. Sometimes instability resulted in gooey, unusable sludge or volatile, explosive mixtures. *I don't think Gavril would want to drink one of those, much as I might like him to.*

Letting the mixture steep, he changed into his frayed black and silver robes. He long ago depleted the mending supplies he had brought with him. *If I ever travel with an entourage, a seamstress will be the first person I hire.* He planned to make the purchase of new robes a priority once the palace gates opened. He heard a rapping, a tapping at the doors of their suite. *Hopefully that will be Lady Milena with the news I desire to hear.*

By the time he finished dressing and entered the parlor, Kale had already invited the knight in. The corners of her mouth turned downward in a frown, yet Kale was almost hopping in glee.

Lady Milena glanced up as Pancras crossed the room. "I have been informed the gates are open. I suppose you'll want to leave immediately?"

"As a matter of fact, yes. I am ready now." Pancras checked to make sure he had sufficient coin in his money pouch.

"I will meet you by the entrance, then. I need a heavier cloak. It's colder than Aita's Purgatory out there. There's talk of dogs stuck to signposts."

Kale scratched his head. "Why do dogs stick to signposts when it's cold?"

"They don't, Kale." Shivering, Pancras knelt before the fire. The cold air permeated the parlor, following Lady Milena when she arrived. "It's a joke."

Lady Milena bowed her head and left. Another blast of arctic air howled into the parlor. Pancras rubbed his hands as Kale joined him in front of the fire. The drak seemed redder than usual.

"Are you sure you don't want Deli and I to go first? She has a fur-lined cloak now, and I don't think it's that cold."

Pancras touched the drak's arm. He felt warmth radiate off him. "How are those lumps on your back?"

Kale shrugged, then craned his neck to look over his shoulder. "I've gotten used to the ache, but they feel tight and are very sensitive. You know, like giant blisters."

"I hope whatever emerges isn't hostile."

Kale's eyes widened, and he looked from one shoulder to the other. "You think something is going to come out of them? Like a giant bug or something? A worm?" He gasped. "Draklings?"

Pancras laughed. "No, no! Nothing like that. It was a joke. A joke! If I were to wager, I would say it might be something nasty, like pus or blood. Maybe you should carry a towel with you."

"You know"—Kale rubbed his chin, nodding—"that drak fortune teller, Oren? He says one should always carry a towel. Everywhere."

Pancras knew Oren but always thought he was more than a little unstable. He made wild predictions about everyone's future, and to Pancras's knowledge, none ever proved correct. He also had a weird obsession with the number forty-two. He cut all his food into forty-two bites exactly. He purchased items only if he could reasonably obtain them in lots of forty-two or negotiate the price to be forty-two talons or pennies.

"I'll be fine, Kale. Lady Milena says there's a clothier near the palace gates. The prince doesn't like to go far for a fitting."

"He's not very nice, is he? Sarvesh cares about all the draks and minotaurs in Drak-Anor. Prince Gavril seems to think the people are a hassle."

Pancras nodded. Gavril did indeed strike him as someone who would leave his people to die if a catastrophe befell Almeria or if the city were under siege. He tried to keep busy so he wouldn't focus on exactly what kind of deal he made to free them from jail and away from the executioner's block.

***

With Pancras gone and Kale working on his puzzle box, Delilah relished the quiet. She caressed the cover of the grimoire before opening it. Over the last several days, it seemed to attune itself to her, if such a thing were possible. The letters and images did not dance as much as they did when she first began studying the tome, and they settled into recognizable patterns, even if she was still unable to quite discern their meaning.

According to Terrakaptis, the book once belonged to a powerful drak sorceress. She found it odd that the language in the grimoire was not written in any form of Drak she recognized. The grimoire was said to have come down from the Age of Legends, so perhaps draks did not speak the same language then as they did now.

The symbols on the page spun as Delilah concentrated on them, finally forming the image of a drak female. Delilah assumed it was the sorceress to whom the grimoire once belonged, Gil-Li the Graven. Appearing to speak, she wagged her finger at Delilah, then closed her mouth. Detailed tattoos on her body glowed when she raised her hands. Bolts of magical energy arced between her outstretched hands, and tendrils of green, blue, red, and gold whirled around her body. Impaling her enemies, spikes of rock erupted from the earth. Boulders tore themselves free from the ground and pelted her attackers, who then charged her with swords drawn.

What am I watching? A vision from the past? Or something she's trying to teach me? Earth magic? Wizards who attended the Arcane University who wanted to learn elemental conjuration and control could specialize in a single element or learn a modicum of each one, but as Delilah was self-taught, pyromancy was the only magic that came easily to her. What she knew of other types of wizardry she learned from other practitioners in Drak-Anor or from books and scrolls they seized from invaders during the time before Lord Sarvesh became their leader.

Delilah guessed the glowing tattoos were Gil-Li's focus. She remembered hearing stories of sorcerers who derived their power from designs emblazoned in arcane pigments into their skin. Delilah could not imagine undergoing the painful and time-consuming process that would obscure her beautiful ebony and crimson stripes. Wearing a cloak for warmth was bad enough.

The sequence repeated. Delilah thought the images conveyed a technique rather than instructions for how to manipulate the earth element.

Delilah studied Gil-Li's movements. The image shifted, focusing on the drak and clearing away the details of her attackers. To create each effect, her hands and arms wove wider and more elaborate patterns than Delilah tended to use, but she had learned through practical application that sort of thing was usually a matter of personal style and preference. Her eyes widened. She realized through the entirety of Gil-Li's gesticulations and stances, one detail remained static: Gil-Li never moved her lips.

She's not talking… she's not saying the words!

Delilah heard tales of wizards who worked magic without ever uttering a single word, but the technique was thought to be lost. Although practitioners of blood magic often evoked without speaking the incantations, the energy they drew from spilling blood was extremely powerful and corrupting, and therefore forbidden. Where arcanists like Delilah and Pancras carefully wove and crafted the effects they desired, practitioners of blood magic erupted in power, barely able to control it. It suited them since they usually didn't care if allies were injured or killed; indeed, they usually expended their allies to harness their power in the first place.

As the grimoire drew her in, Delilah understood. The elaborate gesticulations were not just an affectation of Gil-Li's. They were the words.

"Deli? Deli?"

Delilah's head snapped up. "What?"

Kale knelt alongside her chair. "Are you all right? You were face down in your book. I thought you fell asleep."

"Don't be ridiculous!" Delilah snapped the book shut, wincing as pain shot through her neck and upper back.

"Pancras just got back." Kale helped her out of the chair. "We can leave now, if you want."

"What? Already? He's only been gone—" She rubbed her neck.

"It's been hours, Deli. It's midafternoon."

Delilah stared at the grimoire slack-jawed. She remembered every moment. It seemed like only a few minutes had passed, but if it was already afternoon, she had been engrossed for hours. She found she could visualize the images through closed eyes. Delilah placed the book on the chair, stepping away from it as if it might come alive.

"Yes, let's go. I'm ready to get out of here for a while."

***

The guards, a pair of young humans wearing fur-lined cloaks over their mail armor, waited for them in the main hall. At least, Kale assumed they were young because they appeared fit and their faces did not bear wrinkles. They leaned on their spears, chatting. They perked up when the drak twins approached.

"You must be the draks we volunteered to take into town." The guard with a patchy black beard bowed. "I'm Dusan. This is Mirek." He pointed at the other guard, a gaunt man with sad, grey eyes and wisps of blond hair peeking from beneath his helmet.

Delilah pointed at her brother. "He's Kale."

Kale pointed at his sister. "She's Delilah."

"All right, then." Mirek opened the door, then led them into the snowscape, a field of solid white interrupted only by a row of trees. A steep-sided path led through the snow to the palace gates. Wind howling across the snowdrifts reminded Kale of the mountain gusts that packed snow against the gates of Drak-Anor, sealing shut the city for months at a time. Noting his own woolen cloak provided plenty of warmth, he observed Delilah shivering in the cold and drawing her fur-lined cloak close around her. As he followed behind the humans and his sister, he noticed his feet melted distinct footprints in the snow wherever he stepped.

Kale wanted to show his sister how the snow melted around him, but deciding the humans might react poorly, he proceeded behind the others and kept quiet. He stayed close enough to hear what his sister said over the wind.

"I want to get more winter clothes. Are there shops that have those for draks?"

Mirek nodded. "There must be. Most of the draks live in the Foundry District."

"There are shops there, just on the other side of the main gate to the Commerce District." Dusan saluted the guards at the palace gate before proceeding onto the sparkling white avenue that led from the palace into the city. Dodging a group of children ducking and weaving among snow-covered trees, they avoided the snowball war in progress.

While leading them to the Foundry District, the guards kept to the main roads and avenues. Dusan, the talkative one, related anecdotes about life in Almeria and how he grew up around draks while helping his parents run a farm and livery just outside of the city. He seemed to have a story for every landmark, from the drunken band of brawlers picking fights with everyone who came by the fountain dedicated to Pacha, god of madness and wine, to the mad, old woman who wandered town covered in pigeons, which she threw at anyone who stepped into her path.

Mirek remained mostly quiet. The son of a blacksmith, he grew up in the Foundry District, but he lacked the desire to keep the smithy operating after his father died two winters prior. His eyes scanned the buildings and people, looking for troublemakers and threats. He pointed out important buildings to them as they passed: the Hall of Justice; the Sky Temple dedicated to Tinian, king of the gods; and the Grand Duchess, finest inn in all of Almeria.

Kale nudged his sister. "So that's where it is. Fancy."

Kale noticed the city seemed less busy than it was before the snow, and the people they encountered seemed friendlier and less frantic. He thought at first it was because they had an armed escort.

"Most of the people who are too busy for other folks don't come out when there's this much snow." Dusan stopped by a small fountain at the end of a plaza that featured a sculpture of a curly-haired bearded man drinking from a cup: Dolios, god of commerce and gambling. Giant white beards of ice draped from the spouts high on the wall of the frozen fountain. "Folks have to rely on each other more when it's this cold and snowy, and those busybodies are too selfish to get involved with that."

Mirek pointed to a shop across the way. A tree protruded from the top of the building, spreading its snow-covered canopy over the roof like a parasol. "Several drak merchants are set up in that building. Clothes, tools, handicrafts, that sort of thing. The Howling Siren Alehouse is right next door. That's where we'll be."

"I know we're supposed to keep our eyes on you the whole time, but we'll just be in the way in those shops." Dusan knelt as he spoke to the drak twins. "When you're finished, come join us for an ale, and we'll head back to the palace. You should be able to get anything you want in there. If not, we'll take you somewhere else, all right?"

"Sounds good to me." Kale grinned. If having an escort meant the guards sat in a tavern and he and his sister shopped for the items they needed, he could live with it.

Delilah seemed pleased too. "Fine, fine. Just don't drink all the ale before we get back!"

The shops were arranged around a central parlor. Benches and chairs encircled the tree trunk, and several humans mingled with the draks. Delilah's eyes lit up, and she made a beeline for a corner shop selling jewelry. Kale followed her until he saw the haberdasher.

Hats, hoods, snoods, and bonnets of various fabrics, Kale gazed in wonder at the gamut of adornment from plain to gaudy.

"Hats for draks?" A drak with midnight-blue scales appeared from behind a rack, a wide-brimmed hat sitting on his head at a rakish tilt. He winked at Kale. "We don't need all the fancy pants and frocks and brass-buttoned coats and smocks the humans do, but a fine covering for your noggin"—he rapped his knuckles on Kale's head—"is what we sell for a bargain!"

Kale's mouth dropped open. The dark-scaled drak danced around him, grinning. When he bowed, the feather in his hatband dipped forward to tickle Kale's nose. "So, what'll it be?" The haberdasher slapped his hands together, awaiting Kale's response.

Holding up his hands, Kale backed away. "I think I'm in the wrong shop."

"You didn't want to look at hats, but you walked into a haberdasher?"

"Well, um…" Kale knew any excuse he fabricated would likely insult the shopkeeper.

"Oh, I understand. You're from one of those small villages, aren't you? All the pomp and wonder of the city is too much for you, and I came on too strong, didn't I?" The shopkeeper put his arm around Kale's shoulders. "I know how that feels all too well. I'm from a small village myself. Rockton. Boring place, full of quarries and mines. All but gone now." After pulling Kale over to a mirror, he placed a bonnet on his head. Crowned with a fuzzy green pom-pom, the black-and-red checked pattern on the bonnet matched Kale's scales. Kale's lips curled in derision.

"Hey now, one of my hats will make the females back home ache to raise a clutch with you."

Kale pulled the bonnet off his head, snagging it on one of his horns. Clucking his tongue, the shopkeeper plucked it from Kale's hands. "All right, fine, not your style, eh? Look around, we're sure to have something to suit your fancy."

"I was just curious. That's all. We don't have shops like this back home."

The shopkeeper pulled another hat, similar to the one he was wearing, off a rack, then passed it to Kale. Fashioned from soft, supple black leather, one side of the brim was turned up, held in place with a bejeweled gold pin. A pair of long silvery-black feathers swept back from the crown.

Kale turned it over in his hands, examining it. He noted evidence of fine craftsmanship in the tightness of the seams and weight of the material. Shaped to fit onto a drak's head, as well, it did not snag his horns when he tried it on. Rather, it nestled between them, resting securely on his head.

"Well, that certainly makes my eggs ache." A familiar voice behind Kale startled him. He felt clawed hands on his shoulders. Kali's head appeared over his shoulder, peering at him in the mirror.

"Kali! A pleasure to see you in the shop, as always." The shopkeeper bowed, smiling. "What can I do for you?"

"Not a thing, Calev. I saw Kale come in and thought I'd have a word with him."

Kale turned to face her. "Hello, Kali." Upon removing the hat, he held it out to the shopkeeper.

Kali pulled his arm away. "It's on the house, isn't it, Calev? A gift for our new friend." Kali tossed her heavy, black cloak over her shoulder. Flakes of snow still encrusted the tips of the brown fur lining around the hood.

The shopkeeper's smile vanished. He tilted his head before half-bowing in acquiescence. "Certainly, Kali. Anything for you."

Kali took Kale's arm. "Let's talk a moment, shall we?" After leading him out of the shop and into the parlor, she sat on a bench near the tree. She took the hat from him, then placed it on his head. "It suits you. It makes you look roguishly handsome."

"Thanks." Kale felt his cheeks become hot and his stomach twist into knots. He clenched his fists to keep his hands from trembling."

"I see they let you out. Or did you escape?" Kali kept her hands on his.

"They let us out, with an escort."

"Us? Your sister and minotaur friend are here with you?" Kali's eyes scanned the parlor. "I see neither them nor an escort."

Glancing toward the shop into which his sister disappeared, Kale didn't see her. "Just me and Delilah. Pancras has to stay in the palace when we're out, to ensure we come back. The guards are nice, though. They're waiting for us in the tavern next door."

"There are some decent humans in this town." She picked up the edge of his cloak, rubbing it between her fingers. "All the snow and cold, and you only have this thin cloak and a hat. Aren't you cold?"

"No, I'm quite warm, actually."

"Listen." Kali stroked Kale's arm. Her touch sent shivers up his spine. "My, you *are* warm." She leaned in closer. "Mm. I could enjoy this." Kale shifted in his seat, trying to wrest his arm away, but her grip held tight. "I could use your help with something."

Kale licked his lips, ignoring the dryness in his mouth.

"I'm just waiting on Deli." Kale cast a furtive glance at the jewelry shop. "We're going back to the palace straightaway after she's done."

"That's not a problem. I don't need help until tonight, anyway. Meet me in the undercroft? By the door to the catacombs?" Kali leaned in close to Kale, then nuzzled his ear. "I'll make it worth your while." Pulling away, she smiled. "After dark. After dinner. I'll be waiting for you."

Kale could only nod in reply. He swallowed, watching her leave.

"Hey, was that the drak from jail?" He jumped, startled by his sister's voice.

"Um, yeah." Kale tossed a glance his sister's way. He thought she purchased nothing at first, until he saw the coiled, copper bangles on her arms. He glanced back to the entrance, but there was no trace of Kali.

Delilah pursed her lips. "What did she want? And where did you get that hat?"

"She wants my help with something tonight." He pointed at the haberdasher. "The hat shop is over there. She got it for me."

"Oh." Delilah cocked her head, narrowing her eyes as she examined the hat, then nodded. "It looks good. Let's go get a drink."

Chapter 12

Pancras awoke with a start to the sound of pounding on the suite doors. The fire in the hearth burned low. Rubbing the sleep out of his eyes, he threw another log on it. Although sunlight streamed in through the windows, the pink glow on the horizon announced the coming of dusk.

He shuffled over to the door. "Kale? Delilah. Are you two back yet?" Upon hearing no response, he opened the door.

Lady Milena greeted him. "Trouble with your draks?"

"No, I thought perhaps they returned while I was dozing. What can I do for you?" He stepped aside, gesturing for her to enter.

Shaking her head, she declined. "His Highness demands a progress report. Please accompany me."

"Very well."

Pancras maintained a slow pace while he considered what to say to Prince Gavril. The snow cover outside muffled most sounds, but, as they crossed the stone floors, the stillness amplified the clicking of Lady Milena's armor. In truth, because the snow had thwarted his research, Pancras had yet to accomplish any tasks to further the prince's plan. However, he feared retribution from the prince if he admitted that.

"Are the headaches still bothering you?"

"No, not really." Pancras preceded her down the spiral stairs, then waited for her at the bottom. "I have a theory about them, but I need some more time before I am certain." Pancras suspected the dark dreams, more severe than nightmares, were the cause, but they had not recurred since his last headache. It was one theory he was curious about; yet at the same time he hoped he would not have an opportunity to test further.

"Prince Gavril is in a foul mood. Be short and direct. I can't imagine you have much to tell him since you haven't had an opportunity to do any research outside of the palace yet, but he was insistent." Lady Milena returned the salutes of passing guards as they entered the main hall. She led Pancras to the antechamber where Prince Gavril waited.

The prince appeared haggard. Stubble covered his face, and disheveled hair shot in all directions. Dark circles under his eyes, and loose, wrinkled clothing completed the look. He sighed, glancing up, when Pancras and Lady Milena entered the room.

"Ah, it's about time. Leave us, Captain. I wish to speak to the necromancer alone."

Pancras winced. Although he had admitted he once had been a necromancer, he planned to avoid mentioning it in light of her hostile reaction in the catacombs. Lady Milena's face, a stony mask, revealed no emotion, however. She saluted her sovereign, then turned on her heels. Once she closed the door behind her, Gavril spun on the minotaur.

"Tell me you have a solution."

Pancras chewed his lip, shaking his head. "I do not."

"Why not? You've had days."

"I've had days trapped inside the palace while a snowstorm raged. Your libraries are full of poetry and historical texts." Pancras clasped his hands behind his back and paced. The motion reduced his rising urge to throttle the human. "The ritual you've requested of me cannot be found in those sorts of books. If you recall, today was the first day anyone could even leave the palace, and I spent my time tracking down the rest of the equipment I will need."

"You need?" Prince Gavril raised his eyebrows. "Then you know what must be done? Generally?"

"As I said when we first spoke, it is not something I have ever done myself, but I have heard of such magic. Since there is no Arcane University here, I must attempt to discover the ritual myself by working backward from various cures for infertility that priests of Cybele, Apellon, and Aurora use. I plan to speak to them as soon as possible."

"Tomorrow, then?" The prince moved to stand toe-to-toe with Pancras, thrusting his chin up in an attempt to intimidate him. Standing a head and a half shorter than the minotaur, Prince Gavril resembled a petulant toddler demanding treats from his father.

"The humans here in Almeria don't seem overly fond of minotaurs. It may take me some time to ingratiate myself sufficiently to learn such intimate knowledge from them. Then, once I have the knowledge, it might take weeks, or months to discern what I need to create." Pancras explained the steps slowly in the way he would teach a student. "Once I discover the requirements, I must then create, from scratch, that which is needed. I doubt very much I'm going to find any necromancers or witches in town who will sell me the needed components. Otherwise, you would have availed yourself of their services already, I should think."

Prince Gavril threw up his hands, turning away. "Yes, yes. I have already tried the 'remedies' recommended by those charlatans, and none of them did any damn good!" He spun to face Pancras again. "This had better be worth my time and money."

"What I provide for you will work." Pancras wrung his hands. "It may require something from your princess: a hair, a bit of… fluid—"

Prince Gavril waved his hand to dismiss him. "Yes, yes. I hear you've been spotted conversing with her on her morning walks. I trust you'll handle it. Leave me. I have important business."

Pancras bowed, then left the prince to his muttering and pacing. Lady Milena, awaiting him in the main hall, accosted him. "Well, Necromancer?" She curled her lip, sneering. "Ready to return to your chambers?"

Drawing himself up to his full height, Pancras met Lady Milena's defiant, grey-eyed stare. "I can find my own way, if my presence disgusts you that much." Turning, he left her standing alone in the great hall.

Seizing his arm when she caught up to him by the stairs, she moved to stop him.

Pancras snorted, glaring at her through narrowed eyes.

"Please accept my apologies. You have freely admitted to me your past and have done nothing to earn my ire. Sometimes I forget myself in my zeal."

"You have a very forceful grip for one filled with remorse."

Lady Milena released his arm. "I am sorry."

He searched her eyes for the truth, detecting no trace of contempt or malice. *There must be bad blood there somewhere.* "Very well. I shall want to visit a temple tomorrow. Apellon, Aurora, Cybele. Whichever is closest."

"Yes, Apellon is closest. There is no temple to Cybele in the city, of course, but there is one just outside the north gate. They prefer to be closer to the farms, you understand."

They climbed the stairs returning to Pancras's chambers. Lady Milena gazed at the city as Pancras unlocked the doors. "I'll come for you after the morning meal."

Pancras bowed. "That would be fine. Have a good evening, Lady Milena."

She took a step toward him, opening her mouth to speak, but then shut it and nodded. "You as well."

Pancras waited until she left before shutting the doors. Kale and Delilah were seated in the armchairs, with their puzzle box and grimoire, respectively. He first noticed Kale's wide-brimmed hat then the pair of coiled bangles on Delilah's arms.

"It would appear the two of you had a good afternoon."

"You know"—Delilah shut her book while her brother grinned at Pancras—"I think I'm a little jealous of the hat!"

***

After dinner, Kale returned to his room and rummaged through his pack for tools. He secured his bandolier, ensuring all the daggers were in place. When he turned to leave, Delilah blocked the doorway, staff in hand, tapping her foot.

"And where do you think you're going?"

"I'm meeting Kali in the undercroft. I'll be back." He moved to pass his sister, but she wouldn't budge. She held him back, covering the rune on his chest with her hand.

"Just what does she need your help with?"

Kale scratched the back of his neck. "She didn't say."

"Oh well, then, I am definitely going with you." Stepping aside, she let Kale pass.

"With me? You want to go with me?" Kale stared at his sister with his mouth agape.

"I'm not letting you go wandering into the claws of that harpy all by yourself."

Kale didn't try to stop her from tagging along. He knew better than that. On their way out, they passed Pancras heading on his way to the bathing room.

"Where are the two of you going?"

Kale pointed toward the door. "Exploring the palace." Delilah scowled at him.

"I would have thought you explored every nook and cranny by now." Pancras picked up a bottle of ale from the table.

"Some crannies are worth exploring more than once." Kale grinned at Pancras but dropped his smile when he noticed his sister's glare.

"Be careful. I'm heading into town early tomorrow, so I shan't wait up for you."

Delilah pushed her brother. "That means we need to be quiet when we come back."

Pancras nodded. "That will help." He disappeared into the bathing room.

Kale and Delilah proceeded down the hallway. The snow cover over the city reflected the light of the King and Queen upward, emitting glare almost bright enough to cast shadows from the nearly full moons. Standing on tiptoe to see over the wall, Kale observed thin curls of smoke drifting upward from most of the chimneys in the city. He imagined people huddling around their hearths, struggling to keep warm.

His sister pulled her cloak tighter. "Not going to tell Pancras where we're really going, huh?"

"We're meeting her in the palace's cellar. I don't know for sure that we're sneaking out. Besides, I don't want to worry him, all right?" Kale looked one last time across the city before stepping down the spiral stairs.

"The undercroft? Great. More dead things." Delilah stomped along behind him. She slapped her feet, clicking her claws on the stone in an obvious attempt to annoy Kale. He raised a finger to shush her.

"You know, you can stay upstairs if you don't want to come. Pancras says there aren't any more dead things in the catacombs. Well, there are, but none that are moving around." Kale peered into the hallway from the bottom of the stairs to find a guard walking away from them.

Delilah pushed him forward. "Whatever. Let's just get this over with."

Neither the guards nor the palace staff paid the draks any mind as they made their way past the main hall and to the corridor that led to the undercroft. Delilah grumbled under her breath the whole way.

"Are you going to be like this all night?"

"Yes."

Adjusting his hat, Kale turned the corner. He expected to see guards posted at the cellar doors, but there were none.

"Fos!" Delilah lit the skull atop her staff after they proceeded through the door.

The undercroft itself appeared untouched since their last visit.

"I'm supposed to meet her by the door to the catacombs." Kale led his sister through the undercroft to the door. The body of the zombie Delilah destroyed was gone, but the scorch mark where the corpse burned still marred the floor. He tried the door handle. It was locked.

"See? She probably just wants you to let her in so she can rob the place." Delilah leaned against one of the arches, picking at one of the fetishes on her harness. Kale knelt down by the door, then opened his tool pouch. The rudimentary lock, designed to keep the casual wanderer at bay, proved itself no match for someone who actually knew how to pick locks.

With a click, the locking mechanism disengaged. Upon opening the door, he noted the pile of bodies he expected to find on the other side were nowhere to be seen. *I guess Deli really wiped them out.* The lingering stench of burned flesh in the air mingled with the musty odor.

"I was wondering when you'd show up." Stepping forward, Kali emerged from the shadows. Kale recognized her dark cloak as the same one she wore when she met him in the shop. Raising her brow, she clicked her teeth when she saw Delilah. "Backup, or a chaperone?"

"Protection." Delilah leveled her staff at Kali. "From you."

Laughing, Kali pushed the staff up and away from her. "You think so little of me. Three of us will make this easier. Come on." She motioned for them to follow her into the catacombs.

Kale pulled the door shut behind them. "Where are we going?"

"Yeah, and why?" Delilah took her brother's arm, pulling him to a stop. "What do you need Kale for?"

Kali faced them. Spreading her hands, she smiled. "It's very simple. You're new in town. You have stripes. Obviously, you have talents the average working drak around here doesn't have."

Kale rubbed his arm. "What do our stripes have to do with anything?"

"Probably nothing. Children of Destiny? Isn't that what all the old draks call you stripeys?" Kali put her hand on Kale's shoulder. "It doesn't mean anything, but there are a lot of draks who think it does. You can be an inspiration to them."

Kale brushed her hand off his shoulder, then stepped alongside his sister. "We don't want to be an inspiration to anyone. Besides we don't believe all that talk about destiny. It's all superstitions and nonsense."

"Tell us what's going on, or we'll head right back upstairs." Delilah locked her arm with Kale's.

"There's a seedy underbelly to this city." Kali leaned against the wall. She picked her teeth with one of her claws. "Do you know about the mines?"

Kale shared a confused look with his sister. They both shook their heads.

"Deep below, under the catacombs, there's quite a few mines. Of course, humans being short sighted and impatient, they linked the entrances with the catacombs and various other underground places. They own the mines."

"So? What do they mine?" Kale wished she would get to the point. He wanted to stare in her blue-flecked yellow eyes and hold her hands, but he had difficulty reconciling his desire with his distrust of anyone who beat around the bush.

"Salt mostly." Clenching her fists, she leaned toward them. "It's not what they mine. It's how they mine it. There's a thriving slave trade under Almeria. I know it. The prince knows it. And too damn many humans know it and don't do anything about it."

Delilah tapped the butt of her staff against the ground. "I don't like slavers. But what do we have to do with this? You don't have draks around town who can help you?"

"Yeah." Kale nodded at his sister. "That hat guy gave up this hat with only a word from you. Don't tell me you don't have influence around here." He agreed with his sister on the slaver issue, though. He didn't like it when even the oroqs kept goblin slaves before they were driven out of Drak-Anor.

"Well, sure, but"—Kali smiled a lopsided grin and stroked Kale's arm—"how honest do you want me to be?"

Delilah pulled Kale's arm away from Kali. "Completely. Or we don't budge."

Regarding them for a moment, Kali licked her lips. "All right. Fine." She nodded. "I consider you, both of you, more expendable than the draks I know around town. You don't have any ties around here, so if something goes wrong and you get captured or killed, it'll be easier for me to save my own skin. But I meant what I said. I think you probably have skills and talents most of the draks around here don't have. Am I wrong?"

Kale didn't know what kind of skills or experiences draks in Almeria had, but he would bet money none of them had fought dwarves or oroqs or had ever charged into battle flying on the back of a dragon.

He looked back at Kali. "No, you're not wrong about that."

"Okay, so what's the plan? What are we doing? Freeing the slaves? Wiping out all the slavers?" Delilah leaned on her staff, awaiting Kali's response.

Kale grinned. "I knew bringing you along was a good idea." He could count on Deli to do whatever it took to accomplish their goal, even if the plan was hers. He felt more confident in his own abilities with her alongside him.

Delilah snorted. "Like it was your idea."

"I hadn't intended for us to free all the slaves right now. I've only just learned the way into the mines through the catacombs and sewers." Kali stepped forward, ducking under an arch-spanning spider web. "Think of this more as a scouting mission."

***

The deeper the three draks traveled into the catacombs, the staler and fouler the air became. Mingled with the decades-old scent of decay, fresher odors seeped in from the sewers. Scratching sounds and squeaks in the dark told Delilah they were not alone, but Kali dismissed them as rats or possibly very large spiders.

I hope he's right about that. I can handle those. If we're being stalked by ghouls, that's another story. Delilah kept her misgivings to herself and her eyes on Kale. Her brother seemed enamored of this orange-scaled drak. *And maybe he should be. None of the females back home seem interested in getting to know him.*

Kali stopped at a three-way intersection. She pointed down the left passageway. "If you go that way, you'll end up near the city market. There's a loose grate that leads into one of the water runoffs. If it's not full of water, you can follow it all the way to the market. We're going this way." She pointed to the right.

"Have you ever been to the mines before?" Kale kept pace next to Kali. Delilah followed them, her staff providing enough light for them to see several burial niches ahead. Once, she thought she saw something move in the shadows, but when they reached the spot, she discovered a rat's nest.

"No, but I've heard stories. I haven't been arrested for anything bad enough to warrant imprisonment in the mines yet. They'll also send you if you rack up enough debts you can't pay. I've even heard they send soldiers out west, toward the wastes, to kidnap draks and dwarves when too many prisoners die."

It sounded unbelievable to Delilah. "How do the people tolerate this? Don't they care? Pancras said the princess was nicer than the prince. Doesn't she care?"

Kali looked over her shoulder at Delilah. "I don't think the princess knows. She and the prince have never gotten along. Her father sent her down here to marry Gavril as part of some political deal. The people? As long as it's draks and not humans, the ones who know or suspect just don't care. But the lords like to keep it a secret. No one asks too many questions."

After what seemed like hours to Delilah, they came to a bricked-up wall. Kali directed their attention to the pile of broken bricks lying alongside an opening near the bottom. "This used to connect this part of the catacombs to the old iron mine. It ran dry, so they bricked up the access. All the bodies in this area are miners that died on the job. Hired dwarves, draks, humans too. We can get to the salt mine through here." She dropped onto her belly, then wiggled through the hole.

Kale gestured at the gap. "You go first, Deli. We'll need your light in there."

Delilah dropped to the ground, pushed her staff through the hole, then followed it. Kali helped her to her feet, clapping her on the back after she stood. The tunnel formed a perfect semi-circle over the flat floor just a few inches above them.

Kale went last. As he crawled through the hole, his cloak snagged on a piece of masonry. Jerking it free, he smacked his back against the bricks. Delilah heard him whimper, but he lay still, unmoving.

"Kale? Kale!"

Wincing, he pushed himself up. "I'm okay. It's all right. Those lumps are sensitive, you know?"

Kali backed against the wall, viewing the twins through wide eyes. "What lumps? Do you have some sort of disease?"

"It's a long story. Nothing contagious." Sighing, Kale rotated his shoulders and twisted his back to ease his aching muscles. "Do you think these were dug by dwarven digging machines like the one we saw under Ironkrag?

"No idea, I wasn't with you. Go get Pancras and ask him." Delilah brought the top of her staff around and flipped Kale's cloak off his back. The lumps oozed a viscous, cloudy fluid. She noticed flaps of flesh underneath the peeling skin.

"You've busted them open, Kale. There's something inside."

"What?" Kale craned his neck, whipping his head from side to side trying to see what his sister saw.

"You didn't tell me you were sick." Kali made a warding gesture, moving farther away from the twins.

"I'm not. I went through a chaos rift before we went home, and strange things have been happening to me. That's all. Nothing for you to worry—ow!"

Kale yelped when Delilah poked the flesh around the mound. More fluid oozed forth.

"No wonder it hurts. Whatever is in there is crammed in. Give me one of your daggers." Delilah wedged the butt of her staff in the bricks. She bent Kale over, then pulled him around so she could get a closer look.

"Stop, Deli! I'm fine."

"Don't be a baby, Kale. I've seen worse than this. We need to get this taken care of. Kary, Kali… whatever your name is. Come over here and help me. Take his hand or something. Keep him still." Delilah held out her hand. "Kale. Dagger. Now."

She felt him slap the hilt of one of his throwing daggers into her open palm. Although unaccustomed to seeing open, gaping wounds on her brother, she'd seen plenty of draks run through by dwarves or oroqs. Dismemberment, evisceration, beheadings, they were all worse than this. She probed the wound on Kale's back with the dagger. The flesh flaps within strained against the skin and scales surrounding them. She poked at one of the flaps with her claw.

"Hey!"

"Did that hurt?"

"Not really. It felt really weird. Did you stick your claw in my back?"

Gulping, Kali averted her eyes. She appeared about to spew her last meal all over the tunnel. Delilah chortled. With a flick of the dagger, she slit the skin around the flaps.

Kale screamed. The flaps burst forth from the slit. Unfolding, they spread into a wet, leathery wing. Delilah's eyes widened in wonder. She repeated the motion on the other side of his back. Kale cried out a second time, and another wing unfolded. Fully unfurled, they hung down past the base of his tail and reached the brim of his hat.

"How's that?"

"What is it?" Kale's voice quivered in pain. "What did you do?"

Glancing up, Kali gasped. She dropped Kale's hand, falling to her knees. "Great Rannos!"

"Kale, this is amazing." Delilah released her brother. After straightening himself, he craned his neck to see over his shoulder.

Reaching around his back, he touched the appendages. When he fluttered them, sticky ichor flew like a dog shaking water off its fur. Delilah covered her eyes from the spray. He turned to his sister. "Are those wings?"

Delilah nodded, laughing.

Kale craned his neck to see the other side and flapped his wings again. "That is fantastic!"

"Wait until Pancras sees this!"

"Terrakaptis should see this!"

"Do you think I can fly?"

"Can you carry me when you fly?"

The draks talked over each other in their excitement. "We have to try these out!"

"Pacha's blue bollocks!" Kali shrieked. "Doesn't this strike either of you as a little strange?" She crawled backward away from the twins until she trapped herself in a corner.

Kale giggled. "I'm just happy it's not a worm or a boggin bursting out of my back to eat me. This is great. I can breathe fire now, I have w—" He gasped, covering his mouth with his hands. "I'm a dragon!"

"You can breathe fire?" Kali worked her way up the wall until she stood upright again. Delilah noticed the wicked-looking curved knife in her hands. "I thought you were just talking big when you said you burned a minotaur to death."

Kale spun, inhaling. After pushing Delilah back, he exhaled. Flames shot down the tunnel, burning away cobwebs. Delilah put her arm across Kali and held her back. Eyeing the orange-scaled drak and her dagger, she shook her head.

"Okay, Kale. That's enough. It's getting hot and hard to breathe." Delilah coughed and blinked her eyes, making them tear to alleviate irritation caused by the smoke.

Kale turned around again, facing the two females. His grin split his head in two. "Well? What are we waiting for? Let's get going!"

***

Kale felt great, better than before he went to Ironkrag to help the dwarves with their ghoul problem. His back stung a bit where Delilah cut him, but the ache he had been living with was gone. He arranged his cloak to hang down his back between his wings. Extended, they scraped the sides of the tunnel. He couldn't wait to test them outside to find out if he could fly.

Continuing on, he couldn't help but have a spring in his step, but Kali did not seem eager to walk alongside him. *Oh well, she'll come around. I hope.* Glancing over his shoulder, he observed the two females. Delilah kept her eyes forward, watching for oncoming threats. In contrast, Kali cast furtive glances behind her, like a frightened animal seeking an escape.

Kale tried to put her at ease by smiling every time their eyes met, but it only seemed to agitate her further. As the tunnel sloped downward ending in a sheer drop, he put aside thoughts of assuaging her fears.

Delilah kicked a rock over the edge. It clattered against the bottom after what seemed to be a short fall. "If we hang-drop, I think we'll be all right. I don't know how easy it will be to climb back up, though."

Touching her shoulder, Kale moved past Kali. She recoiled at his touch, averting her gaze and pressing herself against the tunnel wall. He leaned over the edge, spotting the bottom. The area below them appeared to be a small room alongside a larger passage. Kale knelt to feel the wall below the edge. His sensitive fingers felt crevices and irregularities in the rock face that would provide easy purchase for drak claws.

He swung his legs over the edge and hopped off before anyone could stop him. Kale spread his wings. Catching the wind, they slowed his descent, although the sudden jolt made his new joints pop audibly. Wincing, he landed before flapping his wings to ensure their function. Apart from some new soreness, they seemed to have performed as he expected. Chuckling, he waved for the females to follow him.

While he waited, he took stock of the area. A pair of steel rails ran the length of the square, timber-reinforced passageway that connected to both ends of the room in which he stood.

Delilah climbed over the edge, then tossed her staff down to Kale. "Catch it!"

Upon seizing it, he set it aside. Allowing herself to fall, she tucked her knees, rolling as she landed. He offered his sister a hand, helping her to her feet before waving to Kali. "It's not far. There's another passage. It has rails in it."

Kali girded herself, then dropped. After Kale helped her to her feet, she brushed herself off. "All right, then. Let's get on with this." She entered the passageway, then knelt by the track. "We're definitely in the mine now. I think this is an unused spur." She pointed down the passageway. "See how the rails are bent? How they don't join up exactly? Mine carts don't handle misaligned rails well."

Delilah looked one way and then the other. "Which way should we go?"

Kali sniffed the air, pulled out a lump of chalk, and marked the wall near the floor. She pointed to the left. "That way."

"What makes you so sure?" Kale glanced to the right. The passageway appeared the same in both directions. Obviously, they didn't lead to the same place, but he wouldn't know how to determine which way led deeper into the mine.

"The breeze is flowing that way." Kali pointed to the right. "If we follow the foul air, we should find the operating portion of the mine."

The farther they followed the straight passageway, the more evidence they found of its disuse. They traveled through several sections with missing tracks, and they squeezed past a rockslide in another area. On the other side of the partially collapsed tunnel, the dark grey walls of the passageway became streaked with white, and Kale tasted salt in the air. When he stopped for a moment, he heard the faint sounds of picks on stone.

The tracks led them to a vertical shaft in which they found ropes hanging from a pulley system. When Kale saw a glow from below, he signaled for his sister to extinguish the light from her staff. The sound of digging echoed in the chamber. First dropping to their bellies, the three draks crawled forward, then peeked over the edge of the shaft.

A broken lift lay at the bottom, probably a hundred feet down. Bony legs, long since picked clean of flesh, protruded from under a rusty, upturned mine cart. From his vantage point, Kale could not identify to whom the legs belonged, drak, human, dwarf, or otherwise.

Kale expected the mine to be dark. However, the floors and walls of white salt reflected lantern light, giving the atmosphere an eerie glow. Carrying a load of white rocks in a bucket that almost eclipsed him, an orange-scaled drak shuffled into view. Kale felt Kali bristling alongside him as the drak passed under them.

Flinching at the crack of a whip in the distance, he continued with his bucket of salt until the trio could no longer see him. Kale reached over the edge, running his hand along the wall of the shaft. It felt much smoother than the previous ledge. Tucking his wings, he rolled onto his back to assess the pulley system. Although the metal appeared rusted and the ropes seemed intact, experience taught him that looks could deceive.

"Can you reach the ropes?" Kali pushed herself away from the edge.

Kale stretched as far as he dared, but the shaft was too wide. "I don't think we could climb that one, either. It's too smooth."

Delilah agreed with Kale's assessment. "Getting down isn't the problem. It's coming back up. I don't want to stay down here forever."

"There are other ways out, but I agree with you." Kali chewed on one of her claws. "Dammit. My sources told me this was a sure way in."

"What if we go back to the room and take the other passage?" Kale leaned over the edge of the shaft again. He heard cries of pain echoing up from below. "Maybe it circles around."

"It's worth a shot."

Chapter 13

The trio found the alternate passage in worse shape than the one they explored first. The misaligned track seemed to have been twisted by an angry giant. Delilah could not ascertain their position relative to the palace after following the narrowing passageway's twists and turns. The timbers reinforcing the ceiling were rotten or missing in many places, and after ten minutes of following where it led, it was clear the three draks were no longer in a mine tunnel, per se. Deep scars covered the walls, as though some creature dug its way into the mine.

Delilah shone the light of her staff overhead, peering at the grooves in the wall. "I don't think this is going to take us back into the mine. Whatever caused these gouges is something I don't think we want to meet."

Kali ran her hand across the gashes. "I agree. My source was wrong. This was once a way into the mine, but it's useless to us. We should go back to the surface." Slumping, she leaned against the wall.

Upon hearing a scraping sound echoing through the tunnel, Delilah felt a chill run down her spine. She swept her staff in the passageway, shining light into dark corners, searching for the source of the sound. She heard the scratching again, but this time chittering and the sound of skittering appendages followed it.

"We should go."

Kali drew her dagger. "I agree. There's something in here with us."

The three draks broke into a run. Delilah's clawed feet slipped on the hard floor of the tunnel, but Kale seized her arm and kept her from falling. From the scrabbling behind them, it was clear that something, or several somethings, gave chase. Turning the corner at breakneck speed, Delilah skidded across the tunnel, her head ringing upon impact with the rail.

"Dammit!" Grabbing her head, she staggered to her feet. Gleaming teeth appeared from within the darkness just before the multi-legged creature darted forward, hissing.

"Deli!"

"Get back, Kale!" Delilah raised her staff and closed her eyes. Her head throbbed, yet she managed to focus and draw magic to her. "*Synnefotone shifone!*"

She leaped backward, colliding with Kale and Kali. A cloud of flashing, whirling blades appeared in the beast's path. The creature squealed as the swords flayed its flesh. Seizing her brother and Kali's arms, Delilah spun them.

"Run!"

Leaving Delilah's whirling blades to reckon with the toothy beast, they raced to the room through which they entered the mine. After shoving her staff between her back and her harness to secure it, Delilah leapt at the wall, her claws finding purchase in the rock. Clinging to it, she scrabbled with her feet but failed to find leverage enough to climb. Alongside her, Kali jumped onto the wall and climbed upward like a crab crossing a rocky shore.

Delilah felt Kale's hands pushing on the bottom of her feet. "Go Deli, go!" Finding her footing, she climbed. Kale climbed alongside her, offering his hand when she missed a handhold. Kali waited at the top, pulling them up when they were within reach.

The three draks paused at the top of the wall to catch their breath.

Kali slapped Delilah on the shoulder. "Impressive spell."

"Thanks, remind me to tell you how I used it to escape a dragon's belly sometime." She grinned at the other drak, smacking her brother on the knee. "Let's get back. I need a drink."

The journey back through the tunnels and catacombs seemed shorter to Delilah than the initial trip. Kali stopped them when they reached the door leading from the catacombs to the palace's undercroft.

"I know we didn't really accomplish anything, but I appreciate your help. I'm going to try to find another way into the mines."

"If there are draks enslaved down there, Deli and I want to help, right?"

Delilah couldn't agree more. Although she still didn't trust Kali's intentions where it concerned her brother, she approved of any plan that freed draks from enslavement. "Absolutely. We'll make some inquiries of our own as well."

"Be careful who you talk to." Kali tilted the lid of one of the ossuaries near the door. "We can use this as a dead drop"—she chuckled—"to exchange information. Sorry about earlier, Kale. I wasn't expecting the wings." She pulled Kale close and nuzzled his neck. "I'll be seeing you around."

Kali melted into the shadows. Delilah smacked Kale when she noticed her brother panting. "Come on. Let's go to bed. It's probably late."

***

The drak twins were not as quiet as they thought they were when they returned to the suite. Pancras pulled his pillow over his head to drown out their excited giggles and hushed conversation. When sleep returned, the shadow returned with it, enveloping him in his dreams and raging that it couldn't provoke the minotaur into using his magic. In the dream world Pancras felt trapped, buried under a veil of hate and fury, unable to move, unable to wake.

When he finally awakened, he felt the throbbing, pounding headache at the base of his skull had returned.

Groaning, he rolled out of bed, then pulled on a set of robes. He fitted both parts of his focus to the tips of his horns and straightened his jewelry before exiting his bedchamber. The light of the sun reflecting off the snow-covered city bored into his eyes like lances of fire. Closing the door to the suite behind him, he left the draks to break their fast alone.

He met Lady Milena in the main hall. Her scale armor gleamed in the light, as if freshly polished. Although he averted his gaze, he knew the second he stepped outside, there would be no respite from the pain.

Pancras hated being right.

Squinting against the glare, Pancras pulled up his hood and kept his head down while he and the lady knight tromped through the snow. Overnight a new dusting covered the hard-packed path. It reminded Pancras of the time when one of the bakers spilled several bags of imported flour all over the market square in Drak-Anor. The light breeze blew the dusty snow in whirling clouds, coating their cloaks in fine white powder.

Located in the hilly residential area behind the palace atop one of the tallest hills in the district, the Temple of Apellon enjoyed unobstructed sunlight for most of the day. Like the Foundry District, a border of high walls surrounded the residential area, and most of the individual estates within the district isolated themselves behind their own walls. Now bereft of leaves, trees lined the avenues. Servants, bundled up in thick woolen cloaks, cleared snow off the walkways and paths leading to sprawling homes. Pancras scraped away snow with his hoof, half expecting to find the surface of the street he exposed paved in gold.

Columns reaching toward the sky surrounded the temple, the House of Light Eternal. A peaked, fabric canopy covered the vast open area at the center of the structure, allowing light in but keeping weather out. The open sides of the house of worship did not keep the wind from blowing snow in, however, and Pancras observed several young attendants clearing the inside with shovels and brooms and building a wall of compacted snow around the interior.

A man wearing thick, white robes and a furry hat stood at the center of the temple near the altar directing the acolytes to areas where they should concentrate their cleanup efforts. Pancras shaded his eyes with his hand as he and Milena entered the temple proper.

No matter where Pancras looked, the design of the temple's interior drew his attention toward the circular white marble altar streaked with veins of pink. Apellon, depicted by the sculptor as a young man with flowing, golden hair and lips parted in perpetual song, stood at the center of the dais. The god of light, healing, and the arts, held a lyre before him and gazed at the sky.

"Arnost!" Lady Milena held up her hand in greeting, approaching the priest. He spun to face her. The corners of his eyes crinkled, and his mouth opened in delight.

"Milena! You've been away too long." Pinning her arms to her sides, he enwrapped her in a hug. Milena's cheeks flushed, and her lips formed a thin, straight line. Holding her shoulders, Arnost stepped back to admire his sister.

"You look splendid! Why have you not been by?"

Milena extracted herself from Arnost's grip. "My duties have kept me busy. That's why I'm here." She jerked her head toward the minotaur.

Arnost noticed Pancras for the first time since he entered the temple. "A minotaur! What brings a minotaur to Apellon? Perhaps you need to give voice to the music within?" He circled Pancras, looking him up and down.

Pancras put his hand across Arnost's chest, bringing the priest to a halt. "Nothing like that. I'm doing research, and I need the opinion of a healer."

Narrowing his eyes, Arnost reversed course, walking backward around the minotaur. "Yes, of course you do. I see a darkness within you, a place the light of Apellon does not reach."

Pancras venerated Aita, goddess of the underworld, but he didn't think that made him an especially dark person. He didn't twist her word in the way of many death cults that ascribed to a belief where the natural state of all things in the world was to die, and the sooner the better. Arnost's intense, pale-hazel eyes sent a shiver down Pancras's spine. When the priest reached for his golden lyre, the holy symbol hanging around his neck, the minotaur caught his arm.

"It's not for me. Is there somewhere we can speak privately?" He hoped Arnost would agree to move out of earshot of the acolytes and Lady Milena.

"There are no secrets from the light of Apellon." Arnost backed away from Pancras, narrowing his eyes in suspicion.

The minotaur fought to keep his voice steady. "There is nothing sinister about this, but the prince desires some measure of confidentiality where his affairs are concerned." Pancras hoped that stating his intentions truthfully would draw less scrutiny to the details of his deception.

Arnost rubbed his hands on the front of his robes, flicking his eyes to his sister then to Pancras. "Well, if it's for the prince…"

Lady Milena took that as her cue. She approached the nearest acolyte, then took him by the shoulder. Leading him away from the minotaur and the priest, she nodded to them.

Pancras leaned in close to Arnost. "It is a most delicate matter, you understand. A member of the court is dealing with fertility issues. They enlisted me to help, but it's a little outside my area of expertise." He put his arm around Arnost's shoulders and toyed with his golden lyre symbol.

"Ah yes. A delicate matter indeed. One that many nobles do not wish to discuss publicly. I understand." Arnost fidgeted with his robes, then shuffled his feet, appearing to inspect the ground. "We deal with this from time to time. Is this a matter of performance or something else?"

Pancras cleared his throat, grimacing. "The noble in question is reluctant to be too specific, but I am certain it is not an issue with the act itself. Rather it is the result of the act, if you take my meaning."

"Ah, yes." Arnost rubbed his chin. "There is a treatment. Just a moment." He circled the altar, keeping one hand on the pedestal as he paced. "I'm trying to remember."

Pancras drew his cloak around him. The wind picked up, flapping the canopy above them. Swirling snow showered the interior of the temple with crystals of ice that glittered in the morning sun. Acolytes flurried to sweep the accumulation off the marble steps. Sun glare reflecting off the snow, burned his eyes, making them water, and it did absolutely nothing to aid his throbbing head.

"It was an ointment, to be applied internally, um… all the ingredients were to be mashed and mixed with an oil, a boiled oil of… the castor bean! Yes, I'm sure that was it." Arnost, pinching the bridge of his nose, squeezed his eyes shut.

Pancras lifted up the hems of his robes and brushed off the snow while he waited for Arnost to gather his thoughts. He already understood that the herbal infusion probably could not be reverse engineered. He would have to acquire information on contraception as well. *That's not going to seem suspicious at all.*

"Thorntree?" Arnost blinked, tilting his head. "No, no, no." He laughed. "That's for the opposite thing!" He scowled. "Philanderers." He resumed his trek around the pedestal, muttering to himself. He reappeared from behind the statue of Apellon, holding a finger in the air. "Faerie Candle! Er, black snakeroot, if you prefer. Yes, that's it. Mash up black snakeroot, lime ash, and winter cherry in boiled castor oil. Then have the lady in question apply it liberally to… the"— regarding his feet, he cleared his throat—"a… affected area."

Pancras made a mental note to look for thorntree. "I presume an herbalist would have all this?"

"Oh yes, well, except for castor oil. You might have to procure the beans, press the oil yourself and then boil the oil to remove impurities and refine it."

"Of course. Of course." Pancras clapped Arnost on the shoulder. "Thank you very much. There is an herbalist or apothecary in the city, yes?" Pancras assumed there must be one but appreciated confirmation and directions.

"Oh yes, more than one I think." Arnost furrowed his brow, looking upward. "Not quite sure where they are, though. I've never had cause to seek them out."

Pancras smiled and offered Arnost a curt nod. "I suppose Lady Milena would know."

"Milena? Oh, I doubt it."

At the sound of her name, Lady Milena thanked the acolyte with whom she conversed and returned to Pancras and Arnost. "What won't I know?"

"Where an herbalist is located." Pancras wanted to find out first what solutions priests of Cybele and Aurora suggested before they sought for one.

"Of course I know where the apothecaries are."

"Milena! Surely you don't mingle with the commoners—"

"Let's go." Milena took Pancras's arm and led him away from Arnost.

"Milena, wait! Don't go yet. It's been so long."

Lady Milena closed her eyes. Pancras saw her lips moving as she counted in silence to herself before spinning on her brother. "You would do well to remember the commoners are not some contagion, brother. They are the backbone of the realm, not the ground beneath your feet. You ought to mingle with them yourself instead of looking down upon them from on high."

Blushing, Arnost kept his eyes fixed on his sister. After a moment, he nodded, regarding the ground. "You're right, of course. My duties keep me isolated from the people, Milena."

"Mine do not. Goodbye, Arnost."

Pancras followed Milena out of the temple. Part of him felt bad for Arnost, but he took comfort in knowing that he wasn't the only one with whom Lady Milena was curt.

When they reached the bottom of the hill at the foot of the temple, she slowed her pace, allowing Pancras to catch up. "Where to now, Pancras? The apothecary?"

"Not yet. Is there a temple to Aurora? You said the one to Cybele was outside of the city, yes?"

Milena rubbed her temple. "It is really necessary to speak to a priestess of Aurora?"

Pancras understood the cause of her reluctance. Temples dedicated to Aurora were rarely formal structures like the Temple of Apellon. In small towns and villages they were simple shrines tended by one or two women, often those with less-than-wholesome reputations among the self-righteous. In larger cities, like Almeria, they were often compared to brothels, and certainly, they served a similar purpose. Aurora celebrated lust and the physical aspects of love, however, and did not view the expression of faith as something to hide or of which to be ashamed. The worship of Aurora made some people uncomfortable.

"I want to be sure I'm acquiring the correct reagents and materials. I don't want to make several trips back and forth in the cold and snow." He lifted up his hoof to brush away impacted snow from the bottom of it with his finger. "It's uncomfortable."

"Very well." She gestured for him to follow her. "There are several shrines, I hear, in various brothels, but I expect you seek the temple proper."

"Yes, indeed." While Pancras didn't rule out the possibility a priestess tending a shrine might possess the knowledge he sought, he considered the high priestess of the temple itself a more reliable source of information. Also, the temple would more likely maintain a library containing resources from which Pancras could study. In contrast, the priests of Apellon usually kept only books of hymns, and, more often than not, the central repository appeared small, because musicians who performed during worship borrowed the books for practice.

Pancras considered asking Milena about her brother to make conversation as they walked, but her pinched expression and rigid posture suggested it would not be a welcome topic. *Perhaps I will invite her to dine with the draks and me tonight when we return to the palace.*

***

Kale awakened before his sister, not an unusual occurrence whenever she conjured. She didn't tax herself too much when they explored the mines, but the magic coupled with the running and climbing were enough to send her straight to bed after she filled her belly.

Pancras had already departed by the time Kale awoke, so he took advantage of the empty parlor in which to spread his wings and examine them carefully. He wanted to do it as soon as they returned from their expedition, but his grumbling belly and Delilah's protestations that he wait until Pancras awakened delayed his exploration of them.

They reminded him of Terrakaptis's wings, on a much smaller scale, of course. He flapped them a few times, taking note of which muscles they required. He found if he concentrated, he could move each individually, and he was sure that with practice using them would become second nature.

Jumping up into the air, Kale flapped his wings as hard and fast as he could. He hovered for a few moments before falling back to the ground. His wings caught the air, but he was disappointed that even gliding was a skill he needed to practice. An idea formed in Kale's head. Grinning, he climbed onto the table. Looking down at the floor, he realized he still wasn't far enough above it, so he pulled a chair onto the top of the table and climbed on its seat.

"Higher. I need to get higher." His eyes searched the room, stopping on the chandelier suspended from the ceiling above the table. He stretched, but his fingertips brushed only the bottom. Jumping, Kale seized one of the lowest arms of the fixture. He heard a crack from the ceiling just before flakes of stone rained down on his head.

The chandelier held, however, and Kale kicked his legs forward. He swung back and forth, building momentum, despite groans of protest by the chain holding it in place. When it reached its apex, Kale let go and spread his wings. Catching the air, he kept them open, gliding across the parlor.

His breath quickened with excitement. Upon realizing he descended slower than he sped toward the double doors, his eyes widened. Despite swinging his legs and flapping his wings to slow his forward momentum, he plummeted from the sudden loss of lift. Hitting the floor, he rolled across it before slamming into the bottom of the doors.

"Ow."

Kale's head spun, but he found the cool stone comforting. He rolled over on his stomach, freeing his wings from underneath him. After taking a moment to catch his breath, he stood up and tried again.

Rubbing her eyes and yawning, Delilah exited their bedchamber just as he climbed onto the table. Glaring, she put her hands on her hips. "Just what in the name of Maris's bloody spear are you doing?"

"Getting used to my wings." Kale jumped, grabbing the chandelier again, but the support gave way. The entire fixture fell, accompanied by a shower of debris from the ceiling. Kale tumbled backward onto the table, shattering dishes and launching the chair into the air. He rolled to the side in a desperate attempt to avoid being flattened by the fixture.

Delilah clucked her tongue, helping her brother up. "You broke the bloody room! Next time throw yourself off a building. I'm trying to sleep!"

"Sorry, Deli." Kale brushed himself off. He jiggled the chandelier where it lay on the table, overturning a pitcher in the process. Red wine ran along the surface of the table, soaking into the lace runner before dripping onto the carpet. "Do you think they can fix this before Pancras gets back?"

***

Beholding Aurora's Sanctuary, Pancras appreciated the architectural work of art. The building, a tall, pink-and-blue, spiral tower, thrust into the sky. The spirals led his eyes toward the onion dome adorned with gold ridges at the top and a red banner fluttering on the spire above it. Flanked by two round evergreen shrubs, the bulge at the base of the tower marked the point of entry or foyer. A golden seashell decorated the arched, black entry door.

Pancras turned his attention to the sounds of the city market wafting in his direction: vendors barking and innkeepers promising warm fires and mulled wine to soothe chilly shoppers. He barely noticed the man who, nearly slipping in the snow, passed him.

Milena stood next to Pancras, eyeing the tower. "I hate this building. Had I not sworn an oath to keep you in sight whenever you were outside the palace, I would not be going in with you."

"You could stay out here. I will tell no one, and there isn't anywhere for me to escape." He sympathized with Milena's discomfort. Something about the building made him uneasy. It was, without a doubt, the most colorful building he'd seen during his stay in Almeria.

Her sidelong glare conveyed all he needed to know about her feelings on the idea. Clearing his throat, he entered the building. A circular hearth with a roaring fire dominated the parlor. Red banners covered the walls, and multi-colored rugs woven in chaotic, sweeping patterns covered the floors. Statues of Aurora, each depicting the nude goddess in various contortions of ecstasy, stood in alcoves between the banners. A short hallway led out of the room to a corridor that appeared to curve around the inside of the tower.

A woman tending the fire glanced up when they entered. Her golden locks reached almost to the floor, and a shimmering gown the color of fresh pine needles draped her body. After turning a log, she bowed to Milena and Pancras. "Welcome to Aurora's Sanctuary. Have you come to seek shelter from the cold? Instruction in love, perhaps?" She cast an appraising glance at Pancras. "Or perhaps, you're simply lost?"

Sighing audibly, Milena appeared to search for a spot devoid of nude female sculptures to rest her eyes. Pancras offered the priestess a smile. "None of those. I need to speak with a priestess about a very delicate matter, in private, please."

"Not too private. You must remain in my sight." Milena seemed to settle upon staring into the fire.

The priestess took Pancras by the arm. "Fear not, lady. I shall not steal your lover from you."

"My—he is not my lover!" Clenching her fists, Milena stepped toward the priestess.

"No?" The priestess squeezed Pancras's arm. "Then I may steal him away after all. Minotaurs are so strong. So big."

Pancras felt his face grow hot. "I am not here for that, either." He gestured toward the hallway. "Please."

He accompanied the priestess into the tower proper. Milena followed them, keeping her distance. The priestess stroked Pancras's arm as they strode. He noticed she smelled like flowers, as if she'd just come from the meadow. Murals on the walls illustrated various positions of lovemaking, and Pancras thought he heard moaning coming from the room they just passed.

"I am Oksana, Second Divine of Aurora."

He lowered his head before speaking to reduce the risk Milena would overhear. "I was hoping you had a text I might read or borrow that deals with treatments of various ailments like infertility. I've been tasked with something of a rather delicate nature, so we're trying to keep this quiet."

The corners of Oksana's mouth downturned slightly, and the inner corners of her eyebrows raised. "Oh, no. We have nothing to help you conceive with the lady. Minotaurs and humans simply cannot have children."

Rubbing his nose, Pancras stopped, then faced the priestess. "Again, we are not lovers. I cannot tell you for whom I seek this solution. It's confidential, you understand. That's why this… person has turned to an outsider for help."

"My apologies." Pressing her palms together, Oksana bowed her head. "I thought you were just being coy. Minotaur-human relationships are not unheard of, but they are frowned upon here in Almeria. We try not to judge. Aurora is concerned with love, the expression of love as pleasure, not with whom you choose to express those passions."

Pancras lowered her hands. "I appreciate that. Have you something that can help me? Or perhaps know of a remedy?"

Oksana wrung her hands while chewing on her bottom lip. "I believe we have such a text. The high priestess would have specific knowledge, but she is occupied with worship at the moment. Disturbing her would be a grave affront to Aurora."

Pancras glanced back at Milena. The knight stood almost at attention, with her hands clasped behind her back. He felt her eyes boring into him. "I do not wish to disturb your high priestess. I can find the solution in your texts myself. If I might be permitted to view them? Perhaps borrow them?"

"I can fetch them for you, but I do not think I can allow you to borrow them. You said you were an outsider?"

"Yes, but I am staying at the palace." He took her hands, enveloping them within his own. "I'll be here all winter and should only need them for a few days. Perhaps, if I make a monetary donation, to thank you for your assistance?"

Oksana's smile wrinkled the corners of her eyes. She tilted her head. "Donations are always welcome, but there are only three copies of the Codex of Passion. It would have to be a very generous donation, indeed."

Pancras reached into his pouch and fished for one of the gems he brought from Drak-Anor. Not particularly concerned with type, he focused on size. The emerald he produced equaled that of a small berry. Allowing it to catch the light while rolling it in his hand, he showed it to Oksana. Her eyes widened in amazement. Pancras pressed it into her hand.

Oksana bowed her head, touching his hand to her forehead. "If you'll return to the parlor, I will fetch for you the texts we have."

"Thank you, very much."

He returned to wait alongside Milena. He noticed her perspiring despite the cool air within the tower. "Does this place make you that uncomfortable?" He wiped a bead of sweat from her forehead.

Milena swatted at his hand, then wiped her brow. "It does, but not for the reasons you think."

"Care to elaborate?" Pancras rubbed his hands in front of the hearth. The heat from the fire felt nice. Although he was covered with fur, and his new, thicker robes helped keep him warm outside, the bitter wind cut through even the thickest of fabric.

"Not really. I'm not a prude, but I have had to make certain sacrifices." Her eyes lingered on a statue of Aurora that depicted the goddess with her head thrown back, arms spread and reaching for the heavens. The goddess was always depicted as voluptuous, yet perfectly proportioned, at least by the standards of the sculptor.

"A vow of chastity can be difficult." Pancras was chaste by circumstance, not by choice, but he understood why someone might choose to take a vow of that nature.

"That is not it. I have no desire to discuss my love life, or lack thereof with you."

Pancras let the matter drop. He did not wish to antagonize Lady Milena, but he thought she did herself a disservice by internalizing her stress. In his youth, he did the same thing, but he later found, after he moved to Drak-Anor, that even merely voicing his frustrations to a sympathetic ear helped them seem less severe.

He had high hopes the Codex of Passion would offer a solution based more in his skill in the arcane arts than the salve Arnost offered him. Salve and ointments were fine, but he didn't think any of the information he gleaned from the priest of Apellon would be useful, except for the tidbit he let slip about thorntree. Plus, any ointment or salve he made would likely yield a shorter-lived solution than he desired.

The last thing Pancras wanted was for Prince Gavril to feel he needed to hunt him down.

Thinking about the prince and the curse he wanted made his head hurt. He was thankful, at least, for the lower light levels. His headache continued unabated, but being outside in the sun amplified the discomfort. He supposed he should have asked Arnost about it.

Oksana returned with the codex about the time Pancras tired of standing. The red leather-bound book featured gold leaf embellishments. She held it as a mother cradling her newborn child. "Take good care of this. Your donation is much appreciated, but should this be damaged or lost, there is nothing that will spare you from Aurora's wrath."

Well acquainted with the value of sacred texts, particularly bound codices, Pancras sought to handle the tome with care. "Do you have something I can protect this with? I'd hate to slip and drop it while returning to the palace."

"I'm sorry, we do not."

"There's a market stall nearby that may sell what you want." Milena pulled on Pancras's arm. "We need not take more of her time, Pancras."

The minotaur bade the priestess farewell before following Milena out to the street. Fumbling, he cradled the codex with one arm while he flipped up his hood. The glare seemed stronger now that the sun rose higher in the sky.

Milena led him down the street to the market. The north end featured more craftsmen and fewer food and produce vendors than had the area he explored with Kale and Delilah the day after they arrived in Almeria.

With Milena's help, Pancras found a hand-tooled leather satchel in which he could carry the Codex of Passion. The security of the strap across his shoulder eased his mind. The last thing he needed was the ire of a goddess. He knew he could not ask Aita for aid if he angered Aurora; for the task he was bound to undertake for Prince Gavril was borderline an affront to the Princess of the Underworld. He felt he owed it to Kale and Delilah to see to their safety during their journey, and he planned to return them home alive and well.

The winter wind picked up, and patrons of the market pulled their cloaks and robes tighter as chilly air coursed through the streets. A bank of grey clouds approached from the west, like a juggernaut rolling down the mountains. The clouds appeared laden with snow, promising a fresh delivery before morning.

"We should go back to the palace. Cybele can wait." Milena shielded her eyes with her hand, looking into the sky toward the approaching weather system. Other Almerians shared their desire to seek shelter. The bustle of the market and city streets increased with people rushing to complete their daily tasks and stock sufficient supplies to provide for them through the coming storm.

Pancras agreed with Milena that cutting their expedition short was the wisest course of action. He had collected more than enough material to last for the remainder of the week, if need be. "Indeed. The storm won't."

Like lazy dandelion seeds upon a summer's breeze, light snow began to fall as they reached the palace gates. The delicate beauty of the flurries soon gave way to darker skies and howling wind that delivered a curtain of solid white from the heavens.

Chapter 14

Kale had not yet finished cleaning up the parlor when Pancras returned. He didn't notice the worsening weather until the doors opened and howling wind followed the minotaur inside. Delilah slapped her hand on the pages of her grimoire to keep them from fluttering in the gale and hunkered down in her armchair. Snow swirled inside the parlor as Pancras struggled to shut the doors.

"The weather turned quickly. I don't recommend you and Delilah go out to—" Pancras turned, staring open-mouthed at the chandelier lying in pieces on the floor. "What happened?"

Kale extended his wings, fanning them slightly, then rose from the spot where he had been picking up bits of shattered plates. Over the course of the morning, he discovered his wings added a bit of lift, allowing him to stand and straighten more smoothly and rapidly than when he used only his hands and knees to aid him. "I was trying to practice flying."

"Flying?" It was then that Pancras noticed Kale's wings. He pointed, then covered his face with his hand. Flopping in the vacant armchair, he braced himself. "I don't suppose you could bring me wine or an ale before you tell me this story?"

Kale picked up one of the few unopened, unbroken bottles of ale and brought it to Pancras. He folded his wings behind him to avoid blocking the heat from the hearth. He noticed Pancras carrying a new satchel, containing something large and square, over his shoulder. "Guess what the lumps I was growing on my back were?"

Pancras took the ale, then leaned forward. His exasperation gave way to curiosity. "You grew wings? You can still breathe fire?"

"Yes. It's getting easier the more I practice."

Delilah shut her book. "I told him the next time he wanted to practice flying, he should go jump off a building."

Pancras touched Kale's shoulder, urging him to turn around. Kale displayed his wings to the minotaur, allowing him to unfold and manipulate them. Finding the membranes sensitive to the minotaur's touch, he bit his bottom lip to keep from giggling.

"This is extraordinary." He let Kale turn around again. "They support your weight? You can actually fly with them?"

That was the one thing Kale had not accomplished. Yet. "No, just gliding. I think I'll be able to with practice, though." He shifted his gaze to the windows, noticing the storm fiercely raging. The snow sticking to the windows resembled dirty grey paint. Even inside their suite, the howling wind made itself heard, venting its fury on Almeria. Kale expected they would be trapped inside for several days. Again.

Pancras placed his hand on Kale's forehead. "How do you feel otherwise? You're still warm."

"I feel great!" The minotaur's palm felt cool against his scales. "As good as ever, really." He recognized his body temperature ran hotter than before his exposure to the rift, but he no longer felt feverish. He rather enjoyed not having to wear heavy cloaks and robes to protect him from the snow; yet he worried about what would happen when the weather warmed up in the spring and summer. One could always bundle up in the cold, but there was a limit to what one could remove in the hotter months, and draks often wore nothing but their scales.

"Amazing!"

Kale shuffled his feet, looking over his shoulder at the dinner table. He wished Pancras and Delilah knew some magic that would clean it up. They worked out a good system for the bathing vessel, but Delilah informed him in no uncertain terms that even if she knew a conjuration that could clean up broken plates, she would not help him.

"Someone is supposed to be by later to put the chandelier back up. I think. They shouted at me with a lot of words I didn't understand, Pancras." Kale rubbed the back of his neck. "It should have held my weight. It's not my fault the palace servants can't do their jobs properly and everything in here is junk."

"We'll work around it. In the meantime, I have studying to do. Try not to break anything else." Pancras picked up his bottle of ale, then retired to his room.

Delilah resumed reading her grimoire, dismissing Kale with a wave of her hand. "Back to work!"

Kale stuck out his tongue at his sister, but in truth, he couldn't blame her for not wanting to help him clean up. He would feel the same way in her place. He just hoped the palace staff would not refuse to feed them now. He found his grumbling stomach a poor companion while he worked, and he wanted to silence it.

***

The storm seemed to linger with purpose over Almeria. For three days it raged, dumping prodigious amounts of cold, wet snow on the city. The first night, Kale occupied himself with repairing the damage he caused, albeit palace servants performed a good deal of the actual work. After that, he had only his puzzle box.

Delilah with her grimoire and Pancras the Codex of Passion studied their respective volumes in front of the hearth. Upon flipping past all the graphic descriptions of the variety of positions best used for conception or contraception, Pancras finally located the section which focused on remedies for various maladies. He wondered for whom the Codex of Passion was intended, as he doubted the people who would be most interested could make sense of the overly formal language used throughout. He supposed, perhaps, the illustrations were meant for the less educated.

Still, with only three volumes of the codex in existence, Pancras doubted the knowledge contained within was truly intended for common folk. *Perhaps it's an instructional book for the priesthood.* Aita's priesthood kept many texts in its temples, focused mostly on death rites, body preservation, and methods of dealing with corpses that refused to die. Pancras was not considered a priest himself. Even though he venerated Aita as the goddess of death, he did little to spread her word, mostly because he considered it the responsibility of the bonelords, the best of whom travelled Calliome helping those with incurable, terminal ailments pass into the next world according to their wishes. The worst of the bonelords turned their backs on the true teaching of Aita, perverting it. Proceeding without regard for their subjects' readiness to make the journey on their own, they focused their life's work on filling her realm with the most souls possible.

The Codex of Passion contained valuable information in the section dealing with contraceptives, however. From what Pancras surmised, there was a sect of the priesthood of Aurora known as the Ever-Flowering Devoted. They made it their singular purpose in life to spread the physical pleasure of Aurora to as many people or creatures as they could and wished not to become impregnated while doing so. They were sensualists in the extreme and believed that unplanned pregnancies hindered their goals.

The Ever-Flowering Devoted wrote extensively on techniques to prevent conception and in some cases render the priest in question completely barren. For males the technique involved a sort of surgery. Pancras thought the process sounded much like castration, although the descriptions in the codex weren't clear on the actual details of the procedure. For females, however, the instructions were much easier to follow and involved the creation of a fetish. This fetish was to be inserted after which it would dissolve and release its potent magic. It was a temporary measure, but Pancras expected, given enough time, he could modify it to have a permanent effect.

The thought turned his stomach. From his few interactions with Princess Valene, she seemed honorable and certainly more pleasant than her husband. He wasn't sold on the fetish insertion portion of the instructions, either. The task involved some measure of consent on the part of Princess Valene, consent that would fall to Prince Gavril to obtain. Pancras got the impression the prince wanted to be as hands-off as possible.

Still, it was a start.

***

Delilah feared the snow would never stop. With Kale hopping around trying to learn how to fly, she found it difficult to concentrate on her grimoire. Every time she brought an image into focus and concentrated on its lesson, Kale made noise or bumped into her or knocked something over, causing her to lose the image and begin again. Moving into the bedchamber offered no respite because he was so loud.

By the third day, however, she learned to tune her brother out. She spent several uninterrupted hours studying images of Gil-Li weaving magic in silence. The more she studied the forms, the more she understood how this type of magic was possible. Even her dreams centered on Gil-Li and the new concepts she was learning.

She wished eagerly for an opportunity to practice this new technique.

On the morning of the fourth day, Kale woke her early. "Deli! Deli, you've got to see this. There's so much snow!" Tugging on her arm, he tried to get her to leave the bed. She snarled, pulling the covers over her head. Kale jumped up on the mattress. He yanked the covers off her before pressing his snout against hers. "Get up, Deli! It's like those times we were snowed in in Drak-Anor, except there's a whole city out there!"

He jumped off the bed, then sped into the parlor. Delilah waited until the bouncing of her stomach subsided, then rolled out of bed to join him. Frigid wind blew in through the open parlor door, prompting Delilah to retrieve her thickest mantle from the bedchamber. She tightened it around her before joining her brother. Kale climbed up on the top of the wall in the outer hallway. Steadying himself with his wings, he gazed out over the city.

The brisk morning air cut through Delilah's cloak like an icy knife, and when she exhaled, her breath formed a fog. She giggled, noticing Kale's breath hovering around him like his own personal cloud. Far in the distance, puffy clouds floated in the crystal blue sky, and Almeria lay as still as death. Smoke rose from chimneys across the city, collecting to form a dark haze, which hung in the air above Almeria. Delilah located the streets only by finding the separation between roofs.

"Isn't it great, Deli? It's like a painting!"

Shivering, Delilah regarded the scene. "Great, Kale." She turned around, then returned to their parlor. She wanted only one thing: to sit in front of the fire bundled up in as many warm furs and blankets as possible.

After a few minutes, just as Delilah felt warm again, Kale came in from outside, letting in a fresh blast of icy air. Grumbling, she hunkered down further, burying herself in the furs covering her armchair. She knew it would be several more days before the guards would be willing to take them into town again. She vowed that when they were finished with their business in Muncifer, she would find a warm place and never leave it.

***

Kale wanted to leap off the castle wall to test his wings. He was certain the thick covering of snow on the ground would provide sufficient padding if something went wrong, but both Delilah and Pancras insisted he wait until conditions were such that they could supervise. He didn't see what the big fuss was about. He knew he could glide. He just didn't know how far yet. The question was if he could achieve true flight. In his mind, there was no better time to practice than when the ground was covered with a natural cushion.

Since his antisocial sister growled when he spent too much time practicing flying in the parlor, he decided to check Kali's dead drop. The puzzle box had stymied him for the time being. He didn't know if the other drak could get a message to him in the bad weather, but he didn't have anything better to do.

Every guard he encountered asked about his wings. After the third time telling the entire story about the chaos rift, omitting the part about how he could now breathe fire, he wished he had worn a cloak to cover them. He didn't like the way it made him look like a hunchback, but he also tired of telling the story and having to assure all the humans he wasn't contagious.

He slipped away into the undercroft without arousing suspicion from the guards. Most of them were more concerned with staying warm than with where one little drak went exploring. He found a note written in Drak inside the ossuary. Appearing inscribed with an ink-dipped claw, Kali's writing flowed with broad, deliberate, yet precise, strokes.

Kale,

I found another route, a little longer, but from a more reliable source. She said it will take us right into the active part of the mine, though we might have to deal with some vermin first. I'll check the ossuary every night for your reply. I put ink in the box for you.

Bring your sister if she wants to help.

—Kali

Upon locating the bottle of ink, he replied in Drak.

Kali,

We'll try to get away tonight after dinner. If not, then tomorrow.

Keep warm.

—Kale

After his search for a rag bore no fruit, Kale used his leg to wipe excess ink off his claw. He placed the ink and paper back in the ossuary, closed the lid, and then returned to the upper levels to update Delilah. Upon his return, he found his sister and Pancras dozing by the fire. Gratefully avoiding their wrath from awakening them with an icy blast from the door upon his return, he silently thanked Tinian for calming the wind. Kale tiptoed through the parlor into the bedchamber he shared with Delilah and stared at his puzzle box upon the table. It seemed to mock his failure in discovering the secret to unlocking the fourth side.

Kale rummaged through Delilah's pack instead of continuing his exploration of the box and opened the lexicon she used to learn the common trade language. *Maybe I can read myself to sleep too.*

A specter of the past rose out of Pancras's dreams. A furious, screaming, skull-headed man marched toward him. Convinced of his own superiority, the short man, ranted and raved, waving his flanged mace to punctuate sentences. The words spewing forth sounded like gibberish to Pancras.

The skull-headed man stalked closer, looming larger with each step until he towered over the minotaur. He raised his mace to strike Pancras who cowered in the corner. Aiming at the minotaur's head, he brought down the weapon with a mighty overhead swing, but Pancras moved away at the last moment.

Deep inside, Pancras knew the event in his vision never occurred. Yet, lacking the power to escape, he watched it unfold. Again and again the skull-headed man swung at Pancras, and again and again Pancras moved away at the last moment. The man's screaming rants became a high-pitched keen before his features melted away. After dropping his mace, he offered a fur-covered hand to the trembling minotaur.

He recognized the familiar face accompanying the hand that pulled him to his feet.

"Thanos? Is that you?"

"I have missed you, Pancras." The other minotaur embraced him. Warmth Pancras had not felt in decades filled his body, and he felt a stirring within he thought was long dead.

"Thanos, how did…" Holding the minotaur at arm's length, he studied him. Thanos smiled, then moved to kiss Pancras. Thanos's bottom jaw clattered to the ground. Eyes, clouding with decay, slid out of their sockets and down Thanos's cheeks.

Pancras screamed, shoving Thanos away. The minotaur gurgled as Pancras's hands penetrated his lover's chest.

Worms writhed and wriggled from the holes. Instinctively, Pancras wove the magic that took him away from Thanos so many years ago. He felt shadowy claws scratching at the back of his mind, wrapping themselves around his brain, and extracting the magic. The tips of his horns glowed with brilliant emerald light. Tendrils of dark-green smoke swirled around the rotten corpse, lifting it up and devouring it with raw power.

"Thanos!" Pancras gasped, falling out of the armchair. The chair upended with a crash, but thick carpet and the furs and blankets under which Pancras slept muffled the sound of the impact.

After Delilah awakened with a start, she glanced around the room, bleary eyed. "Who's Thanos? Is someone here?"

Wiping tears from his cheeks, Pancras extracted himself from the tangle of blankets, then righted the chair. "No, no one. Sorry, bad dream." He patted Delilah on the arm, then peered out the window at the long shadows creeping across the streets. "It's getting late. Perhaps we should see if dinner is ready?"

She yawned, nodding. "Good idea. I'm hungry. I'll get Kale."

Pancras had not thought about Thanos in years. When he was a youth in Muncifer, he and Thanos lived together and made plans together as young people in love do. During Pancras's final years at the Arcane University, however, Thanos became jealous of Pancras's dedication to the arcane arts. He pledged himself to a mercenary company preparing for a lengthy expedition into the Western Wastes on the other side of the Dragon Spine Mountains.

Promising to wait for each other until after their respective tasks were complete, they parted ways. Pancras waited two years after finishing his apprenticeship, but the mercenaries never returned. After making some inquiries, he learned they were thought to have been wiped out by giants in the mountains.

Pancras left Muncifer the very day he learned of Thanos's demise and had never returned. *And now I'm going back to give money to the people who forced us apart.* The vivid nature of his dream shook him to the core. He rarely remembered dreams, and when he did, they never involved the rotten corpses of people he knew. He never dreamed about the dead. Reaching up, he removed both components of his focus from the tips of his horns. He had promised Kale and Delilah he would no longer sleep with them on, but, of course, he hadn't planned to fall asleep by the fire.

Dinner was a quiet affair. Ascertaining by each drak's body language they had after dinner plans, Pancras decided to let them be. Stopping them would be too much work for too little gain, and if they kept themselves busy and didn't burn down the palace or rip chandeliers out of the ceiling, who was he to complain?

The Codex of Passion awaited him after dinner. He was almost ready to return it, but there were a few more notes he wanted to take and a few more passages he wanted to revisit. After he completed those tasks, all that remained was to confirm a few things with a priest of Cybele and to gather ingredients. In his heart, Pancras knew giving Prince Gavril what he wanted was wrong. He would make the prince happy, though, because he planned to make him believe he got what he wanted. The dilemma involved making the effect last long enough to convince Prince Gavril that it worked. Pancras needed to bide sufficient time for the snows to melt, all of them to leave Almeria, and reach a safe distance before the prince discovered the ruse.

***

"I noticed you didn't bother telling Pancras where we were going."

Smiling, Kale held the door to the undercroft open for his sister. "What's the point? He'd just worry or want to go with us, and we can move faster without him. Besides, he's too big for some of these tunnels, and he looked terrible. You said he had a bad dream or something?" Kale couldn't remember the last time he had a nightmare. Most of the dreams he remembered were about silly things, like being chased by giant fruit or being held down by fuzzy rocks while they tickled his feet. He asked Oren about his dreams once, but the drak fortune teller was hardly helpful, predicting he would likely die choking on a piece of moldy fruit.

Upon entering the catacombs, Kale paused to check the ossuary. He found only the inkwell; the note was gone.

"So what?" Delilah illuminated her staff. "She's got a new route for us that isn't going to be a dead-end-waste-of-time?"

"Yes, she does." Kali stepped out of the shadows. "I'm glad you were able to make it. Word is they brought a new batch of slaves in just before that storm. New slaves are stronger and will be able to fight back."

Kale took point as they moved through the catacombs. Kali directed him with taps on his shoulder when they needed to take a new turn. "So what do we do if we free a bunch of slaves? Lead a revolt and kill all the slavers? Deli and I can't just flee the city if things go bad."

"You won't have to. We'll lead them back here to the catacombs. There's a network of sympathetic folk who have cellars that connect. They'll hide them and give them shelter for now. Slavery is illegal; the only way they get away with it is because most humans don't care about draks."

Kale didn't know many humans. Mirek and Dusan seemed nice, and there were a few others who came to

Drak-Anor over the years who didn't seem to think draks were some sort of vermin. "Not all humans are bad."

"True enough, but there are enough who think if you're not a smoothskin, you're little better than an animal, and there aren't enough willing to stand against them. They think it's not their fight." Kali tapped Kale on the shoulder, then pointed down a cobweb-filled corridor. Shadows shrouded the burial niches, and the odor of the graves permeated the air.

Darkness encroached upon the light from Delilah's staff. Kale cut away the cobwebs with one of his daggers, but the preternatural silence unnerved him. "Shouldn't there be rats or something?"

Kali held up her hand signaling them to stop. "You're right. It's too quiet."

"You said there'd be some small vermin. I don't hear any."

Delilah thrust her staff between them, illuminating the corridor ahead. "I'm cold. It's cold in here, more so than it should be, I think."

The trio stiffened when they heard scraping against the stone behind them. Upon turning in unison, they faced a cadaverous form with stringy black hair and burning red eyes. Glaring, it ran its overgrown fingernails along the walls before licking its long, pointed tongue along its knife-like teeth.

"That's not a small vermin." Kale took a step away from the creature.

"Ghoul." Delilah pointed her staff at it.

Hissing, it lunged.

"Run!" Turning, Kale grabbed his sister's hand. The three draks tripped over each other in their haste to flee. Kale heard the ghoul chasing them. Its long legs closed the distance, but he dared not look back. In the periphery of his vision, Kale saw a grimy, skeletal arm swipe at Delilah's cloak, rending the fabric.

Skidding to a stop as they rounded the corner, Kale pulled Kali and Delilah around behind him.

He inhaled.

Just as the ghoul loped into view, he unleashed a gout of flame into its face. Falling to the ground and clawing at the inferno covering its head, the ghoul screeched a high-pitched wail. Kale continued exhaling fire, engulfing the ghoul in flames, until he could exhale no more. The ghoul scratched and clawed at the flames, rending its blistering flesh.

Continuing to burn, the ghoul's rotting flesh sizzled and popped. The creature's wail of anguish diminished, and soon after, it stopped moving.

Kale put his hands on his hips, regarding the blaze. "Ha! Nasty thing."

He felt someone tap his shoulder.

"What?" Kale turned around. Delilah and Kali pressed backward against him. The stench of rotting flesh hit him like a punch to the stomach, and he fought the urge to vomit. Beyond them, he saw dozens of glowing red eyes in the darkness. A translucent pea-green shape emerged. The human knight wearing battered armor moved on legs that resembled ragged stumps. Using the tip of his spear, he lifted the visor on his helm. His left eye glowed in the darkness. The right one was but a jagged hole.

The apparition pointed his spear at the three draks, uttering words in a language Kale didn't understand. The ghouls behind him hissed in response. Then, they charged.

***

Pancras closed the Codex of Passion, then returned it to his satchel. Satisfied he acquired all the information useful for his purpose, he pulled on his heaviest robes and stepped outside. The light of the waning moons in the clear sky cast a cool glow on the city, and a strong breeze sculpted the snow on the ground into gentle drifts. The Eye of Tinian, a hazy blue, oval-shaped formation with red-tinged edges rose high in the sky, a reminder of the ever-watchful nature of the king of the gods, even when snow and ice blanketed his wife, the Earth Mother, during her winter slumber.

"Taking an evening stroll?" Princess Valene, wearing a heavy, fur-lined, red overcoat over her floor-length, shamrock-colored gown, joined him at the wall, her ever-present goblet steaming in the chilly, night air. The light of the King and Queen reflected off the jewels dangling from her ears.

"I do not often come up here at night, but Gavril is being particularly annoying this evening, and I had to get away. Are your companions too much for you to handle tonight as well?"

Pancras chuckled. "No, I just wanted to get some fresh air. Drak-Anor is mostly underground, so I don't get to see the night sky often. I sometimes forget to stop and look at the world around me."

"My husband doesn't actually value your services, you know. If it were up to him, he'd run all the draks and minotaurs out of the city."

Princess Valene revealed nothing he didn't already know. Curious, however, to learn where she headed with her commentary, he leaned on the top of the wall after brushing snow off it. Gazing out over the city in the stillness of the winter night, Pancras heard the songs played by minstrels in nearby taverns faintly drifting upward, but their words were unintelligible.

"You might do well to tell me what he's planning. What are you working on, Pancras?"

So that's your game. He focused his eyes downward, attempting to hide his smile from her. "I can't say."

"Can't or won't?"

"Does it matter?" He turned his head to regard the princess, noting the corners of her eyes crinkling when she sipped from her goblet. He expected she already knew he would not betray his oath to Prince Gavril, but he decided to try anyway. "I don't want to earn a reputation for being untrustworthy by not being able to keep delicate matters confidential."

"Of course not. However"—upon setting her goblet on the top of the wall, she rubbed her arms for warmth—"you may be the first necromancer I've ever heard of who is worried about his reputation."

"Well, I haven't practiced necromancy, per se, in nearly a decade." Leaning against the wall, he leaned on his elbows. Princess Valene picked up her goblet, then moved alongside him.

"Why not? Did you get an attack of conscience? Did you accidentally create a ghost or apparition of some sort from a close friend?"

"I never did that, even when I was active. I always felt free-willed undead were an abomination. I only animated skeletons to help me in my lab, and only then from volunteers. Sometimes, I'd create zombies if we needed them for a battle, but they stunk up the place too much for my taste. I like a clean workspace."

Princess Valene threw her head back, laughing. "You are quite fastidious for a minotaur." She rubbed his sleeve between her fingers. "And, you seem to bathe more regularly than other minotaurs I've encountered."

"Thank you." He bowed his head.

"Who would volunteer to have their skeleton animated? Are the people in Drak-Anor that restless?"

"Dutiful minotaurs who felt proud to continue contributing to the well-being of the city after death. But, after Drak-Anor established formal relations with Celtangate and Ironkrag, I felt it was inappropriate. We'd driven off the oroqs, and enough lives were lost doing so, it seemed… disrespectful." He tapped his hoof against the bottom of the wall, sighing. "I felt like I didn't have a place there anymore, but my friends convinced me otherwise."

"So you learned different magic."

"I didn't have to learn much. I was a generalist before I took up necromancy. Some of my techniques were a little rusty, but I always dabbled in alchemy on the side. Of course, I was helping with the administration of the city, so I didn't have to use much magic for that at all. Politics is dull. Er, no offense."

"None taken." She touched his arm, smiling. "I find it dull too." She drained her goblet. "My parents sent me down here to marry Gavril to seal a political alliance neither one of them has ever taken advantage of." She sighed. "I love our children dearly, but that man… he's"—chuckling, she regarded her feet—"never mind. I should not speak of such things with you."

Shivering, she tucked her goblet in one of her coat pockets. Placing a hand upon Pancras's arm, she met his gaze. "I hope whatever you're doing for Gavril does not put you in conflict with me or anyone I respect. It would be a shame for us to become enemies."

"It would indeed."

"Good night, Pancras. Sleep well."

"You as well, Your Highness."

Chapter 15

Get behind me!" Kale jumped in front of his sister and Kali as the ghouls charged. He didn't know how frequently he could breathe fire, but incinerating a pack of ghouls before they ate him seemed like a good time to find out. Upon feeling his throat burn as he inhaled, he unleashed a torrent of dragonfire into the corridor ahead of him. The ghouls erupted in flames, deafening the trio with their high-pitched wails of agony. The passage filled with inky, black smoke.

"*Synnefotone shifone!*" A swirl of azure energy surrounded Delilah. She pulled her brother alongside her by the strap of his bandolier. A cloud of flashing, swirling blades manifested between the draks and the pack of ghouls. With a thought, Delilah sent them hurtling into the inferno.

The apparition howled in rage when the blades passed through its body. However, it advanced on the three draks, leaving its minions to burn in the conflagration. Because Delilah did not know if her incantations could dispatch an incorporeal entity, she followed Kale and Kali's lead when they turned and ran.

In the aura of cold that surrounded the apparition, Delilah's breath appeared as puffs of fog as she ran. The ancient ghost's screams of fury followed her as it gave chase.

"We need to get away from this thing!" She felt unhelpful stating the obvious, but she hoped Kali would develop some sort of plan since she seemed familiar with the catacombs under the city.

Kali paused long enough to open a door, pulling Kale inside. She slammed it shut after Delilah passed through. "I'm open to suggestions!"

Delilah threw up her hands. "Great. How do we kill something that doesn't have a body and is already dead?"

She pointed her staff at the door when she saw the arms and head of the apparition poke through it. Desperately seeking inspiration, she glanced around the small, cramped compartment, noting it featured only a stone sarcophagus in the center. She herded Kale and Kali to the far side of it.

"I was hoping you had a plan bringing us in here, Kali. This is a dead end." Neither the blades she conjured nor Kale's dragonfire seemed to have an effect on the ghost. The area was too small in which to throw a fireball at it. They were almost out of options. *This is what I get for concentrating so much on fire and conjurer's tricks.*

"I don't think you should say 'dead' when we have a ghost chasing us, Deli."

The apparition pushed its way through the door, flashing a jagged-toothed grin upon discovering the cornered trio. Delilah wracked her brain, hoping an idea would present itself, anything. *Maybe I can distract it.*

She leveled her staff at the skull of the specter. "*Kalee'steen enoch leetiké goyna!*" Azure tendrils swirled, forming a furry ball with legs and teeth. With a pop a boggin appeared, but not a glowing blue boggin she used for carrying messages. She conjured a real, flesh-and-blood boggin out of the air with her sorcery. As she continued gathering threads of aether, more yipping boggins appeared, covering the floor and the sarcophagus. They hopped from foot to foot, clicking their sharp teeth in anticipation.

"Boggins?" Kali's voice strained. "Are you planning to feed it?"

As if on cue, the boggins snarled, springing toward the apparition. Leaping to attack, they passed through the sickly olive mist of its body. The ghost stabbed with its spear, impaling one of the boggins. It shuddered, squealing. Its fur changed from black to grey, and its body became gaunt and withered. Two other boggins leapt toward the desiccated husk of their brethren, then tore it apart. The ghost turned away from the draks, stabbing another boggin. The rest of the pack continued their attack on the apparition, snapping their teeth as they passed through it.

"Run!" Delilah dashed around the sarcophagus, then threw open the door. She hesitated, looking both ways for approaching ghouls.

"Right, go right!"

Heeding Kali's instructions, Delilah proceeded to the right. The yipping of the boggins and screams of the ghost faded as she ran. Within moments, both Kali and Kale caught up to the sorceress. "Do you know where we're going?"

"Yes! Keep going, three more niches and then left. After that, we'll come to an open grate in the floor."

With Kali in the lead, they neared the grate. From the odor, Delilah knew it led nowhere she wanted to go.

"Get in!"

Kale grimaced, pinching his nose. "Down there? Does stink repel ghosts?"

"Don't be a baby!" Kali dropped to the floor, then disappeared into the opening.

"We should've stayed in the palace tonight, Kale." Delilah cast a furtive glance down the corridor whence they came, searching for signs of the ghost. A screeching wail told her it was on the move again.

Kale dove headfirst into the hole. Delilah followed, swallowing her reluctance. The short drop from the grate turned into a slimy slide, jolting her tailbone when she landed. She scrabbled against the rock trying to control her descent with only the scant illumination from her staff to guide her. When she reached the end of the slide, she sailed through the air, plunging into the cistern near Kale. A wall of frigid, foul-smelling liquid shocked the air from her lungs, filling her nose and mouth. After fighting her way toward the surface, gasping and choking, she swam to the others.

Iron rungs set into the wall led up to the catacomb slide. Kale and Kali paddled toward a corridor on the far side of the cistern. Delilah caught up to them, relieved when she felt packed earth beneath her feet. In the corridor, the sewage stood only a few inches deep.

"Are we anywhere near where we're supposed to be?" She wrung out one of the hairy fetishes on her harness before removing her dripping cloak to wring it out as well. Delilah shivered, fearing her bones might snap from her violent tremors. She watched her brother making a sour face before he gagged and spat toward the cistern.

Kali studied the corridor for a moment. Counting on her fingers, she appeared to make mental calculations. "No, but I think I can get us back on track. I wasn't counting on an undead infestation."

"I thought Pancras said there weren't more undead in the catacombs, Deli."

Delilah bit her lip, nodding. Pancras indeed said that, but he also said he couldn't be sure. Her eyes widened when she realized he napped earlier in the day without first removing his gilded horn tips.

Kale huffed. "I'll bet he necromatized in his sleep again."

"Necro… what?" Kali eyed Delilah then Kale, furrowing her brow in confusion.

Kale rubbed the back of his neck. "Pancras has been having bad dreams lately, I guess. He might've animated some undead accidentally in his sleep, but I thought he wasn't wearing his focus anymore when he slept, Deli?"

"He forgot to take off his golden horn tips when we dozed this afternoon."

"Wait, wait." Kali held up her hands to silence the twins. "Are you telling me your minotaur friend created these undead?"

Delilah pursed her lips, glaring at her brother. It didn't seem fair he blamed Pancras since they weren't sure that's what happened.

"Maybe." The twins answered together.

Kali covered her eyes with her hand, shaking her head. "Let's just get to the mines and do what we came down here for. Maybe that thing will stay up in the catacombs."

That suggestion suited Delilah fine. She put aside her worry about returning to the palace and concentrated on the task at hand. She knew she would have better luck dealing with slavers than with a vengeful ghost.

**

The circuitous route by which Kali led the twins to the salt mines took far longer than Kale thought she intended, based on her grumbles. Although, he couldn't say for sure how much time they spent in the sewers, it seemed like their tromp through near freezing water took half the night. By the time they reached drier corridors, both Kali and Delilah were shivering hard enough to make their teeth chatter. He tried holding both of them close to warm them while they proceeded, but they kept tripping over each other's feet.

Soon, the deep, rhythmic pounding of the mine echoed in the dark. In a way, it reminded Kale of home. In Drak-Anor, someone was always digging to expand or renovate. The dormant volcano in which they lived contained no precious stones, per se, but digging through the hardened lava required many of the same tools. Recent trade agreements with the dwarves brought many new tools and techniques to

Drak-Anor, and the draks and minotaurs could finally fully express themselves in the architecture of their homes.

The air felt thick and almost briny; yet the stench of refuse from the water through which they waded clung to the fur linings of their cloaks. Kale worried his sense of smell would be permanently tainted by the odor.

Kali held up her hand, indicating they should stop. Crouching low to the floor, she peeked around the corner before waving Kale and Delilah forward. She stopped Delilah before she turned the bend.

"Kill that light."

Delilah extinguished her staff, and together with Kale, crept forward behind Kali. Ahead, they found a wooden walkway with a railing attached at about the height of a drak's head. The tunnel in which they stood formed a three-way junction with the corridor. Kali dropped to her stomach and belly-crawled forward until she could see over the edge of the walkway, then signaled for Kale and Delilah to join her.

Attached to the wall near the ceiling, the pathway overlooked a cavernous, white-walled chamber. Below them, Kale spotted workers pushing carts laden with white blocks to and fro. Translucent stones set in sconces similar to the lighting in the palace illuminated the cavern. Thin, wispy clouds clung like puffs of cotton to the ceiling, and Kale tasted salt in the air.

Kali pointed toward the left, motioning for Kale and Delilah to fall in behind her. The trio followed the downward angle of the catwalk around the side of the chamber, down a set of stairs, and into a corridor carved into the rock. The surface of the stone felt gritty beneath Kale's feet. Fine white powder clung to the scales of his fingers as he ran them along the walls. He licked one of them clean. Salt.

Encountering tool alcoves and storage rooms at regular intervals along the corridor, they had no trouble concealing themselves from patrolling guards and workers as they advanced deeper into the mine. They found their way to an antechamber off the main cavern in which half-a-dozen orange-scaled draks chipped away at the rock with hammers, chisels, and picks. Kale noted the color and pattern of their scales closely resembled Kali's. A salty crust covered the dull, cracked scales of the diggers, a contrast to Kali's shiny, smooth, and supple scales. The draks appeared on the verge of starvation, and their breaths came in ragged gasps.

One of the older ones spotted them. His eyes lit up, even as Kali held her finger to her lips to quiet him. She pulled him into their hiding spot.

"Kali? Is that you?"

"Father!" She pulled the old drak into a tight hug. "I've come for you. Where are the others?"

"It is not safe. You should not be here, you should not have brought—" He glanced at the twins. Wide-eyed, he dropped to his knees. "These are your allies, with stripes?" He prostrated himself before Kale and Delilah.

Kale coughed, shuffling his feet and averting his eyes as Kali helped the old drak stand upright. Meanwhile, Delilah studied a chip in the wall, scraping at it with her claw and then tasting the salt.

Kali gestured to the twins. "This is Kale and Delilah… I… I forgot their clan name—"

"Windsinger." Kale smiled before averting his eyes.

"They've come from Drak-Anor. They're going to help me free the clan."

"Clan? Your whole clan?" Delilah pulled Kali aside. "You said we were going to free a few draks. How are we going to smuggle a whole drak clan out of here?"

The others in the room now stared at them. Kale wanted to be anywhere but the center of a drak clan-mass rescue.

"Yes, my whole clan." Straightening, Kali held her head high in defiance of Delilah's disbelief. "For too long have the Firescales toiled in bondage to the human who owns these mines. I mean to kill him and free my people. You're here now and can't get back without me, so you might as well help."

"Firescale? You said your name was… oh." Kale buried his face in his hands. He never wanted to get involved in a full-scale revolution, even it if was against just one human.

"Kale." Kali placed her hand on his shoulder. Kale peeked at her through his fingers. "I lied about my name because I have to in the city. I can explain why later, but I need your help. Your sister's too. Nothing has changed."

"You didn't tell us you needed a whole clan spirited away!" Delilah tapped the butt of her staff against the ground for emphasis.

"Someone's coming." One of the other draks in the room rasped the words, pointing at the hallway. From the heavy footsteps and rattling of metal, Kale guessed it was one of the guards. He, Delilah, and Kali ducked back to their hiding place behind a boulder as the others scrambled to look busy.

"What's all this then?" A corpulent human with a whip draped over his shoulder waddled into the room. "I hear talking when I should hear digging!" He lashed his whip, striking Kali's father across his shoulders. Blood welled in the welt it drew across his back before he fell to the ground.

Kali's breath quickened before she drew her daggers. Kale seized her arms to keep her from leaping out of their hiding place and onto the human. When the human cracked his whip again, Kali strained against Kale. Flapping his wings to keep his balance, he dislodged a rock. It clattered across the floor.

The fat man smiled, turning in the direction of the sound. "What have we here? Layabouts?" He strutted toward them, licking his lips as his mouth spread in a wolf-like grin.

Kali elbowed Kale in the ribs. Grunting, he faltered, loosening his grip on her. She sailed through the air, howling in rage. The human gasped at the sight of the armed drak hurtling toward him. Landing on the human's ample chest, she plunged her daggers into either side of his neck.

Gagging, he clutched at his throat. He gasped for air as blood spurted from the wounds. Kali held tight, snapping at his face, tearing chunks off his nose and ears. He staggered backward, gurgling. Kali yanked one blade from his neck, the blood of her victim painting the once white walls of the antechamber crimson. She plunged the dagger into his face, piercing his skull. Pushing with her feet, she leapt off his chest. The human fell backward into the wall with blood pulsing from his ruined neck and face before sliding to the floor.

Licking the blood from her lips, Kali landed in a crouch near Kale. He glanced over at his sister.

Delilah squeezed her eyes shut. "Bloody hell."

***

For a moment, Delilah sympathized with Kali. She felt a pang for the father that cast her and Kale out. *If it were my father lying there, what would I have done?* As the fat guard slid down the wall, unconscious, his lifeblood spilling onto the floor, Delilah realized what would likely happen next: they would have to fight their way out of the mine with a clan of malnourished, sickly, exhausted draks in tow.

Staying in bed the rest of the winter sounded like an excellent plan.

Kali clapped her hands to gain the attention of the other draks in the antechamber, then helped the nearest ones to their feet. "Up you get! This ends now. We're getting out of here, and these draks, these Children of Destiny are going to lead us."

The draks moved with renewed vigor, even as Delilah cringed, hearing Kali put her and Kale on a pedestal. They never believed they were special because of the circumstances of their hatching. They were just draks with stripes who tried to live their lives and look out for each other.

"Kale! Talk!" Delilah waved her brother over. After pulling him close, she lowered her voice to avoid being overheard. "What are we going to do? This is already out of hand."

Kale glanced over his shoulder at the assembled clan. "I guess we lead them out, Deli." Grinning, he clapped her shoulder. "Today we get to be heroes!"

The sentiment made Delilah want to gag. She was all for doing the right thing, but in this instance, it felt as if they were duped into helping. She promised herself a nice, long chat with Kali when this was all over. *Oh yes, there will be a reckoning.*

"All right, fine." Delilah tapped the butt of her staff on the ground to get everyone's attention. "We're going to do this quickly and efficiently. No vendetta killings. I don't suppose anyone can tell me how many guards there are and where they're located?"

Kali's father raised a shaky hand. His daughter dabbed at the wound on his back with a piece of torn cloth. "Four, maybe five guards. They're lazy and cruel. Mighty Slayers such as you will have no trouble with them."

Four or five? How do they control a whole clan of draks?

"It's the crystal sentinels we'll need to watch out for."

Delilah's head snapped toward him. "Crystal what?" She had heard of them, of course, arcane constructs, automatons. She'd never seen one in person but she had heard they were strong and tough.

"The crystal creations of Volos."

Kale checked the corridor for any other guards approaching. "Who's Volos?"

The assembled draks muttered, making warding gestures. Kali threw the bloody rag she used on her father's wounds to the floor. "Volos runs the mine. He's not the owner, but he's in charge. They say he's a fiendling, an evil sorcerer that drinks blood and keeps fertile drak females in cages so he can eat their eggs."

Kale gulped as the color drained from his face. Delilah growled deep in her throat. She checked the corridor with her brother.

"I don't think that's true, Kali. Just stories made up to frighten children." Kali's father stood, groaning with the exertion. He waved her away. "I'm all right for now."

Delilah double-checked the corridor again before motioning for the draks to follow her. Kali helped her father, and Kale brought up the rear. Delilah kept her staff readied as she moved forward. Another antechamber lay ahead to the right. Just before she reached the doorway, she signaled for everyone behind to stop, then she peeked around the corner.

The unoccupied antechamber appeared to be someone's living quarters. A footlocker sat at the end of a wooden bed lashed together with rope. Delilah also noticed the corner of a desk, just to the side of the doorway. Waving everyone on, she then ducked around the corner to search the desk.

She found various documents she couldn't read, but from the careful way the writing was arranged in columns, she figured they were important. She took them, then returned to the group. Kali's father perked up when he saw the papers in her hands.

"Did you find their records? May I?" He held out his hand. The drak sorceress passed the papers to him. "These are mining manifests documenting shipments of rock salt to the surface, import records of mining tools, and this one looks like payment records."

"We might be able to use these to prove how we were enslaved." Kali inspected the documents, then handed them back to Delilah. After stowing them in her pouch, the sorceress checked the corridor again. She led the draks onward after determining the path was clear. The corridor seemed to run along the perimeter of the mine, sloping downward toward the bottom level. Delilah didn't have a particularly great desire to see how deep the mine went, even though she wanted to ensure they freed every drak slave. She did not plan to return to the mine after she left and tried not to worry about the repercussions of their actions.

Several minutes passed before Delilah saw another room ahead. Slowing their pace again, she crept toward the room. The sounds from within indicated it was an occupied sleeping chamber. She spared a moment to glance within.

Rows of stacked cages contained two to three draks each huddling together. Most were sleeping, but some were awake. Their eyes darted this way and that like trapped animals watching for predators. She motioned for Kali.

Upon approaching Delilah, Kali peered around the corner.

Delilah held her head close to Kali and spoke softly, "Have someone go in there and tell them we're coming in. I don't want them getting all excited and making a lot of noise."

"Understood." Kali returned to the group of drak miners, then selected one of the stronger-looking males to precede them into the slave quarters. After a moment, he came out, giving the all-clear.

Delilah counted more than three dozen caged draks. Some seemed near death with dehydration and the near-starvation conditions in the mine taking the ultimate toll. The sight made her reconsider her decision not to kill every slaver and overseer they came across, but she knew that would be a hollow victory.

"This is worse than anything the oroqs ever did to us or the goblins back home, Deli." Noticing Kale's tear-stained cheeks, Delilah pulled him into a hug.

"Unlock the cages, Kale. We're getting them all out. Kali, keep them calm. Save the grandiose speeches about our stripes for after we get out."

Kali and Kale went to work waking and freeing the draks while Delilah monitored the corridor. Some of them were weak enough to require help merely leaving their cages. While the process dragged on, Delilah heard a clicking, clacking sound approaching.

"Something's coming, hurry up!"

Kali's father cocked his head. "It's a crystal guardian. They're like giant crystalline spiders that patrol the corridors when the guards sleep. We must flee!"

"Nuts to that!" Delilah unfastened her cloak, dropping it to the floor. "Kale!"

Her brother joined her, drawing two daggers from his bandolier. Delilah glanced over her shoulder at Kali. "Get them out, get them ready to move. Kale and I will handle this thing."

I hope.

***

"Do you know how to fight one of these things, Deli? I've never seen a spider made of crystals before." Outstretching his wings, Kale rolled his neck. The clacking from the corridor grew louder by the second. The sound echoed in the salt tunnels, making it difficult to determine how far away it was.

"No idea. We'll improvise."

Kale was used to ad-libbing in battle with his sister. That was, in fact, their primary strategy. They always employed it against known enemies, however. He didn't like not knowing what to expect.

He didn't have to wait long. The crystal construct skittered into view. Eight legs propelled a blocky body topped with a small head that glared at them with beady, red eyes. Made of sharp angles and jagged protrusions, the giant spider appeared to have been birthed from a geode. The sentinel reared on its four hind legs, slashing at them with the front two. Tucking his wings and rolling, Kale dove forward. He slashed at its legs as he passed, but his daggers glanced off the hard, crystalline body.

Delilah skipped backward, smacking its legs with her staff. Blue tendrils swirled around her head. The construct stomped its hind legs, trying to impale Kale beneath it. Coming up behind it, he jumped, flapping his wings to gain altitude. He landed on its back, seizing one of its legs for balance. After it skittered forward, it stabbed at Kale's sister.

Flames poured from Delilah's staff, washing over the sentinel's head. Holding fast to its leg, Kale swung out of the path of his sister's attack. The absence of reaction from the crystalline spider unnerved him. It seemed unnatural a creature bathed in fire would not howl or scream, although, he supposed the sentinel was not a creature and he couldn't think of a reason why its creator would make it feel pain. Grunting with exertion, he used his wings to maintain his hold when the sentinel, its head glowing red from the heat, lunged toward Delilah.

From his perch, Kale viewed Kali holding back some of the draks. The rest shouted encouragement. Another blast from Delilah highlighted a dark spot where the construct's head met its body, a chink in its crystalline structure. He sprang forward, then drove one of his daggers into the gap.

The crystalline spider bucked, unseating Kale. Utilizing his wings to remain airborne, he landed upright on its back.

He pulled his dagger free from the crevice, then stabbed it again.

"Kale, get clear!"

Heeding his sister's command, Kale allowed the construct to throw him. He glided down the corridor away from it. The shockwave from a fiery explosion rocked the passageway, flinging the crystalline spider against the ceiling. Delilah hurled another ball of fire at it. The impact snapped off three of its legs before the creature collapsed.

It thrashed where it lay, but Delilah, unrelenting, engulfed it with magical fire. Kale followed suit, breathing dragonfire on it. He felt Delilah's flames washing over him as the crystals of the sentinel glowed red and then melted, but aside from it burning his harness, he felt no discomfort from the fire.

Neither let up until they reduced the spider into a glowing, quivering puddle on the corridor floor. It hardened into a discolored mass as it cooled.

Kale brushed the charred remains of his bandolier and harness off his scales. His scorched daggers were little more than misshapen lumps of the metal from which they were forged. He picked one up off the ground, holding it with two fingers. "Well, I can't use these anymore. Your fire burned the hilts off, Deli."

"I got you with fire?" Delilah rushed to her brother. "Are you hurt?"

Kale patted himself down. "No! I didn't feel a thing. Looks like I'm immune to fire now!"

"It makes sense. If you can breathe it, why would it harm you?" Kali approached the twins, whistling. She viewed the remains of the crystalline spider. "Ready for an encore performance? Father says there's at least three more of those things. Plus guards, and Volos."

Delilah slumped, leaning on her staff. "If we must. Just once, can't the bad guys turn tail and run?"

Kale gathered his sister in a hug, lifting her off her feet. "Come on, Deli! They're going to sing songs about us when we're done!" Kale heard the whispers among the sickly draks they rescued. They wondered who these striped draks were, why one of them had wings and breathed fire like the dragons of legends. Where did Kali Firescale find them? Were they sent by the gods?

Chuckling to himself, Kale led the group onward, giving his sister a rest. *In a sense, the gods did send us. Terrakaptis, the child of a god encouraged us to come on this journey with Pancras. Maybe he knew!*

***

Delilah felt it was unwise to encourage hero-worship among the former drak miners. They weren't out of danger yet. She couldn't deny, though, Kale's grandstanding seemed to energize and encourage the sickly and frail draks to follow behind them. Many grabbed picks and hammers as they found them, preparing to fight for their freedom and that of their comrades if necessary.

She glanced over her shoulder at the group. If they encountered serious resistance or another sentinel, and the weak ones tried to fight, she didn't want their slaughter on her conscience. A hiss from Kale startled her. Glancing up, she barely avoided bumping into him while he was motioning for them to stop.

Kale pointed at a room up ahead. "I checked it out. There's guards in there. Four of them, sleeping."

For a moment, Delilah thought about throwing a couple of fireballs in there. *Burn 'em all.* Resisting the urge to indulge her dark side, she relayed the news to Kali, who nodded, then drew her daggers.

"Wait here, I'll deal with it."

She scampered past the drak twins before Delilah could protest. After a few moments, she returned, blades dripping with blood. She bared her teeth in a feral grin. "They won't be bothering anyone." She focused her attention on the others beyond Delilah. "If you want something pointier than a hammer or pick, go on in and take what you want. The guards won't be needing them."

A handful of the healthier-looking draks moved ahead into the room. They returned with swords. One carried a pair of bone-handled, leaf-bladed daggers.

He knelt before Kale, holding the daggers up as an offering. "To replace the ones you lost in battle."

Kale accepted the weapons, transferring them to one hand. He pulled the drak to his feet. "Thank you, I'll put them to good use."

"Slay your enemies with their own weapons. We'll make them bleed."

"Let's go." Delilah didn't want the bravado to continue on too long. The fight with the crystalline spider took more out of her than she was prepared to admit to anyone, and she suspected they wouldn't be able to just waltz out of the mine without further confrontations.

"That should be all the guards save the one who is on duty." Kali joined the drak twins at the front of the group. "Father says there should be one more group of miners. They're digging the lower level tonight. Across the main hall." She pointed ahead and to the right. "Maybe we'll get out without finding Volos."

Shaking her head, Delilah squeezed her eyes shut. She thought her eyes would pop out of her skull if she squeezed any harder. *Now we're sure to run into him.*

Chapter 16

Kale could see his sister working to hide her exhaustion. The battle with the sentinel taxed her arcane power; she needed rest. He hoped if they ran into more trouble, it would be the final guard or even the fiendling. Either was sure to require less effort than another one of those crystal guardians.

He worried about crossing the main hall, even though most of the guards were now dead, according to Kali's father. The group would be in the open, exposed, and most of the draks moved slower than he liked. They tried to keep up, tried to act like they were ready for a fight, but he recognized some of them were on the verge of collapse from exhaustion. His own lungs burned, not from the dragonfire, but from the salty, dry air. It chafed his scales, and especially itched the bottoms of his feet.

Kali motioned for everyone to stop. Delilah leaned on her staff. She labored with each breath.

"All right, we're here. According to my father, the corridor to the lower level is straight across the main hall. I didn't see any patrols, no crystalline spiders, no guards, nothing, but I think we should cross as fast as we can."

"I'm ready." Kale glanced back at his sister and the other draks. "I think we should rest a minute though." He worried about the other sentinels because an enemy unseen was more dangerous than the ones seen. He hoped Volos was far, far away from the mine. *Maybe he was out at a tavern when that last storm hit. He's probably still there, getting drunk off warm ale in his belly. Warm ale sounds good.*

"Let's go, Kale." Delilah dismissed his look of concern with a wave of her hand. "When I pass out after we're back at the palace, just leave me alone for a few days, and don't draw funny faces on me like you did last time."

Kale worried his sister would collapse in exhaustion before they returned to the palace.

"Pass out?" Kali looked from twin to twin. "Why is she going to pass out?"

"I'm not!"

"If she pushes herself too hard, uses too much magic at once, it drains her. Wizards can burn themselves out completely." He tapped his temple. "Messes them up in here too."

Delilah shoved her brother. "I'm not going to overdo it that much. Let's get going. If we run into this Volos guy, just hit him with your bad breath."

Kali knitted her brow. "All right, I'll go first. Delilah, bring the rest. Kale, bring up the rear." She didn't wait for a response before rushing into the main hall. After a few moments, Delilah led the rest of the draks. They loped along behind her. Kale bounced from foot to foot waiting for the last to pass him, then followed at the end of the line.

From the bottom, the main cavern was even more impressive than from the catwalk at the top. Straining to see the wooden walkway from which they first entered, he thought the clouds seemed thicker than on the night they first scouted the mine. Not even Deep Road was large enough to have clouds, at least not the parts Kale explored. In the distance, he heard the click-clack of one of the crystal sentinels on its patrol.

As he proceeded, his eyes searched the walls of the cavern for signs of the crystalline spider. Kali and Delilah were already across, safe in the corridor that led to the lower level. Half of the other draks had crossed safely. Kale finally spotted it high on the wall, halfway across the cavern as he dove for the entrance to the corridor. When he poked his head out to monitor its position, he noticed that it moved away.

Turning, he stopped in his tracks at the somber scene of several draks weeping and cradling dying loved ones in their arms. Kali knelt in front of her father. The old drak lay collapsed on the ground, wheezing. She pleaded with him.

"No, we've come so far! I promised I'd get you out. I promised!" Leaning over, she pulled his head into her lap. He reached up with a shaky claw to stroke her cheek.

"You must… leave me, Kali. I tried to… be strong. I won't make it now."

"We'll rest here for a moment. Catch your breath. I promised you I would get you out of here!"

"You… did." His arm dropped away from her face. After gasping one last shuddering breath, he lay still.

The drak who gave Kale the daggers knelt alongside Kali. He stroked her arm. "The run was too taxing for many of them."

She met his gaze, her red-rimmed eyes flashing in the light. "It was the only way. If we'd lingered, one of the crystalline spiders would've spotted us."

"No one is contesting that. They're old. The mines are harsh. Many of these draks were waiting in those cages to die. Because of you, they died free."

Delilah approached Kale, then pulled him into a hug. They watched in silence as the draks laid their loved ones side-by-side, spending one final moment with them. Kali nuzzled her father's cheek. After crossing his arms over his chest, she stood. A line of blood stains crossed her legs where her father had lain.

"Let's finish this."

Kale squeezed his sister. "Right."

They found the stairs leading to the lower level nearby. Carved into the rock, they surrounded a central shaft containing a lift and pulley system similar to the one they viewed the first night they scouted the mines. Kali explained the lift carried rough ore to the surface, and she cautioned using it would make too much noise.

The stairs were just wide enough for the draks to proceed and feel secure. Kale couldn't imagine how a human or minotaur could navigate them without falling to their death. As they approached the bottom, Kale heard the sounds of picks on rocks.

"Come on, lizards! I want to see those scales bleed!" The guttural voice punctuated his words with the crack of a whip. Kale darted into the chamber from which he heard the sound. Five draks hammered away at the rock on various ledges while a tall human paced, cracking his whip for emphasis. He wiped his glistening bald head with a dirty rag before turning on his heel to pace the other direction.

Spotting Kale, he cracked his whip as a gap-toothed grin spread across his face. "Well, well. Here's a new one. Come to make troub—"

The human's grin fell when the others turned the corner. The tide of draks cut him off mid-scream, falling upon him in a rush of picks, shovels, teeth, and claws. The draks working the wall turned their picks and hammers on their shackles and chains upon witnessing the drak mob beat down their tormentor.

Kali helped free the chained draks from their restraints. She climbed up on one of the ledges. "Behold the Firescale clan. Free at last!"

Cheers and applause rose from the assembled miners. Kale felt a swell of pride in his chest. He felt that for the first time in his life, he did something important. Something good. Mocking laughter and slow, deliberate clapping from high above them cut short their revelry.

On a catwalk overlooking the room stood a crimson-skinned man in gleaming, golden armor. His black hair, pulled back, revealed a pair of twisted horns which rose from his temples.

"Very good. Very good. Be proud. You've disrupted my mine." He leaned forward, placing his hands on the railing. "Where will the people get their salt? You probably don't even know all the things it's used for."

"How dare you act the victim!" Kali balled her fists, glaring up at Volos. "You've enslaved the Firescale—"

"Oh please. These draks are paying their debt to me. Elantan the Grim made a legally-binding contract with me—"

"Three hundred years ago!"

Volos laughed, wagging his finger at her. "The debt is not repaid. I pay every worker here."

A drak stepped forward from the crowd. "You pay us pennies and then charge us talons for food and equipment!"

Cries of "Robber!" "Slavers!" "Gods-cursed fiendling!" rose from the crowd. Volos's jovial facade fell away.

"Get back to work, or I will have you all killed!"

Delilah climbed up on the ledge with her brother. "We're taking these draks away from you. We owe you no debt, and from what we've seen and heard, none of these draks do, either. Anyone who did died long ago."

"The terms of the repayment were clear: all generations will be indebted to me until the debt is paid. No matter. You had your chance." Volos pulled a thick rod from his belt. Kale heard the familiar click-clack of approaching sentinels.

The draks near the stairs shouted in alarm. They pushed into the room, scrambling to get away from the approaching crystalline spiders. Kale jumped, flapping his wings, but still lacked the strength to truly fly. He landed on the ledge where Kali stood.

She grabbed his hand. "Thanks… for trying."

Delilah swore under her breath when Kale failed to fly. She observed the smug fiendling directing his crystal constructs from on high as they butchered the draks nearest the stairs. Both Kale and Kali leapt into the fray with their daggers, pulling weaker draks away from the crystalline spiders, and slashing at their spindly legs in an attempt to hold the sentinels at bay.

She tapped the butt of her staff against the ground, pulling strands of aether together. They swirled around her like an azure tornado. "*Synnefotone shifone!*"

Delilah willed the cloud of whirling blades into existence right behind Volos. The fiendling jumped in alarm as they blocked his escape route. Delilah continued drawing on her magic. The room shifted out of focus, and blackness crept in at the edges of her vision. She blinked, attempting to clear her sight, then pointed her staff at the fiendling's feet.

"*Ophayra!*"

A ball of fire streaked forth from her staff, impacting the bottom of the platform directly underneath Volos. The explosion shook the room, cracking the stone supports that held the catwalk in place. Fire danced along the bottom, burning the wood and filling the top of the chamber with smoke. Salt dust raining down from the ceiling stung her eyes.

Through the haze, Delilah saw draks hacking and chipping away at the sentinels with their mining tools. Although the tools were made for digging through stone, the taste of freedom so close lent the miners strength enough to damage the crystalline spiders. She squeezed her eyes shut as a wave of blackness passed over her, threatening to steal her consciousness. She gritted her teeth, opened her eyes, and focused on the platform again.

"*Ophayra!*"

Delilah sent another fireball rocketing toward the structure. The impact and resulting explosion shattered the wooden flooring under Volos, showering flaming splinters across the chamber. Plummeting, Volos screamed. He smashed into the back of the guardian engaged with Kale and Kali before he bounced onto the ground where he lay motionless. Delilah allowed herself a smile and staggered toward him, leaning on her staff for support. Several of the older draks seizing the opportunity, surrounded the limp, broken form of Volos. They blocked him from Delilah's sight, but she didn't need to see him to know what half-a-dozen miners flailing picks and hammers would do to him.

Kale and Kali maneuvered the crystalline spider they fought into a corner. Kale unleashed dragonfire in its face while draks clung to its legs, holding them in place to keep it from impaling him. The rest of the draks continued to attack the other sentinel as if it were a rich vein of ore and freedom was the wealth they sought to acquire.

Delilah slipped, tumbling off the ledge. Her staff skittered across the floor, kicked far from her reach by the dozens of draks dodging attacks by the crystal guardians. She crawled in a feeble attempt to reach it, but stopped when her hand closed on a hard, cylindrical object: Volos's focus.

She felt the power coursing through the rod. Holding it in her hand, she pushed herself upright, sitting with her back against the wall. When she closed her eyes, she saw through the eyes of the crystalline spiders as they skittered, stabbing and slashing at their attackers. Her view shifted, and she saw another sentinel scurrying down the stairs to join its brethren in the fight.

Her vision clouded. The draks fighting in front of her became vague shapes in the mist. Squeezing her eyes, she poured all her thoughts, all her remaining strength into the rod. *Stop. Sleep.*

Kale grunted when the crystalline spider's leg caught him across the midsection. He snapped his mouth shut to keep his dragonfire from burning the draks who clung to the appendage that shoved him across the room. He tumbled into Kali, knocking her on top of him. Flaming debris showered down on them from above, and Kale spread his wings as a canopy to protect them.

The spider raised its leg, seeming intent on driving it through the two draks. Then, shuddering, it paused. It stepped backward away from them, lowered itself, then folded up its legs.

The draks cheered. After rolling off Kale, Kali helped him to his feet. The other sentinel disengaged as well. While he picked up his daggers off the ground, his eyes scanned the room. Many draks, a third of their total number, lay dead or bleeding. The combined metallic tang of blood and the salty scent of the air created an unpleasant, acrid taste in Kale's mouth.

"Hey, do you see Deli?" He stopped short to avoid stepping in a ruined pile of fiendling. Gagging, Kale averted his gaze, giving the mound of beaten flesh a wide berth. He found Delilah sitting against the wall with her head lolling.

"Deli!" Kale raced to his sister, skidding to a stop. He fell to his knees at her side. Although her eyes were closed, a smile spread across her face.

"Go 'way. Sleep now."

"Deli! We did it! The crystalline spiders stopped attacking! We won!" He shook Delilah in an attempt to rouse her; yet he recognized the signs of exhaustion from expending so much energy during the fight.

She pushed him away, then held up Volos's rod. "I did it. Go 'way."

Upon rising, Kale's eyes met Kali's. He noticed the dark trails from her tears staining her cheeks. She snatched him up in a bear hug, lifting him off the ground, then spun. Her touch ignited a fire in him, a warmth he rarely felt. He leaned into her embrace, holding her until someone behind them coughed.

The drak who, earlier, gave Kale his new daggers held Delilah's staff. One of the skull's teeth was missing. "I believe your sister lost this."

Kale took the staff from the drak. "She'll be thankful you found it."

"Paz." Kali put her arm around the stout drak and squeezed. "We did it."

He nodded. "Perhaps." He smiled at her, then faced Kale. "We still must lead everyone out of the mines. Your sister, is she…?"

Kale glanced over his shoulder at Delilah. "She just needs rest. I don't think she's hurt."

"We'll help her." Kali took Kale's hand. "There shouldn't be any more guards, right?"

Paz rubbed his arms, chewing his lip. "I think we took care of all of them, but it's hard to say for certain. We shouldn't linger. I don't trust that the crystal sentinels are truly dormant."

"Deli said she stopped them." Kale pulled Kali over to Delilah's sleeping form. He knelt alongside his sister, then lifted her arm. "She has that fiendling's rod." Despite pulling on it, he could not wrest it from her fingers. Even in her sleep, she kept a tight hold on it.

"I do not know how such wizardry works. We should leave quickly, at any rate." Paz took stock of the room, observing draks binding their wounds and tending to their dead and dying. "Our people's strength may fail if we give them a chance to rest now." He rubbed his belly. "Though, perhaps if we could find the food stores, we might be able to linger there long enough to restore some strength, hmm?"

Kali squeezed Kale's hand. "I'll scout around, see what I can find. If the others have the strength, see if they can climb up, back to the main chamber."

Kale nodded and shook Delilah again. "I'll lead them up."

After picking her up, Paz threw Delilah over his shoulder. Kale took her staff, and together they led the surviving draks back to the stairs. Casting furtive glances, the draks passed the motionless crystalline spider in the center of the landing. Kale's gaze wandered to the draks they left behind. He did not like the idea of abandoning the deceased miners, but they didn't have the resources to take them along for a proper burial.

The other draks noticed Kale's lingering glances at the dead. One of the older females laid her head on Kale's shoulder. "Grieve for them, but do not concern yourself with their empty shells. They reside with Rannos now. This place is their tomb but not their final resting place."

Chewing on a strip of dried meat, Kali waited for them at the top. "I found their larder. No wonder these humans are fat. There's more than enough for all of us." She led the group across the main cavern, then underneath the tunnel by which she and the drak twins entered the mine.

With Paz's help, Kali distributed the food, cautioning the draks against eating too much, too fast. Kale forced himself not to wolf down his ration in front of the others. After he ate, he roused Delilah.

"Time to eat, Deli. You have to wake up enough to travel. You can sleep all you want when we get back to the palace."

She glared at him with half-closed eyes. "Can't we just stay here until morning? Pancras won't miss us."

Kale pressed a strip of dried meat into her hand. Despite her protests, Delilah ate it. Kale made sure she ate a second piece before he helped her up and passed her staff to her. She secured it in her harness.

They journeyed up through the mine tunnels and corridors without further incident. The weary draks followed Paz and Kali, leaving the tunnels of salt behind. Kale recognized the route they traveled took a different path than the one they used to enter the mine. Snippets of overheard conversation between Paz and Kali indicated this was the route by which they were supposed to arrive, had they not been chased by the ill-tempered apparition and his ghoul minions.

Kale dreaded re-entering the catacombs, and he hoped Kali would lead them back another way, even if it meant spending a few days away from the palace. *Deli can always send Pancras a message to let him know we're all right.*

The upper levels felt noticeably cooler than the bottom of the mine. At a word from Paz, small groups of draks split off from the main one. When the last group left for their safe house, Paz and Kali clasped arms.

"Thank you, cousin. We'll have a few drinks soon."

Kali pulled Paz into a hug. "We will, as soon as the streets are clear enough."

Abruptly, she pulled him around her, then pushed him to the side. Kale saw the translucent form of the spectral knight, brandishing his spear, pass through the tunnel wall. He advanced toward the draks.

Kale regarded the daggers in his hands. They seemed woefully inadequate, and fire seemed to have little effect on the apparition.

Delilah groaned. "Not him again."

***

Delilah hoped she possessed enough energy to create one last distraction so they could flee the apparition. If nothing else, the evening's adventure taught her that she possessed the power but not the diversity to combat the terrors of the wider world. Her most powerful destructive magic barely scratched the crystal constructs, and apparently, the most she had accomplished against the specter was to annoy it.

Paz brandished a sword he took from the dead guards, but Delilah knew using it would do no good. He glanced over his shoulder at her. "I hope you have some tricks under your scales for this thing."

"This foe is beyond me." Delilah hated admitting that. "Run."

"What?"

"Run!"

She pulled him by the arm and fled, trusting her brother and Kali would follow. The apparition cursed in its ancient language and gave chase.

"Ahead, to the left! We can get back into the catacombs that way!"

Following Kali's directions, Delilah hoped no ghouls waited for them. *That thing is probably herding us toward them.* She took the first left, grabbing the corner to maintain balance as her claws skidded on the ground.

"Run! Faster! Look for—sloping passage—the right. It should—just ahead!" Kali shouted in between gulps of breath.

Delilah found the passage to which Kali referred. Ahead, piles of rubble narrowed the tunnel. Beyond them, the tunnel widened, appearing more structured. Burial niches lined the sides of the corridor.

The catacombs!

Leaping, she cleared the first pile of rubble, but she tripped over the second one, falling nose first into the ground. Fire erupted in her knees as the rough surface scraped away some of her scales. She felt two pairs of hands pull her up. Pushing them away, she turned to face the specter.

"Deli, what are you doing?"

Delilah pointed her staff at the ceiling junction between the old tunnels and the catacombs. Laboring through exhaustion to draw magic to her was like pulling a rope through a narrow hole, but she strove to do it once more.

"*Ophayra!*"

After the ball of fire exploded against the ceiling, the heated backblast knocked all four of them to the ground. The collapsing ceiling filled the corridor with dust and rubble, sealing off the catacombs from the tunnel.

Coughing, Delilah pulled Kale to his feet. "What good will that do, Deli? It can come through walls."

"Yeah, but it's slower until it gets free." *I hope.* "Run!"

The apparition raged, screeching. Not wanting to press their luck waiting to confirm her supposition, they increased the distance between it and them. *I hope that'll delay it enough to let us evade it.*

Sprinting, Kali led them through the catacombs. Although the hallways seemed familiar to Delilah, with the many twists and turns they took, she couldn't be certain of their exact position. Finally, she recognized a door ahead.

"Do you think that thing will follow us into the palace?" Kale threw open the door to the undercroft. It appeared undisturbed, just as they left it.

"It didn't follow us into the mines." Delilah figured it was either unwilling or incapable of leaving the catacombs. She watched the corridor.

Paz hesitated by the door. "We should go our own way, Kali. Get back to the Assassin's Dagger."

"I'm not certain we can evade—" A ghostly spear penetrated the wall, piercing Kali's shoulder. The grim specter followed behind it. Cutting short her strangled wail, the ghost lifted her off the ground. She clutched at the spear, but her hand passed through the spectral weapon. The skin around the wound made by the spear lost its shine, blackening.

"Kali!" Kale and Paz cried out simultaneously. By reflex, Kale threw a dagger. The blade passed through the specter's head, embedding itself in the wall.

As soon as Delilah attempted to draw upon her arcane abilities, the world went dark. She felt her pulse rushing like a river in her ears and her heart beating in her chest with the rhythm of a hammer on steel. Still, below that, she felt power.

Her blood.

She grabbed at her skinned knees. Blood magic, forbidden by the Arcane University, was widely known to be vile, corruptible, and unpredictable. However, Delilah was not a guild mage, and although she had witnessed its power, she had never used it. Desperate and on the verge of unconsciousness, she justified the decision her usually rational mind would have never considered.

Delilah drew upon the power of her own blood. Her vision cleared, and the world snapped into sharp focus. She saw the tendrils connecting the spirit of the dead knight to Aita's realm. Shouting, she pointed her staff at the specter.

A swirling lance of crimson energy blasted forth from her staff through the skull's eyes, twisting into a single ray. Smashing into the specter, it enveloped it. The ghostly knight's mouth opened in a scream of pure anguish. In a flash of green and red, it exploded.

Ectoplasm sprayed in every direction, coating the draks in gooey mucus. Kali dropped to the floor, holding her hand over her ruined shoulder.

Delilah fell to her knees. Her hands shook, and her whole body tingled with electricity. She wiped the ectoplasm off her snout, flicking it into the corner.

"Wow, Deli. I didn't know you could do that!" Kale whistled at his sister, kneeling by Kali. The orange-scaled drak writhed on the ground, groaning.

"I shouldn't have done that." The power called to Delilah. She felt it all around her, coursing through her veins, and the veins of those around her, Kale, Kali, Paz. She even felt it, albeit faintly, coursing through the veins of all the humans in the palace above. Pancras, the only other practitioner of the arcane arts in the palace, stood out like a beacon, a beacon with a dark shadow.

"It is destroyed?" Paz offered Delilah his hand. She shrugged, using her staff to help her rise.

"I guess? I don't know.."

"Paz? She's hurt bad."

Kali screamed when Kale touched her shoulder. Scooping her up, Paz cradled her head. "I know a healer. I can get her there faster."

Kale touched Kali's face, but his wide eyes locked with Delilah's.

"Go. Find us at the Assassin's Dagger when the streets are open." Paz shifted Kali's weight in his arms. Kale glanced from Kali to his sister and back again.

"I'm going with them, Deli."

Kale's voice penetrated the fog of Delilah's head. The power faded, leaving her numb. Her legs felt like leaden weights. She scrunched up her face trying to bring him into focus and trying to parse his words.

"I have to know she's going to be okay. Tell Pancras I'm fine. I'll catch up with you as soon as I can."

Delilah opened her mouth to respond, but words wouldn't come. She found herself nodding and watching her brother leave with the other two draks. She shuffled through the undercroft, her tail dragging on the floor, and a single thought running through her head over and over.

I shouldn't have done that.

***

Pancras slept soundly for the first time in days. When the door to the parlor slammed shut, he awoke with a start, sitting bolt upright in his bed. He ran into the parlor.

"Where's Kale?"

"Hey, why are you naked?"

Pancras opened his mouth to protest, recognizing only then that he left his robes in the bedchamber. He heard Delilah slurring, and he noticed her glassy eyes appeared unfocused. He knelt to examine her. In addition to being coated in a thick, gooey substance, dried blood crusted her legs below the knees. A thick rod protruded from one of her belt pouches, and she teetered on the edge of unconsciousness.

"Delilah, where's Kale. What happened?"

She put her hand on his shoulder, swaying from the effort. "I shouldn't have done it. Wait, no. Kale. Told me… something. He's fine. Yeah. That other drak got hurt. He's with her. He's fine. I sleep now."

Delilah's eyes rolled back in her head, then she crumpled. Lurching forward, Pancras caught her before she hit the floor. He carried her into the bedchamber. Upon a cursory examination of her legs, he concluded she was not severely wounded; the blood appeared to be from skinned knees. He peeled back her eyelids with his thumb, seeing only the whites of her eyes.

It wasn't the first time he'd seen a mage collapse from exhaustion after taxing herself. After cleansing the blood off her legs and bandaging her knees with some of the supplies they brought from Drak-Anor, he covered her up and let her sleep.

Pancras deduced the late hour of the morning from the amount of sunlight streaming into the room. The absence of Kale's noisy early-morning activities explained why he slept late.

After eating, he checked on Delilah. The drak sorceress was fast asleep and seemed not to be in distress, so he shut her door, returning to his experiments. The Codex of Passion gave him enough information to get started; however, he wanted to confirm a few suspicions with the priests of Cybele before beginning in earnest.

It was nearly dusk by the time Delilah awoke, emerging from her bed to find nourishment. Engrossed in his experiments, Pancras did not notice he worked away the day. In a way, it felt like the busy times in Drak-Anor before helping Sarvesh manage the city became a regular part of his schedule.

Delilah, wearing that same distant expression as she had that morning, slumped in her chair at the end of the table and chewed on a piece of day-old bread.

Drumming his fingers on the tabletop, he waited for her to notice him or become annoyed. When he could wait no longer, he broke the silence. "Would you care to tell me what you got into last night? I cannot believe your injuries came about from just exploring this palace."

"I used… blood magic, Pancras." Delilah's voice quivered, and even from across the table, he noticed tears welling in her eyes. She flung her piece of bread across the room. "Blood magic!"

Pancras rubbed his horn while studying her face. Of all the responses she could have offered, that was one he had not expected. *We fought a bunch of nasty spiders in the undercroft.* Or *we found more zombies in the catacombs.* Or *we snuck out and got into a bar fight.* Anything but '*I used blood magic, Pancras.*' In all his years practicing necromancy, he never succumbed to the temptation to use blood magic. He did not want to judge her too harshly, however. He never knew Delilah to be wantonly cruel or destructive. Something terrible must have happened.

"What happened that made that seem like a good idea?"

"We went through the catacombs with Kali to free the slaves—"

Pancras held up his hands. "Whoa, whoa. Slaves? What slaves?"

"The drak slaves in the salt mine. They had almost the entire Firescale clan enslaved. It was terrible. There was a fiendling in charge and these crystalline spiders…"

Pancras covered his face with his hands, resting his elbows on the table. Delilah continued rambling, and he caught snippets of ghouls, Kali's father, slaughtered humans. The story flowed from her like water from a burst dam. He rapped his knuckles on the table to get her attention. Nothing made sense, at least, not the way she told the story.

"Look, I'm going to try to not worry about any of what you just told me as long as the prince or anyone else here in the palace doesn't come looking for your heads, okay? Just tell me about the blood magic." Whatever that other drak got them into sounded like it was a lot of trouble. If they helped her with her problem and no one came to complain to the prince about it, Pancras figured he would be happier and safer not knowing about it himself.

"There was a ghost or something in the catacombs." Delilah put both her hands on the table and looked down her snout at him, as if she were explaining to a child. "We killed all the ghouls, but nothing we did hurt this thing. It chased us through walls and everything. When it stabbed Kali, I was already so tired from all the fighting in the mines, I didn't know what to do." She sat back in her chair, slumping down so far only her head remained above the table. "It just happened. I was desperate. So tired. I just wanted it to go away.

"So I exploded it."

Chapter 17

Delilah wanted to crawl in a hole and die. To the lay person, in the story she related to Pancras, she saved their lives. She knew, however, tapping into blood magic was the first step down a dark path with no redemption, only madness and death.

Leaning forward on the table she buried her face in her arms. "I don't want to go crazy and die in a rampage!" She felt weak for wailing and crying. *And I let my brother go off with two strange draks, and now I'll never see him again, and I'll be dead after you have to kill me because I'm going to go crazy—*

Delilah felt Pancras put his arm around her. He held her while she cried. When there were no more tears, she sat up, then wiped her nose. She nodded her thanks, reaching for another piece of bread to calm her turbulent stomach.

"I'm not an expert on the matter, Delilah." He reached over her for a pitcher, poured wine into a glass, and then handed it to her. "If it was in the heat of the moment, a reflex to save those you cared about, and something you did not choose to do consciously in an effort to increase your own power or destroy innocent lives, I don't think you've crossed the point of no return yet."

"You're just saying that." Delilah convinced herself megalomania was the next step. She contemplated it as she chewed the tough crust of bread. Despite being leftover from the morning, she found it tasted delicious. *I wonder if megalomaniacal overlords employ skilled bakers.*

"No, I'm not. You're not cruel. You're not ambitious. I've never known you to be so." He squeezed her shoulder. "It was an act of desperation, right?"

"You got that right."

Pancras lifted her head to meet his gaze. He smiled. "I don't think you have anything to worry about as long as you don't use it ever again."

"It was so easy. I felt so much power. It was like… it was like it wanted me to use it." She knew how that sounded. Magic, an elemental force of the world, didn't have desires.

"I've heard that is how it is."

She finished her piece of bread and drained the goblet of wine. It burned descending her throat, but it warmed her belly. "I was unprepared for what we encountered down there. At home, fire solved almost everything. I didn't have anything useful against ghosts or the crystal sentinels they used in the mines."

Pancras helped himself to some wine. He swished it around in his mouth before swallowing. "You're sure it was a ghost you exploded?"

"It was some dead human knight. He was greenish, and we could see through him. If that wasn't a ghost, I don't know what it was."

"There are several different types of incorporeal undead. Ghosts, specters, wraiths. All terrible in their own ways, but what they do and how they do it varies." He sat back, covering his mouth with his hand. "You say it was in the catacombs and was accompanied by ghouls?"

His comment triggered her memory. She jumped up from the table. "Wait here!" She rushed into the bedchamber to retrieve the rod she took from Volos. When she returned, she placed it in front of Pancras.

"I just remembered: you need to figure out how to attune yourself to a new focus, one you don't wear while sleeping."

"What?" Pancras poked at the rod, then regarded Delilah, furrowing his brows in confusion.

"Every time you've fallen asleep with those gold tips on your horns"—she pointed at his focus—"you have had bad dreams, and undead showed up. Three bad dreams with them on; three times undead have attacked."

Pancras touched the gold on the tips of his horns. "I've gotten used to being hands-free—"

"The fiendling in the mines used this rod to control his constructs. I used it to shut them down. Maybe you can attune yourself to it and use it as a focus, or maybe I can help you make something new. We have time. I need to make Kale one of those light gems anyway."

Pancras picked up the rod to examine it. "Perhaps you're right. We need to dawdle away the winter. I can't do what this prince wants me to do. It isn't right."

Delilah still didn't know exactly what kind of deal Pancras made to get them out of jail. He wasn't one to go back on his promises, so if he didn't want to go through with it now, what the prince wanted must be pretty bad. "Is there something I can do to help?"

Pancras laid the rod on the table, then scratched his chin. "No, I don't think so. Not at the moment. I can't do anything until we can go out into the city. There are many reagents I need to locate and purchase. Perhaps you can help with that." He removed the gilded tips from his horns. "In the meantime, I'm going to work on attuning myself to a new focus."

For a moment Delilah thought Pancras intended to work through dinner. The bell on the food lift rang, and he perked up. "Oh, food!" He laughed. "I almost forgot."

Delilah helped him bring out the trays and set them on the table. The aromas and sights of fresh, hot stew that smelled of herbs and pepper and fresh, crusty bread set her stomach rumbling again. When their bellies were full, Delilah and Pancras retired to the armchairs in front of the fire.

"It's been a long time since I've done this." Pancras sipped from a goblet of wine while he examined the rod.

"You and me both." Delilah attuned herself to her staff almost as soon as she learned she could focus arcane energy. It wasn't the staff, per se, but rather the lizard skull on top of it. For years after she and Kale were cast out of their clan, that skull was her constant companion, a source of comfort for a young drakling scared of the world and everything in it. Now, it helped her fight back against that world and all the things in it that wanted to kill her and her companions.

Pancras set the wine goblet on the floor and held the rod in the palms of his hands. "Let's get to work!"

***

Kale's arms burned from fatigue, trembling while he held Kali. Paz worked to unlock the door. The basement of the safe house opened directly to the catacombs. It belonged to a once-influential family, according to Paz. Even though they no longer participated in affairs of court, their property still accessed the catacombs, and they were sympathetic to the plights of non-humans in the city.

Paz flinched when someone inside the dwelling opened the door. Holding a lantern, a bent old human with one eye peered out. "I thought I heard someone scratching at this door. What's all this fuss, little draks?"

"She's wounded. She needs a healer."

"Oh bugger." The old man stepped aside, then held the door open, allowing Kale and Paz to bring Kali inside. "Put her there on that cot." Constructed of stone not unlike the catacombs, the walls and floor of the cellar appeared cleaner and better maintained. The two draks laid Kali on the cot in the corner as she groaned, writhing in pain.

"Tinian's ever-watchful eye, boy! You've got wings!"

Kale chuckled, looking over his shoulder and flapping his appendages. "I sure do."

"Wings and stripes. Truly he is a Child of Destiny, touched by the gods." Paz fell to his knees, prostrating himself before Kale. "We would never have escaped the mines without his aid."

Kale stepped back, rubbing his arms. Turning his head toward Kali, he coughed. "Yeah, please don't do that."

The old man held his lantern over Kali and examined her shoulder. "Hm. This is an odd wound, what caused this?"

Kale pulled Paz to his feet before joining the old man by Kali. "It was a ghost or something. It stabbed her with its spear."

"Hm. Undead. A ghost? Are you certain?" He touched the flesh around the wound, eliciting a new round of whimpers from Kali. "Ghosts usually don't harm people like this."

"Well, he was translucent, floated, and was in a very bad mood."

The old man lowered his lantern. Taking Kale by the arm, he led him to the stairs. "I guess some ghosts could be angry enough to hurt folk." He shook his head. "It doesn't matter. My wife will know how to treat it. Come upstairs, I'll get you some mulled wine. We have warm beds for you and your friend."

Paz followed the old man. Kale eyed Kali. He did not want to leave her behind, even though they were in the same building. He waved to the two on the stairs. "I'll be along shortly."

The old man shrugged, then disappeared with Paz. "Dalenka! Up, woman, we have guests!"

Kale sat on the edge of Kali's cot. Stroking the back of her hand as he held it, he noted how supple her scales felt. She turned her head, moaning and shifting in discomfort. Opening her glazed eyes, she offered him a weak smile.

"Hey, you stuck around."

"Yeah. I told Delilah to let Pancras know what was going on. He's probably going to be mad, but I just…" Kale turned his head away, giving her hand a squeeze. He shrugged. "I just couldn't leave you. I had to know you were going to be okay."

She smiled. "Aw, you do care." Wailing, she clutched her shoulder. Kale heard someone stomping down the stairs. A portly, silver-haired woman dressed in a sleeping gown, holding an oil lamp and muttering to herself entered the cellar.

"Oh by Apellon's lyre… Ludomil wasn't making things up." She placed her lamp on a shelf near the head of the bed, then knelt at Kali's side. She placed her hand on the drak's forehead. "How are you feeling, dear?"

Grimacing, Kali raised her arm. "My shoulder feels like something is eating it from the inside out. My whole arm is numb." She regarded Kale. "Sorry, I know you were holding my hand, but I couldn't feel it."

Dalenka pushed Kale away. "Go upstairs. You'll be in the way down here, Drak. I'll take care of her."

Kale hesitated, eyeing Kali. Only after she nodded her assent did he shuffle toward the stairs, intent on overhearing as much as possible. However, since the old woman hummed to herself and muttered as she worked, Kale resigned himself to remaining ignorant.

Kale found Ludo and Paz seated at a table. In the flickering light of the lantern, dancing shadows crossed their faces. Kale felt a chill from the wall of white that covered the windows, blocking the moonlight. A small fire crackled in the hearth.

"How deep is the snow?" Kale glanced at the top of the window, but he didn't see a gap that might indicate the top of the drifts.

Ludo sipped from his mug. "Oh, you can't go by that. It's been crusted over with ice and snow for weeks now. It's only about as high as you out there. I'll have a path carved out to the street by midday. I worked on it all day yesterday."

Paz drained his mug, then licked his lips. "Oh, so good. I haven't had anything stronger than dirty water since I was sent to that damn mine."

Ludo slammed his mug on the table. "I've been trying to tell the prince about that accursed place for years. He doesn't care. Just because you're short and have scales, everyone thinks they can push you around. Well, my family still remembers the draks have been part of this world longer than we have. It just isn't right!"

"We have?" Kale heard stories about how the world was created, but the stories included little about how the various peoples all came to be. He pulled out a chair, climbing up to sit with Ludo and Paz. Ludo poured steaming wine into a mug, then handed it to Kale.

Spices in the mulled wine tingled in his nose and mouth, warming Kale's throat as he drank. "Well, I think we shut the mine down. That fiendling guy is dead and so are all the guards."

Paz bowed his head. "We lost many, but all the Firescales are free now."

"Volos? You killed Volos?" Ludo chuckled, raising his mug. "Burn at the end of Maris's bloody spear, you son-of-a-bitch!"

Paz raised his mug. "I'll drink to that!"

"He'll roast on a spit in the infernal realms, that one will." After refilling their mugs, he raised his own again, nodding at Kale. "To the slayer of Volos! May he ride Tinian's steed to everlasting glory!"

Kale felt his face become hot. "I think my sister killed him, or maybe all the miners that hacked him to bits with their picks. I didn't fight him at all."

"To your sister then!" Ludo and Paz drained their mugs. Ludo, laughing, refilled them again.

The heated wine made Kale's head swim. Unaware of the time, he figured it must be nearing morning. His eyelids became heavy, and his belly felt warm with the wine he poured into it.

After finishing off the jug of wine, Ludo showed Kale and Paz to their beds. They were made for humans, and without his sister to share his, Kale felt as if the huge expanse of mattress would swallow him up. His trepidation evaporated when his head hit the pillow, and he drifted to sleep to images of a smiling Kali holding his hand and guiding him to his dreams.

***

Attuning to the rod went easier than Pancras expected, although the rod itself, a single piece of hardwood, perhaps oak or ironwood, with a simple brass cap affixed on one end, was rather plain for his tastes. From what Pancras deciphered, the runes scratched into the wood appeared related to the control of arcane constructs.

Pancras preferred flashier implements: an ivory scepter or polished bone with a cap depicting a mouth or a geometric design. He decided the runes would have to go. Attunement took most of the evening, but when he went to bed, he felt confident it would work as well as the gilded horn tips he had used for decades.

In the morning, he planned to let Delilah sleep while he took his midmorning constitutional in the cold and tracked down Lady Milena. The sorceress, however, had other plans. He found her already awake and studying her grimoire in the armchair by the time he dressed and emerged from his room.

"Feeling better today, Delilah?" Pancras opened the food lift and removed the tray the servants sent up while he was still in bed. He poured himself a goblet of mulled wine.

"I'm no longer exhausted." Without looking up, she turned the page.

The answer wasn't exactly the response Pancras sought, but he decided to let the subject lie. "I will be just outside if you need me."

Delilah closed her grimoire. "I'll come with you, if that's okay."

Although her wanting to join him surprised Pancras, he didn't have a problem with Delilah tagging along. However, he didn't think she would find the experience particularly invigorating. Together, they entered the corridor. Scattered clouds covered the skies over Almeria. A light breeze scattered wisps of snow off the tops of the buildings, but it didn't add to the chill of the morning air. Pancras leaned on the ledge and stared at the city.

"So what do you do out here every morning?" She brushed some snow off the ledge, watching it drift in the wind, then climbed upon it to sit beside him.

"Contemplate the upcoming day, admire the city, try not to drive myself insane wondering what you and your brother are up to."

Delilah laughed, playfully punching Pancras in the shoulder. "We don't go out looking for trouble."

"Nevertheless, it seems to find you." In truth, Pancras tried not to be sick with worry for Kale. Almeria was a far different city than Drak-Anor, and it wouldn't be hard for one lone, unfamiliar drak to disappear or find himself on the wrong end of a cutpurse's blade.

Pancras's ears twitched upon hearing the telltale sounds of Princess Valene approaching. She rounded the corner with her customary goblet of heated, mulled wine. A slight hesitation and hitch in her step revealed her surprise upon finding Delilah alongside Pancras, but her face was a mask of boredom. From outward appearances, it was as if Princess Valene always encountered a minotaur and drak during her morning strolls.

"I see we are not alone this morning, Pancras."

Crossing one arm over his chest, the minotaur bowed. "Good morning, Princess. May I present one of my companions, Delilah of Clan Windsinger?"

Delilah waved hello. The Princess pursed her lips, growling deep in the back of her throat. Clearly, she expected Delilah to hop off and bow. "An unusual name for a drak."

"Yeah, well, when half your clan wants to hide you away out of sight and the other half wishes they'd smashed your egg before you hatched, you have to forge your own identity."

Pancras closed his eyes and coughed, hoping Delilah was a figment of his imagination. However, upon reopening them, he still saw her there.

"Indeed." Princess Valene sniffed, raising her head. Silently, she regarded the drak, then sipped her mulled wine. She turned her attention to Pancras. "Apart from introducing me to this rude creature, have you any interesting thoughts for me today?"

"I would never presume to know what you would find interesting, Your Highness." Pancras felt the tension in the air.

Princess Valene sniffed, eyeing the drak. "So you, Delilah. Why did half your clan wish to commit infanticide? Surely that is more interesting than Pancras's newfound desire to walk on eggshells."

Pancras caught himself before he sighed in resignation, turning to gaze at the city again. He prayed silently to Aita for Delilah to find enough tact not to insult the princess.

"Draks with stripes are revered. Twins are feared. My brother and I are both." She scratched at a blemish in the ledge. "You might say our clan was conflicted. They didn't kill us at birth but cast us out as soon as we were old enough to fend for ourselves. They didn't even allow our parents to name us."

Pancras knew the bare bones of Kale and Delilah's story but not many details. They didn't talk about it unless they were asked, and he had never wanted to pry.

"So you chose your names yourselves?" Princess Valene took a drink of wine and nodded. "Hm, I do not know much about draks, apart from how poorly they've been treated in Almeria. They seem to be held in ill regard here, for reasons I cannot fathom. Back home, in Vlorey, we find draks to be skilled craftsmen and tinkerers."

"Yeah, around here some people treat draks like slaves. Or worse."

Pancras nudged Delilah. She shot a glare of a thousand knives at him. He tilted his head.

"Yes, well. Obviously hyperbole is a trait draks share with humans. Have a good day." Princess Valene left them without giving them a second look.

Delilah smacked Pancras on the arm. "Why'd you push me? I could've fallen!"

"It's a bit bold to compare the people of Almeria to slavers in front of one of its rulers. It's downright…" He couldn't find the word. Rude seemed an understatement.

"That's what they are, Pancras!" Delilah hopped off the ledge, poking him in the belly with a clawed finger. "The big salt mine under the city? They were using drak slaves to mine the salt. Slaves!"

Pancras first became aware of the slaves in the hidden salt mine when Delilah told him of her brush with blood magic, and Almeria wasn't the first city in which exploitative industry was concealed from visitors. He stood listening while Delilah lectured him about the events of their expedition with Kali, and he tried to maintain a neutral expression. Some parts of the story seemed unbelievable, but he knew Delilah well enough to know that although she might lie for a prank, she never lied if she was passionate about a cause or angry.

He knelt down and held her by the shoulders. "I believe you. Freeing slaves is always a good thing. Just try to interact with the princess with a bit more tact next time. We may need her as an ally very soon."

Delilah smacked his hands away. "Why? What's this all about anyway?" She waved her finger in his face. "And don't tell me you can't tell me."

Pancras intended to tell her just that. "I… am unable to discuss the terms of my agreement with Prince Gavril."

Delilah screeched, throwing up her hands, then stormed away. Shaking his head, Pancras stood up and dusted off his robes. "This day is certainly starting off well."

***

Delilah grumbled, scuffing her feet on the floor as she hastened away from Pancras. She wasn't sure why she was angry. *It's the blood magic. It's affecting my brain!* She scuffed faster, as if she could outrun her own thoughts.

When she left Pancras, she went in the opposite direction from that of the princess. She desired not to encounter more drak-hating people today. The corridor led to familiar halls. She and Kale had truly explored the entire palace, except for the wing containing the royal living quarters. Almeria's palace contained no less than four banquet halls, along with various sitting rooms furnished with plush chairs, roaring hearths, and colorful rugs and tapestries.

Most of the sitting rooms remained empty. The snow kept visitors and guests away from the palace, and the solitude Delilah found in one of the empty sitting rooms suited her.

She pulled a chair closer to the hearth and climbed into it. By reflex, she reached for her grimoire and then smacked herself on the head. She then realized she left her staff behind as well. A chill born not of cold came over her body.

Oh well, who's going to come after me here? She drummed her fingers on the arm of the chair and sighed. *I probably should go back. I could be doing something. Anything.* Instead of leaving, however, Delilah pulled her legs up in the chair and let the crackling warmth of the fire lull her to sleep.

While she slept, Delilah's dreams took her back to a desperate battle between the denizens of what later became Drak-Anor and the dwarves. She and Kale crouched behind a boulder. A dwarven battering ram slammed into the Deep Road Gate while oroq defenders rained arrows down upon the invaders. The thunderous roar of the lightning cannons Delilah and Kale constructed for their home's defense cut down vast swaths of dwarves, but the stout warriors attacked in a never-ending tide.

Nearly spent, Delilah clutched at a wound in her side. Kale ripped a strip of fabric from the tunic of a dead oroq lying near them, then pressed the cloth against the wound.

"The boss is coming. We just need to hang on a little while longer." Her brother winced as an oroq backed into him. The grey-skinned warrior glanced down at the draks, sneering. He spat, then growled. He head-butted the dwarf he battled, knocking the hairy invader off his feet.

Delilah didn't like oroqs. They were brutish bullies. If they didn't have dwarves to fight, they often focused their attention on the draks and goblins who lived in the area. The Overlord felt they were too useful in fights to get rid of.

"Little draks too weak to fight?" The oroq taunted them, then backhand swung his sword, beheading the dwarf in front of him. Upon separating from the helmet as it spun through the air, it landed at Kale's feet with a splat. The coppery scent of blood combining with smoke and ozone from the lightning cannons hung thick in the air.

Kale kicked the dwarf's head away from him. Delilah grimaced, picking up her staff. Tapping the butt against the ground, she fought to still her trembling muscles as she summoned more magic.

"*Synnefotone shifone!*" Tendrils of blue aether gathered around the sorceress, and her eyes sparkled, turning bright turquoise. The wound in her side threatened to overwhelm her, and she felt her focus fade. In the periphery of her vision, a dwarven axe descended toward her brother's head.

Exhausted, Delilah's arcane power waned, yet one source called to her. She drew upon the magic in her blood, digging her fingers into her side to encourage the wound to seep and flow. Gritting her teeth against the pain she pointed her staff at the dwarf about to cleave her brother. The turquoise tendrils swirling around her staff darkened, turning purple, then red, as a bolt of crimson light shot forth, vaporizing the dwarf.

She jumped up on the boulder, spinning her staff, then slammed the butt end into the rock. With her free hand, she drew a wide arc. The swirling, vaporous tendrils of magic flowed into the ground. She raised her hand toward the sky.

Spikes of rock erupted from the ground, impaling dwarf and oroq alike. The tang of blood, running down the spikes and forming streams, filled the air. Drawing upon the power of their deaths, arcane energy surged into Delilah, flowing like floodgates opening after a torrential storm. The spikes continued growing until they formed the arms, torsos, and legs of great stone constructs. After ripping themselves free from the earth, they smashed obstacles in their way.

Delilah turned her attention to the dwarves manning the battering ram. Drawing more power from the bleeding dwarves and oroqs around her, she drained the life force of each one. The color drained from their flesh, and their skin first sagged, then sank. After she finished, the air around the battering ram shimmered, then burst into flame. Screams of the dwarves mingled with groans of the dying, and Delilah reveled in the power she drew from their deaths.

She felt the air grow thin as the expanding inferno consumed the cavern. She kicked away a claw scratching her leg, basking in the energy of each of her enemies as the blaze consumed them. Annoyed by the interruption, Delilah directed her attention to the clawed hand wrapping around her ankle. Her brother stared up at her, his face gaunt and eyes cloudy white.

"Deli—stop—you're killing—" Kale choked, gasping as his body burst into flames. His scales blackened, then peeled away from his bloody muscles. Finally, they, too, burned away, revealing his charred skeleton.

Delilah awoke with a gasp. She fell out of the chair, slapping at her legs to free them from Kale's skeletal grasp before remembering she was in Almeria.

She crawled over to the upended chair, then pulled herself to her feet. Delilah set the chair upright, holding on to it for support while she caught her breath.

"You're cracking up, Deli-girl. It was just a dream. That's not how it happened. Just a dream."

Racing out of the sitting room, she headed toward the chambers she shared with Pancras and her brother. Judging by the flurry of activity she saw in the city from the walkway, she realized she slept away most of the morning. When she did not find Pancras in the suite, she picked up her staff and made herself comfortable in her armchair. She opened the grimoire, taking comfort in its weight as she lost herself in its pages.

***

Under the ministrations of Dalenka, Kali made a swift recovery. The wound was deep, but with bed rest and the attention of a skilled healer, it started to mend within a day. Kale left her side only to eat, sleep, and help Paz and Ludomil carve a path through the snow to the street.

On the third day, Kali got up and about. She wore a sling to immobilize her arm, but she seemed well enough. Paz left to ensure the rest of the miners they rescued transitioned to their new lives. Ludomil put Kale to work hauling firewood from the cellar up to the hearth.

Kali patted the mattress next to her. "That's three loads already. Rest a moment."

Kale sat on the bed, whacking Kali with his wing as he tried to position it behind them. "Sorry."

She laughed, pushing his wing out of the way. "You've been watching over me like a celestial guardian."

Rubbing his arm, Kale chuckled. "It didn't seem right, just leaving you. Now that you're well, I really need to get back to Pancras and Delilah. I'm not supposed to be out without an escort."

Kali took Kale's hand, resting her head on his shoulder. "What's that all about, anyway?"

"I don't know. Part of the deal Pancras made to get us out of jail. He won't talk about it."

"Will you help me get into the palace? I need an audience with the prince to talk about this slave thing. The mine owner will no doubt be petitioning him as soon as he can get to the palace." Kali nuzzled Kale, nipping at his ear. "I'll make it worth your while."

Kale giggled, pushing her away. "You keep saying that."

She pulled his hand into her lap, intertwining her tail with his. "Well, what do you want?"

Kale observed minotaur females and fiendlings in Drak-Anor trying to get their way with what Sarvesh called "feminine wiles," but drak relationships were different. Mating was not a recreational activity for draks; clutches of eggs required dedicated care and were not taken lightly. "You've done enough really. Staying in the palace all the time is really boring. I should be thanking you for giving us something to do."

"You'll help me then?"

"Of course."

Kali tackled him, pushing him onto the bed before straddling him. She pressed the tip of her snout against his. "You're all right, for a twin."

Kale laughed, trying to squirm out from under her. She held him tighter than he thought possible with the use of only one arm.

"You can't get away." A smile overtook her face. "Do you know what I want?"

"No. No, not really." Kale wasn't sure he was ready to find out.

"I want to go with you. Wherever you go. Take me away from this city, this place." She stroked his cheek, running a claw along his jaw. He failed to suppress a shudder.

Kale figured Pancras would go along with that, but he wasn't as sure about his sister since she didn't seem to like Kali much. Whether she felt genuine dislike or jealousy, he didn't know; however, he hoped she would put her feelings aside in deference of his happiness. "I would like that."

Chapter 18

Pancras worried when Delilah insisted her brother was fine alone in the city. She refused to conjure a boggin to get a message to him, and his attempts at replicating that type of magic fell short. He resigned himself to checking and rechecking his notes until word came that the city was open again.

Lady Milena offered to find a guard to return the Codex of Passion to Aurora's Sanctuary for him, but Pancras felt it would be disrespectful to have a guard return such a sacred text. He believed she welcomed any excuse not to return to the temple.

"Where is your other drak, Pancras? I have only seen the female lately." Lady Milena pulled her cloak around her as they prepared to exit the palace. It was a question Pancras dreaded hearing. He had hoped no one would notice Kale's absence.

"He hasn't… been… feeling well. I have him on bed rest." He rubbed the tip of his horn before realizing the gesture betrayed his nervousness. He scratched his head instead, hoping she wouldn't notice.

"You are a terrible liar. Did he sneak out of the palace before the last storm?"

"Sneak?" Pancras chuckled. "I really wouldn't know. I've been so involved with my research for the prince—"

"Yes, yes, this project about which you can say nothing." Milena waved her hand to silence him. She seemed content to drop her inquiries as to Kale's whereabouts.

"Hands off me, ya longshanks!" A familiar voice shouted from the palace entrance. Pancras observed the guards grappling with a short, hairy man. Upon spotting Pancras, he pointed at the minotaur. "There! Ya see? I'm supposed to be here, fools! I got caught out when the storms hit."

The guard dragged the dwarf to Pancras and Milena. "Here, he says he knows you."

"Indeed, this is the dwarf who traveled to the city with us."

Milena sniffed, crinkling her nose in distaste. "He was not with you when you were arrested?"

Pancras detected the odor of cheap ale, sweat, and vomit on Edric, the likely source of Milena's disgust. "No, as I recall, he was elsewhere, gambling."

"Aye, been stuck there ever since! Unhand me!" He shoved the guard, then straightened his tunic.

"We have another bedchamber. Delilah is there now. Get yourself cleaned up, and stay out of trouble. I have to go into the city for a bit."

Milena jerked her thumb toward the hallway that led back to Pancras's living quarters. "Show him the way. Make sure he doesn't leave. I'll relieve you when I return."

After saluting, the guard escorted Edric toward their suite. Pancras was surprised the dwarf turned up. *He's probably out of money now or on the run from the gambling den owners.* He pulled up his hood as they trudged out into the snow, feeling exposed without wearing the gilded tips on his horns. Unaccustomed to the weight on his hip, Pancras felt as if the rod Delilah gave him pulled him to the right.

Snow covered the city deeper than before. The solid mass reached the middle of the first-floor windows of most buildings. Trekking through the streets resembled walking underground, except for the bright glare from above. The wind blew feathery puffs of snow across the tops of the carved chasms.

Pancras noticed makeshift steps carved into the snow leading down to the doors of most buildings. The snow cover muffled the sounds of the city despite the crowds of people going about their business.

After returning the Codex of Passion to Aurora's Sanctuary, Pancras treated Milena and himself to mulled wine from one of the street vendors. They sipped it from wooden tankards while he wandered the market, looking for herbalists and artisans.

By afternoon, he located the ingredients he needed and arranged for their delivery to the palace. A metalworker agreed to create a new, more ornate cap for his rod. He decided to wait until he had more time to commission someone to create new horn tips. Until then, he would suffer with bare horns.

"I would say this has been a productive day."

Milena drained the rest of her mulled wine. Her cheeks reddened from the cold wind, and her eyes squinted against the sun. "It's getting late. Your draks aren't going to be happy; they can't get much done before dark."

"They don't need to do anything. Anyway, it's best if they stay in today." Pancras considered going to the Assassin's Dagger to search for Kale, but he didn't have any leads on his location. Finding the cold intolerable, he changed his mind about staying out longer to conduct a search. He hoped Kale would find his way back to the palace sooner, rather than later.

Pancras needn't have worried. As they headed down the avenue leading to the palace, he and Milena caught sight of Kale, his wings unmistakable even from a distance, and Kali. As they caught up with the pair, Pancras noticed Kali's arm in a sling, and he knew he would finally get more information about the ghost of which Delilah spoke.

"You're late, Kale."

"And without your escort, I see. We'll have to have a chat about that."

Pancras surmised from Lady Milena's tone more amusement than anger about Kale's disregard of Prince Gavril's decree.

Kale spun toward the sound of their voices. "Pancras! Lady… Knight lady! Did Deli come home?"

Pancras turned Kale about face and continued their march down the avenue. "Yes, she did, and we have a lot to talk about. Edric has returned as well."

"Kali wants our help petitioning the prince. She wants to make sure the slave owners don't get to blame everything on the draks."

Milena stopped Kale, placing a hand on his shoulder. "Slave owners? What do you mean?"

Pancras removed her hand from Kale's shoulder, again turning him to face in the direction they traveled. "I'm sure we'll hear all about it soon enough. Might we proceed indoors, please, where the environment is more conducive to conversation?"

When they finally reached the palace, Pancras stomped his hooves to loosen the impacted snow and shook accumulated frost off his cloak. He almost believed he would never feel warm again.

"All right, Draks." Milena knelt in front of Kale and Kali. "Tell me about these slaves."

Kali launched into a tale of how the Firescale clan had been enslaved for generations in the salt mine under the city and how she escaped last year, vowing to free her people.

"And when I saw the striped draks in our city, I knew the time had come. With their help, we defeated the overseers, slew Volos, and freed the Firescales! Never again will the blood of my people grease the tracks of Almeria's salt mine." Kali stood with one hand on her hip and her head held high.

Milena stood up, pursing her lips. "Slavery is illegal in Almeria. These are serious charges. Can you pr—"

"Lady Milena! Lady Milena!" A guard ran down the hall toward them from the throne room. "You're needed immediately. Lord Reznik is in a mighty fury. Prince Gavril is requesting your intercession."

Milena glanced at Pancras. "Reznik owns the salt mine. It looks like the pot has been stirred. You'd all better come with me." They rushed toward the throne room. As they approached, Pancras heard a voice yelling, although he understood only part of what the man said.

"Ruined… Years of work… My investment… Families!"

Milena threw open the door. A wiry, bald man stood with one foot on the throne dais, pointing his finger at Prince Gavril. Spittle flew from his mouth as he ranted. Princess Valene sat back on her throne, rolling her eyes and sighing loudly enough to be heard over Lord Reznik's voice. The guards stood with their spears pointed at the man, ready to strike him down if he moved aggressively toward the prince.

Prince Gavril stood upon noticing their arrival. "Ah, Lady Milena. Perhaps now we can have some order."

Pancras stood aside, giving her a wide berth. He wasn't sure why she was needed when the prince was attended by guards who stood ready to protect him. Placing her hand on the hilt of her sword, she approached Lord Reznik. His eyes flicking down to her weapon, he stepped down off the dais, then bowed.

"I didn't come here to cause trouble."

"Oh yes you did. You have a grievance you wish to air." Prince Gavril returned to his throne, then seated himself. "But now that your better is here, perhaps you will exercise the self-control to speak in a civilized manner."

Lord Reznik noticed the new arrivals. His eyes fixated on Kali. His face flushed, and he pointed a trembling finger at her. "You! You're the cause of this, I know it! Seize her! Seize her now! She's a murderer and a thief."

The guards stood motionless. With the wave of the prince's hand, they snapped to attention. Prince Gavril yawned, covering his mouth with the back of his hand. "You forget your place, Reznik. I rule Almeria, not you. The guards obey my commands, not yours."

"Your Highness, if I may." Milena turned toward the prince, then saluted. "This drak has accusations of her own against Lord Reznik."

Princess Valene perked up. "Oh, this should prove interesting. I would very much like to hear what this drak has to say, my husband."

Gavril cast a sidelong glance at his wife, sighing. "Very well, I shall indulge you." He leaned forward, turning his attention toward the draks. "You are fortunate my wife has a soft spot for your kind."

He clapped his hands. A servant appeared carrying a tray laden with goblets of wine. He took one, passed it to Princess Valene, then took one for himself. "We will hear Lord Reznik's tale of woe first."

Kale tapped Pancras's hand. The minotaur turned his attention to the drak. "Delilah should be here too. She was with Kali and me in the mine."

Pancras nodded, clearing his throat. "I beg your pardon, my lord, lady, Your Highnesses."

With an exaggerated sigh, Prince Gavril shifted his gaze to Pancras. "Yes?"

"I'm told there is one more drak that should be here for this."

"I will send a guard to fetch her, Your Highness." Milena bowed, then approached the throne room doors. She opened them a few inches to call to a guard, spoke to him briefly, then returned. "She should be along shortly."

"Proceed, Reznik."

Princess Valene cleared her throat. "If this other drak was involved, we should wait, my husband."

Lord Reznik huffed. He opened his mouth to speak, but a glare from Princess Valene was enough to stifle him. They waited in uncomfortable silence for the guard to fetch Delilah. Kale shifted from foot to foot, his claws clicking against the stone. Lord Reznik glared at the draks, but he kept his distance, cowed by Lady Milena's presence.

Pancras desperately wanted to know the history between the two nobles. Lord Reznik struck him as a bully, but he appeared thoroughly fearful of Lady Milena. The man's eyes widened, like a deer caught on the open road in the path of a runaway cart, whenever she adopted a threatening posture. When Kali rubbed her slung arm, Pancras noticed the wound on her shoulder. He hoped when this business was all over they would tell the whole story about the ghost they allegedly encountered.

***

Delilah sprinted behind the guard, following him to the throne room. When he knocked on the doors to their suite, she was so thoroughly engrossed in her grimoire, that it took a naked, dripping wet Edric shouting from the doorway of the bathing room to rouse her attention. Although the guard said only that Lady Milena and Pancras needed her, she decided not to waste time by sauntering there.

Upon the guard opening the doors, her stomach knotted at the sight of Kale alongside Kali and Pancras. Lady Milena stood between the draks and another human, a nobleman, she guessed, judging by his finery and fur-trimmed cloak. With a hand on her sword, Lady Milena stood at the ready, and her eyes regarded the man like a boggin waiting for a mouse to cross its path. Prince Gavril and Princess Valene were seated on their thrones, flanked by their guards.

"Ah, this must be the other drak." Princess Valene nudged her husband. "You may proceed, Lord Reznik."

Delilah stepped alongside Kale, then nudged him. "It's about time."

"SILENCE!" Prince Gavril half-stood, clutching the arms of his throne. "The draks will not speak until Lord Reznik has given his testimony."

Adjusting her grip on her staff, Delilah bowed her head in apology, then stepped behind Kale. She guessed the human would spin a tale of woe regarding violent, monstrous draks. She was not disappointed.

"Your Highnesses." Lord Reznik bowed. "I am a poor, humble businessman."

Princess Valene snorted.

He ignored her. "But the other day, a grievous assault was launched upon my mine. My workers were slaughtered, murdered by bloodthirsty draks. The mine's manager was so badly beaten, his own mother would not recognize him. Months of production wasted. Thousands of crowns of product ruined! And for what? To sate their appetite for mayhem, for destruction. I demand justice, beginning with the ringleader of these draks!" He pointed at Kali again. Kali snapped her teeth, leering. He flinched, snatching back his arm, despite the distance between them affording her no opportunity to follow through with her threat.

Princess Valene curled her upper lip. "Did you bring evidence of this slaughter?"

"Evidence? What… what sort of evidence?" It was clear Lord Reznik did not expect his claim to be challenged. "Volos carried a rod of office. We could not find it. I believe the draks took it as a prize. Search them!"

Delilah noticed Pancras shifting his weight to adjust his robes, pulling them across his legs. Kali stepped forward, spreading her cloak with her arm. "You're welcome to. Just watch where you touch my tail, Human."

"I think it's obvious she has nothing hidden on her." Princess Valene gestured to the advancing guard. "What else, Lord Reznik?" Kali returned to her original position.

"Is that not enough?" He clasped his hands behind his back.

"Identify yourself, Drak, and tell us your tale." Princess Valene gestured to Kali.

Kali stepped forward, taking a deep breath. "I am Kali Firescale, sometimes known as Blackclaw. Three hundred years ago, the leader of our clan, Elantan the Grim, made a pact with the ancestors of Lord Reznik. In exchange for the dissolution of our debt to him, we would supply workers for his salt mine. For three hundred years, his family kept us as slaves, taking more Firescales whenever it suited them, working them to death—"

"Slaves! Pah! You were paid a fair wage."

The guard to the right of Princess Valene stepped forward, leveling his spear at Lord Reznik. Princess Valene cocked an eyebrow in disapproval. "Kali Firescale has the floor now, Lord Reznik. You had your say."

Their intention to give audience to Kali surprised Delilah. She expected Lord Reznik's testimony to be taken at face value and Kali's to be dismissed.

"Yes, we were promised a wage. By the terms of the contract, two copper pennies a day. However, what Elantan failed to tell the rest of the clan leaders and what Lord Reznik and his ancestors kept from us was that we would have to pay for food, lodging, and equipment. These tallied tens of talons a week. Far more than we were earning! Our debt increased the more we worked."

Princess Valene ordered her guard back to his post. "It's not quite slavery if you were getting paid, but it certainly sounds like the terms were misleading. Anything else?"

Kali glared daggers at Lord Reznik. "Plenty. Draks were worked to death in starvation conditions. When too many died, men were sent to collect more from our villages in the mountains. Our villages are surrounded by human guards, making sure we're always ready to be pressed into service. I escaped with the hope of finding a way to free my people, and when I saw these two striped draks"—she gestured to Kale and Delilah—"I knew the time was right."

Delilah shifted, regarding the floor. She hoped Kali would make her case without involving Kale or her. Her brother spread his wings, reaching forward to take Kali's hand.

Kali glanced over her shoulder at Delilah. "Our elders tell us stories about striped draks. How they carry the favor of the gods. When Kale's wings grew while he was helping me, I knew it was a sign from Rannos that our victory was preordained."

Delilah suppressed a laugh. Kali was certainly aware that Kale's wings were completely unrelated to freeing the slaves. She hoped Pancras hadn't revealed to the prince or princess their true origins.

"This is utter nonsense." Lord Reznik took a step onto the dais. The guards adjusted their stances and readied their weapons. "These sla—The workers went on an unfounded, murderous rampage."

Prince Gavril nodded in agreement. "Well, certainly I'm not prepared to take the word of random draks who wandered in off the street over a member of this court."

Delilah withdrew from her pouch the papers she took from the mine. "You won't have to." She waved the records in the air. "I have documents here that show the wages the slaves were paid in addition to the expenses they were forced to bear." She hoped that's what the papers showed. She never took the time to verify what Kali and her father told her during their escape.

"Lady Milena, if you would?" Princess Valene gestured toward Delilah. The sorceress handed the papers to the knight. She leafed through them.

Lord Reznik spun on Delilah. "How did you acquire those?" Pointing a finger at her, he turned to Prince Gavril. "You see? Thievery! I am the victim of murderers and thieves!"

"The evidence of these documents is clear. The draks were paid insufficient wages to cover the expenses they were levied. One of these papers is a personal note from Lord Reznik addressed to the miners calling out Volos by name and referring to the miners as 'vermin slaves.'" Glaring, Lady Milena took a step toward Lord Reznik, then brought the papers to Princess Valene. The princess examined them, fighting to keep her ever darkening expression neutral.

When she finished reviewing them, contempt and disgust painted her face. Her lips formed a thin line, and her eyes flashed in anger. "Lord Reznik. Slavery is forbidden in Etrunia. This was clearly a slave revolt." She turned her glare on her husband.

Prince Gavril clucked his tongue. "I am shocked, Lord Reznik. Shocked, I tell you." He sighed an exaggerated display of contempt. "I suppose I must punish you." He yawned, waving his hand in the air. "You are hereby stripped of your titles, Reznik. Be gone."

Delilah snorted. A noble without a title was still a wealthy man. *He'll probably buy his way back into influence before the end of the year.* Kali stepped backward to her position alongside Kale. Delilah sneered as the female drak's tail intertwined with Kale's.

Reznik sputtered, turning his head to glare at the draks before snapping toward the prince and princess. When their eyes met, Delilah snarled.

Princess Valene stood. "Furthermore, I decree that your lands and properties are forfeit, to be sold at auction, the proceeds of which will be given to the draks of Firescale Clan as restitution for three centuries of mistreatment, and you are banished from Almeria, forthwith, upon pain of death." She sat down again, crossing her arms over her chest. "Although, execution of that sentence is commuted until such time that the roads out of town reopen. Lady Milena?"

Fixing her eyes on the princess, Delilah blinked as she replayed the princess's words in her head. A smile crept across her face. Reznik's bald head turned beet red, and Delilah thought she noticed a vein throbbing in his temple.

"Yes, Your Highness." The knight stood at attention.

"Escort Reznik back to his estate. He is permitted one change of clothing and sufficient funds to purchase lodging at a modest inn in town for the rest of the winter. See to the administration of his estate until the proper arrangements can be made and ensure Reznik's thugs are removed from the drak village as soon as possible. Take him away."

"It shall be done, Your Highness." Lady Milena bowed before seizing Reznik by the arm.

After snatching his arm away from her, Reznik spun to face Princess Valene. "This is an outrage! The Council of Nobles will hear of this. You will—"

Lady Milena stepped forward, drawing her sword and then laying it across Reznik's neck. "The Princess of Etrunia, a sovereign of Etrunia, has spoken. You have been dismissed. Exit with me or you will be carried out and left for the carrion eaters."

Reznick's mouth moved in wordless rage as he trembled. Lady Milena stared at him, setting her jaw. She might as well have been a statue, so unmoved was she by his outburst.

"Give me an excuse, Reznik."

Prince Gavril clucked his tongue. "You've been stripped of your lands and titles Reznik. Milena is the captain of the Royal Guard. You know no one will question her if she runs you through right here. Not after what you did."

Throwing up his hands, Reznik stalked out of the throne room. Kali cheered, hugging Kale. She reached over his shoulder to pull Delilah into an arm-crushing group hug. Kale's wing slapped Delilah's face as she tried to extract herself from the tangle of arms, wings, and tails.

"Now, all of you except the minotaur, get out!" Prince Gavril stood and pointed toward the doors. "Minotaur, come with me. I wish to speak to you."

***

Once they returned to their living quarters, Kale no longer could contain himself. He whooped and hollered, alternately jumping up and down and hugging Kali. She nuzzled his neck, nipping at his ears as their tails intertwined.

"You know, I'm happy, too, but do you have to do that out in the open?" Delilah shoved her brother as she passed. She picked up her grimoire, then flopped into her armchair.

Kale felt his face become hot. "Sorry, Deli."

"What in the name of Pacha's blue bollocks is going on—" Edric stepped out of the unused bedchamber, his jaw dropping upon seeing Kale and Kali. "By the burnin' hearth of Adranus… now there's three of them, and one 'em's got wings!"

"Edric!" Kale crossed the room to hug the dwarf. For the first time since they knew each other, Kale noticed the dwarf actually smelled clean. To Kale's amazement, the dwarf had groomed his beard, and he wore clean, albeit threadbare, clothes.

"Enough, enough." Edric pushed Kale away. He shuffled over to the other armchair and sat down next to Delilah. "How do we get ale around here?"

Kale approached the food lift, and then he pulled aside the tapestry. While the light streaming through the windows faded, it felt too early yet for dinner. He rang the service bell, opening the door. The lift and tray were still down in the kitchens.

He stuck his head in the hole. "Hey, send up ale with dinner!" His request met with cursing.

"Fancy system you have here." Kali carried a chair from the table over to Delilah and Edric to join them in front of the fire.

"So, spill it. Don't leave me wandering in the dark like an elf underground. What's all this I hear about a mine and slaves and fighting that I wasn't a part of?"

Kale brought over a chair setting it in front of the hearth. "It's Kali's story, really. Deli and I were just helping." With Kali already seated in between Delilah and Edric, Kale had to settle for the space next to his sister or the one next to Edric. He chose the one near his sister.

Delilah closed her book. "Miss Drak there tricked us into helping with her little slave revolt. Once I realized what she was up to, it was too late to back out."

"Deli, that's not really fair." Kale placed his hand on Delilah's arm. She shook him off.

Kali held up her hands. "No. No, she's right. I did deceive you initially. I didn't know if I could trust you. My people went through a lot. I didn't survive by being stupid."

Turning her head, Delilah glared at Kali. "It didn't strike you as stupid to deceive a sorceress?"

Kali turned her hands palms up and smiled, shrugging. "I didn't know how powerful you were. Do you know how many hedge wizards wander through town trying to pass off peasant tricks as high sorcery? Until I saw you in action, I had no way of knowing whether or not you were drunk on Pacha's wine."

Kale chuckled. Delilah had a point about Kali keeping the truth from them, but when it really mattered, she was forthright. Personally, he didn't mind helping; it beat sitting around in the palace watching his sister read all day.

"My brother likes you a lot more than I do." Delilah hopped down out of her chair. "Next time, just tell me the truth." Carrying her grimoire into the bedchamber, she slammed the door behind her.

Kale seized the opportunity to trade the dining chair for the much softer armchair. Kali climbed in with him. It was snug for the two of them to sit in it together, but she seemed to want the physical contact. It reminded Kale of when he and Delilah used to sleep cuddled together as hatchlings.

"So, fine. You want to mount her, and your sister hates her." Edric kicked his legs against the chair. "Now tell me what bloody happened!"

Kali told Edric the story of her clan, how they were duped into working in the mines, and how she conspired to free them. She told him of Kale and Delilah's involvement. With rapt attention, Kale watched her tell the tale.

"And now that we've freed the slaves, Kali is going with us to Muncifer!" Kale squeezed Kali's hand. Edric wrinkled his nose, scratching through his beard to his chin.

"That's still the plan, eh? A change of scenery might be good. I don't think I can go back to the gambling houses here anyway."

"I've never been to Muncifer." Kali squeezed Kale's hand in return.

"Neither have we, me and Deli, I mean. Pancras is from there, I think. He and Deli have to go there for some business with the Arcane University." Tired of Almeria, Kale wanted to get back on the road. He wished Delilah could magic up some good weather for them to travel.

"I heard Muncifer was a dwarven city before the Sundering." Edric yawned. "When the world cracked, the mountains split open and exposed it. Most of the dwarves died. Then, when the world healed, the city remained on the surface, and minotaurs repaired it. Now it's mostly humans and minotaurs, but I think there are a couple of drak clans living in the area too. No more dwarves, though."

Kale cocked his head. "You'll be the only dwarf there?" That sounded sad. Kale wasn't sure he would want to live where he was the only one of his kind.

"Nah, of course not. There will be dwarves there, but they'll be immigrants, probably. Just like the minotaurs and draks here, right?" Edric moved to stand when the bell rang from the food lift. After extracting himself from Kali, Kale set the platters and pitchers on the table. Delilah emerged from her self-imposed exile to help. The smell of food ignited a hunger Kale wasn't aware he had. The last meal he consumed was when they broke their fasts that morning, and the excitement of the day kept his mind off food. Now that it was in front of him, he couldn't wait to dig in.

***

Pancras followed Prince Gavril to his antechamber as the three draks headed back to their living quarters. Because he knew the topic the prince likely wanted to discuss, he formulated his response as they strode.

The minotaur spent a lot of time thinking about how to solve Prince Gavril's problem and an equal time calculating how to make it appear he fulfilled the prince's request without actually rendering Princess Valene barren. The only sure conclusion he had reached thus far was that he needed more time.

Prince Gavril shut the door behind them, then sat in an armchair. Flickering candlelight cast sinister shadows that danced over his eyes like dark faeries on a midsummer's night. Drumming his fingers on the arm of his chair, he eyed Pancras. "All right, enough of this nonsense with the draks. What is your status?"

Bowing, Pancras cleared his throat. "I've taken my research as far as I can with the limited resources I've been able to access and given the storms we've had. I have acquired the materials and equipment I need to begin some rudimentary work, but I would like to verify a few ideas with the priests of Cybele, discretely, of course, before finalizing anything."

The prince leaned forward. "Do you have a time schedule?"

"Three to four weeks minimum, possibly more if additional storms come and I'm unable to procure additional materials in a timely fashion." In truth, Pancras could perform all the experiments he wanted to conduct in about a week, but he counted on Prince Gavril's ignorance of wizardry to pull off his deception.

"Acquire the materials now before the next storm."

"I would, if I knew what I needed. This is not an exact science. I am attempting to replicate a very messy, obvious effect in a way that leaves no outside traces. I'm essentially creating new magic so this affliction cannot be traced back to you." *Or me.*

"Well, what does all this entail?" Prince Gavril furrowed his brow. Pancras almost saw the gears grinding in the prince's head.

"Currently, it appears the method with the most promise is a fetish of some sort, to be inserted into the va—subject. It will release its magic, rendering her—"

"She'll have to insert it?"

"Or you. I think it would be inappropriate if I did it. There would be talk." Pancras suppressed a chuckle at the thought of having such an intimate encounter with Princess Valene. He didn't find women attractive, and human women possessed far too little fur for his taste and lacked horns or hooves. Human feet always made Pancras squirm.

"There is no other way?" Prince Gavril chewed on his fingernail. He rose from his chair, then paced the room.

"None that I am aware of at this time. Further research may prove illuminating." If Prince Gavril was as squeamish as he suspected about touching his wife, Pancras hoped he would be more open to slower progress.

"Then do the research you need." Gavril spun, sweeping his cloak behind him. "But finish before you're scheduled to leave. You need to go to Muncifer, yes? I will not allow your departure until your task for me is complete."

Pancras borrowed a phrase from Lady Milena, bowing. "It shall be done, Your Highness."

Chapter 19

It took several days after the reckoning of Reznik before the five occupants of the suite learned to accommodate each other's routines. With the addition of Edric and Kali, the living quarters were too busy for Delilah's taste, and she took to carrying her grimoire out to one of the vacant sitting rooms to study.

She never saw servants tending the hearths in these sitting rooms, but a roaring fire always waited for her. Delilah suspected it was some sort of enchantment. Ever-burning torches were not unheard of in Drak-Anor, and she supposed that same magic could be adapted to keep a hearth burning eternally for someone with sufficient wealth.

Reading in front of a crackling fire relaxed her, and she found herself often dozing while she studied her grimoire. She learned to hold the book in such a way that it wouldn't drop onto the floor if she accidentally fell asleep, and the armchair ensconced her comfortably when she truly wanted to curl into a ball and nap. There was no place for Kali to sleep except in the bed she and Kale shared, and while draks were used to sleeping together in groups, Delilah had become accustomed to solitude or only her brother's presence at most. It was a good day for a nap.

She awoke to several guards reaching for her. Before she could cry out or move, they grabbed her snout and arms, lifting her bodily out of the chair. Another guard bound her legs. Despite squirming and her best efforts to wrench herself free, the humans overpowered her. They wrapped leather straps around her snout to muzzle her before putting a sack over her head. After they bound her hands, they carried her out of the sitting room.

Because Delilah spent much of her life navigating dimly-lit underground passageways, she could visualize the route they took even though she couldn't see. They navigated several sets of stairs down near what smelled like the kitchens and larder. The next staircase took them into an area Delilah did not immediately recognize. She concluded, from the musky, stale odor that permeated the vicinity, she had been taken to the undercroft.

The men stopped, whispering amongst themselves. After pushing her up against a cold, stone wall, they raised her hands above her head, then locked them in shackles. She tried to shout at them through the muzzle and sack, but they ignored her and left. In the distance she heard the drip-drip-drip of water and the sound of a door being shut and locked.

Delilah felt the tendons and ligaments in her arms stretching as she hung. In time, first her shoulders ached, then her arms. Leaning back, she rested the top of her head against unyielding stone, but letting it hang forward stretched the muscles in her already aching neck. Initially, her legs felt free, but when she tried to move them, she realized shackles held them too.

Despite twisting and turning, Delilah found no relief from her discomfort, and the muscle fatigue brought pain. Tears welled in her eyes, and even though she tried to remain calm, her breathing became quick and labored. *What did I do? Did Volos work for the princess?*

The sack over her head allowed no light to enter, and in the pitch black, she had no means of keeping track of time apart from the dripping water. She became keenly aware of the dryness in her throat, as well as her need to relieve herself, an urge brought to the forefront by the incessant drip-drip-drip.

Kale. Kale, hear me! Delilah had heard stories of twins who shared an almost telepathic mental connection. Acknowledging the act of reaching out to her brother in her mind as one of desperation, Delilah thanked Rannos no one could see her blush in embarrassment. Often she empathized with her brother, and sometimes they finished each other's sentences when their minds were on the same track, but she never thought they had a psychic connection.

At any rate, she didn't hear back from Kale. Delilah felt as if her arms would pop out of their sockets, and knives of fire sliced the muscles in her shoulder. Her muscles trembled with fatigue, and she felt her tears soaking into the sackcloth around her neck.

Finally, the door opened. She heard several pairs of footsteps approaching, as well as one pair of what sounded like hooves on stone. She lifted her head in hope. *Pancras?*

"As you can see, we have one of your draks." The voice belonged to Princess Valene. "I know you are plotting something with my husband, Pancras. I also know threatening your life will have no effect. So, I offer you this: the truth for the life of this drak. Tell me what you're plotting, or I will kill Delilah."

***

Pancras winced at the sight of Delilah hanging in shackles from the wall. A guard positioned near the drak pointed his spear at her chest. Princess Valene, with Lady Milena alongside her, crossed her arms, awaiting his response.

Pancras licked his lips, reaching up to worry his right horn. In response, the guards around him raised their spears, but Lady Milena gestured for them to stand down.

The minotaur lowered his hands. "First, I will have you know I hold you in the highest regard, and it was never my intention to bring harm to you. I would like to know if you have mistreated my friend in any way before I answer."

"Fair enough. I will show you, because I like you." Princess Valene gestured to the guard nearest Delilah. He pulled the sack off the drak's head. Delilah blinked her eyes. Dark lines stained her cheeks where tears had fallen, but she appeared otherwise uninjured. He noted the muzzle straps wrapped around her mouth. *A wise precaution.*

Delilah's eyes followed him as he paced the room, as did the spears of the guards. "You may not want everyone to know what I am about to tell you, Highness. If you doubt the loyalty of anyone in this room, you may wish to send them away."

Princess Valene considered Pancras's words. Her eyes flicked to Lady Milena and then to Pancras. "Very well. Guards, leave us. Lady Milena will protect me." The guards hesitated until Lady Milena nodded her assent.

Pancras waited until after the guards exited and Lady Milena closed and locked the door behind them before he approached Delilah, laying his hand on her cheek. Her eyes pleaded with him. It didn't matter to him if she wanted him to stay silent and sacrifice her or tell the truth to relieve her suffering. He couldn't bear contributing to her pain.

"Your husband's deal with me was this: my freedom, and that of the draks, in exchange for a hex to render you barren." He sighed, letting his hand slip away from Delilah's cheek. He turned to face the princess, to look her in the eye. "I have been stalling for a few weeks now, trying to develop a way to make it look like that's what I was doing but without bringing any actual harm to you."

"Indeed?" Princess Valene clasped her hands behind her back. She eyed Pancras, her emerald eyes flashing in the dim light. "I am to believe this?"

"You asked for the truth. He seeks legitimate grounds for divorce, grounds that will enable him to remain in power and seek a new wife, one who is more… open to his advances."

Lady Milena jerked her head up, fixing her eyes on the princess. "Do you think—"

"Silence!" Princess Valene paced, moving her lips in silent thought. "A mistress, were she made public, would cause him to forfeit his wealth." She stopped face to face with Pancras. "What is your plan?"

Pancras shuffled his hooves, regarding the ground. "I don't have one yet."

"We need to force him to show his hand, to reveal his plot. No one will believe the testimony of one minotaur, and an outsider at that." Lady Milena stepped alongside Princess Valene and took her hands. The princess pulled them away from the knight, shaking her head.

"I could confront him, in front of the court." Pancras didn't like the thought of sticking his neck out, but he didn't see any other options at the moment. "He'd likely order my death right then and there. I want protection."

"Some of the Royal Guards are more loyal to me than to him."

Lady Milena nodded. "I could ensure all who served that day were loyal to you."

Pancras glanced at Delilah. "Do you suppose you could release my friend? I will cooperate with you fully. I swear on my life I will."

Princess Valene resumed her pacing. "Very well. Milena, help him."

Lady Milena and Pancras worked at freeing Delilah from her restraints. She whimpered when Pancras moved her arms to free them from the wall.

"His reaction would be key. He is not a man of even temperament, and it is unlikely he could control his reaction to an extent that would conceal his true mind."

Pancras knelt to remove Delilah's muzzle, but she threw her arms around his neck, hugging him before he accomplished his task. When finally she was freed, she opened her mouth to speak, but she managed only a hoarse whisper.

The minotaur glanced toward the princess. "I've found it impossible to rely on what you think someone's reaction will be."

"I could tell my guards to watch him closely. See if he has already chosen a mistress to replace you, Highness." Lady Milena untied the restraints securing Delilah's feet.

"I doubt he'd be foolish enough to keep her in the palace. If he leaves, however, it would be best if you would attempt to put a loyal man on his retinue of guards."

Taking Delilah's hand in his, Pancras met her gaze. "I am so sorry this happened. I tried to keep you and your brother uninvolved. You weren't supposed to get hurt."

"It was nothing personal… Delilah, was it?"

The drak sorceress narrowed her eyes, baring her teeth at the princess. Pancras squeezed her shoulder.

Princess Valene paid no heed to Delilah's response. "I needed the truth from Pancras. If you need a healer, one can be arranged." Princess Valene pulled Lady Milena aside. "Pancras is not to leave the palace until we have arrived at a solution."

"What?" He stood up, then faced the princess. "I may need additional supplies to continue the ruse."

"Send your draks to retrieve them. I have a feeling keeping them confined to the palace is more trouble than it's worth."

"What—" Delilah croaked, "What about Dusan and Mirek?"

Princess Valene cocked her head at Lady Milena.

"The two guards I assigned to escort the draks into town."

The princess nodded her understanding. "They won't be needed. I do not believe the draks will abandon Pancras here." She eyed the minotaur, the drak, and the Captain of the Royal Guard in turn. "I needn't say this, but I will anyway: speak of this to no one. Lady Milena, you will be our liaison. I have the utmost faith in you."

Lady Milena saluted, bowing as Princess Valene left the room. She escorted Pancras and Delilah out of the dungeon and back up to their living quarters. Delilah tugged at Pancras's sleeve to get his attention before they opened the doors.

"My grimoire. I think it was left behind in the sitting room where the guards captured me."

"Which one? I can retrieve it for you." Lady Milena dropped to one knee to meet Delilah at eye level.

"I'd prefer to get it myself."

Pancras understood Delilah's trepidation in allowing someone else to retrieve the grimoire for her. Handling powerful books of magic could be dangerous for the lay person, and there was no guarantee Milena would recognize it for what it was.

"Very well. I insist on escorting you. Most of the guards are probably aware you were taken to the dungeons. Not all will yet be aware that you have been released. It's safer if I'm with you."

Delilah hesitated, glancing up at Pancras before exiting. Lady Milena stood, then followed her.

Pancras headed to the suite. Standing outside the entry doors, he straightened and smoothed his robes before entering the parlor. Kale, Edric, and Kali sat in a circle in the center of the large rug playing a dice game. Kale glanced up when Pancras entered.

"Is everything all right? Where's Deli?"

Pancras jerked his thumb toward the door. "Everything's fine. We just had a minor emergency. Delilah had to leave her grimoire behind, so she's retrieving it. She'll be along shortly." To Pancras's relief, Kale accepted the explanation and didn't inquire further.

By the time Delilah returned with her grimoire, dinner arrived, and they ate while listening to Kali and Edric one-up each other with the outlandishness of their stories. After dinner, Pancras elected to retire early. After shutting the door to his bedchamber behind him, he sorted through all the materials he acquired to create the cursed fetish for Prince Gavril. He decided to create some sort of protective fetish instead, in case their plan to confront the prince about his plot went awry.

Pancras familiarized himself with the abjurations required to create such protective objects during his studies in necromancy at the Arcane University. Wizards often used these amulets to protect themselves from the various evil forces they sought to control. Although the undead Pancras created were always mindless, and so less dangerous that intelligent undead, he still lost control on occasion, particularly in his youth.

After a thorough examination of his supplies, he picked up a quill, ink, and paper. He had acquired sufficient equipment already, but he would need different materials and reagents. Smiling to himself, he wrote a list for Kale and Delilah, feeling confident the situation would improve now that he had the support of the princess.

***

Over the next several days, the weather remained pleasant, though cold. Most streets were sufficiently cleared of snow as to be passable, and Kale and Delilah reveled in their newfound freedom to come and go from the palace as they pleased.

Upon splitting Pancras's list between them, Delilah and Edric searched the marketplace for the esoteric reagents and materials, while Kale and Kali searched for the more common items. Most humans and minotaurs they encountered gawked at Kale's wings, their stares making his skin crawl. Despite the discomfort they caused while they grew and difficulties attaining comfortable sitting and sleeping positions, he liked his wings. In Drak-Anor, he never felt like he stood out as an individual. He was always "Delilah's brother." Feeling pride in possessing a unique attribute, he interpreted the stares from townsfolk as envy.

The four met for lunch at one of the taverns near the marketplace, relishing the variety of meat-filled pastries served there. After lunch, Delilah wanted to return to the palace. "I'll take all this stuff back to Pancras. Keep out of trouble, and come back at dusk. I don't want to have to come looking for you."

Kale dismissed her concerns with a snort. None of the plans he and Kali made involved danger, and they all agreed to keep Edric out of gambling dens. "Yeah, yeah, we won't be much longer. I just have one more errand to run for Pancras, and then we'll be back."

The minotaur had given Kale the old tips he used to wear on his horns. He wanted them melted down and remade. The process of melting them would release the magical energy that bound them to Pancras, so that the gold could be fashioned into ornamental tips. Kale wasn't sure he liked the idea of releasing magical energy, but both Delilah and Pancras assured him it would be perfectly safe. Still, they counseled him not to mention anything about wizardry to the jeweler and to commission new ones if he had to, using the old ones as trade if they couldn't be reused.

"I need the best jeweler in town, Kali." Kale patted his pouch feeling the gold horn tips within it.

"That would be Icos the Elder in the Foundry District. They say he can see a fly's footprint on a rock and has the steadiest hands in Etrunia. I know the way."

"I'll bet he can't hold a candle to a dwarven jeweler." Edric tossed a silver talon to a vendor selling ale and picked up two bottles from the snowbank.

"Well, I don't know any dwarves making jewelry in Almeria, so old Icos will have to do." Kali led the way, exiting the marketplace. They made their way through the snow-covered streets toward the Foundry District.

Although his wide-brimmed hat adequately shielded his eyes from the sunlight above, he squinted to keep snow glare from blinding him. Enjoying the warmth of the sunlight against the brisk winter air, Kale spread his wings to increase the surface area upon which the rays of the sun fell. The changes he incurred passing through the chaos rift seemed to be permanent, and he found he enjoyed never feeling cold. He pitied the people who required heavy cloaks and coats in order to function at even a basic level in severe weather. By the way they all complained about it, even bundled up, they never felt warm enough.

Kali took them down a familiar road. He recognized the signs of the Sleeping Viper and the Assassin's Dagger ahead. Upon turning down an alley across the street from the tavern, they found themselves in snow as high as their hips. Kale pushed ahead of Kali and Edric. With every step forward, the heat from his body melted a path for them to follow.

Icos the Elder's shop protruded from the side of a dwelling as if the builders changed their mind about the design of the building halfway through its construction. Featuring its own entry door separate from that of the residence, the tower climbed to the second floor of the structure. A conical roof hung over the row of tall windows composing most of the second floor wall.

Kale heard a bell at the top of the door jingling as they entered. Sitting cross-legged in a chair near the entrance, a grey-furred minotaur chewed on the end of a long-stemmed pipe. His horns curved up and outward, reaching half-again the height of his head. Flicking his ears toward the newcomers, he turned to face them.

"Are you Icos?" Kale removed the horn tips from his pouch.

"The Elder." The minotaur's smooth baritone voice sounded like it belonged to a much younger individual.

"I have some jewelry that needs to be remade."

Removing his pipe from his mouth, the minotaur stood. He held out his hand, casting an eye toward Edric. "Mind you don't touch anything, Dwarf. Most of these creations are works-in-progress for paying customers."

Kali pulled Edric away from the jeweler's workbench. Kale dropped the horn tips into Icos's open palm. Grunting, the minotaur weighed them in his hand. He moved to the workbench, clopping across the wooden floor. After tossing the pipe onto the bench, he held up one of the horn tips, peering into it.

"Where'd you get these, huh? I can feel the magic in them."

Kale wasn't sure how to respond. Pancras didn't say anything about the possibility someone might detect their arcane characteristics. "My minotaur friend's a wizard. He doesn't need those anymore but wants another pair that's similar and just ornamental. You know, to put over the tips of his horns."

"Hm. Vain fellow." He blew into the gold tip, then tapped it against his own horn. "What does he want, exactly?"

"Something fancier, I think. But no dangly bits." Kale improvised. Pancras instructed him only to have them melted down and recreated. Kale figured Pancras still wanted to appear well-dressed, even if he no longer used them as his arcane focus.

"I can do some embellishments. Maybe some rose gold in a knot pattern or a rope pattern. Give me a week. Pay half now."

Kale nodded, reaching into his pouch. Pancras had given him some gemstones to use with the hope that a jeweler would accept them as payment. He fished around before withdrawing a rough, translucent forest-green gem. "Will you take this in trade?"

"Hm? Give me that." He took the rough gem from Kale. "Do you know what this is?" He hefted the fist-sized rock in his hand before examining it using equipment on his workbench.

"Not really. Emerald, maybe?"

"No. Looks like a kind of garnet. This is worth far more than the work I'm going to do."

"Oh, well," Kale dug in his pouch. He found a handful of crowns and twice as many talons, but nothing in between. "I don't have enough crowns, probably. I can bring something else later. I have more, just not with me."

Icos set the stone on his workbench. "I'll hang onto this as a deposit. Bring me three hundred crowns, or the equivalent, when you pick this up, and I'll give you the new tips and this one back."

Kale noticed Kali gesturing to him, but he ignored her. "Fine. I'll be back in a week."

Holding up his hand, Icos spread his fingers. "Five days is fine."

Later, after they left the shop, Kali seized Kale's arm. "Are you insane? That rock was probably thousands of crowns! You'll never see it again!"

"That's what Pancras gave me to pay with." Kale shrugged. "Icos will give it back when I come back with real money." His expertise was in locksmithing and trap-building, not gemology and jewelry. "Let's get back. I'm getting hungry."

***

Delilah, pleased they acquired everything Pancras needed in one trip, hummed to herself on her way to the palace. Kale,

Kali, and Edric could spend their remaining time in town throwing dice or visiting all the taverns in Almeria for all she cared as long as she could resume her study of the grimoire. The business with the salt mine and Pancras's plotting with the prince or the princess distracted her from learning the lessons contained in her gift from the Earth Dragon.

She felt on the verge of discovering the trick behind silent casting, if only people would stop interrupting her study time. The grimoire revealed its images to her swiftly now, and she lost herself in it after concentrating only a minute or two on a page.

Images of the battle returned. Drawing a dagger over her palm, Gil Li closed her eyes. When she opened them, Delilah noticed they glowed red. Gil Li made a fist, then squeezed blood through her fingers. Her enemies exploded in clouds of blood and gore. Upon raising her arms in triumph, fire and lightning raged around her. The image shifted.

A crowd of humans and draks cheered at Gil-Li riding a horse down the street. Suddenly, a rock flew from the crowd, striking her in the head. After touching the wound, she stared at her blood-covered fingers. She pointed at the mob, in the direction from which the rock came. Seeking to punish her tormenter, she unleashed a ray of fire into the crowd. The man who threw the rock tried to flee, but Gil-Li burned his legs with fire. When he fell to the ground, screaming in agony, she struck him again and again and again with lightning, electrocuting him until nothing but a charred corpse remained. Ovation from the people shifted to screams of outrage and fear. Gil-Li destroyed them all, calling down fire and lightning from the sky until nothing survived.

The image shifted again. Endless graves surrounded Gil-Li, and rain deluged around her. The drak fell to her knees. Then, the image of Gil-Li in the graveyard grew distant, revealing the scorched plain that surrounded it.

The message the grimoire conveyed was clear.

Delilah turned the page. The letters and markings before her swirled together, forming a new set of images. Gil-Li faced yet another shadowy assailant. Her tattoos glowed, and tendrils of blue, red, gold, and green aether surrounded her like a rainbow whirlwind. Moving her lips while weaving her arms, she traced a knotwork pattern in the air before her. Wispy aetheric tendrils trailed her movements, until spikes of earth, erupting from the ground, impaled her attackers. The image shifted, focusing on Gil-Li's lips as she chanted. While studying the image, Delilah tried to mimic the patterns Gil-Li's mouth made.

"A… koda… geo… sea…" She had not quite deciphered the words of Gil Li's incantation. Understanding the consequences of not using the precise words exactly as Gil-Li said them, she continued to study the movement of her lips. The wrong intonation risked yielding no result or a catastrophic failure. "That's not quite right, Deli-girl." It had been a while since Delilah mastered new arcane effects. Most of what she knew she had taught herself from scrolls and books liberated from invaders of their home before the foundation of Drak-Anor.

"A… kida… geo… sis." The words felt closer but still not right. She nodded, glad she had not channeled arcane energy while trying to mimic Gil-Li's incantation. Mispronunciation in the heat of the moment killed many hedge wizards and other self-taught practitioners of the arcane arts.

"Akeeda! That's it! Akeeda… something. Gee… oh— Geiosis!" Every fiber of her being told Delilah she got it right. She *knew* it. She felt excited, but disappointed at the same time. The snow cover would make any demonstration she might offer less than impressive, and she doubted either the prince or the princess would appreciate her tearing up the palace grounds just to show off.

After a month of diligent study, her dedication to the grimoire paid off. She learned different magic than that to which she was accustomed. She snapped the book shut and hopped off the chair, running off to tell Pancras or Kale about her accomplishment. *Some things are just too good to keep to yourself!*

***

The needle darted in and out, trailing shimmery, silken thread as Pancras sewed the final stitches. Oblong, phallic, and almost obscene, the fetish looked the part it would play. He hoped the abjurations with which he planned to infuse it would hold. The construction of arcane fetishes was an exact art. One suitable for necromantic curses would, more often than not, not function for protective abjurations such as one might use to defend a child. The structure he incorporated in the interior of the fetish would prove more important than its outward cosmetic appearance.

Upon hearing a thud followed by cursing outside his bedchamber, he jabbed his finger with the needle, flinching when the commotion interrupted his concentration. He laid the fetish on the table. Sucking on the injured digit, he entered the parlor to see what the commotion was about.

He found Delilah sprawled on the floor with her legs tangled with Edric's and Kale's. Her grimoire lay open, face down not far from her. Kali regarded the writhing pile of limbs as she held her snout shut with her hands, her quivering sides betraying her laughter.

"Is everything all right out here?"

"Stupid Kale and Edric!" Delilah extracted herself from the pile, then retrieved her grimoire. "I return with news, and they're in the middle of the floor doing… something!"

"We were wrestling, Deli. Edric said even with my wings, no drak could pull down a dwarf who braced himself."

Rising, the dwarf dusted himself off. "It wasn't a fair contest. Yer sister interfered."

"I had you. You were going down even before she ran into us!"

Pancras tried to ignore their bickering over whether Kale won the contest. He turned to Delilah. "You have news?"

She held the grimoire aloft. "I did it! I actually learned something from this book!"

The news didn't surprise Pancras, but Delilah's enthusiasm about it did. "I should think an ancient tome like that holds many secrets in its pages."

"Earth magic, Pancras. You don't understand. This isn't like reading a set of instructions. It showed me how to make spikes of rock erupt under my enemies!"

"Earth magic? Are you sure? I thought it was lost during the Sundering."

She opened the book, then set it on the table. Pancras leaned forward to examine it. Instead of finding arcane text, however, the swirling patterns and eddies he saw made no sense to him. Even a brief glance threatened to make his head throb and vision swim.

"Does it always look like that?" Pancras had never encountered a tome so ensorcelled, but he trusted the Earth Dragon not to confer a gift if it were harmful.

"Until you learn how to concentrate and look at what the pages are trying to show you." She turned the page to share another set of swirling, shifting symbols. Blinking to clear his vision, he placed his hand on her shoulder. "I'm sure you will unlock all its secrets in time."

His eyes returned to the grimoire, as if drawn to it. *A tome of lost magic*—The bell on the food lift rang, signifying the arrival of another dinnertime. For a brief moment, Pancras considered returning to work, but the tight rumble in his belly reminded him he had been working nonstop since breaking his fast that morning.

Edric's bravado dominated their meal. It was obvious to Pancras that everyone had been indoors for far too long. He wished for some way to speed up time or alter the weather so they could be on their way again; yet what awaited him in Muncifer filled him with trepidation. Traveling on the open road was one of his least favorite activities, but Almeria, snow, and political scheming wore him down.

He put the final touches on his fetish before turning in for the evening. The ritual to infuse it would start tomorrow. He hoped the draks and the dwarf would allow him some uninterrupted peace for however long it would take.

Chapter 20

The next day, Pancras kicked them all out after their morning meal. He handed each of them twenty talons. "I need to be free from interruptions for the rest of the day. I don't want anyone coming in here until after dusk!"

"What are we supposed to do all day?" Kale dropped the silver coins into his pouch with a satisfying jingle.

"Drink, gamble, go to the market. I don't care!" He shut the door, then locked it.

Edric counted the coins in his hand, put them in his pouch, and saluted as he left them. "I know just the place. I'll come back with triple his money!"

"Fat chance of that." Kali snorted, shoving the coins in her pouch. She regarded the twins. "Well?"

Delilah held up her book. "I am going to study."

"Oh, come on! We have all day and sixty talons between the three of us." Kali pulled on Delilah's arm. "Don't be boring."

Delilah dropped her coins into Kale's hand. "Sixty talons between the two of you. You'll thank me when I unlock magic that will enable me to teleport us all to Muncifer with the snap of my fingers."

Kale took hold of his sister's arm. She pulled against him, but the combined might of Kale and Kali kept her in place. "You really need to stop touching me, both of you."

"Deli! Take a day off! There's so much of Almeria we haven't seen yet."

Delilah shook herself loose. "Go jump off a tower!"

Inspired by Delilah's suggestion, Kale ran past her. "If I jump off the wall, will you come with us?"

"What? Are you insane?"

Shaking his head, Kale spread his wings. "I've been practicing." He lied, hoping Delilah didn't see through his deception. He climbed up on top of the wall, holding onto a column to steady himself. When a gust of wind threatened to catch his hat and blow it off, he handed it to Kali. "I'll be back in a flash!"

The snowy ground seemed much farther away now that he stood above it, preparing to throw himself off the palace wall. *I can't back out now. I'll look really stupid.* After stepping away from the column, he shuffled sideways giving himself enough room to extend his wings to their full span. Kale inhaled the brisk morning air. The chill lingered, burning in his lungs.

Then he jumped.

For a moment, Calliome rushed toward him, promising to envelop him in powdery white fluff before thrashing him against the unyielding ground. Arresting his fall, a gust of wind caught his wings, stretching their leathery skin like sails on a ship. He soared on the current, gaining altitude. Almeria's zigzagging city streets, low district walls, and plains beyond the high city walls lay before him like a relief map painted white.

People in the streets pointed at him. Waving, he banked, wheeling one hundred eighty degrees to return to the palace. Flapping his wings propelled him higher aloft. Soon, his back tightened with fatigue from taxing barely used muscles, and the palace seemed far beyond his reach. When he could no longer flap his wings fast enough to maintain altitude, he descended rapidly.

Kale plowed into snow drifts in the palace garden, showering a plume of white powder into the air. Although he tucked and rolled, his forward momentum propelled him head over tail through the icy precipitate. Slamming to a stop into the base of a snow-covered fountain, he viewed the frozen waterfall pouring from the cherub's vase, a moment suspended in time. The snow hissed, steaming, as his body melted its way to the ground, ultimately, leaving him in a soggy, muddy puddle.

***

Wide-eyed, Delilah and Kali watched Kale jump, drop, and then soar above Almeria. Kale waved at someone in the street below, whom Delilah imagined noticed the creature flying above was clearly not a bird. It surprised her when the guards in the watchtowers didn't shoot arrows at him. He plummeted right after turning toward the palace.

Kali ran toward the staircase. Delilah followed, witnessing her brother crash into the ground in a cloud of snow. They stumbled down the stairs in their rush to reach Kale, pausing only for the guards to open the palace doors.

When they reached him, they found Kale sitting in a puddle of mud at the base of a fountain. His wing tips were drooping, and he rubbed the top of his head.

"Are you hurt?" Delilah offered him a hand, then pulled him up.

"Not really." He regarded his muddy feet, shaking off the muck.

"I brought your hat." Giggling, Kali handed it to him.

He put it on his head, sighing. "I almost had it there for a minute."

Delilah wanted to berate him for being irresponsible enough to jump off the palace wall, but she reconsidered. *It may have been foolish, but he got me outside like he wanted.* She patted his shoulder. "I'm sure you'll figure it out with practice."

"I guess I should practice more while there's still snow, huh? I imagine crashing into the ground once it all melts will hurt a lot more."

"Yes, but not today." Delilah pulled up the hood of her cloak. "You wanted me outside, so here I am. Where are we going?"

Kali put her arms around the twins. "I know this place in Old Town. It's run by a drak, and she makes the most amazing pies. Meat pies, sweet pies, you'll be in Cybele's Pastures with one bite."

***

With the draks and Edric out from underhoof, Pancras relished the quiet. He briefly considered bathing and spending the entire day drinking wine in front of a crackling fire, but he decided to be true to his purpose and complete the fetish. It was crucial to their plan to expose Prince Gavril, and he didn't want to be the weak link in the chain.

Shutting the door behind him, Pancras approached his makeshift workbench and set the fetish upon it. Aesthetically, it revolted him. The more he looked at it, the more he thought it resembled a dried-up piece of excrement. The art of creating an aesthetically pleasing fetish was not something in which Pancras was skilled; he crafted magic, not art. However, it needn't look pretty to do its job.

Pancras picked up the fetish, holding it like one of the hollowed-out, painted bird eggs artisans sold at Muncifer's spring market. He prepared himself to begin the painstaking and time-consuming task of infusing it with arcane energy. Closing his eyes, he concentrated, but despite his best effort, Pancras did not feel the threads of aether.

His eyes snapped open, and, chuckling, he picked up his rod. He was not yet accustomed to consciously holding his arcane focus. Pancras closed his eyes, then tried again.

Arcane energies flowed through his focus and into him. Pancras spoke the words of protection under his breath as he directed the energies into the fetish. Concentrating on the intonation of repetitive words while directing energy could be uninspiring, but Pancras found the repetition relaxing. He knew his goal, and he knew what steps to take to achieve it. That sort of certainty brought him confidence and motivation.

The words became a mantra for Pancras. He felt the magic swirl and twist around him, pouring into his focus, through him, then into the fetish. Protective abjurations felt bright, clean, and pure. On the periphery, Pancras sensed darkness. *Probably from all the necromantic research I've been doing.*

Through closed eyes, he perceived colors as he worked. Gold, silver, the azure of a clear sky. Darkness seeped in at the edge of his vision, like claws reaching from behind him. The darkness clouded his vision, blotting out the colors of the abjuration with which Pancras attempted to infuse the fetish.

Pancras chanted the words louder, hoping to drown out the hiss that now accompanied the dark haze. A miasma of shadow filled the room, coalescing from the magic he drew together. Burning eyes stared at him from the mist, and shadowy claws reached for his throat.

With a strangled gasp, Pancras stopped chanting. He staggered backward, clutching at his neck as the eyes followed him, boring into his head.

"You have resisted too long, Necromancer. No more."

Pancras fell to his knees, coughing. An icy chill crawled down his back as the shadow enveloped him. In his hand, the rod turned to ice, freezing the flesh of his hand. He cried out. Choking, he flung the rod across the room. It clattered to a stop against the far wall. The shadowy mist vanished as Pancras collapsed, gasping. Darkness overtook him.

When he regained consciousness, he found himself lying on the floor with his head on a pillow and the blanket from his bed covering most of his body. Groaning, he rolled over.

He viewed Kale seated on the edge of his bare bed, fiddling with his puzzle box.

"Oh hey, you're awake. We found you on the floor. No one was strong enough to get you into the bed, so we just covered you up there."

"What happened? What time is it?"

Kale set down his puzzle box, then hopped off the bed. He helped Pancras into a sitting position. "Midafternoon, I guess. We were hoping you could tell us what happened. Delilah and Kali went to find a healer."

"Midafternoon?" Pancras rubbed the crick in his neck. Sleeping on the floor ignited a bevy of aches and pains in muscles he didn't often use. His head felt like an army of dwarves marched inside it. "Only a few hours, then."

Kale snorted. "It's been a day since we found you there."

"Oh." Pancras crawled over to his bed, then used it to pull himself up. He regarded his workbench. The fetish, now a twisted mass of blackened goo, sat on top of it. Hesitant to touch it, he retrieved his rod from its resting place on the floor. "How did this get here?"

"I don't know. Except for the blankets and pillows, we left the room the way we found it. Don't you remember what happened?"

Pancras searched his memory. The last thing he remembered was being glad for the peace and quiet and starting the ritual to create the fetish. He studied the room, then shoved the rod into his belt. Save for the ruined fetish, his tools seemed undisturbed.

"Nothing. Something must have gone wrong, but I have no idea what." Rubbing the base of his horn, he staggered into the parlor. Kale followed him.

"Have a seat. The girls should be back with a healer soon."

Pancras sat in an armchair, realizing he felt chilly as the warmth of the crackling hearth heated his bones. Wisps of fragrant smoke wafted from the fire, and he noticed the curling, black remnants of an aromatic sachet someone had tossed into the fire.

"Where's Edric?"

Kale climbed into the armchair his sister normally claimed. "He said he was going down to the public baths. Kali was using ours, and he didn't want to wait."

Pancras leaned his head back and closed his eyes. He was certain the ritual he attempted was correct. *Perhaps I made an error constructing the fetish?* The warmth of the fire lulled him into a fitful sleep, and he next awoke to a human poking him.

"Well, he's not dead."

Pancras rubbed his eyes, yawning. The throbbing in his head lessened, and when his eyes were able to focus, he recognized the human priest, Arnost, peering over a pair of thin spectacles at him.

"I can see that." Delilah shoved Arnost to the side, then wiped Pancras's chin with a rag. "You had us worried. How do you feel?"

Pancras yawned again and stretched, narrowly missing Kale's head as the drak ducked under his arm. Kale eyed him over the side of the chair. "Not bad, actually." He stood up. "Yes, pretty good. Did I sleep long?"

"No, just a few hours. This time." Kale offered him a goblet of wine.

"Let's not be hasty." Arnost took the goblet before Pancras could drink. "Your scaly friends said you were unresponsive when they found you. That is a matter for some concern."

Pancras waved his hands, dismissing Arnost's worry. "I was trying to make a protective fetish. It's been a long time since I've performed abjurations. I'm sure it's just backlash from a miscast, nothing more." The theory sounded reasonable to Pancras. He didn't recall ever forgetting the event of a miscast before, but he was older than the last time one occurred.

Arnost held up the golden lyre, the symbol of Apellon, from around his neck. He chanted in a low voice, waving the symbol over Pancras. Curling his lips, the minotaur stood, but Arnost pushed him down again into the chair.

"I still sense darkness within you. It is most unnatural."

"I'm sure we all have things in our past which taint our souls." Pancras stood again. This time, Arnost allowed it. The minotaur joined Delilah, Kali, and Edric at the dining table. After sitting alongside the dwarf, he picked up a hunk of bread. "How long did we live under old bonehead? We were surrounded by evildoers and the wicked for most of our lives. It's bound to leave a mark, a stain, if you will." Pancras didn't need some addle-minded human mystic to tell him that the past could leave a scar.

"That is not what I am sensing. You would do well to allow yourself to be thoroughly examined. Something is not right."

Pancras poured himself a goblet of wine. "Very well. When I have the opportunity to venture into the city again, I will come see you. Yes?"

Arnost blinked, looking from the drak twins to Pancras and back. "I think this situation is more serious than that."

"Until my task here is complete, I have been confined to the palace under order of the princess." Arnost's assessment bothered Pancras. The dark dreams, the spontaneous appearances of undead in the catacombs, his inability to remember anything about the ritual he just performed, all pointed to some sinister interference. Pancras didn't want the distraction. He was so close to completing his task and ensuring their freedom to depart Almeria on time.

"Then perhaps I should look you over now." Licking his lips, Arnost wrung his hands.

Delilah threw a hunk of bread across the table at her brother. "Do you really think something is wrong with him?"

Kale caught the chunk in his mouth. Pancras frowned at their antics, snatching the next piece of bread out of the air. "There's nothing wrong with me."

Kale chased his bread with a gulp of wine. "I don't know. Forgetting stuff and necromancing in your sleep. It can't hurt to check, Pancras."

With Kali and Edric present, Pancras did not want to discuss the strange goings on that seemed to follow him from Drak-Anor. He pushed himself away from the table, then shuffled toward his bedchamber. "Fine. Come along, Human."

Pancras didn't wait to see if Arnost followed him. He half expected the human to sputter and leave. He knew his behavior was unreasonable, but at the moment he didn't care. The more Kale and Delilah conjectured that something might be wrong, the more Pancras felt certainty that something indeed was.

Arnost shut the door behind him. He clutched the golden lyre around his neck. "Perhaps you could sit down?"

Pancras sat on the edge of his bed and prepared himself for what he expected to be a waste of time. The sort of magic the faithful practiced differed from the sort he practiced primarily in technique. Where the arcane energies Pancras harnessed were flashy and obvious, Arnost's divination would be subtle with few outward effects. Divinations and many healing charms provided perfect cover for charlatans, and Pancras had encountered many such people during his life who professed to be people of faith.

The human held the golden lyre symbol above Pancras's head as he hummed a repetitive drone. The symbol flared, bathing the room in golden light. Pancras held up his hand to shield his eyes, feeling the warmth of the light washing over him.

"The light of Apellon reveals much that is hidden."

Pancras felt something stir within him. The room dimmed, darkening at the edges of his vision. The darkness crept in around him, and he felt his chest tighten. The light from Arnost's symbol flared; yet the darkness overtook Pancras. His muscles convulsed, and he flopped backward onto the bed. His mind spiraled into a void.

***

Delilah's head snapped toward the bedchamber door when a clatter arose from behind it. Light flooded from the gap beneath the door as a moaning wail rattled the walls. She leapt out of her chair, snatching up her staff as she raced toward Pancras's room. As she left, she heard Edric advising Kali.

"Leave the wizarding problems to them, Lass. You don't want to crowd the room if things go bad."

Throwing open the door, she squinted against the blinding light. Rising from Pancras's prone form on the bed was a dark figure, a hole in the light. It loomed over Arnost with black, smoky wings and shadowy claws.

It snarled at Delilah when she entered the room. "This one is mine. You will all march in the Undying Legion before the end."

Delilah pointed her staff at the shadow demon. She gathered arcane energy while deciding what effect might defeat the creature and at the same time minimize the potential for backblast and collateral damage.

Kale seized her shoulder. "Deli! That's the… thing! The one we fought under Ironkrag!"

Arnost raised his symbol of Apellon higher. "Be gone, demon! Flee from the light, foul creature of darkness!"

The shadow threw back its head, laughing. "Your antiquated notions of power hold no sway over me." It reached forward, snatching the golden lyre from Arnost's hand. Crushing it, the demon extinguished the light. Darkness engulfed the room.

Delilah heard the clatter of Arnost's symbol hitting the floor. "*Dapane phlogone!*" She directed a stream of fire toward the creature, hoping she aimed high enough to miss Pancras. The flame poured across the room, but the darkness surrounding them smothered it.

"No!" She heard Pancras's voice coming from the area in front of her, then noticed a faint verdigris glow through the shadow. The minotaur groaned, then Delilah heard his hooves hitting the floor.

"*Exoria! Apothoun tis daimonikees dynameis!*" A burst of green light flooded the room. Spinning, the shadow demon screeched. Tendrils of greasy black smoke swirled around it.

Covered in emerald aether, the shadow diminished. Kale moved to help Arnost, whom he found on one knee in front of Pancras's bed, to his feet. Shadowy tendrils whirled around the room, buffeting Pancras and launching papers and linens into the air.

Darkness engulfed the room once more for a brief moment before it disappeared.

After the green glow from Pancras's rod faded, he held one of his bedposts to steady himself.

Arnost plucked the remains of his golden lyre from the floor. "You cannot tell me that was 'nothing.'"

Delilah and her brother helped Pancras regain his footing. His room lay in shambles with most of his laboratory equipment upended or smashed. He held his head, sitting on the edge of the bed. His cheeks appeared sunken, and his eyes stared ahead, unfocused. For the first time, Delilah noticed Pancras seeming haggard and aged.

"Do you know what that thing was, Pancras?" Delilah sat next to him on the bed.

"I think Kale is right. It was the shadow demon we encountered under Ironkrag."

"I thought we destroyed that thing." Kale pulled over a chair from the small table. "Did it follow us here?"

"I have never encountered a demon before." Arnost looked up from his ruined symbol. "It did not feel as foul as I expected."

For all the talk about Sarvesh being a demon of flame and fury and all her time spent under the various ill-tempered overlords of her people before Sarvesh became their leader, Delilah did not think she had encountered a true demon before, either.

Pancras confirmed Arnost's suspicions. "I do not believe it was a demon. Some sort of shadow creature bound to a more powerful master, for certain. But a true demon? No, I don't think so."

"What was it then?" Arnost grunted, failing to bend his golden lyre into its original shape.

Delilah directed her attention to her brother and Pancras. "It's that thing you fought under Ironkrag? How did it get here?"

Pancras stood. "How it followed me here is a question I cannot answer right now."

"Is it gone?" Kale hopped off the bed, steadying Pancras through the doorway and to the dining table. Edric was deep into his second helping. Kali turned her head toward them, narrowing her eyes.

Pancras sat down at the table, then poured himself a goblet of wine. "That is a question Arnost will have to answer."

"At some point, you should probably tell us non-magical folk what's going on." Edric tossed a bone across the table, missing the bowl appropriated for detritus. He took another rib for himself from the roasted rack in the center of the table.

A wave of guilt passed over Delilah. It hadn't occurred to her that Kali and Edric might not understand what just happened.

Pancras motioned for Arnost to join them at the table. "I think we should all take a moment to discuss it. Wouldn't you agree?"

**

Arnost sat alongside Pancras and drank the proffered goblet of wine before he responded. "Yes. Yes, I think that is wise."

Pancras refilled Arnost's goblet, then topped off his own. "Before we left Drak-Anor, Kale, Edric, and I dealt with a mob of ghouls that had been bothering the good dwarves of Ironkrag. We found they were apparently being led by a shadowy creature, which I dubbed a 'shadow demon' for lack of a better descriptor. It seemed to draw its power from a nearby chaos rift and a bloodmaw."

"What's that?" Kali tossed a hunk of bread to Kale after taking one for herself. Arnost continued working to reshape his amulet while he listened.

"A creature of chaos. Mostly teeth." Pancras knew about such creatures from his studies at the Arcane University, but he had never seen one before that encounter. "Otherworldly creatures aren't really my area of expertise. Unless I'm forgetting something, we never directly defeated the shadow-thing. I"—Pancras chewed on his lip, shifting his eyes to focus on the table—"I assumed it was destroyed when I closed the rift."

"I got thrown through the rift!" Kale spread his wings. "It made me grow wings and breathe fire. I felt sick for a long time before that, though."

Arnost glanced up from his golden lyre. "You passed through a chaos rift?"

Delilah nudged her brother, spilling his wine. "It explains a lot about him."

"It was after that when my disturbing dreams began. More than mere nightmares, they were more vivid and unsettling than those. I can recall very little detail, but they all ended with me spell casting. I would awaken and learn of yet another outbreak of undead."

"Yeah, yeah! That zombie at the tower." Kale flicked wine off his fingers in the direction of his sister.

"And the undead in the catacombs." Delilah smacked her brother's hand.

"The dreams didn't come every night, and I don't remember dreaming at all when I slept without wearing my focus. I woke up with pounding headaches many mornings after that." When Pancras listed the instances aloud, they seemed like more than just coincidence, even though the occurrences all happened over the course of several months.

"Did you see what happened to this shadow creature? Did it touch any of you? What happened when the rift closed?" Arnost gestured for Delilah to pass the bread.

Pancras rubbed the back of his neck. "The rift vanished in a flash of light. I felt something slam into me and was thrown to the ground. What did that thing say in my room? Something about the Undying Legion?"

Arnost scoffed, "Idle threats, I'm sure. The Lich Queen's army was called the Undying Legion. Anyone who fell in battle against her army would rise again the next night and join them as they marched across the land. She was defeated long ago."

Pancras was a young minotaur when she met her final defeat at the Battle of Badon Hill. Her armies mostly rampaged in the plains north of the Celtan Forest, so he heard only exaggerated stories by the time they made their way to Muncifer. He always fancied she had a personal vendetta against Vlorey and the kingdoms of the north.

"I heard she was called the Witch Queen until the humans and elves killed her. Then she came back as the Lich Queen." Kali tore into a rib, smacking her lips as she wolfed down the meat.

Edric chuckled. "Leave it to the tall folk to muck up killin' somebody."

Pancras had heard that story as well. "I also heard she planned to be killed as the final part of her ritual to grant her immortality as a lich."

Occupying decaying bodies, liches retained all the power they possessed in life. They grew hardier and more difficult to destroy as their decomposition progressed, and they required the destruction of life to sustain themselves. Because he never could reconcile his personal beliefs with creating intelligent, self-aware undead, Pancras had limited his practice to creating automatons like skeletons and zombies.

Kale drained his goblet of wine. "So this shadow-thing? It was a minion of the Lich Queen, maybe?"

Pancras glanced at Arnost. The human nodded. "It's possible. A remnant biding its time."

"It's gone now, right?" Kali talked around a piece of meat.

"Without my amulet"—Arnost held up the twisted remains of his golden lyre—"I cannot say for certain, but it seems likely."

Unconvinced, Pancras found the whole affair anti-climactic, and he suspected he and Arnost merely drove away the shadow creature temporarily. He didn't want to push the issue, however. He wanted to finish this business with the prince before undertaking another challenge.

"Regardless, I hope the shadow demon stays away until my task here is done."

As they finished dinner but before excusing himself, Arnost promised to check in on Pancras in a few days. The shadow's words gnawed at Pancras's insides. The Lich Queen and all her minions had been silent for decades, and he feared if one caused trouble now, it wasn't just a remnant. The implications boded ill for the future.

***

After dinner, Kale sequestered himself in his bed chamber with the puzzle box and Kali. Pancras busied himself cleaning up the shattered remains of his laboratory, Delilah buried her snout in her grimoire, and Edric went off looking to entice a few of the guards into throwing some dice with him.

"Maybe you can help me figure out the rest of this puzzle box." After setting it on the table, Kale showed Kali how the sides he'd already figured out worked.

"What does this thing do?" Kali lowered herself to eye level, peering at the box.

"Clicks and whirrs? I don't know. There's probably something magic inside it, if I can figure out how to open it."

Narrowing her eyes, Kali sat up. "How do you know there isn't something dangerous in there?"

Kale's wings fluttered. "Terrakaptis wouldn't give me something dangerous."

"So, you have to figure out each side? How did you know where to start? Does it matter?"

Kale thought for a moment. "Well, I just picked a side." He scratched his head. "I don't know that it matters as long as I work on one side at a time."

"How long have you been trying to figure this out?"

"Since we left home…" Kale chewed his lip. "A few months on and off."

Kali picked up the box before rotating it in her hands to view each side. "It would be terrible if you started in the wrong place."

The thought that he had chosen the wrong approach to solving it from the outset never occurred to Kale, but since Kali mentioned it, he wondered if that was the reason he found the box's responses underwhelming. The two spent hours examining every side of the puzzle box, but they could not determine whether one side bore importance over the others. They worked far into the night, only stopping when Delilah entered with the intention of sleeping, exaggerating her bedtime preparations. Kale sighed. He left his puzzle box on the table; it would be waiting for him in the morning.

Chapter 21

As Pancras yawned, stretching, he realized he slept through the night without experiencing upsetting dreams or dark thoughts. He suffered no disturbances whatsoever. Hopping out of bed, he pulled on his robes, then entered the veranda to gaze at Almeria. For the first time since he left Drak-Anor, the minotaur felt refreshed and energized upon awakening.

Dark, puffy clouds glided on the wind at the edge of the horizon, but the skies over Almeria were blue and clear. The crisp winter air carried the scent of burning hearths, and although the breeze made him shiver, the day seemed bright and cheery.

He hoped he could conclude his business soon. They couldn't leave, of course, until the snows started to melt away, and winter in Etrunia could be unpredictable. Still, the sooner he didn't have to worry about Prince Gavril's whims, the better. At the very least, he and the draks would be free to enjoy what the city had to offer, and perhaps, they could get to know Edric better. Pancras regretted they hadn't included the dwarf in any of their plans, but he seemed content to find his own entertainment.

The familiar cadence of Princess Valene's soft footfalls approached from the right. Pancras greeted the princess with a bow. "Good morning."

"It is so far. How goes your… research?" The princess sipped from her customary steaming goblet of mulled wine.

Pancras cleared his throat. *So much for the good morning.* "There's been a mishap."

Princess Valene narrowed her eyes, frowning. "How bad?"

"Catastrophic. I have to start over, including acquiring new equipment." Saying the words aloud hammered home the extent and severity of the damage caused by the shadow demon.

Princess Valene's mouth became a thin line before she turned away from Pancras. Steam wafted up from her goblet, mixing with the fog of her breath while she regarded Almeria in silence.

"I don't want to know what happened, and we do not have time for you to start over." The princess turned to face Pancras. "We have to confront Gavril today."

"Today?" Pancras's eyes widened. "Why? You've discovered something new?"

"My agents have informed me that they've waylaid one of Gavril's spies. In addition, they've located the woman with whom Gavril has been involved. I'm told she's quite eager to cooperate in exchange for leniency. Treason carries a serious penalty: death."

Pancras's mind wheeled with the revelation. He didn't like the idea of confronting the prince with only the bare bones of a plan and without his protective fetish. *And our discussion here is not treasonous?* "You don't really need me then, do you?"

The princess dismissed his question with a wave of her hand. "Your testimony will strengthen my case against him. I want you to confront him with his vile plan in court."

The minotaur did not relish being trapped in the middle of a power play between the rulers of Etrunia, although he appreciated the logic in confronting Prince Gavril with all the evidence against him in a public forum.

Princess Valene took a step forward to meet his gaze, her eyes flashing with fire. "Understand this: I reward loyalty. I will ensure you leave Almeria free and in time to make your journey to Muncifer. You will receive no such promise from my husband."

Pancras held up his hands, then stepped away from Princess Valene. "I understand your position. I gave you my word that I will cooperate with you, but I require assurances that no matter what happens, the safety of the draks and the dwarf will be guaranteed."

The Princess's expression softened. "I can't make any promises, but as long as they don't interfere, I will do what I can. I will inform Milena and the guards loyal to me as well. I shall send her for you when we are ready."

Pancras nodded, bowing. "I will make preparations. I'll be ready when she calls."

***

Delilah, sitting in her chair in front of the fire with her grimoire, breathed a sigh of relief when Pancras didn't seem to notice her on his way to the veranda. Sharing a room with Kali and her brother lent itself to neither a good night's sleep nor quiet study.

She found solace focusing on the grimoire. Making sense of its ever-changing text became easier the more time she spent with it. The book whisked her away to another battlefield. Delilah grinned, amused by the thought of Gil-Li the Graven spending her whole life fighting battles. *Of course, I may be seeing images she wants me to see and not actual history.*

Gil-Li stood on a rocky outcropping overlooking a blasted meadow. Any vegetation that might have grown there had long since burned away. Mist obscured the faces and forms of the army marching over the plain in lockstep toward her. Her tattoos glowed with arcane energy, then the earth erupted beside her. The motions and form of the invocation seared themselves into Delilah's mind. Humanoid shapes of rock and earth tore themselves loose from the ground, towering over Gil-Li. They jumped down from the outcropping, meeting the army head-on.

Flames erupted from Gil-Li's tattoos, forming a whirlwind of fire around her. Moving ahead of the rock giants, the fiery tornadoes cut swaths through enemy ranks while the lumbering stony brutes pounded the enemy with boulder-sized fists

Although, impressed by the carnage Gil-Li unleashed, Delilah did not understand the objective of this particular lesson. She had heard stories of wizards of sufficient power devastating entire armies and laying waste to entire regions. Shifting, the image focused on Gil-Li summoning the creatures of stone. Delilah followed her lip movements as she invoked the effect she desired.

"Kaleesie… gee… stoche-e-a-key."

She knew the words weren't quite right, but she figured they were a close approximation. Delilah tried again, but a blast of cold air from outside broke her concentration. She glared at Pancras, but the minotaur didn't seem to notice. When he plopped into the chair next to her, its wood frame groaned, protesting his lack of finesse.

"Is Kale up?"

Delilah closed her grimoire, shaking her head. "I doubt it. It's just you and me, unless Edric is being very quiet in his room."

"Wake everyone. I have urgent news." Pancras pushed himself out of the chair and checked the food lift while Delilah roused everyone else. Kale was the only one of the three who wasn't bleary eyed and reluctant to leave the warm confines of their feather beds. Meanwhile, Pancras poured mulled wine for everyone and spread the variety of pastries and cured meats provided by the kitchen on the table.

The berry-sweet smell of the wine and the smoky, briny aroma of the meats made Delilah's stomach grumble and her mouth water. After filling her plate, she took her place next to her brother, who fumbled with a sweet roll.

Pancras tapped a knife on the side of his goblet to get everyone's attention. "I have been informed that, essentially, my research here is done. I still can't go into detail, but the princess wants to meet with me in the throne room this afternoon, in the presence of the prince."

"So what does that mean for us?" Flecks of food flew from Kale's mouth as he talked around a mouthful of pastry. Delilah smacked him on the shoulder, scowling.

"If things go as planned, the princess will guarantee our safe departure in time to arrive in Muncifer before Spring's Dawning." Pancras watched Kale layer slices of cured meat on a hard roll.

"What of the prince?" Edric drained his goblet of mulled wine in a single gulp, then refilled it. "I don't reckon he'll go along with that, will he? I've heard he's a right prat."

"I doubt he'll go against the princess." Kali cocked her head. "We hear she's the silent power behind the throne. She pulls the strings while he dances and squawks like a mother hen."

Delilah chuckled. She hadn't interacted much with Prince Gavril, but he struck her as the type who liked to be louder than everyone around him, despite the cost of his effectiveness.

"This meeting might be unpleasant for the prince. I want everyone packed and ready to leave."

Delilah stopped with her goblet halfway to her mouth. She turned her head toward Pancras. "We can't travel yet. The snow is too deep."

"We may have no choice but to flee the palace after this afternoon. I'm certain if things go our way, the princess will allow us to stay until we can travel, but if things do not go our way…" Pancras left the thought lingering over the table like a storm cloud.

Delilah slammed her goblet, sloshing wine onto the table. "You need to tell us what's going on, Pancras. I think we can all keep a secret, if that's what it takes. We haven't asked a lot of questions about the deal you made, but now you're talking about us fleeing the palace. We deserve to know what's happening!"

The drak sorceress wanted Pancras to be the one to explain the situation. Murmurs of assent circled the table. Delilah didn't care what the humans did to each other, but she knew she would have to deal with all sorts of questions from Kale once they were alone. The minotaur slumped in his seat, nodding. "Very well. I suppose it's better you hear it from me than from rumors that might start if things go poorly this afternoon."

Pancras sipped his wine, then took a deep breath. "In exchange for our freedom, such as it is, and these very fine accommodations, the prince tasked me with cursing his wife, the princess."

Edric grunted. Kale stifled a gasp.

"I won't go into all the political details of the situation. He wanted me to make her barren so he could easily divorce her and marry someone else. I agreed rather hastily in my desire to escape the jail, but upon reflection, I cannot go through with it."

"So, what have you been doing this whole time?" Kale couldn't understand why the prince would want to divorce Princess Valene.

"Stalling. I tried to create a protective fetish to use during the inevitable confrontation, but that shadow demon saw to it that I failed."

"Maybe we should come with you, then." Kale snatched another sweet roll from the plate that passed from Kali to Edric.

Delilah nodded in agreement. "The three of us will deal with the nasty humans, and Kali and Edric can make sure our escape route remains open."

Pancras held up his hands. "No! No, we're not planning an assault on the throne room. I'm going there to have a conversation with the prince and princess. That's all."

"I still think Kale and I should go with you. We've come this far together. Besides, the princess already knows I know."

"Yeah, and we're just tagging along like hungry mongrels, right?" Edric huffed before draining another goblet of wine.

"Hey, that's not true!" Kale glared at the dwarf. "The way we've been fed here in the palace, how can you say you're hungry?"

"It's probably best I go alone."

Ignoring Pancras, Delilah eyed Kali. "You know how to get around without being noticed. Maybe you and Edric can work together to make sure we have a way out, just in case things do go wrong."

Kali nodded, glancing over at the still-grumbling dwarf. "Sure. Everyone already associates Pancras with the two of you. If Edric and I show up in the throne room, it might put everyone on edge. We can make sure the way out through the undercroft remains clear."

Pancras rubbed his forehead. "Fine, look, just promise me you'll follow my lead, all right? The prince's moods can be volatile. Just let him rage, if that's what it comes to. The princess has given me assurances she'll back me up."

After they finished eating, everyone busied themselves packing up their clothing and possessions in case they needed to beat a hasty retreat. By the time they finished, the sun had passed its zenith. Edric, Kale, and Kali passed the time betting on dice while Pancras paced, wringing his hands and rubbing the base of his horn. Delilah tried to study her grimoire, but she could not concentrate amid the nervous tension in the air.

Upon hearing a knock at the doors, occupants of the parlor fell quiet. Pancras let Lady Milena enter. She studied the draks and dwarf. "Dare I ask what is going on?"

Pancras gestured to the room. "We've made preparations to leave… just in case."

"I would say that's an unnecessary precaution, but under the circumstances, perhaps it is wise." Lady Milena put her hand on Pancras's shoulder. "Let us go, Their Highnesses await."

Delilah closed her grimoire, then hopped off the chair. She shoved the tome in her pack, then picked up her staff, while Kale checked his bandolier of daggers and straightened his hat.

"What are they doing?"

Pancras glanced down at the drak twins. "They're coming with me."

Lady Milena shook her head. "I do not see how their presence will improve the situation."

Delilah poked her in the stomach. The armor the knight wore under her tabard didn't budge. "Hey, my brother and I stick with Pancras, no matter what. It's Kale's fault we're even in this mess."

"Hey!"

Albeit she told a half-truth, Delilah did not intend to be left behind if she had any say in the matter.

"If things get out of hand and there is violence, I cannot protect them if they get involved."

After kneeling before them, Pancras took the drak twins by the shoulders. "Like I said, let me do the talking. I want you there for support, but you are not to interfere, no matter how bad things seem. Everything is taken care of. We have a plan. Lady Milena, the princess, and I will handle everything."

Delilah grunted, smacking Pancras's hand away. "We know how to behave ourselves." She wasn't about to promise to stand by and do nothing if these humans decided they wanted Pancras's head.

Lady Milena threw up her hands. "Fine. Act only out of self-defense, or I can make no guarantees. We need to leave. Now."

***

Pancras followed Milena into the throne room. He motioned for Kale and Delilah to follow behind him, but not too closely. He knew this confrontation would not be pleasant, and he hoped the presence of the draks would help keep things from spiraling out of control. *Assuming they don't lose control themselves.* Pancras trusted in Kale's ability to hold back his sister but not in Delilah's ability to control her temper.

Prince Gavril sat with one leg draped over the arm of his gilded chair. Princess Valene slouched in the chair next to him, glancing at her husband with a mixture of disgust and disdain. Guards leaning on spears flanked the throne dais.

"Ah, so, Minotaur, you have news for me?" Outstretching his hands, Prince Gavril approached Pancras. "Shall we convene in my antechamber? No need for the rest of the court to hear our business."

"That's unnecessary, Your Highness. My news concerns Princess Valene as well." Pancras hoped a public confrontation would temper Prince Gavril's reaction to bad news.

"Does it?" Princes Gavril clenched his jaw. Glaring, his left eyelid twitched.

Pancras glanced past Gavril to the princess, finding not a hint of emotion in her expression. She straightened, keeping her eye on them. "I am disinclined to fulfill your request. I find the idea that you commissioned me to curse the princess vile and reprehensible."

Prince Gavril's face turned bright crimson. "You dare—"

Pancras nodded, watching the princess for her reaction. "I can compensate you for your hospitality, but I will not curse her. I will not make her barren."

"Lies! Slander! Kill him!" Gavril snarled, backing away. He glared at his guards, then at the knight. "Lady Milena, slay this treacherous beast!"

"Gavril!" Princess Valene stood, clearing her throat. "Dear Husband, is this minotaur's accusation true?"

"Lies!" Gavril pointed at Pancras, ignoring the princess's question. "Lady Milena, I order you to do your duty. Obey me! Kill him!"

Dropping her hand to the hilt of her sword, Milena stepped in front of Pancras. "No. I will not. He has done no wrong. Killing him does not serve the realm."

"You. Are. Relieved." Prince Gavril dismissed her through clenched teeth. He held out his hand. "Give me your sword. You are a disgrace to the Royal Guard."

After drawing her sword, Milena held it before her as if presenting it to him. She dropped it on the ground. Prince Gavril spun around. He snatched one of the guard's spears.

"Pancras—" Delilah stepped toward him, but Pancras silenced her with a wave of his hand. He couldn't see Kale, but as Gavril approached him with the spear, he didn't have time to worry about Delilah's brother.

As Prince Gavril prepared to drive the blade into the minotaur's gut, Pancras stepped backward. He seized the rod in his belt. "*Skia veema.*"

The spear passed through the space where Pancras previously stood. The minotaur stepped out from behind Gavril's throne. Princess Valene gasped. The guards near her leveled their weapons.

Prince Gavril spun. His face reddened with fury. "Your foul tricks will not save you!"

"It's over, Your Highness. There is no need to continue this." Pancras grabbed the nearest halberd leveled at him, pulled it out of the guard's hands, and then smacked the man across the belly with the haft. The guard fell backward, coughing.

Descending the dais, the necromancer held his rod before him. Prince Gavril lunged at him once more as a blast of azure energy intercepted the guard advancing on Pancras from his right. He heard Lady Milena shouting at Kale and Delilah as he dodged a thrust from the prince. The tip of the spear thudded against the stone steps of the dais.

After kicking the haft of Gavril's weapon out of his way, Pancras pointed his rod at him. *I need to put a stop to this before it goes too far.* "*Angigma tou tafou!*"

A sickly green ray shot from Pancras's focus, striking Prince Gavril and enveloping the monarch in a layer of frost. The color drained from his face as he fought to move. Wispy, decaying hands grasped at his legs, slowing his approach.

The minotaur took hold of the haft of the prince's spear, holding it tight as he circled the prince. "Your plans are laid bare. Stop this madness!"

"Gavril!" Princess Valene's voice echoed in the throne room. "Guards! Stand down!"

Pancras's knee exploded with pain as a halberd slashed into the tendon in the back of it. Shrieking, he fell to one knee. The prince wrenched his spear from the minotaur's grasp.

In an attempt to keep the drak sorceress from unleashing her fury upon the guards, Lady Milena wrestled for control of Delilah's staff. He heard a human voice cry out as Kale bounded past him, twin daggers flashing in the light.

Prince Gavril threw his spear toward Pancras.

"*Aspida tou ravematos!*" A shield of energy appeared in front of Pancras just as the spear reached his chest. Snapping it in half, the barrier arrested the projectile's momentum.

***

Delilah leveled her staff. Blue wisps swirled around her body as she prepared to unleash the full force of her magic on the humans.

Milena seized Delilah's staff, redirecting it toward the ceiling. "No! I cannot protect you if you destroy half the throne room!"

Kale slashed at a guard who moved to grab him. He saw a flash of emerald energy from Pancras. The prince, now weaponless, scrambled backward away from the minotaur.

"Stop this! I command you!" Princess Valene's voice again echoed throughout the throne room. With unwavering purpose, she stepped down off the dais toward her husband. While Milena held Delilah at bay, the princess directed the guards to resume their posts near the thrones.

"You have betrayed me!" The prince pointed a shaking finger at his wife. "This is a coup! You conspired with these beasts to overthrow me!"

Princess Valene slapped her husband, snapping his head back. He fell to his knees, clutching at his cheek.

"Silence! I know about Baroness Moravec. Think of this as a transition of power."

Kale watched the prince open and close his mouth in silent protest. Princess Valene held the badge of office he wore around his neck as an amulet. She rubbed her thumb over its design.

"It is you who has disgraced your office. All your schemes, your conniving… you wanted this marriage, Gavril. You and my father." She yanked the emblem from his neck, snapping the chain.

"Arrest him." Princess Valene ascended her throne. After taking her seat, she gestured toward Pancras. Still kneeling, the minotaur used his hands to staunch the flow of blood from his injured knee. "See to the minotaur's wounds, Lady Milena, and escort the draks back to their chamber."

Kale wiped his daggers on his cloak and returned to his sister's side. Delilah squirmed out of Lady Milena's grasp. "We're not leaving Pancras."

While maintaining his hold on the laceration, the minotaur stood, albeit crookedly. He faced Princess Valene and bowed. "I can see myself out, Your Highness, with your leave."

"Bind your wound, Pancras. We will discuss the ramifications of this debacle later."

Prince Gavril lashed out at one of the guards struggling to lock shackles around his wrists. His blow caught the man below the chin. The other guard bashed him in the back of the head with his cudgel. He crumpled to his knees, glaring upward at Pancras.

"There will be a reckoning for this, Minotaur. Make no mistake."

Kale pulled Pancras away before he could retort. Based on the minotaur's labored breathing and the speed at which the crimson stain spread across his robes, Kale concluded his friend lied about the severity of his injury.

They returned to their suite, ignoring murmurs and furtive glances from palace servants loitering in the hallways and courtiers who came to see the cause of the commotion. Kale took heart in Pancras's apparent lack of concern for the princess, and although he did not understand who were truly their allies in all this, he felt confident Pancras did.

"I'll send for a healer." Lady Milena helped Pancras through the doors into their suite and into one of the armchairs in front of the hearth. Edric and Kali glanced up from their game.

"Can't you go to a meeting without getting cut up?" Snorting, Edric threw his dice.

Kali hopped down from her chair, then raced over to Kale. "What happened? Are you all right?"

Kale nodded, hugging her. "Fine, I'm fine. Pancras was injured, and the prince was arrested."

Delilah pushed past them and climbed into the chair next to Pancras. "I'm fine, too, thanks."

"I'll post a guard for your safety. Permit no one entry until I return." Lady Milena closed the doors behind her.

Kale locked them after she left. He faced his sister and Pancras. "What now?"

***

Pancras pulled up his robes to inspect his wound. It burned like fire and oozed dark blood. The gash on the back of his leg missed his knee by no more than a finger width. A bit lower and the halberd might have sheared off his lower leg. He clasped his hand over the laceration.

"Kale, I have strips of cloth in my room. In a box on the table, I think. Could you bring them here?" Pancras needed time to think without Kale pestering him for their next move. He had expected Prince Gavril to react poorly, but not violently.

"What happened?" Kali rested her hand on the arm of Delilah's chair.

"Are you in or out, Kali?" The dwarf rattled the dice for emphasis.

"Dolios curse your dice, Edric!"

Pancras cocked his eyebrow, glancing over his shoulder at the dwarf. Edric shrugged before pouring more ale for himself. The minotaur chuckled. *Some things never change.* "The prince reacted… poorly when confronted with his own treachery. He attacked us."

Kale returned with the bandages. "They're not going to throw us in jail again, are they?"

"I don't trust these humans, Pancras. We need to leave." Upon taking the strips of cloth from her brother, Delilah hopped out of her chair. "Now."

Pancras shook his head. "We should wait until we hear from the princess. We don't need a mob of Gavril's supporters hounding our steps."

Delilah mumbled something under her breath. Pancras thought it sounded like a threat to destroy the entire city. Although he didn't think she could follow through, he put a hand on her shoulder to calm her.

"It will be all right, Delilah. We must trust the princess."

Kali cleared her throat. "He has a point. Princess Valene has been sympathetic toward non-humans in the city in the past. If she's helping you, she's a damn sight more trustworthy than the prince."

"Nobody asked you, Kali." Delilah worked to bind the minotaur's knee.

The orange-scaled drak huffed. Kale led her away. Pancras rubbed his forehead, focusing on a log crackling in the fire. He stared at the dancing flames, losing himself, until Delilah tightened the bandage, shooting a wave of pain through his thigh.

"Sorry."

"Delilah may be right." Pancras winced as he stood. He patted the sorceress on the shoulder, offering her a smile of thanks. Hobbling toward the tapestry depicting the Battle of Badon Hill, his thoughts turned to the shadow demon.

Perhaps it's truly gone. I did not feel its touch fighting the prince. Hearing the draks bickering in the background, he focused on the tapestry. Captivated by the individual threads composing each picture, Pancras followed a gold thread as it wound around the picture until he lost it before focusing on a different thread heading in a new direction.

Much like our lives. He fingered his focus, secure on his belt. The minotaur turned to regard his friends. Edric still sat by himself, fidgeting with his dice while he drank. Kali stood near Kale observing the twins arguing over their next move. The air carried Delilah's huffs of disapproval in reply to every one of Kali's suggestions.

Smiling, Pancras felt warmth spread in his heart at the familial scene. "It's time to take action."

His words silenced the room. All eyes turned to him.

"It's dangerous to stay here. I think we should take our chances on the road. We'll buy tents on our way out of town and put this place behind us."

The minotaur limped over to the draks and put his hand on Delilah's shoulder. "No longer will the humans decide our course. Gather your things."

Heraldy of Andelosia

Free City of Celtangate

Free City of Ironkrag

Principality of Etrunia

Heraldy of Andelosia

Duchy of Muncifer

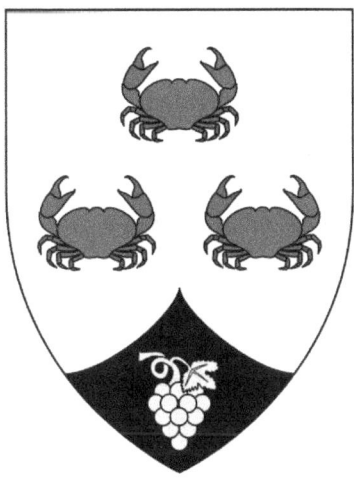

Free City of Vlorey

Arcane University

Hans Cummings
Author/Publisher

Author of the fantasy duology: The Foundation of Drak-Anor: *Wings of Twilight* and *Iron Fist of the Oroqs* as well as the Zack Jackson science fiction series, Hans Cummings published his first novel in 2011. Two of his short stories appear in Fear the Boot's Sojourn speculative fiction anthologies. He is Nuvo's Best of Indy — Best Local Author 3rd place Honoree for 2014 and 2015.

In addition to his writing blog http://vffpublishing.com, Hans maintains a gaming blog http://doctorstrangeroll.wordpress.com.

Hans earned a Bachelor of Arts degree in English from Indiana University in 2006. He grew up in Indiana, Germany, and Virginia and returned to Indiana when he was 21. He currently lives in Indianapolis with his wife. Hans's hobbies include tabletop and video gaming, cooking and smoking meat, and igniting young people's curiosity and passion for science and exploration.

Learn more about this and other works by the author at:

HansCummings.com/

Use Facebook? Find him at www.facebook.com/vffpublishing